NOT SO DIFFERENT

A Funny Story According to Arëk

(an Alien from Schmec)

By Bec Johnson

ISBN: 978-1-963949-67-4 (Paperback)

ISBN: 978-1-963949-68-1 (Hardcover)

Printed in the United States of America

Bec Johnson
Email: arek.chelsey@gmail.com

Dear Reader,

I'm super excited you're here! I can't wait to introduce you to Arëk, my goofy surfer alien friend from planet Schmec. You're going to love him as much as I do! And guess what? This is only the first book in the series of Arëk's hilarious (and sometimes dicey) adventures. So, stay tuned for the sequel. Rumor has it there might be pirates!

Before you dive into this awesome story, I want to thank you, my new friend. Thank you for picking up my novel and saying to yourself, "This Bec Johnson chick is going to be my new favorite author! I can feel it in my bones!" And you won't be wrong! Be prepared to fall in love with fun characters from all over the Universe as Arëk tells his new friend, Axl, about people he's met during his travels. You may laugh a little and maybe even cry a little. But for sure, you'll want to go with him on his next adventure.

This story began as a short one-pager for my daughter, Chelsey, just for fun. But chatty Arëk kept talking about his adventures until the short story was over two hundred pages long! At that point, I thought, what the heck! Let's call it a novel and get it published. So, here we are. You, me, Arëk, and a stellar good time! Thanks again for hanging out with me!

Your new awesome friend,

Bec

Acknowledgments

This book would not be possible without the loving encouragement from my wonderful hubby, Josef. You are my rock, the beat of my heart, and the reason I finished this book. God really showed off when He gave me you! I love you so stinkin' much, my Boo!

To my parents, who raised me to believe that I can do anything, thank you! God blessed me big when he gave me the best parents in the Universe!

Mom, I'm so proud of you for writing your story! You are a beautiful bright light in this dark world! I can't imagine how many lives you've changed for the better, just by being beautiful, amazing, wonderful YOU.

Daddy, your faith surpasses any faith I've ever seen. No matter what that ugly old enemy throws at you, you crush him under your feet. You are an awesome example of what a soldier of Christ should look like.

To my brother, Paul, the funniest guy I've ever known. Through ups and downs, curveballs, and plot twists, we will always be a great team. I'm proud of the awesome man you are! I love you, brother!

To my kids, Austin, Lexi, Chelsey, and Tripp, the characters in this crazy book, I LOVE YOU! I miss you. I pray for you. I hope you smile when you see your names in this story and can read between the lines. I pray every day for God to hug you and kiss you for me. You will always be my first true love.

And one more humongous shout out to my awesome readers! Thank you for joining my crazy little circle of friends!

Prologue

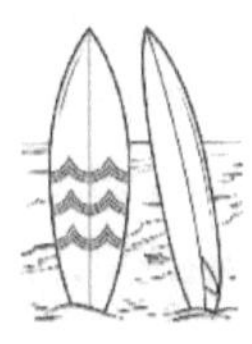

A stranger strolls up beside me on the beach, looking like he could use some directions.

Aloha, brah!

The man says hello and takes in the evening scenery around him.

Perfect night, huh? The sky is amazing! You're welcome to take a seat.

He thanks me for the friendly gesture and sits in a lounge chair next to my hammock.

So, I'm guessing you're not from the islands, based on the leis around your neck, your suitcases, and the jet lag circles under your eyes. Have you ever been to the islands before?

The man shakes his head no.

No? Oh, dude, you'll be so glad you bought the ticket! This place will give you an entirely unique perspective of the Earth. The clear blue water, colorful flowers, green landscape, year-round warm sunshine, and stars so bright and innumerable, it's nearly impossible to wrap your mind around, brah.

The man agrees with a nod as he looks at the ocean, the sky, and the landscape around him.

I've been lying out here in the hammock for hours, totally mind-blown at the awesomeness of the Universe. You know, I've admired the night sky from tons of different places, but there's nothing like the view from a beach in Hawaii. It just feels a little closer to Heaven somehow, wouldn't you agree?

Again, he agrees with a nod. He doesn't seem to be much of a talker, so I lead the conversation.

And besides the scenery, there are so many cool things to do and learn here, like siphoning the water from the coconut that tripped you on the way to the beach. FYI, coconut water always tastes better out of a crazy straw. I don't know why, but somehow, it's true. My bestie always keeps a corkscrew and two crazy straws in her backpack for such coconut emergencies. You know, I bet that Chuck dude on *Castaway* would totally have been stoked to open a FedEx package containing a corkscrew and a crazy straw. I mean, seriously, what are you supposed to do with ice skates and divorce papers on a lone island? Not super practical. But back to the crazy straw since you gave me "a look" a second ago. Whose life isn't happier with a crazy straw? Think back to your childhood when simple things made everything better.

The man raises his eyebrows and shakes his head in agreement.

Ah, see? You just had a good crazy straw memory, didn't you? It made you smile a little, didn't it, brah! Sometimes, you've got to bring back the simple stuff.

The two of us look at the ocean, where a couple of dudes are night surfing.

Surfing is another awesome thing that makes the islands great. Just about everyone here knows how to surf, even little kids and dogs.

You should see the pooches on boards looking cool in their sunglasses and bandanas. My buddy, Chelsey, taught her dogs and her capuchin monkey how to surf. They're all better at it than I am, embarrassing as it is to admit. But in my defense, they have the advantage of being born here, while I was born where there are no oceans. But since I'm a beach dweller now, my goal is to become as excellent a surfer as my bestie. She's a beast on the waves, brah! She makes it look so easy and cool. Chelsey is the perfect picture of a Hawaiian surfer girl. Long wavy blonde hair, green eyes, forever tanned and always in the water. I'm glad she's not from the city. This is a much cooler hangout. I love it here.

So, anyhoo, back to what I was saying about the sky earlier. It's totally covered with stars tonight! I mean, look at it, brah! It looks like you could reach your hand into it and pull out a thick, black, glittery glove! This might sound kind of coo-coo for coconuts to you, but it reminds me of when I watched the *creation* of your stars, your moon, and the sun a long time ago. That was an experience I'll never forget! According to this old guy I know called Nuuk, your stars were created about a million years after the big "God created the heavens" thing. Nuuk knows all kinds of cool stuff. But you know what was even more awesome than watching the making of all that? Watching God create your planet! Dude!

The stranger turns his focus on the ocean waves to look at me with an expression that said, "What did this guy just say?"

The creation of Earth was the wildest thing I've ever seen, and I've been around long enough to see a lot of incredible things! I don't know what lit God's fire that day. Maybe He was just feeling inspired to create something epic. I don't know, brah, but it was quite a show, let me tell you! He just said what He wanted, and it all just formed out of *nothing*! Those six days were the weirdest six days I can remember, as far as time goes. A couple of the days seemed like regular days and some of them were like month-long days. Come to think of it, one of the days seemed like a decade long. It was weird, dude. Anyhoo, back to the important stuff. God clearly put tons of time and deep thought into planning your planet.

The man tilts his head and opens his mouth to speak for the first time since he arrived, but I keep talking. I can tell his brain is screaming overload.

You should feel enormously important. Do you want to hear how He did it? How He created Earth and your solar system in less than a week? It's super cool and exciting, brah! Only God could pull off something that mind-blowingly awesome. Oh, I know, you've probably read the Bible and how it describes the creation, but have you ever heard about it from someone who saw it happen?

The man closes his gaping mouth and shakes his head to clear what he could only have imagined hearing, due to the jet lag, he's sure.

I love telling this story. It was awesome, dude! So, are you interested? I'll take the "this guy's crazy, but I'm really curious" look on your face as a yes. But first, why don't you go get settled in your hotel and grab something to snack on? Peanut M&M's are always a brilliant choice, or maybe a sandwich if you're extra hungry. Then we'll meet back at the hammock in, say, thirty minutes?

The stranger can't seem to pronounce words. So, he shrugs his shoulders, and gives the "why not" hand gesture.

Cool! I'll go grab a snack, too, and a couple of smoothies for us. Do you like berry or orange smoothies? Pineapple? Banana? Banana, it is. See you in half an hour, dude.

The stranger stands up, grabs his suitcases, and walks toward his rental car. He looks back at me, wondering what he's gotten himself into.

1

Dramatic Introduction

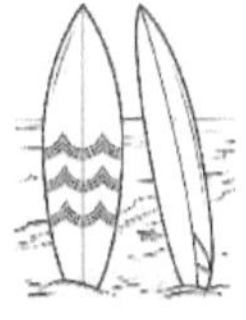 *About thirty-seven minutes later, the stranger rejoins me on the beach.*

Brah! I see you brought peanut M&M's. Excellent choice! They'll go perfectly with your smoothie. Here, try this.

The man takes a sip of the smoothie and nods his head in delight.

I know, awesome, right, brah? The best smoothies in the world are made right here on our humble little island. Cheers!

Ok, now back to the story. Let me "set the stage" before we get in too deep. Have you ever watched a 3-D space movie or been in a space theater, planetarium, or some other cool place that offers you a realistic view of space's enormity?

The man shakes his head no while popping a couple of M&M's in his mouth.

No? Well, you totally should sometime! It'll blow your noggin'! But until then, and for tonight's purpose, you'll have to just do your best to imagine space on your own. Just close your eyes and open your mind as far as you can open it.

The stranger reluctantly closes his eyes after rolling them at me.

Ok, now try to picture the massive… vastness… of space. Note that no manmade facility or movie can truly simulate what I am about to describe. You seriously must remove the borders of your imagination and set it free to get the full picture. Ready, brah? You are about to envision… the creation… of Earth. DUN-DUN-DUUUNNN…

Keep your eyes closed. Picture the darkest darkness you can imagine. No light of any kind and no sound. Only the blackest darkness and the most deafening silence. Are you there? It's totally empty and void. There is nothing, only darkness and silence. Darkness. And silence.

Then, suddenly, in the thick darkness, you feel a big, powerful, and all-consuming Presence. It makes you powerless, and you have no control over your body anymore. You lose the strength in your legs and fall to your knees! You don't know why, brah, but you start to cry, like ugly cry, because whatever this is takes full control of your emotions, your senses, and feelings! It fills your heart so full of its own emotion it takes over you! You feel like you can't breathe or think because this Presence, this thing, fills up every inch of you, your lungs, your mind! It fills all the space surrounding you! Your skin tingles and your hairs stand on end! You feel heavy and weightless at the same time! It's like nothing like you have ever experienced, known, or felt! It's bigger than you can understand, more powerful than you can handle in your own strength, yet you're not afraid, brah! You don't feel defensive or threatened. Contrarily, you feel loved, warm, and more alive than you've ever felt!

Then, this Presence speaks! Its voice BOOMS with authority! It rumbles all over the space around you and inside you. The sound is louder than the most deafening thunder you can imagine! You look for the One who demands attention, but you can't see Him, although

He is clearly there all around you! Words can't escape your lips, but your mind is pleading to see His face! It's crazy, brah!

Finally, the Voice, the all-consuming Presence, reveals Himself, and you know you have heard the voice of God Almighty! You cry with joy and praise as you fall on your face in worship. You still have no control over your mind or body. It's all heart and spirit. You have connected with the Spirit of God, dude! You are a guest in His space, His time, and His Presence. Now, you are about to witness the Great Creation!

Keep your mind in this setting. Never ever forget how awesome, powerful, and true God is, but also know God is tender and has a loving sense of humor. The Bible even says He laughs, which makes sense since we laugh and are made in His image.

The following is my version of events. I watched it from a great distance, along with like a zillion other wide-eyed spectators, including Heaven's angels. It was so spectacular! I could see it as if I were close by. You'll wish you had been there, too, after I tell you about it. It gives me goosies thinking back to that week! So amazing is our Creator!

Ok, so grab your M&M's and your awesome smoothie, and strap in, dude. Back… into the darkness… we go.

2

Creation

Like any builder or architect, God had to choose the perfect place in all that darkness to start his project. Everything He does has a purpose, so the placement was intentionally chosen. With the location decided, He began the construction of Earth. But first, "LET THERE BE LIGHT, BRAH!"

Now, this light that God commanded on day one of creation wasn't some big light bulb with a chain hanging from it waiting to be turned on. This light was God's light, a special supernatural light emanating from Him. It's like it was his "working light" for the task at hand.

Out of all the many options, God decided the planet would be round, like a beach ball. With that decision made, His thunderous voice spoke into the darkness and commanded "water." Clear liquid began to seep out of an invisible globe. Then, He did something that threw me for a loop. He smiled and chuckled, then spun the ball like a pro would a basketball with His huge finger! I thought He was just goofing off with His new creation, but it turns out He did it for a reason, like everything else He does. Go figure, right? He held the liquid ball spinning on His finger until it slowed down to just the right speed. Then, He carefully set it in the perfect place in space where it continued to slowly spin on its axis. Dude! It was the coolest thing! A tiny drop of water out in the middle of the Universe, spinning! Everybody watching couldn't wait to see what God was going to do next. It was "edge of your seat" excitement!

After that, He added a separator to divide the water above the Earth from the water on the Earth. A.k.a, the sky or atmosphere. The sky's number one job is to protect the Earth from the psycho heat of the sun, which will be created here shortly. But I believe, since the Bible says all of God's creation praises Him, the sky goes beyond its assigned duties and creates beautiful sunrises and sunsets to show its gratitude to its Maker. It's a cool bonus for the folks on Earth, too. Everyone loves the sunset, am I right, brah?

Next, God wanted "land." At the sound of His imperious voice, an enormous solid mass obediently floated to the top of the water. It would eventually, after the Great Flood, split off into several separate pieces of land. They're now called continents and islands.

God then commanded self-reproducing trees, grass, flowers, vegetables, fruits, and other vegetation to start growing from the ground. He's so clever that He thought to grow distinct kinds of vegetation on various parts of the land mass. One, because God has an awesome imagination, and He likes variety. Two, because He also created various landscapes and temperatures, knowing the land mass would eventually split off and float to separate places on the globe. He decided some areas would be sandy deserts and some would be mountains covered with tall trees, valleys, and gorges. Some would be covered with ice, and others would be tropical, with waterfalls, flowers, jungles, and beaches. The Earth was becoming colorful, scented, and delicious!

Then, the next command roared thunderously. God said He wanted "light." Out of the darkness appeared a bright, fiery light, a star known to you as the Sun. After it was set in its purposefully chosen place, God swirled His finger around the sun, causing the newly decorated liquid ball to move with His finger. So, the globe not only spun in circles, but it also spun around the sun. With the sun in place and the spinning globe moving all the way around it, part of the globe became dark and the other light. Welcome, night and day. Then He tossed the "moon" into the equation, giving you a planet-stabilizing, tide-controlling "night light" so you can see and surf in the dark. Thoughtful, right? God also thought it would be cool to sprinkle zillions of stars and funky space lights out there for you and your neighboring planets to enjoy. It was a spicy little touch to His decoration in space! He's so creative, brah! The Artist of all artists, for sure!

Fish and birds were next. God commanded all kinds of sea creatures to fill the water and every kind of bird to fill the skies. Suddenly, the dark blue water was alive with every shape, color, and size of fish, sea creature and subaquatic plant. It didn't take long for whales to start jumping out of the water and for dolphins to play in the enormous waves the whales created. God also designed fish and creatures down in the deep, dark water, but you don't want to meet them! There's some crazy stuff down there, dude! Have you seen that super creepy fish with a lightbulb floating in front of its terrifying face? I'm glad it's not a surface fish! Anyhoo, the sea was alive, and so was the sky!

Coming out of every direction, birds of thousands of varied species flew. They stretched their wings and soared over the water and land, expressing their gratitude to their Creator. The trees became immediate homes, as did caves, holes, and even the water, for the ones who weren't created to fly. Some of the birds squawked, and some of them sang beautiful tunes. Many were blessed with bright, shimmering colors, and others would appear plainer.

The creation of the animals came next and, dude, it was so hilarious! God instructed His angels to attend. He had a blast conjuring up all the different animals with all their sizes, shapes, designs, and colors. Then, He ordered the angels, who are super serious creatures, to vocally teach each animal its voice. God must've been feeling His comedic oats that day because it was side-splitting! I don't think I've ever laughed that hard before! Those unemotional, enormous warrior angels imitated the voices of all the animals. You should have seen it! It was awesome! There were so many animals! Some of them, you still see in today's time, and some are long gone now. It was like the world's first zoo! Hysterical and *noisy*! It was such a fun day, brah! I thought for sure God was finished after all that work and imagination, but He kept going! You know God, the original overachiever, having a fun time!

The most magnificent of all God's accomplishments, though, was the first human being, "Man," God called him. For this part of Earth's artistry, the Great Creator insisted on being alone with Jesus and the Holy Spirit. The angels were dismissed to give the Trinity privacy. Man's intricate design would be God's most complex and beloved work. He wanted zero distractions. It was clear that Man was already cherished by God, even before he was made. God put a lot of thought into how to make him perfect. In fact, He told Jesus and the Holy Spirit that He wanted to make Man in their own image. That's beyond awesome, dude! That's like, *whoa*!

You should have seen the intensity on God's face and the way He smiled and softly hummed a catchy futuristic Pharrell song He called "Happy" while He created Man. God made a mud pie and carefully formed each part of him with His hands until he was flawless. When Man was exactly how God wanted him, He looked at him with tears in His eyes. He cupped his face with complete affection, then breathed His Spirit into him, and the man came to life! The very first CPR, dude! I couldn't believe my eyes!

"Our masterpiece!" God exclaimed to Jesus and the Holy Spirit. Then He named him Adam, after the red earth of Eden from which he was formed.

Man's creation was an extraordinary moment for God. It was an honor to watch. I cried tears of wonder and amazement while God cried tears of love and adoration. It was like God gave birth.

Adam and God were besties from the very beginning. They walked around the Garden of Eden, the beautiful place God gave Adam to live in. They talked and laughed all the time. They got tickled at the funny names Adam gave the animals and at the goofy things the critters did. Can you imagine how much fun Adam and God had just chillin' together? God's the best, dude! He even placed Adam in charge of protecting the Garden from anything uninvited or menacing. This was a crazy important assignment for Adam because Eden was a special place to God. Adam knew his Creator had total confidence in him to take care of the Garden and its inhabitants. He aspired to make Him proud.

Adam loved his life with God. He felt so blessed and honored by everything God had given him. But he was still missing one thing. Another human to hang out with. Every other creature in the Garden had a matching mate of their own kind. God was sensitive to Adam's feelings. He knew Adam noticed he was the only human in the Garden. God also knew Adam would need a mate to populate the Earth, which would also provide the way to bring Jesus into the human world down the timeline. Because, you know, God knows *everything*. So, God decided to surprise him with a most excellent gift. One day, God caused Adam to take a long nap. While he was out, God sneaked one of Adam's ribs out of his body and created a girl! I don't know how He did it, dude. But He did, and she was smoking hot! When Adam woke up from his nap, God introduced him to his new companion, a.k.a. "wifey for lifey." Adam was totally stoked about her! Did I mention she was smoking hot? He named her Eve, meaning "life." A pretty name for a pretty girl.

Everything was gravy until Adam and Eve messed up. Bad! They got into a wad of trouble with God. You've heard about the day when Adam totally slacked off from guarding the Garden. He was probably checking out Eve's bodacious curves when he should've been protecting his lady and the homestead from gangsters and thugs. Because you know, by that point, Lucifer had become jealous of God and His relationship with Adam. And, like an idiot, Lucifer decided he wanted God's job. We all know how quickly his plan took a nosedive. God said, "Uhhh, no, jerk face, I don't think so! You're FIRED!" So, Lucifer became a "fallen angel" who now lives on Earth and who's commonly known as Satan, the bonehead who is *still* trying to win! It cracks me up, dude! He's so dumb!

Anyhoo, back to Adam and Eve's screwup. While Adam was *not* doing his job, Satan snuck into the garden in his snazzy serpent outfit. He spun a colorful lie to Eve and Adam, convincing them to eat the one and only fruit in the Garden that God had said they couldn't have. The one fruit that would mess up their lives forever. Adam, you had one job, brah! ONE JOB! The worst failure of all time, hands down! And then he tried to pin it on hottie Eve! Unbelievable!

God was so hurt and disappointed in them that He kicked them out of the Garden of Eden! Hardcore! I wasn't around that day to see it for myself, but my pal, Fletch, saw the whole thing. He said it was devastating to watch God lose His best bud and to see Adam so disappointed in himself! Eve was drowning in shame, too. She even lost her hotness on eviction day. Strange phenomenon how sin makes you ugly.

Adam and Eve's new life was *hard*! Once sin became a thing, everything on Earth went to crap! Those two had been accustomed to a cushy lifestyle in Eden. Now, they had to get their hands dirty and do tough manual labor to put food on the table. And raising those brats of theirs was no easy job either, with Satan breathing down their necks every second of the day. One of their sons even became Earth's first murderer! He killed his own brother, dude! The world had changed from the beautiful place God had created to a horrible, sin-filled place reflecting Satan's hatefulness. Sickness and death also came with the price of Adam and Eve's mistake, for people and animals. It became a totally different place than the one God had originated for humans. You guys were supposed to live forever in perfect health and happiness. Your first ancestors totally screwed everything up for you. It sucks, dude.

Heavy sigh.

Well, anyhoo, that's how the creation of planet Earth happened. Pretty awesome, huh?

So, what's your name, brah?

The man finally speaks.

Axl? Cool name!

My name is Arëk, pronounced "Uhh-REEK." I live on the planet Schmec. It's about a zillion miles and two wormholes away from Earth. Minus the wormholes, I added that for effect. God created my planet ages before He made Earth and the other planets in your galaxy.

Hey, whoa, dude, what's with the judgmental face suddenly? I thought we were buds. I introduced you to the world's best smoothie. Ok, ok, I already know, it's the "other planet" thing, right? Oh, come on, Axl, you don't think you're alone in the Universe, do you? I mean, after all, God isn't limited to just a small space and a few tools to work with. He's GOD! And He's not limited, period. Everything, *all* space, belongs to Him. He *made* space! Remember the awesomely narrated "darkness to creation" story you just heard a few minutes ago? God's created all kinds of stuff in zillions of places. The Milky Way is just an itty-bitty speck in the big scheme of space. There are lots of us out there, dude, and most of us are pretty stinkin' cool! Especially me.

I smile in jest, but Axl doesn't seem to appreciate my humor.

Axl, bro! You're still making a judgy face. Dude, come on! Humans had to get the ideas for movies and stories about "aliens" and "Martians" and "E.T." somewhere, right? You hang out with us all the time and don't even know it. This brings up a good opportunity to point out how your depiction of us in movies is not only inaccurate but a little insulting and a bit nauseating. We are not slimy, vicious, brain-probing weirdos. I mean, look at me! I'm just a super cool and incredibly good-looking surfer you could've met on any beach. Plus, I gave you all my red M&M's, brah! What horrible, hostile, slimy alien would give you the best ones? Look, you guys obviously want there to be other planet life, or you wouldn't obsess and fantasize about it so much. We're clearly fascinating to you! I bought a t-shirt in a gas station in some little podunk town in Texas, like ten years ago, featuring a goofy little green alien. He's giving the two-fingered peace sign, wearing Ray-Ban sunglasses and its own t-shirt, saying, "I don't believe in humans." Earth totally has an alien obsession! Surely, you believe in us, at least a little bit! How can you believe in Bigfoot and not us? I mean, seriously, brah! Bigfoot?

Anyhoo, you'll just have to get used to the fact that we're here. God created us, too. There are many galaxies, planets, and universes in space. Most of the planets have "people" living on them and have been there for much longer than your planet or mine. One of God's favorite past times is to manifest stuff. And let me tell you, He has a vivid imagination and quite a sense of humor! Some planet beings favor in appearance, some look different, and some of them, WOW! *CRA-CRA!*

God has fun creating, especially the goofy stuff. I mean, look at human beings! HA! I'm kidding! Smile, brah! My best friend is from Earth, remember? So, I'm a little partial to humans. As I mentioned at the beginning of our conversation, her name is Chelsey. You are going to love her, dude. Hopefully, she'll come and hang out with us in a bit. We'll talk about her behind her back until she gets here. My adventures with Chelsey are the coolest part of my life.

So, anyhoo, is your interest peaked about the "rest of us?" I've got tons of awesome stories, dude. It'll be fun. Are you hungry for real food? M&M's can't be enough after your long flight. There's a little Mexican food joint just up the road from the beach.

Axl asks, "Mexican?"

Yeah, I know, kind of odd, right? This family from Mexico moved to Oahu like ten years ago. They changed our lives with their food, brah. I kid you not! You like chips and hot salsa? They've got this insane Habanero salsa that'll set your soul on fire, dude! It's serious! You like guac?

Axl nods his head yes and smiles.

Cool, me too. Oh, hey, I forgot to ask you earlier, do you surf, brah?

Axl shakes his head no.

You mean, *not yet*. We'll catch some waves tomorrow! I'll show you the basics. It'll change your life! There's nothing like it.

We arrive at Garcia's Mexican Restaurant and sit at my usual corner table by the window. Chips, tongue-burning salsa, and guac are served.

Alright, dude, are you ready to hear about my world?

3

Intro To The Universe Schmec

I'll begin by telling you about my planet, Schmec.

Let's start with the practical stuff to ease you into it. Schmecums are what my people are called. As you can see, we are not the ridiculous, hostile "little rubbery gray men" humans depict in your movies. I've seen blue people, yellow people, several other colors of people, and a few rubbery-skinned people, but not little rubbery gray people. Nor have I seen ugly, warty, creepy, hostile, vicious nightmarish aliens who want to suck your brains out or blow up your planet like Marvin the Martian. Got it? Cool! Now that we've got Hollywood out of the way…

Dude, this salsa rocks! We're going to need more chips ASAP!

Axl agrees with a mouthful. I wave to get someone's attention.

Schmecums, like humans and most other Universal beings, are male and female, but we don't reproduce like humans. I'll get to that. We blend in with the species of whatever planet we happen to be on. Same as every other species, including yours, believe it or not. I know it sounds crazy, brah, but just hang with me. As you can see,

Schmecums dress in similar fashions as you, we eat like you, go to school like you, and talk a lot like you.

Most of the planets teach English as a foreign language class in school because so many of us spend time on Earth. I'm hoping that one day, your schools will teach the languages of other planets since humans frequently travel the Universe. I'll get to that, too. Your people have had to learn our languages the hard way, kind of like tossing a kid in the pool and yelling, "Swim!"

The restaurant owner comes to the table.

Aloha, Mrs. Garcia! Your salsa is amazing tonight! Oh, this is my new friend, Axl. Axl, meet Mrs. Garcia, the owner of this place.

Axl extends his hand for a handshake smiling with a mouth full of chips.

Hey, Mrs. G., can you keep the chips and salsa coming for a while? And maybe a smidge more guac?

Mrs. Garcia pats me on the shoulder, winks at both of us, and walks toward the kitchen.

So, back to Schmec. Here's where you and I are a little different. You know how I told you God has a wild imagination? Here's a good example. Humans have skin color, whether it's beige, brown, dark chocolate, white, or something else. When I'm in my natural form, I'm sort of iridescent. My skin looks like a moving liquid, but it feels pretty much like yours does. It changes from one shiny color to another in different lights, and it's kind of see-through.

Axl almost chokes on his iced tea.

Are you laughing at me, dude?

He makes a complete sentence for the first time since his arrival. It turns out he's a smarty pants.

No, wise guy, I'm not shiny like a *unicorn*!

I throw a chip at Axl. He's still trying to recover from his previous choking episode but still manages to chuckle at me.

As you can see, I have two eyes, like you. The exception is my irises change color depending on the light, my emotions, or my temperature. They may appear in any variety of colors and sometimes more than one color at a time.

Another sarcastic question from my new companion.

No, dude, not like *vampire* eyes. Moving on. I have hair, but it's not like yours. It's kind of like Silly Putty. I can change its shape however I like, and it also changes color depending on my emotions.

The questions are flowing in now.

No, I don't need gel. It works without gel.

Now he wants to touch my hair. This guy!

Yes, you can touch it *once*. Dude, don't overdo it!

Another annoying question.

Yes, your hair would be like mine if you went to Schmec. You'd look just like me, dude, only not as handsome, obviously.

We both laugh and scoop up more salsa.

Anyhoo, as you can see, we're really not so different. I think God thought if all the beings were at least somewhat alike, we could relate to one another if we ever met. You know, things in common. Like chips and salsa. And cool hair.

He reaches toward my head.

No, you can't touch it again.

Mrs. Garcia arrives with more chips, salsa, and guac.

Mrs. G., you are the best! Mahalo! When are you going to let me teach you to surf?

She shakes her head no.

Never? What about Chelsey? She'll teach you.

Another head shake no and she smiles.

Are you kidding me?

Mrs. Garcia responds in Spanish and says Chelsey is a much better surfer than I am and giggles.

Ok, you're right, she is better.

I smile at Mrs. G.

I think we're ready to order. Dude, you've never had enchiladas until you've had Mrs. G.'s enchiladas. Sound good?

Axl shakes his head with an emphatic yes.

Enchiladas is what we'll both have, then, Mrs. G. And don't be stingy with the green sauce, if you know what I mean.

I wink at Mrs. Garcia because she knows I love that green sauce. She nods and walks back toward the kitchen.

So, here's some information you might find strange. Unlike humans, who are "born" from their mothers, Schmecums are… hmm, let me think of how to explain this to you. Ok, picture the bright, colorful, dancing Aurora Borealis or Northern Lights. Do you have the visual, brah? Schmecums appear as lights falling from the bright "Aurora Borealis" in the sky. This happens once a year when the whole population of Schmec gathers and celebrates the occasion with music, dancing, food, and games.

When it's time for the "arrivals," the lights slowly reach the ground. When the lights fade away, there stand about a thousand new Schmecums. Instead of arriving as babies, we start as young adults, approximately the equivalent of age twenty. We don't grow, mature, develop, and change as the years go by like humans do. We arrive fully developed and intelligent. We do, however, still go to university to be educated about other planets and their cultures. We don't have "biological" parents, which I think is very cool about humans. We do, however, live in groups together in houses like Earth families for a few years after we arrive.

The Schmecums, who have been around for a while, take on a parental role like Earth parents and look after the newer ones. I say "newer" because "younger" doesn't really apply since we don't age. That's right, brah, I'll look this awesome *forever*.

Axl smiles and slightly rolls his eyes.

Our government system is quite different from yours. Whereas Earth's leaders are Presidents, Kings, Queens, or Emperors, we have Dragos. Every fifty years, a new Drago steps into office. The Schmecum appointed for a future Drago position is indicated when he or she arrives in a red light instead of the normal blue. When the Schmecum has lived fifty years, he or she steps into the position of Drago. The current one retires to live as a regular citizen.

Life on Schmec is timeless. We live on and on and on. We only use times and dates to keep records. I can remember when humans lived for hundreds of years. As I mentioned before, the original plan for humans was to live forever like us. But, as I pointed out earlier, humans are famous for playing with destruction. Your ancestors started destroying their lives early on, which in turn, messed things up for you, which sucks. Living forever is actually pretty cool, dude. You see a lot of fascinating stuff over time, and you meet lots of cool people.

When our planet starts getting overpopulated, many Schmecums move to less crowded planets. You'd be surprised how many Schmecums live on Earth. As a matter of fact, Earth is populated with lots of different Universal species. They live normal Earth lives, like humans, holding jobs and going to school. You've seen them working at Walmart, hospitals, post offices, FedEx, schools, police departments, Pizza Hut, you name it. You just didn't know the difference because we're just like you, dude. God made every species to be able to blend into other planets' cultures, styles, and appearances with no problem. Your next-door neighbor could very well be from another planet. Your friends or coworkers could be. The people you invite over for cookouts could be. Your *girlfriend* could be. And I'll bet not a single one of them has tried to suck your brain out, have they?

I make a loud sucking sound with a crazy face. Axl throws a chip at me, making us both laugh.

Some of the Universal beings living on Earth are even famous! You know some of them, and don't pretend to be surprised when you hear who they are! Pay closer attention to a couple of your favorite American talk show hosts. Ellen and Fallon? What about those old-school British bands from the 1960s? Ever wonder about the Beatles? I'll bet you never suspected your spunky President Trump was not from Earth. But guess what! All the people I just mentioned are from a great planet called Pathub.

Axl stops chewing and stares wide-eyed at me.

No, dude, I'm not kidding. Are you familiar with an old rock star who used to bite the heads off bats back in his prime? Yes, Ozzy! That crazy hellion is from planet Fasi. HELLO! Like you haven't wondered!

Axl admits that is true.

You'll also recognize the Queen of planet Zooch. She's an iconic American punk rock artist and fashionista who's married to superstar Blake Shelton. Gwen may not be the most obvious alien on Earth, but she's an alien just the same! I wish I had her digits, dude. I love me some Gwen!

Axl says, "No way! What about Blake?"

Blake's an Okie, dude. I'm pretty sure that's it.

Axl seems relieved.

There is a famous children's book author whose strange rhyming characters are real folks from planet Zax. Does Dr. Seuss ring a bell?

Several of your favorite and most famous comedic actors are from the planets Hootie and Gomah. It should be no surprise if you really think about it. They're the ones who get the kookiest, most outrageous parts in movies. We all love the weirdness of Jim Carrey and Johnny Depp. Planets Hootie and Gomah.

These people are only a handful of the out-of-this-world residents living on Earth.

Axl's reactions and expressions during this conversation are MOST entertaining for me. I wish I could video him and show it to him later. I think he'd have a good laugh. I know I would.

Here's some information you might find surprising. There are also well-known *humans* who spend a lot of time on other planets, too. Nate Bargatze, one of your funniest and most dry-humored comedians, stays with friends on planet Tate sometimes. He's a big hit there with his comedic life experiences. He also taught the residents there how to make pancakes. They think he's the funniest dude in the whole Universe.

The King of Rock and Roll quickly moved to planet Yaboo after his unfortunate little "accident." Yep, Elvis is still in the building performing with his youth renewed.

Axl's mouth gapes open again.

Yep, it's true, brah. Several planets in Yaboo's galaxy have healing and youth-renewing powers. I saw him in concert about five years ago, singing like he did in his twenties. Scouts honor!

Several Oscar-winning actors and famous musicians spend quite a lot of time on planet Ceb. It's very peaceful there, with lots of meditation, spas, and beautiful scenery in which to relax. If you're stressed out, Ceb is the place to be.

But don't get me wrong, brah, celebrities aren't the only Earth people who visit other planets. Regular folks travel around the Universe, too. I met two brothers named Derick and Drew in Japan about a year ago. They go to planet Pi in the month of Jow to compete in the week-long "Survival of the Fittest" competition. They say it's a fun and welcoming planet on which they wouldn't mind building homes and settling down someday.

Tracie, a well-known fitness trainer for celebrities in New York City, frequents the gorgeous beaches on planet Hanky. It's the perfect escape from her fast-paced city life.

Matt, a semi-pro tennis player from Sydney, Australia, takes biannual trips to planet Samien. Twice a year, he leaves the tennis racquet at home to ski on lavender snow-covered mountains. He says his favorite thing is to watch the planet's five moons dance across the sky while the sun sleeps. Plus, he says the food there is delicious, and the miniature people are friendly.

Dusty, a successful businesswoman who I met in Paris, France, goes to planet Bloosh once a month to get away from the stress of her busy life. She tells her business partners she needs to take an undisturbed break for a few days. So far, she hasn't had to explain where she goes.

These are a tiny fraction of the people I know in Earth's population who spend time or live on other planets. There are thousands!

Mrs. Garcia arrives with plates of steaming rolled chicken enchiladas covered in bubbling cheese and green chile sauce, along with perfectly cooked refried beans and Spanish rice.

Oh, Mrs. G., you've outdone yourself again! Dude, you have no idea what's about to happen to your taste buds! Your life is about to be changed forever! Mahalo, Mrs. G.! Can we get more chips and salsa, please?

Dude, did you know that Earth people are the only space beings not taking full advantage of the wonderful ability to travel the Universe? Would you like to know why? I'll tell you. Many humans are convinced Earth is the only planet in the Universe with life, which is a little egotistical, in my opinion.

Another reason Earth people don't travel to the Universe is denial. Some choose to believe space travel is something they can only wish will happen *someday*. Surprise! It's been happening *every* day for ages! More people know about it than you would think, although it's been kept a secret for some reason. Example: Your United States government is not trying to figure out how to travel to other parts of the Universe. They've known how and have been doing it for a long time. And I'm not talking about the moon or their hopeful "one-way trip to Mars." I mean, come on, you had a Pathubian as your American President! They know about space travel! And he's not Earth's only outer worldly leader, either.

Do some research on a couple of European countries, Australia, and China!

Axl looks up at me with a mouth full of enchiladas and surprised eyes.

Oh, yeah, I'm totally serious! Universe travel is nothing new, dude. I think everyone should know about it and have the opportunity and the choice to travel the Universe if they want to. There is so much out there to see and experience! And since so many of your people won't share their knowledge of how it's done, I'm going to spill the beans, as you goofy humans say. Speaking of beans, aren't these the best refried beans you've ever tasted?

Axl enthusiastically nods his head while chewing.

Mrs. Garcia arrives with more chips and salsa and asks about the enchiladas.

Oh, my gosh, Mrs. G., they're the best ones yet! How do you make them better every time?

Mrs. G. smiles, shrugs her shoulders, and walks back toward the kitchen.

So, you want to know how you do it? Travel? It's easy, brah. Magic is not required. A rocket is not required. Belief is the requirement, mainly. Sound crazy? It's not, brah. Anyone can do it.

However, God is *not* a fan of what humans have done to their own planet, so He's not going to let humans mess up someone else's world, too. So, say a person decides they want to see what else is out there. And, for some reason, they can't seem to leave the Earth when they are doing everything correctly, technically speaking. In such a case, the struggling person might check their motives.

God would probably keep a person with less than ethical motives on permanent "stand by," if you know what I mean. The naughty kids have to stay at home, per God. But the good kids who want to experience and enjoy more of God's amazing creation with no nasty ulterior motives get to go! Sounds fair, right?

So, it's up to you. Do you want to travel to space, dude? See everything else out there? I'd be happy to show you how. I know all the cool spots.

Axl's imagination is in overdrive, and he asks if Mrs. Garcia is an alien.

No, silly, Mrs. Garcia is from Mexico! Not everyone you see now is an alien, dude. Ha-ha!

I love this guy!

4

Zooch

So, before we discuss the technicalities of space travel, I think I'd better give you a heads-up on what you'll see on some of the planets. You know, to minimize the shock. I'll cover five or six of them to provide you with a good spectrum. Let's start with Zooch, a pointy star-like planet. Warning, dude, I cannot describe the Zoochians with a straight face.

I'm cracked up thinking about it. Axl smiles in anticipation.

Zooch is a weird one, brah, way out there! They're totally eccentric people, but they love to laugh and have a good time. The Zoochians blend into any society like the rest of us, but when they are in their true form, they look a little… bizarre. They're tall and lanky, with an average of seven arms and three legs. Believe me when I say they are *special* dancers!

Axl almost spits out a bite of Spanish rice in laughter at me and the visual.

Competitive swimming is popular with the Zoochians. They have a natural advantage, being hatched from gigantic eggs in the water with all those arms and legs. You should see them in competitions, brah. Once those arms and legs turn into propellers, they could challenge a sailfish in the Atlantic!

I lose it, and Axl laughs out loud at the thought of their swim caps and propellers.

Oh, dude, it gets better! They have two hairless heads, each having an independent brain. This special feature can cause the Zoochians to be indecisive, self-argumentative, and clumsy, as you can imagine. To add to their odd situation, each head has a big eye on the back, along with the two on the front. They have a windshield view and rear-view mirror view at the same time.

Axl squeezes his eyes shut and laughs out loud.

There's no sneaking up on those dudes!

We both laugh.

I think they're one of God's "mad scientist" experiments. Zoochians don't seem to notice how unusual they are, though. They're happy people who get along just fine. They are perfect role models for making the most of every day.

Mrs. Garcia comes to the table and jokes that we're having too much fun. She also tells me the restaurant is now closed for the evening and sets the ticket on the table.

Thanks, Mrs. G. Here you go (handing her my credit card).

Axl reaches for his wallet.

No, dude, it's on me this time. I'll finish up with Zooch, and then we'll pick it back up tomorrow.

The people of Zooch are big fans of American junk food. They are not opposed to empty calories and carbs! Pizza, Double Stuf Oreos, corn dogs, and string cheese are some of the favorites. Oh, and green Jell-O. They love green Jell-O because it looks like their friends on planet Yao. I've never been to Yao, but my friend Spoink says the Yaos totally look like green Jell-O. But without the nuts and fruit cocktail inside.

Axl tries not to spew out his tea.

Zoochians also love the styles, clothes, and hats often worn by humans on Earth. Hats are a popular accessory since everyone is bald twice over. You'll also see an occasional terrible wig or crooked toupee. It's *epically* bad, dude.

Axl laughs.

The Zoochians have a Queen, as I mentioned before. *LOVE HER!* Queen Zumkii, or Gwen Stefani, as she is known and adored on Earth. She's been Queen of Zooch for about seven hundred years. Her people love her, and she loves them. When she decides to step down from being Queen, she'll choose her replacement.

Most queens on Zooch stay in office anywhere from four hundred to a thousand years. In the history of its government, there has only been one bad ruler, and she didn't last long. Queen Hech was a total curmudgeon who was unanimously "voted off the island" for banning music and dancing. Hech currently lives contently alone in a Himalayan cave, where she can be as grouchy as she wants to be.

So, let's stick a cork in it until tomorrow. We'll get a good night's sleep and then meet up again in the morning, what do you say? There's a great breakfast place just up the street from your hotel. They make awesome banana pancakes. Meet you in the lobby at about 8:00, brah?

Axl happily agrees.

Cool! Hey, Axl! Welcome to Hawaii, dude!

He smiles, and we part ways.

5

Cozy

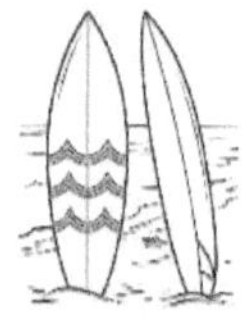

Axl is sitting on the couch in the lobby when I walk in right at 8:00 a.m.

Aloha, brah! Did you sleep well?

Axl tells me he slept wonderfully.

Awesome!

We exit the hotel lobby and take a short walk down the street.

Hey, so I never asked what you're doing in Hawaii. Are you here for work or vacation?

Axl says he's here to get away from everything.

The islands are the best place in the world for a relaxing escape, brah! How long are you staying?

Axl holds up three fingers and adds, "Weeks. Maybe longer."

Dude, you will feel totally reenergized after three weeks or so. Are you ready for some delicious pancakes?

We sit in the restaurant, look at the menus, and wait for the server.

Axl tells me he dreamed about the Zoochians last night. I laugh.

Dude, just wait until you see them in person. They are quite an experience! So fun!

The server approaches the table.

Aloha, Leilani! How's your kupuna kāne doing? I heard about his heart attack.

Leilani thanks me for asking, tells me her grandfather is recovering well, and then asks for our order.

I think we're going to have Haikili's famous banana pancakes and fresh pineapple juice.

Leilani nods and walks back toward the kitchen.

Are you ready to hear about some of the other planets, dude?

Axl leans forward in his seat.

Cozy is a beautiful and serene planet. Its beings are unimaginably more beautiful than any other species. They have bodily features resembling those of humans, only they have a white glow around them. They never age, don't reproduce, and never die. The original Cozyens are the only Cozyens and will ever be the only Cozyens. Crazy, huh, brah?

Cozyens are not big talkers. In fact, they are silent most of the time except when they are heard singing in their forests. They sound like angels, thousands of them at a time. Cozy, along with Ceb, is a planet visited often by humans because of its natural spas, waterfalls, vegetation, and clean air.

Cozy is also known in every galaxy for its fragrance. The flowers are considered kissed by God, brah. Millions come from all around every year to see and smell them. The flowers apparently have healing and rejuvenating powers, too. You can eat them, bathe in them, or have them massaged into your skin. It's been said that it is impossible to leave Cozy with any ailments, including wrinkles or sagging skin. It's popular with the ladies, as you can imagine. The planet seems so perfect, it's labeled as God's own personal garden and sanctuary. Perhaps it is His other-than-Earth version of a Garden of Eden.

Cozy's government is simple. There has only been one leader in the history of the planet. His name is Bandi. He was appointed by God, not the people, thousands of years ago. The Cozyens are such peaceful people that there have never been any problems. Bandi is a very loving and gentle being who takes excellent care of his planet, its inhabitants, and anyone who visits Cozy. The best thing about him, though, is he's like a gazillion years old and plays hacky sack! Totally awesome, right?

Axl says, "Wow!"

Leilani brings our pineapple juice and syrup. She announces the pancakes should be out shortly.

6

Rondo

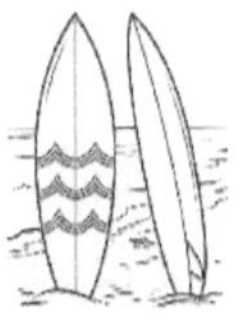 Ok, dude, one more planet before we eat some amazing pancakes.

Rondo, nicknamed "Planet Basketball," is a tiny, fun planet. One of my favorites! Everyone on Rondo is physically active and in love with Earth basketball! Like Cozyens, Rondoans are also like humans in appearance. Kind of. They have similar features besides their blueish-colored skin and three rows of sharp teeth on the top and the bottom of their mouth.

Axl's eyes widen.

Oh, don't let it scare you, brah. The Rondoans are completely harmless. They just look like they could eat you. No worries, dude, they don't eat humans. They're totally chill.

Axl looks freaked out. I better move on.

Rondoans are never seen without an NBA jersey, ball cap, shoes, or other NBA gear. Sportswear is the only apparel sold and worn on Rondo. Do you like basketball, brah?

Axl enthusiastically says, "Yes."

Yeah? Do you play?

Yes, he does! Highest scoring point guard in his high school to date. Impressive!

Cool! Then you'll love Rondo!

The San Antonio Spurs are a favorite team on Rondo, although two of the Spurs starters are from planet Harley. I bet you never suspected, did you? Here's a fun fact, dude. During the NBA Playoffs and Finals, at least half of the crowd at the games are Rondoans! SOLD OUT TICKETS, thanks to the otherworldly fans!

Axl says, "No way!"

It's true, dude! Rondo is a fanatical place! Everything there has a basketball theme or name, including restaurants, foods, streets, stores, schools, and styles. Every resident shares a name with an NBA player or legend. Stephen Curry, Paul Pierce, Derrick Rose, Michael Jordan, Kawhi Leonard, and Tony Parker, to name a few.

Foods like Maverick Burgers, Laker Smoothies, Tim Duncan Donuts, Bulls Pizza, and, of course, Celtic Fajitas are some of the planet's most popular foods.

Trail Blazers Elementary School, J. Kidd Preschool, Thunder High School, and Magic Johnson University are some of the schools on the planet. Much of the curriculum includes basketball analogies, lessons, and examples featuring the sport's legends and history.

Rondo's media technology far surpasses Schmec's or Earth's. High tech big screens light up every home, business, and street with basketball games and half-time reports. And neither would be as exciting as they are without the Universe's favorite sportscaster, nicknamed Hoops. He is an Earthborn Rodoan legend! This guy was a star player in college and was drafted into the NBA. But before his first professional game, he injured both of his knees and was unable to play. During recovery from several surgeries, he was invited to announce some games and join in halftime shows. That's when he decided to become a sportscaster. Now, he has the largest fan base of any sportscaster in the Universe, including Earth. We love you, Chuck Barkley, but Hoops has you beat, brah.

Axl chuckles and says he loves Charles and Shaq.

Like Earth, Rondo has a President, only theirs is called an Equon. In fact, Rondo's government is set up a lot like yours, only without all the boxing matches between Republicans and Democrats. Everyone gets along and agrees, with a few exceptions from time to time. Political problems seem to be resolved in a friendly manner. Earth should take a few pointers, just saying.

Axl nods in agreement.

My only advice for you when you visit Rondo is to pack your jersey and be prepared for scrimmage! Everyone on Rondo plays basketball. And they're good. Really good.

Leilani brings heaping stacks of banana pancakes and tops off our pineapple juice.

This looks amazing, as usual. Please tell Haikili mahalo!

Leilani nods and walks to the kitchen to give Haikili my message. He spots me across the restaurant and gives shaka. Axl and I give shaka in return before digging into our breakfast.

7

Smithers

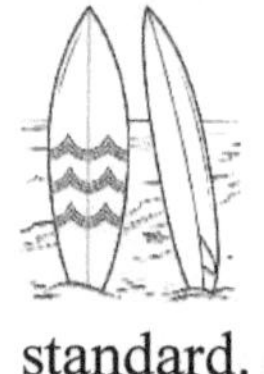

Axl says these are the best pancakes he's ever eaten.

It's crazy, right, brah? No other pancake holds up to this standard.

Axl nods in agreement with a mouthful, then asks about the next planet.

The next place I'm going to tell you about is straight-up crazy, dude! Smithers is a square-shaped planet and is known as the "intellectual" planet in my galaxy. It's famous for its geniuses, inventors, scientists, and discoveries. Its beings are pretentiously stuck up and snotty because they feel superior to every other species in the Universe.

Axl raises his eyebrows.

Seriously, brah, they're a trip! God created them with unusually large bulbous heads, which barely accommodate their exceptionally large brains. Their brains can store five hundred times more memories, thoughts, ideas, and intelligence than any other species' brains. One hundred percent maxed out capacity. As far as looking like humans, well, not so much. Beneath their colossal heads are thin, pale green, rubbery bodies. They have three arms which are always loaded down with books. And bearing the weight of the books and the humongous head are two deceptively strong skinny legs.

Axl laughs with a mouthful of pancakes.

Dude, I'm telling you, the Smitherines are something else!

They know every language from every galaxy. And there is nothing mathematical they didn't come up with first, from the problem to the solution. Since their brains work overtime, they are so full of ideas and inventions they can't keep up. They thoroughly enjoy rubbing their intelligence and inventions in everyone else's face. Smitherines are absurdly obnoxious, brah. They're not sociable with other planets, which is fine with everyone else. Most people from other planets can't stand to be around them because no one likes to be treated as if they're inferior or stupid. I imagine God puts the Smitherines in check occasionally to knock the huge chips off their shoulders.

Axl agrees and says it sounds like they need it.

Smithers has no government system. Everyone there is too busy minding their own business, studying, inventing, or problem-solving to pay attention to what the next guy is doing. Smitherines are loners. Go figure, right? They grow their own food, build their own houses, and make or invent everything they need from the planet's abundant natural resources. It's like they each live inside their own little bubble. There is no need for a hierarchy or government.

I'll tell you a funny story about the Smitherines later.

8

Laya

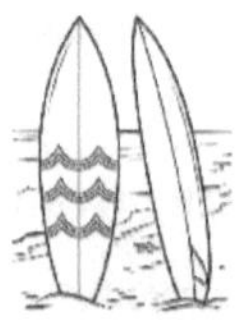

One more before we get the check and head out?

Axl nods yes and insists on paying this time. Cool.

Alright, Laya is an egg-shaped planet, spoken of with high regard and admiration. Layans are rescuers. They're awesome, brah! Some species think they're angels. God created them with a heart for helping others. Layans are small beings, standing a whopping thirteen and a half inches high, and their strength is mind-boggling. They resemble a small cartoon alien I once saw on your Cartoon Network. They're light yellow in color with two arms, two legs, antennas on their head, and a long tail with acute motion sensory.

Axl looks at me with doubt while taking his last bite of pancakes.

No, dude, I'm not kidding. They look just like your cartoon.

Their rescue missions are unmatchable by any species or planet. They've even done some rescue missions on Earth, although you guys had no idea it was happening. A good example is your Leaning Tower of Pisa. Although its tilt appears only slight, it would have fallen completely over had it not been for the intervention of some

Layan tourists. They saved a lot of lives, not to mention a now historical monument.

Some of their rescues on Earth and in other areas of the Universe are less renowned but no less important. They saved eleven kids from drowning in a river in Australia earlier this month. They also saved an entire apartment building from splitting in two during an earthquake in California recently.

Last weekend, a lady and her grandmother were walking to their car after shopping at a mall in Paris when they were attacked by two muggers. A Layan spotted the situation from across the parking lot and rushed in to save the women. The funny part is he appeared in his natural Layan form! HA! I guarantee those muggers will never forget the cartoon alien who foiled their crime!

Axl laughs.

Laya is also known for saving entire species at times. You should see the dinosaurs living on Laya! You'd probably recognize them, brah. They're *yours*!

Axl chokes on his pineapple juice.

It's true, dude! When the Earth started changing after the Great Flood, minimal food supply became a problem for the dinosaurs, and they started dying out. The Layans asked God if they could take them to Laya. Of course, He said yes. So, they brought a big team to Earth and transported the dinos back to their planet. What a shame to let such a unique species die off! Apparently, the big guys are happy there. The Layans treat them like giant pets! Pretty cool, huh?

Axl tells me I'm full of crap. Doubting Thomas!

No, brah, I'm telling you the truth! We'll go there sometime, and you can see for yourself. It'll be a great story to tell your friends!

Laya is another planet without an organized government. I suppose God didn't feel they needed a leader since they're self-initiators, driven to serve others.

Axl's expression says he doesn't care about the Layan's government.

Dude, are you still stuck on the dinosaur thing? It's the truth, I swear, brah!

I laugh out loud at Axl's judgy expression.

Leilani brings the check, and Axl hands her a credit card. Once the receipt is signed, we exit the restaurant.

9

Fasi
Meet Chelsey

What do you say we head to the beach, brah? We can grab a smoothie at the smoothie shack and chill for a bit. I'll even give you the hammock.

Axl likes the idea, and we drive to the beach.

I introduce Axl to a blueberry-mango smoothie. It will, without question, rock his morning. We get comfy in the hammock and lounge chair to continue the story.

Alright, brah, Fasi will be the last planet I tell you about for now. I've given you a lot of info to process so far.

Axl agrees but appears interested to hear more.

Fasi was known for its bad reputation until a few years ago. No one dared go there. It was the only known planet in the Universe whose inhabitants considered every other species an enemy, especially humans. They expressed unbearable hostility and hatred for Earth, brah.

Axl asks why.

I don't know why they despised you guys so much. They were a bunch of mean, ruthless heathens. That much, I know. I had a not-so-wonderful experience with the Fasians before they changed. It's a dicey little tale. I'll back up and give you a little history before I jump right into it.

Axl sits up in the hammock with anticipation.

Several years ago, I went to Ireland to see Bono and U2 in concert. I scored backstage tickets, which I was super excited about. I had the whole experience planned out in my head. I imagined being pulled up on the stage to sing with the band and then becoming buds with them backstage after the show. I knew when the band met me, we would have an awesome connection. Because, well, I'm awesome.

Axl rolls his eyes and shakes his head. Then he sarcastically asks if I became best friends with the famous Bono. I don't like his attitude.

Unfortunately, the concert was canceled because Bono got the flu.

Axl says he's guessing I didn't become best friends with Bono then. I'm beginning to question his friendship. His sarcasm is disgusting.

Anyhoo, after a few days in Ireland, I decided to visit America before going back to Schmec. My intention was to go to Memphis, Tennessee for some blues music and BBQ. But somehow, I ended up in this quaint little beach town on Oahu instead.

Remember earlier when I told you all it takes to travel in space is to believe in it? Well, it's true, mostly. Believing is the first part. Your thoughts take you where you want to go. If you want to go to Earth from Schmec, you concentrate your thoughts on Earth. Then, within a few seconds, you're on Earth. However, it is important to focus on a specific location. Otherwise, you could end up somewhere you don't want to be. Like in the middle of an ocean at night. Scared out of your mind. All by yourself in the cold, dark water. Surrounded by sharks...

I drift back to a distant memory.

...which is another story for another time.

Axl opens his mouth to say something, but I add...

Or maybe never. Yeah, probably never, so let's move on.

Axl closes his mouth and snuffs out his comment. He clearly hopes the subject will come back up later so he can get more details about MY HORRIBLE EXPERIENCE WITH THE STUPID SHARKS! BULLIES.

I take a deep breath and continue.

So, anyhoo, Memphis, Tennessee, is where I intended to go. However, somewhere in my thought process, I lost concentration and landed on an island. I realized, when I arrived, I was not in Memphis. But I figured, what the heck, I'll check this place out, too. So, I started walking through the neighborhood where I arrived, in Haleiwa, Oahu. Almost immediately, I saw a cute little blond girl singing and playing in her front yard. She was about five years old and looked and sang like an angel. As I walked down her street, she saw me and smiled the friendliest, most beautiful smile. I waved hello.

She said, "Hi, my name is Chelsey. What's your name?"

When I told her my name was Arëk, her eyes lit up, and she gasped with joy. Then she stood up, ran to me and hugged me! It took me by surprise because most human children are taught not to talk to a stranger, much less *hug* one. But I wrapped my arms around her and hugged her back. When she let me go, she put her tiny hands on her tiny hips and said, "You're *late*! What took you so long?"

I looked at her a little baffled and thought to myself, she must have confused me with somebody else.

"Who are you waiting for, Chelsey?" I asked.

She giggled and said, "*You*, Arёk. You're funny, just like He said."

"I think you must have confused me with someone else, little princess. We've never met until now."

"No, no, no, silly," she said with confidence, "I know you already even though we just met."

Poor thing, I thought, the child is delusional. Probably too much seawater.

"See, watch," she continued, "I'll prove I know you."

I let her go on with this little fantasy because, to be honest, I was curious to see where it was headed.

"You're not from here, are you?" she asked demanding the answer she expected.

"Here, *where*? Your island?"

She giggled.

"No, silly head, *Earth*!"

I looked at her with shock and asked, "Why? Don't I look like I'm from Earth?"

I wondered how this little girl could possibly know. I've always blended in with humans perfectly well, so I was a hundred percent confused.

A few seconds later, I asked the inquisitive Chelsey, "What would make you think I'm not from Earth?"

She giggled and said, "I like you, Arëk, you're funny. I know you're not from here. You can stop pretending. Are you ready to be my friend?"

I'd been visiting Earth for ages when I met Chelsey, and she totally busted me out on the alien thing!

Axl laughs.

First time ever, dude! Humans never question if I'm one of them or not because I look just like you guys when I come to Earth. So, how did this little brat know?

I gave her a puzzled look and said, "I would love to be friends with you. However, I'm curious. How do you know I'm not from Earth?"

Then she *really* shocked me!

She said, smiling, "Jesus told me you were coming. I've been waiting for you, for like *ever* (rolling her big green eyes)! What took you so long?"

My mouth dropped open. Then I thought, well, now I know how I ended up here instead of Memphis. God invokes *His* plans instead of ours sometimes. Just like humans, Schmecums have free will. But occasionally, God pulls a little sneaky detour on me, and I end up somewhere other than where I was headed. It always turns out for the better, so I can't complain.

I told this very intelligent little girl, "I'm *sorry* I took so long, but I didn't know I was coming. So, what exactly did Jesus tell you, anyway?"

"He's been telling me about you since I was born. I haven't told my mommy and daddy about you. They might think I'm coo-coo if I tell them someone from another world is coming to be my friend. You know how grownups are. That's why I only talk to Jesus about you."

"Makes sense," I agreed.

"Anyway, Jesus told me a really nice person named Arëk, from a planet that starts with an 'S,' I can't remember how to say it, is going to come walking down my street while I'm playing in the yard. He is going to become my friend, and we are going to teach each other stuff and make each other laugh. Jesus really likes you. That's good! I wouldn't want to be one of those people who's in trouble with God all the time. Those people have no sense if you ask me."

I had never, in all my centuries, experienced this sort of thing before. How could a tiny little girl possess so much intellect? Most of the five-year-old humans I'd ever seen were busy coloring outside the lines or chasing each other with boogers.

Axl laughs.

I didn't really know what to say, so a wimpy little "Huh!" escaped my mouth.

Chelsey made a gesture with her hand, motioning me to bend down.

She took my face in her small hands and said, "Are you ok, Arëk? You don't look so good. Do you need an aspirin? My great-grandmother, Mam, says aspirin fixes everything. I think M&M's with peanuts fixes everything."

Axl says he agrees with Chelsey.

I couldn't help but smile when I replied, "No, thank you, Chelsey. I think I just need to gather my thoughts for a minute. So, has this ever happened to you before? Jesus arranging a friendship like this, I mean?"

"Nope, I've just been waiting for *you*, goofy head. I'm happy you're here."

She hugged me again. I liked her. It seemed strange how bright and mature she was for such a young child. I was going to have to have a chat with God over the whole deal, though. It would be nice to have a heads-up about something like this. You know what I mean, brah?

So, as oddities would have it, Chelsey became my BFF. We've been together seventeen years now, traveling the Universe and making tons of memories. She's the coolest person I've ever met, dude. I've learned so much from her. And a huge bonus is that she has the most awesome relationship with God. Which, in turn, has helped me to become closer to Him, too.

Chelsey and I decided from the beginning of our friendship to wait for the OK from God to introduce me to her parents. Because, as she said, you know how grownups can be. We were still waiting for the thumbs-up until a few years ago. To be honest, brah, I'm pretty sure we jumped the boat a little early. I'll explain later.

Anyhoo, we felt it might be best for God to prepare her mom and dad for Chelsey's big news. We didn't think the following would go over well: "Mom, Dad, this is my best friend, Arëk. He's from planet Schmec, about a gazillion miles from Earth. Jesus told me when I was born that he would be coming to Earth to become my bestie so we could teach each other stuff and make each other laugh. Oh, and I've been traveling to different galaxies since I was five. Please don't be mad."

Axl chuckles.

Yeah, most Earth parents, especially from small country towns, probably wouldn't smile at something like that. But we had to tell them soon enough anyway because of what happened. The Fasi thing I mentioned earlier.

So, here's where the story I was telling you about begins. Unbeknownst to Chelsey's friends and family, we were together at least five days a week. Sometimes more often. I would go to Earth to see her, and she would go to Schmec to see me. We would go to concerts, movies, sporting events, and many other activities on our and other planets. I have always loved going to places with Chelsey. She's fun, friendly, and automatically likable. Anyone who has ever met her before is always happy to see her again. Plus, she makes me look super cool. I mean, even cooler than I already am.

Axl rolls his eyes and smiles.

10

The Fasi Story Begins

Chelsey's sixteenth birthday fell on a Thursday. Her parents gave her the "cake and presents" celebration after she got her "Happy Birthday" phone call and gift by mail from her grandparents and great-grandparents. With her birthday falling on a weekday, it left us the weekend to do *our* thing.

We planned to go to a huge concert in Los Angeles featuring "up and coming" garage rock bands from around the country. We decided I would go pick her up at her house in Haleiwa, and we'd go together. We had already discovered trying to meet up somewhere neither of us had been before was disastrous, so we vowed not to do it again. Getting lost in a foreign place can be a little scary. We would always meet somewhere we were both familiar with, usually her house or mine.

She was supposed to meet me in her backyard by the big palm tree next to the fence. I showed up, but she wasn't there. Chelsey was habitually late, so I waited for her. Thirty minutes went by, then an hour. But she was never *that* late. I got worried.

I thought myself into her bedroom to see if she was there. She wasn't. In fact, she was nowhere in the house. I thought maybe I had misunderstood the plan, and she was supposed to pick me up at my house, so I went home. No sign of Chelsey. It wasn't like her, brah. She and I talked all the time. She would have told me if she'd changed her mind. We told each other everything. No secrets. And we had made birthday plans! Cool ones!

So, where was my bestie? Something had gone wrong. I asked several of my friends on Schmec if they had seen her, but no one had. I went back to Haleiwa and looked everywhere for her. No Chelsey. I even went to Los Angeles to the Staples Center where the concert would soon be getting underway. No Chelsey. I panicked. Something was wrong, dude.

I decided to search on other planets. I started on Cozy, but no one had seen her. Zooch, nothing. Hootie, nothing. Harley, nothing. I looked everywhere else I thought she could possibly be, but my best friend was nowhere to be found. After searching for several hours, I ended up on the beach near Chelsey's house. I started to cry, and I fell to my knees. Dude, don't judge.

Axl shakes his head and puts his hands up, signifying no judgment.

"God," I begged, "where is she? Please help me find Chelsey. I'm worried! I can't find her anywhere!"

My tears started to sink into the sand. My heart ached, and I felt scared and empty inside. Then suddenly, something felt like a heavy blanket covering my back, followed by the gentlest, most comforting voice.

God said to me, "Chelsey is in danger, Arëk. She needs you. I will help you save her, but you haven't looked far enough. Think, Arëk. Where have you *not* looked?"

And then the "blanket," God's warm hand, was gone.

Axl says, "Whoa!"

Yeah, dude, the whole thing was weird! Like crazy weird!

I sat up and dried my face on my "I'm With the Earthling" t-shirt, an arrow pointing to the left; Chelsey's t-shirt said, "I'm With the Alien," an arrow pointing to the right.

Axl smiles.

I said out loud, "Where haven't I looked?"

I went over a mental list of places on Earth and other planets I'd been to so far.

"I've looked *everywhere*, God!" I shouted in frustration. "Where is she?"

Then, a light bulb lit up in my head. Surely, she wouldn't go to Fasi for any reason, I thought. We've *never* been there and never would! But where else haven't I been?

I said, "God, the only place I can think of where I haven't looked is Fasi, but there's no way. Chelsey wouldn't be on Fasi for any reason, especially without me."

It seemed nutso, dude, but I suddenly felt the weirdest peace about my epiphany. I stood up and took a deep breath.

"Ok, God, I guess I'm going to Fasi. Please protect me. That place is scary dangerous."

I closed my eyes and concentrated on Fasi. I didn't have a choice! I had to find her!

Axl is all ears! He sits further up in the hammock, waiting to hear what happened next.

11

Monsters

When I opened my eyes, I was standing on a hill near the headquarters of the Fasian military. It's located on the outskirts of a city called Krupt. Ironically, but not surprisingly, it's pronounced "cor-rupt." This place definitely lived up to its name, brah.

I had to believe this is where God directed me, so I sneaked up to the headquarters like a ninja. I took full advantage of some super sick Jackie Chan moves I'd waited forever for an opportunity to use. Dude, I have to say, I felt pretty cool as a ninja. But I'd been warned all my life about how cruel and heartless the Fasians were, so I knew I had to stay out of sight. Several soldiers walked past where I was hiding. They were speaking in their native tongue, which I understood only a part of.

When they were gone, I ran to the nearest building and peeked in a window. There was a huge group of them, including what looked like a high-ranking officer. They were all listening intently to him, and I tried to hear what he was telling them. After several minutes, all I gathered was when the three red moons lined up vertically, the prisoner would be brought to the circle of elders. Then, the prisoner would be tortured, if necessary, until she gave up the information they wanted about the Earth's government, military weapons, and any other useful intelligence. The descriptive torture procedure was insanely graphic, so I won't give details.

Axl's eyes widen, and he listens intently.

I watched the officer dismiss the soldiers, and I waited until they were all gone. Then I sneaked around to another part of the compound to try to find out more about this prisoner torture thing they were planning. I slipped quickly around a corner after almost being seen by two soldiers passing by. I caught the gist of their conversation. They talked about the Earthling and how exciting it was going to be to finally have the information they'd been waiting for ages to know so they could take possession of Earth once and for all. My eyes bulged in my head at a couple of wild thoughts. One, "TAKE POSSESSION OF EARTH?" And two, "WHAT EARTHLING WERE THEY PLANNING TO TORTURE?" I really panicked, then! Was the Earthling they spoke of my Chelsey? Oh, God, please, no!

Axl shakes his head and says, "Oh, no!"

Dude, it was an awful feeling!

I slyly crept around corners and buildings until I was on the far side of the compound. Two of the red moons had lined up, and the third one was close. I had to find this prisoner and fast! I was so determined, I forgot how scared I was. I asked God under my breath to lead me to my friend.

I quickly walked through some tall grass, which concealed secret underground tunnels. I reached a stucco-covered hut lit up inside. I listened for voices and heard none, so I sneaked around to the front. No one was inside, so I went a little farther past the hut until I heard voices coming from under the ground. I searched for an opening, and finally, I found it. It was a huge room dug under the grass, but it was modernized like a conference room in a luxurious hotel. I peeked inside. The voices I heard belonged to the elders the officer spoke of. They were discussing the ceremony about to take place. There was no sign of Chelsey, though. I decided I was going to have to wait for the third red moon to align with the others and for the ceremony to start to find out. Luckily, I only had to wait about half an hour in the trees, where I found a good hiding place.

Torches were lit in a big circle about a mile from the military compound, where each of the elders sat on stone seats in front of the torches. Then, from somewhere I couldn't see, a drum started beating in a creepy rhythm, just like in the movies, brah.

Axl's eyes widen even more.

Yeah, dude, cree-py!

Can I interrupt the story for a second to tell you a little about the Fasians?

Axl quickly nods his head yes.

Brah, the soldiers were scary looking! They wore black robot-armored outfits covering ten-foot-tall, freakishly muscled, five-hundred-pound bodies! And their heads housed mean red eyes, mouths full of horrible, long pointed teeth, and minds dreaming of bringing destruction to entire worlds!

Axl's eyes grow to the size of coconuts. Almost.

But, dude, the *elders*! Those guys were *super* scary! They've been around forever, and they are HUGE! They made the soldiers look like kittens! They stood at thirteen or fourteen feet and weighed about seven hundred pounds apiece! The Fasian elders were pitch black-skinned with blood-colored tattoos from the tops of their bald heads to the tips of their toes, with the most chilling images you could ever see! These monsters were consumed with torture and death! Their red eyes and long pointy teeth were ever-threatening, not to mention the blood-curdling curses and spells trickling from their snarling lips! I'm telling you, dude, pure evil oozed out of their pores!

Axl is biting his fingernail.

So, back to the torture party.

At first, the elders were alone. Then, the soldiers filed in, marching in hundreds of synchronized groups. They surrounded the circle behind the torches. There seemed to be tens of thousands of them. I waited and waited, and then finally, the red moons were aligned, and they brought out the prisoner. Her head was covered with a black sack, and her hands were bound together with what looked like a metal contraption of some sort. One thing I knew for sure. Only *my* best friend would be wearing an "I'm With the Alien" t-shirt, and this masked prisoner wore such a shirt.

Axl releases a long exhale, "NOOOOOOO!"

"CHELSEY!" I shouted in my head.

My heart leaped with joy and fear all at the same time, dude. Ok, now what? I knew better than to just jump out of the trees and demand those armed and dangerous soldiers and creepy elders let my friend go. I had to use my head.

"Help me out, God," I kept saying under my breath.

The ceremony was finally underway.

"Be strong, Chelsey," I whispered.

The lowest-ranked elder stood and raised his arms, and the drums stopped. It was creepily silent.

He spoke to the elders, the soldiers, and the prisoner in his native tongue, "Today is a day of victory! The god of the red moons has provided our desired resource. Today, the Fasian nation will have the intel which has eluded us for ages! By the end of this day, we will begin our reign of destruction on Earth!"

The crowd roared in excitement.

Having understood enough to get the gist of the speech, I laughed hysterically inside my head! I covered my mouth in order not to laugh out loud.

"These idiots kidnapped the wrong person!" I almost said out loud.

Axl shouts, "How could you laugh at a time like that?"

Dude, Chelsey didn't know crap about intel or government stuff! She barely even passed her American History class. *I* made a better grade than she did in American History and I'm from another galaxy! There was *no way* they meant to kidnap Chelsey!

She squirmed in her seat.

"Hold on, buddy," I whispered.

Another elder stood up and approached the prisoner. He removed the black sack from her head. Her eyes grew to the size of frisbees when she saw her captors. My friend was scared to the bone!

I knew I had to wait until the right moment to make a move, so I watched anxiously as the standing elder began his interrogation of my best friend. He put his enormous, tattooed hand on Chelsey's head and closed his scary red eyes. The blood red tattoos began to glow on his midnight skin as if they were lit by lightbulbs! At first, I didn't understand what was happening, but then it dawned on me. He was using his evil power to listen to her thoughts and read her mind. He was searching for all the secret government stuff he would *never* find inside that surfer girl's brain. NOT IN A MILLION YEARS!

Axl chuckles.

After just a few seconds, he opened his eyes and snarled at his prisoner. He took his hand off her head and roared like a beast! You didn't have to be fluent in Fasi to know he was furious.

After his fit, he said, "The human hides the information from us. Humans are more powerful than we realized."

Then, with only inches between his enormous face and hers, he looked at Chelsey.

In perfect English, I didn't know they spoke English, he said, "Do you choose to play games, human? I will break your mind and your body until you surrender the information I require of you. Then, I will make an example of you for your despicable planet to see. Earth will suffer worse torment than they could ever imagine because of *your* rebellion. Will you make a foolish decision, or will you cooperate without force?"

Chelsey was crying with fear. She tried to be strong, but this dude was SCA-RY! She told him she didn't have any of the information they wanted, and she didn't understand what Earth had done to possibly make anyone hate them so much. She began sobbing, begging for them to release her. Fasians weren't known for compassion on any level, and they weren't about to start practicing with Chelsey.

An older elder stood up and approached the interrogating elder. They spoke in secret, then the first one returned to his seat leaving Chelsey with the older elder. He walked a slow circle around her, chanting something unknown. Little did he know, Chelsey was a child of God, the Creator of Heaven, Earth, and Fasi! She began to pray out loud.

"God," Chelsey began, "You have never let harm come to me. Well, besides the shark incident when I was a kid, but it wasn't as bad as it could've been. I mean, I didn't die or anything. Anyway, You know I don't have any information for these guys, nor would I give it to them if I did."

She looked up at the chanting elder with contempt, not making points, obviously.

She continued, "God, I ask You to speak to their hearts if they have hearts. Please make them see that Earth is not a threat or an enemy to their planet. Surely, they weren't always this full of hate and rage since *You* created them. Help them to remember how much better their lives were before their hearts were hardened. Protect me and protect Earth, please. Signing off for now, amen."

As soon as Chelsey finished, she looked around the circle and spotted me peeking around the tree. Her eyes widened, and she took a quick, sharp breath. She had a look on her face, shouting, "What in the world are you doing here, Arëk?" or "How did you know where to find me, Arëk?" or "GET ME OUT OF HERE, ARËK!"

The elder stopped in front of her.

"What does a *human* know about *God*?" he said, laughing in insult.

The crowd joined in his laughter.

She looked at him with stern confidence and replied, "Are you kidding me? Are you being serious right now? God is my best friend, well, besides Arëk. And anyway, why wouldn't humans know about God? He made us all, you, me, everyone, and everything."

The elder looked around at the other ancients, who were murmuring to each other in confusion.

Chelsey spoke up and said, "It sounds like you all know God, too, or at least you did at some point. I don't know what happened to you or what caused you to hate. Don't you remember what it was like before your hearts were so hardened toward everyone? When you knew God? He created Earth with as much love as He created Fasi. We're all the same in His eyes, and we should all be the same in each other's eyes, too. Earth isn't your enemy. The hatred in your hearts is."

I was so proud of my strong BFF. The elders gathered for a pow-wow to discuss what was happening. It seemed to take forever. The opportunity to sneak into the circle and grab Chelsey was perfect. But just as I took the first step, I felt something stop me.

God said, "Wait."

I thought, "WHAT? *WAIT?*"

The look on my face must have been a little sassy because I felt a thump on the back of my head.

I rubbed it and said, "Ok, ok, I'll wait. *Ow.*"

Like Chelsey's great-grandmother, Mam, God doesn't take any sass!

Axl chuckles.

The crowd became loud, between the soldiers talking to each other and the elders deliberating. Chelsey looked at me like, "What are you waiting for!" I looked at her with wide eyes and used hand signals to send her a message. First, I pointed to the sky, signifying "God." Next, I pointed to my mouth meaning "said." Then, I held up two fingers to say "to." Lastly, I used the hand-out signal which meant "hold on." She got it right away and nodded to let me know she understood. Chelsey and God are tight, so she was confident in whatever God had up His sleeve.

Finally, the most ancient Fasi elder moved to the center of the circle and raised his arms. Everyone stopped talking and listened.

He said, "The human speaks from the heart of the God whom we abandoned so very long ago to worship the god of the red moons. My heart is torn open like a gaping wound. I had long forgotten about love and forgiveness."

I looked across the circle of elders. Tears filled those glowing red eyes.

Axl looks totally shocked.

Yeah, dude, it was quite a sight, let me tell you! It was so weird watching those enormous monsters cry. You wouldn't think they'd even have tear ducts, they seemed so void of any goodness. God doesn't make anything bad, though, so tears had to be in those big guys somewhere.

The elder continued, "Fasians, something phenomenal has occurred this day. Am I wrong to assume every one of us is affected by this most recent event?"

Heads nodded, and soft nos were heard all over the gathering.

"Then we have a unanimous decision to make. Do we continue with our plans to take possession of Earth and offer up our victory to the god of the red moons, or do we return to the God of our creation?" He paused. "Perhaps we should take a few moments to look at how we have lived since we chose to worship the god of the red moons. We turned to sorcery and evil. We have killed and destroyed innumerable beings, cities, and even planets. We have lost ourselves to a god we created and who has done nothing for us in return. We have become despicable in the sight of the one true God."

More tears appeared on many faces.

Then my BFF piped up, "Excuse me, Mr. Ancient Elder, may I say something?"

He turned to her and nodded.

"I can feel the change and repentance in your hearts, and I can help you to reunite with God. He still loves you as much as when He created you, and I know He wants you to return to Him. He wants to bless your planet and all who live here," Chelsey said.

With a fresh tear running down his tattooed face, he softly said, "How *could* He love us after all the horrible things we've done? And the way we've lived for centuries, worshipping another god? He should make us slaves in His kingdom for all the evil we've done."

She smiled and said, "Believe me, every species in the Universe has messed up sometime or other but God never stops loving us. He is always forgiving, and He loves us no matter what we've done. In fact, when we come to him with a sincere heart, He opens His arms to us. He totally forgets about what we did, as if we'd never done it!"

Like a little kid, the elder's eyes turned tender.

He knelt in front of Chelsey and said, "Are you certain?"

She giggled in joy and said, "Yes, enormous sir, I am certain."

"Then help us, please," he said with pure sincerity.

Chelsey looked at him and said, "Do you think you could maybe uncuff me now?"

The elder responded with embarrassment, "My most sincere apology, yes."

He motioned to a soldier who unlocked her shackles and then returned to his place.

My goofy friend touched the hand of the ginormous elder. Even kneeling, he was amazingly tall.

She said, "Sir, before we go on, I have to tell you something, but don't freak out, ok?"

He looked at her a little apprehensively but told her to go on.

"Did I mention my best friend, Arëk, came here to rescue me? No? Well, he is here, and he had an excellent opportunity to grab me so we could escape. However, he was obedient to God and waited. So, please don't punish him. He was doing what any best friend would do in the situation I am in. Is it safe for him to come out of hiding and join us? He's from Schmec, and he's super cool. You'll love him."

Axl shakes his head no and gives a worried, "Holy moly!"

Yeah, dude, holy moly is right! I thought for sure it was my last day.

The Fasian elder took his time answering her, but finally, he spoke to the soldiers and fellow elders.

"The Schmecum shall be welcomed to the circle."

All nodded in agreement.

Chelsey said, "Arëk, you can come out."

I thought, no freakin' way, dude! You cra-cra! I'm not dying today! But I slowly walked out from behind the tree anyway and joined my friend.

Axl laughs.

I smiled, "Hello, everyone," giving shaka, hoping for acceptance.

No one said anything, but they didn't kill me either, so it was all good.

Chelsey took the initiative and continued telling the Fasi elders and soldiers about repentance.

She said, "Ok, I think it would be easiest if we did this as a group instead of individually since there are so many of you."

The oldest elder looked around to see if everyone agreed.

He said, "We will leave it to your discretion."

"Ok, first, my name is Chelsey. It's easier to be friends if you know someone's name. I'll learn all your names later. Let's get started."

Chelsey closed her eyes and addressed Heaven, "God, thank You for interceding today. A day of possible destruction turned into a day of victory for the Kingdom of Heaven. The Fasians, as a whole, are seeking Your forgiveness for their sins and for abandoning You so long ago. They are truly repentant, God, and they want to come back to You."

After those words, Chelsey looked at the Fasians and said, "If you are truly repentant, as I told God you are, I ask you to repeat after me. "Lord God…, we, the people of Fasi, come to You asking for forgiveness… We know what we have done… and we want to correct it and live better lives from here on… Please accept us as Yours once again… Amen."

Everyone opened their eyes and sighed with relief.

The oldest elder said, "Our new friend, Chelsey, thank you for bringing back to our remembrance the love of God. I apologize on behalf of the entire Fasian planet for kidnapping you. I have to say, though, I'm glad it was you and not another human who would have been a victim of an outrageous crime. We are deeply indebted to you."

Chelsey smiled, "You're welcome, sir. As scared as I was and as awful a situation as this initially was, I'm also glad it was me who you brought here. Not only was my planet saved, but you all came back to God. It is my honor to be the one to help you."

"I'd like to know who was in charge of picking the human to kidnap," I said with a smile that turned into a laugh.

Axl says, "You didn't!"

Chelsey busted out laughing, knowing where I was going with this.

Axl laughs.

"I suppose I don't understand the question," the elder said, smiling.

"Out of the entire Earth's population, Chelsey was your *WORST* option! The very last resort! She doesn't know the tiniest bit about government stuff or military intel! SpongeBob SquarePants would've been a better choice!"

Chelsey and I both bent over and laughed even harder.

The elder laughed at our uncontrollable laughter.

Axl laughs, too, wiping tears out of his eyes.

"I'd like to place blame on the soldier who did the actual kidnapping, but it seems God directed him to Chelsey instead of a military genius," the elder said, still laughing.

"Well, in hindsight, it makes sense. God intervenes at times. But just thinking about the soldier picking Chelsey out of the crowd for your purpose is *hilarious*!" I said, trying to catch my breath.

"It's pretty bad," she agreed.

Axl is still laughing.

The ancient elder said, "You two are funny! I'm happy God sent you both to us. Chelsey and Arëk, please tell everyone you know in the Universe that they are welcome on Fasi. Our planet's reputation is in for a good change."

"We're glad to hear it. I guess we'd better be on our way, though. Maybe sometime soon, we can stop by for a visit. You can give us a tour of the planet, and Chelsey can fill you in on government stuff!" I said, laughing.

Chelsey punched my arm and laughed some more.

Axl rolls backwards, laughing.

"Oh!" I added, "I have one more question. Why couldn't Chelsey transport herself off Fasi?"

"A very long time ago, we conjured up a curse holding anyone who wasn't Fasian, captive here. It was cruel, but it served the purpose of supplying sacrifices for the god of the red moons. Mostly, tourists and lost travelers were caught in the curse. Unfortunately, and fortunately, Chelsey couldn't leave. You didn't realize it, Arëk, but you wouldn't have escaped the curse either. There wouldn't have been a rescue. It just goes to show even more how God planned for Chelsey to be brought here instead of another human. He knew that by sending such a strong representative, there *would* be a rescue for both of you and for Fasian souls. I sincerely apologize again for holding you captive," the ancient elder said.

"I accept your apology again. Make sure you get rid of the curse, though. It's scary to be stuck somewhere," Chelsey said smiling her beautiful smile.

The elder responded, "When we repented of our sins, the curse was automatically broken, along with every other curse we'd spoken. We all felt it right away." He could see the relief on our faces and said, "You two be safe. We look forward to seeing you again."

"God bless you, sir," Chelsey said just before we disappeared.

12

Freaked Out Parents

Axl inhales deeply and lets out a heavy sigh.

Yeah, brah, it was definitely an adventure. But it didn't end there.

I should mention my and Chelsey's Fasi trip lasted only a day for us, but it was three days on Earth. Chelsey's parents were beside themselves! They paced a trail on the carpet, waiting for her to return.

When we walked into the house, Gracie and Micah Wick ran to the door in desperate relief. They grabbed their daughter, hugged her, and sobbed tears of joy. The dogs and monkey jumped on her and begged for her attention like they hadn't seen her in weeks! We wondered why everyone was acting so weird! We thought Chelsey would be in trouble for being a few hours late, so we were surprised they were so happy to see her. We expected her to be scolded, drilled about where she'd been, and possibly grounded for a weekend or something. But hugs, kisses, and tears?

We looked at each other like, "What's up with the pets, and why are Mom and Dad so emotional?"

Finally, Gracie and Micah calmed down and asked Chelsey where she'd been for the *last three days*. We looked at each other with raised eyebrows.

She asked, "What are you talking about, guys? I've only been gone for a day. I'm sorry I'm late. I'll do extra chores for a week to make up for it if you want me to."

They stroked her hair as if to ask, "Are you on the dope, sugar plum? Someone call the rehab!"

Axl chuckles.

Gracie said to Micah, "Something traumatic must have happened!" Then she addressed Chelsey. "Angelfish, you've been missing for *three days*. We're so relieved you're home! We've been so worried! We've had the police and everyone else we know looking for you all this time. I thought maybe another shark…" she trailed off with tears in her eyes, remembering the terrifying encounter Chelsey had with a tiger shark while surfing at seven years old.

Axl's eyes widen.

Yeah, dude, I'll have to tell you about it sometime. It was epically scary!

Axl asks if I was there. I nod yes, and he says, "Oh, man!"

Micah hugged Gracie and said, "She's home. She's safe. Let her explain, ok?"

Once again, we looked at each other like her parents were the ones who needed professional help.

"Can you tell us what happened, baby?" her dad asked.

Chelsey said, "Yes, I definitely want to tell you all about it, but there's something else I want to do first. I think it's time I introduced you to somebody. This is my best friend, Arëk. Arëk, meet Gracie and Micah, my mom and dad.”

They seemed to notice me for the first time standing in the doorway.

“Oh,” Gracie said, slowly extending her hand, “nice to meet you, Arëk, is it?” And before I had a chance to return the gesture, her mom added, “Did you say you’re *best friends*?”

Chelsey said, “Yes. I know I’ve never mentioned Arëk before or introduced you, but there’s a good reason. Can we all go sit down in the living room to talk?”

“Of course, sweetheart,” her parents said together, looking at each other with worry.

The four of us went to sit down for the big surprise.

“Ok, guys, first, I need to tell you, this is not going to be easy for you to hear. Please try to be patient and understanding and… as open-minded as possible,” Chelsey said while looking at me like, “Here we go!”

Her parents sat side by side on the couch, waiting apprehensively for the “sit down” news. I sat next to Chelsey on a large square ottoman, along with two dogs and a capuchin monkey. They were competing for the closeness of Chelsey.

She took a deep breath and said, “Mom, I want you guys to listen to me without saying anything. You’ll probably have a million questions. But please, just this one time, listen until I explain everything, ok? Please?”

Her parents looked at each other, then at me, then at their daughter, who apparently had a big secret.

After what seemed like hours but was only five seconds, her dad said, “Ok, Chels, we’ll listen. Promise.”

Chelsey looked totally nervous but tackled it like a champ. I figured if she could handle being kidnapped and almost tortured by the most brutal, scariest nightmare of all species in the Universe, she could handle her parents. Of course, I don't have parents, so I really didn't know what I was talking about. But I know my best friend, and she's the toughest girl I've ever known. She could do this!

I prayed inside my heart, "Please help her, Lord, this is important to her. She feels like it's the right time to tell her parents. Please help them to be understanding."

I think Charlie, the Border Collie, sensed my concern, as dogs have the keen ability to do so. She licked my fingers and rooted her head under my hand to let me know she was there. It helped to ease my mind somehow.

"When I was born, the *day* I was born," Chelsey began, "Jesus started talking to me. I know it sounds crazy. I don't even know how I understood Him, but I did. He said a guy named Arëk from planet Schmec would come walking down my street while I was playing in the yard. He would become my friend, and we would learn from each other. Every time I went outside to play, I looked for the guy Jesus told me about. It took five years, but he finally showed up. This is him."

She turned to glance at me and then back at her parents.

"I knew it right away, even though he had no idea what was about to happen or why he was even in Haleiwa. Ever since then, Arëk and I have been best friends. I know it's a shocker to hear there is life on other planets, much less that your daughter has been best friends with someone from another planet. But it's true.

"Something else you should know, and please don't get mad. I've been traveling all over the Universe since Arëk and I met. I've been to at least a hundred different planets, and I've met the most amazing people! Or species, beings, or whatever you want to call them. And I've done the most incredible things! I've wanted to tell you for so long, but God hadn't given me the OK I was waiting for. So, please don't think I wanted to keep this from you because I didn't. I had to honor God, and by doing so, He protected me when I was kidnapped by the Fasians. Oh, yeah, that's where I've been today… or the last *three* days, according to you."

Chelsey's parents' eyes grew wide as they inhaled deep gasps.

Against the promise to keep silent until Chelsey was finished, her mother interrupted with tears in her eyes, "*Kidnapped? Universe?* I don't under…"

"Mom, you *promised*!" Chelsey scolded.

Micah wrapped his arm around Gracie's shoulder and held her close to comfort her as their daughter continued.

"So, the Fasians kidnapped me to torture me into telling them all the Earth's government and military secrets. But of course, I don't know any government stuff. And Arëk went there to rescue me, which was super crazy and so brave! The Fasians were furious when I didn't tell them what they wanted to hear. They were going to kill me, but guess what?"

Gracie whimpered, "*Kill* you?"

"Yeah, but it was so awesome, Mom! God stepped in and used me to lead them to repentance! See, they had dumped God and started worshipping and sacrificing to the god of the red moons, which was a totally bogus god that couldn't make them happy.

"The Fasians started hating everyone, especially Earth, for some reason. They've been trying to get all our "military secrets" (air quotes) for ages. Finally, they kidnapped a human who they thought could give them our "military secrets" (more air quotes), but they kidnapped *me* instead. And as we all know, I don't know crap about government stuff. Remember, I barely passed American History and was grounded for like a month for my terrible grades? But you see, God led them to pick *me* instead of a military genius! He had a plan like He always does. The whole nation of Fasi repented and gave their hearts back to God! Isn't that awesome?

"Afterwards, they told me and Arëk we could visit anytime. And they invited everyone else, too. No one is in danger anymore since all their awful curses have been broken off their planet. So, anyway, now me and Arëk are home safe, and everything's good!"

When Chelsey finished explaining, she was completely out of breath. I looked across the room at her mom and dad. They were speechless and perfectly still. They kind of looked like mannequins. It was borderline creepy.

Axl chuckles.

Finally, Chelsey said, "Mom? Dad?"

The only word spoken at first came from her dad, "Uhhh…"

Chelsey asked, "Do you have anything to say or ask?"

(Silence)

"Guys?" Chelsey asked, a little concerned at the distant stares on her parents' faces. "Mom! Dad!" she shouted.

The dogs barked as if to help Chelsey. Her parents suddenly rejoined us and seemed somewhat coherent.

They looked at each other, and then Micah asked Gracie, "An *alien*? He said there would be a visitor, but… an *alien*?"

Chelsey and I looked at each other, then back at her parents.

Then her mom started talking crazy, too.

She answered, "Maybe we misunderstood so long ago. Did He tell us the visitor would be from another *planet*?"

Micah responded with, "No way, *did* He?"

"Maybe we missed that part. Maybe we weren't listening," Gracie kept on.

The two looked out into some great distance, then to each other, then to Chelsey, then to me. I smiled a big toothy smile and wondered what would happen next.

Axl smiles.

Chelsey asked, "What are you guys talking about? What visitor? Who told you about a visitor?"

Her mom replied, "When I was pregnant with you, God spoke to me and your dad. His voice was as loud and clear as I'm talking to you right now. Strangest thing ever."

Micah nodded in agreement.

"God told us the child growing in my womb was extraordinary. Then He told us there were many things about the world and the Universe you would teach us. It made no sense to us, but we continued to listen. Then He told us you would have a visitor at a very young age who would become your closest friend. God said you would know when to present this friend to us because we wouldn't understand at first. Now, I understand why," Gracie said.

"Why didn't you tell me about this?" Chelsey asked.

Her dad piped up and said, "We didn't understand it ourselves, baby. It just didn't make sense. And you never said anything to either of us about a visitor or a new friend. So, we thought maybe it hadn't happened yet, or we didn't understand God's meaning, or maybe God revamped the plan."

"Oooh," Chelsey said. "Well, since we're all on the same page now, I hope you'll accept Arëk for who he is. He is a gift to me from God. I want you to get to know him. And when you're ready, we can take you to his planet, Schmec, and lots of other planets! You wouldn't believe how many humans visit and live on other planets!"

"Slow down, kiddo. We're going to have to take this one step at a time. *Baby* steps," her dad said with an overwhelming sigh. "Little bitty, tiny, patient baby steps."

"I understand. I know you and Mom aren't Universe travelers like I've been for the past eleven years or so," Chelsey kind of joked.

"Oh, and about that," her mom said, "you're grounded! For a *thousand years*!"

"Maybe more!" her dad added.

Chelsey and I looked at each other with wide eyes and deep gasps.

"Mom, Dad, I'm sorry for leaving Earth without your permission! I couldn't tell you, not yet! Please forgive me and try to understand! Arëk and I have been asking God for years to let us talk to you and Dad about this, but He kept telling us to wait. So, I couldn't, right, Arëk?" Chelsey asked with teary eyes in desperation as her dad gave her "the look."

Might I say that dogs aren't the only animals in Chelsey's house with a strange sense of *knowing* something is wrong? Poot, the goofy little capuchin monkey …

Axl repeats, "Poot?"

Yes, dude, his name is Poot because he poots all the time! Nasty little monster!

Axl falls out of the hammock, laughing.

Anyhoo, the monkey ran about seventeen laps at the speed of light around Chelsey, me, Charlie, the Border Collie, and Booger, the Mastiff/Great Dane. Then he ran up and down the ottoman until I thought he was going to have a mental meltdown, running, spinning, and squeaking! He felt Chelsey's panic and about lost his mind in her defense! I was caught between wanting to laugh or sit on him to stop him! I did neither. I just sat there waiting for the next weird series of events.

Axl says he wants to meet Poot.

After the monkey fiasco, I said, "Chelsey's telling the truth, sir, Dad. Can I call you Dad?"

Micah looked at me with raised eyebrows but didn't have a chance to respond before I continued.

"God said we had to wait until the right time," I said in her defense.

I looked at Chelsey, and she had tears in her eyes.

"Please, sir, ask God. He'll tell you. Chelsey has never dishonored you. She loves and respects you more than any other human kid who loves or respects their parents. She hated keeping this secret from you," I said in desperation.

"And besides," Chelsey abruptly stood up and blurted out angrily, "it's not like you haven't kept secrets from me! God told me a long time ago about the plane crash and my sister and brothers you didn't feel obligated to tell me about!"

Her hands flew up and covered her mouth as soon as she realized what she had said.

Axl tilts his head, and his eyes widen.

Yeah, brah, the saga continues! Listen to this!

13

Secret #2 Revealed

All of us displayed wide-eyed, jaw-dropped faces.

Puzzled, I asked, "Brothers? Sister? You never told me you had brothers and a sister."

Axl says, "Whoa, that's major!"

Tell me about it, dude. I was critically wounded, and she could tell. A *secret*? My bestie had kept a big secret from me for all this time? I slowly slumped onto the ottoman. Chelsey had shocked herself. She was still standing with eyes wide, her mouth covered with white-knuckled fingers. Her parents looked at each other first with shock, then apologetically at their daughter.

Finally, her dad spoke up, "Chelsey, honey, we love you. We're sorry. We told you about them years ago, but you were too young to understand. So, we decided to wait for the right time to talk to you about it, and time got away from us. I promise we will tell you everything. But first, let's finish talking about you and Arëk. One thing at a time?"

Chelsey slowly sat down next to me, avoiding my bruised-hearted expression and the exhausted monkey in my lap.

Her dad said, "We've been kept in the dark about your secret, too. Your double life, which has obviously been a mature one, but that's not the point. My point is, we have hurt feelings with you now, too." He sighed, glanced at his wife, then continued. "Baby, I want you to know your mom and I trust you. Really, we do. We've known since you were a tiny little girl that you were exceptional, different, and special. We knew we had to give you a little more space than most parents give their children because of the strange message we heard from God. We've known all along this was supposed to happen. The whole *Arëk* thing. Minus the part where he's from another planet. We just didn't know what to expect or that it has been going on for all this time."

Chelsey's dad gave her the aggravated-parental-one-raised-eyebrow look, then added, "Travelling all over the Universe, Chels, *really*? What does that even mean? What if something had happened to you? On *MARS* or wherever! How would we have known? Can you understand our frustration? Do you hear how ridiculous this sounds? Traveling the Universe? Am I dreaming right now? Are we secretly being punked? *Universe* travel, Chelsey? Those words don't even make sense! You're barely allowed to fly to the mainland by yourself to see your grandparents!"

Micah stood up, threw his hands on top of his head, and started pacing the room.

Chelsey sat quietly for several seconds, trying to choose her words carefully.

"Look, Dad, I understand what you're saying, and I'm sorry it had to be kept a secret. But aren't you even interested in hearing about it? About the Universe and the planets and all the species I've met? About Arëk? About our adventures? About my… life?"

She knew she could turn his disappointment into pride if he'd only listen.

Micah cleared his throat and answered, "Yes, sugar, of course I do. We both do. Just give us a second to catch our breath. This is a lot!"

Micah sat down next to Gracie. He smiled the best he could at his daughter, who had just dropped a whopper of a bomb. Two bombs! He also tried to console Chelsey's mother, who was still off in another world somewhere.

Gracie shook her head to clear her thoughts after Micah kissed her cheek. Then she looked at her little girl, who was suddenly all grown up. Someone, please get Mom a Xanax.

Chelsey knew she'd hurt me, but my wounds would have to wait until later to be healed. Best friends are supposed to understand unconditionally. Parents are a tougher species to deal with. So, I'd wait because I loved her. Besides, I was getting big slobbery kisses of comfort from Booger to make me feel better. Slimy and gross but sweet.

Axl wrinkles his nose at the thought.

Chelsey is her parents' pride and joy. Although her news about her secret adventurous experiences shocked and perturbed them, they knew they needed to be the parents their daughter needed them to be. They knew they had hurt her, too.

Micah and Gracie stood up and hugged their daughter. They smiled at me, nurturing my pain, which was exactly what I needed. Then they sat back on the couch, tried to relax, and told Chelsey they wanted to hear about our big adventures. But to take it slow. Cardiac arrests wouldn't help the situation, they reminded her.

Chelsey and I sat on the edge of the ottoman, excited to fill her parents' ears with our stories. We told them about celebrities we've met, the snobby intellectuals on Smithers, and the crazy Zoochians. They heard about the basketball enthusiasts on Rondo, the many trends other planets have adopted from Earth, and the great friends we've made throughout the Universe. We skipped our wild experience with Fasi until later. It was way too much for Chelsey's parents all at one time, but they were gracious to listen.

They couldn't help but smile at their daughter's glowing, happy face as she shared her life with them. I had a feeling she was forgiven and hopefully ungrounded. The three of us couldn't hold back the laughter at how exhausted Chelsey was after talking at record speed! She looked and sounded like she'd just beat the current record for a race around the world! There's no one like my bestie. She's awesome, dude.

Axl smiles and loudly slurps the last of his smoothie through the straw.

You want another one, dude? They're so good, huh? There's a coconut smoothie you've got to try. Let's take a walk.

14

Flight 179

I continue the story as we walk to the smoothie shack.

After the unexpected disclosure of Chelsey's life outside of Earth, we thought it would be considerate to spend more time with her parents. We wanted to ease their minds and for them to get to know me. Over the next few weeks, they fell in love with me, and I with them. Gracie and Micah invited me to call them "Mom and Dad" if I liked. It touched me deeply, brah.

Chelsey's mom immediately began nurturing me after she learned I had no biological parents of my own. Apparently, it's unacceptable to Earth mothers for someone not to have parents. She hugs me and kisses my forehead every time she sees me. Best feeling EVER, dude!

Micah claimed me from day one because I make him laugh and we pick on Gracie and Chelsey together. He's a cool dude. He moved from Texas to Hawaii about thirty-something years ago, and he still talks with a Texas drawl. I like to give him a hard time about it. I've gotten good at imitating him.

We arrive at the smoothie shack and greet Makaio, the smoothie master. We order pineapple coconut smoothies and watch the surfers. Once the drinks are made, we head back toward our usual spot.

So, where was I, brah? Oh, yeah. Just as they promised, Chelsey's parents shared the tragic story about her siblings, Lexi, Austin, and Tripp. The details of the plane crash and their bodies never being found were still quite painful for Gracie and Micah, even after all those years. But they told Chelsey everything they remembered.

They and the other survivors were rescued from the sinking plane and delivered to an ER in Honolulu for medical attention. It took Micah until the end of the first rescue day to regain consciousness. It was the second day for Gracie. She was prego with Chelsey, by the way.

Axl says, "Oh, wow!

When Gracie woke up, her parents and grandparents were sitting in the hospital room talking to Micah and a doctor. Gracie's grandparents, "Mam and Pap," had been watching the news at home in New Mexico when there was an urgent "breaking news" interruption. An American Airlines passenger jet crashed into the ocean about six hundred miles from Hawaii. The reporter said the passengers on Flight 179 were all accounted for except for three children, who were still missing. When the photos of their great-grandchildren filled the tv screen, Mam got on the phone and called everyone to start praying. Pap called the airline and bought six plane tickets to Honolulu with their "emergency only" Discover card. They knew Gracie and Micah would need family support.

Once Gracie's and her unborn baby's vitals were stable, the doctor delivered the bad news he'd given Micah the day prior. Their children's bodies were not among the survivors. She was assured the government had search teams out looking for them. Gracie lost it! Micah and Gracie's family did their best to comfort her and keep her as calm as possible.

The parents stayed at Gracie's bedside after the devastating news. Mam, Pap and Micah teamed up to get the word out about their kids. There had to be a chance they were still alive. Mam used a phone at the nurses' station to call every prayer warrior she could think of to pray and spread the news.

Micah called the local news station and begged for a spot on the news. A reporter was at the hospital in half an hour to get Micah's statement. Before long, his urgent request for a search team spread like wildfire.

Dude, God caused the story to catch the attention of billionaire and future USA President, Donald Trump. He was on Maui purchasing some property when he heard about the Wick's tragedy. Being a man of power, he knew he could help. Mr. Trump flew to Honolulu and went to the hospital to visit Gracie and Micah.

Axl says, "No way! That's awesome!"

I know, right, brah? Talk about a surprise!

To hear Micah tell it, the whole chattering family became instantly silent when Mr. Trump walked into the room. HA! Apparently, he just started talking to them like they were old friends. He didn't even introduce himself.

Axl says, "Like he needed to! HA!"

Mr. Trump talked to them about regular stuff, then told them he was going to help them find their kids. He made a few quick phone calls, declaring the situation "URGENT." He told one of his assistants to organize a search team and get them in helicopters as soon as possible. Once all the business was taken care of, Mr. Trump sat next to Gracie on the hospital bed. He held her hand and told her and Micah he'd like to meet the kiddos after their rescue. In fact, he invited the whole family to go to NYC and stay at the Trump Tower, all expenses paid. He said he and Melania would love to host them for as long as they'd like to stay.

Axl says, "Whoa, are you serious?"

Serious, brah! He stayed at the hospital for a couple more hours, then got back to his business. He's a cool dude!

Micah was released from the hospital after three days with a few broken bones and a healing concussion. There were no internal injuries, thank God. Gracie had to stay about a week longer. The doctor wanted to monitor her pregnancy and make certain Chelsey was ok. He also wanted to feel confident that Gracie would be mentally stable enough to take proper care of herself and the growing baby inside her.

As soon as Micah was released, he researched contact information for some of the other passengers and flight crew. The ones he found were very supportive and shared what they could remember about the events. Many remembered seeing Austin, Lexi, and Tripp during the flight. But only a handful of them saw the kids after the plane hit the water. No one remembered seeing them in the group of survivors when help arrived. It was like they just disappeared. Micah and Gracie discussed how impossible it was that the kids were the only passengers out of a couple hundred unaccounted for. Why them? And where did they disappear to? It just didn't make any sense.

Only two weeks after the official search for the kids had begun, Gracie and Micah received a visit from a local authority. He told them the Coast Guard downgraded the search status to "Active Search Suspended, Pending Further Developments." Basically, they hadn't *completely* given up the search, but since no bodies had been found, they had to calculate the kids' odds of survival. They decided to call off the search.

Axl says, "Oh, no!"

Sadly, they did, brah.

The "calculation" is configured with software combining statistics and information like the temperature of the water/air and the location of the crash/disappearance. It also considers the weights and heights of the children, what they were wearing, and whether they had access to something floatable. The software determined the kids were not likely to still be alive due to thirst, exposure to the elements, or drowning. There was also the possibility they could have become part of the food chain, God forbid.

It didn't matter what the Coast Guard decided to do. Micah and Gracie were not going to quit. They couldn't give up on their kids, even if the rest of the world did. They knew either the kids would show up somehow or God would give them closure if all options failed.

Axl wipes a tear before it drops.

Her parents' story was not what Chelsey expected to hear. It was much worse. She felt guilty about being upset with her parents for not telling her about her siblings when they'd been living with this painful memory. She was glad to finally know what happened, and it gave her an even more determined drive to find them. She knew in her heart, somehow, some way, Austin, Lexi, and Tripp were alive. And we were going to find them.

15

Quick Getaway To Crumms

Chesley and I brainstormed day after day about how to look for her siblings. We had zero to go on. That made our detective work difficult and discouraging.

Chelsey was extra gloomy one day after an unfruitful day of sibling searching. I suggested we visit one of our favorite spots in the Universe. A tropical planet called Crumms. Chelsey and I discovered it one day when we were bored and looking for something new to do. From then on, it has been our "getaway" planet. Super chill place, brah.

If you enjoy Hawaii or the Caribbean, you'll fall in love with Crumms. The beaches are gorgeous and peaceful like in Hawaii. However, there is a slight difference in how things look there compared to here. Everything on Crumms is at least ten times bigger.

Axl raises a doubtful eyebrow.

Seriously, dude, the trees, flowers, waterfalls, all the landscape is titanic. The people are the only thing our size. They speak a unique language, producing more sounds than words. It's hard to learn. Although the Crummits understand each other, their language seems inconsistent to everyone else. It changes from day to day. It's one of those things you have to see for yourself. To accommodate visitors, they communicate mostly through smiles, hugging, and a loving spirit for everyone-kind. It works.

You know what else is cool about Crumms? The music. You can hear singing day and night, but you can't ever figure out where it's coming from. Chelsey and I have tried to follow the sound on several different occasions, but it eludes us. It's like it doesn't want to be discovered. It's weird but cool, brah! You'll have to check it out sometime.

So, anyhoo, it was a perfect day, like every other day we'd spent on Crumms. We laid on the beach and enjoyed the warm waves. We listened to the relaxing sound of the giant leaves blowing in the trees behind us, and we soaked up the warm sunshine.

Chelsey and I talked about random stuff mostly. Like what bands we would see in concert next or what Spoink and Weasel might be up to. Spoink and I "arrived" on the same day and have been good friends forever. Weasel is a school friend of Chelsey's who she knew would get along perfectly with Spoink, so we introduced them. They've been besties ever since. We run into them from time to time in my hometown of Lixyto. They're always goofing off and barely avoiding trouble. Weasel taught Spoink how to skateboard and hacky sack, and then they introduced their skills to the Schmecums. Now, there are skate parks all over the place.

We laid on the sand laughing at the thought of those two idiots.

Then Chelsey asked, "You know who would love Crumms? Poot, Booger, and Charlie. They love the beach and the water. I think the locals here would love them. Do the Crummits have pets? I don't recall ever seeing any animals on this planet."

"Me either," I agreed.

She continued, "Did I tell you an iguana wandered onto our front steps the other day? He's like four feet long! Big guy! Mom tried to shoo him away and tell him he couldn't stay. But he's still hanging out on the front lawn. I caught Mom feeding him a carrot yesterday. Sucker!"

We both laughed.

"You know my mom. She can't turn an animal away that needs rescuing. What should we name him?"

"I don't know, what's his personality like?" I asked.

"I don't know yet. I do know he's been injured at some point, though. He only has one good eye and lots of scars. I hope people didn't do it to him. It's disgusting how cruel people can be to a helpless animal! He'll be safe with us. I think I'll get him a cool patch to put on his bad eye. We'll have to give him a raunchy pirate name."

We both smiled.

"Pirate lizards are cool! But if I ever run into the jerk who took his eye, I'll give him a piece of *this*!" I said, flexing my sad little biceps.

Chelsey rolled her eyes and giggled.

Axl giggles, too.

"When your mom brought Poot home after finding him all beat up in a dumpster, it was hard to forgive humankind. It's a miracle Poot survived what those stupid guys did to him!" I said.

Axl laughs every time I say the name Poot. What a dude.

"Yeah, he's such a sweet little guy, crazy monkey. I love Mom extra for letting me keep him after she nursed him back to health," Chelsey said, smiling.

"Yeah, your mom's a saint, dude! It was awesome how she rescued Booger just in time, too! He was headed for the doggie electric chair! The Furry Green Mile! I'm glad the lady at the pound called your mom. He's enormous and slobbery, but he's a cool dog. Charlie's awesome, too. I love them all! I wish we had dogs on Schmec."

Chelsey smiled at my sentiment, then became serious.

"Arëk, I really, really, really want to find Lexi, Austin, and Tripp. Do you think they ever think about finding me? Assuming they're still alive somewhere? I'm sure they remember Mom was prego with me, right?"

"Of course! I'm sure they want to find you. Who wouldn't?" I said, smiling with my eyes closed.

She smiled back and said, "Don't you think it's weird that *no one* knows where they are? I mean, it's not like people can just disappear off the face of the Earth!"

After several seconds, we opened our eyes at the same time and turned to look at each other.

"You're brilliant," I whispered.

"We're dumb!" she responded. "Why didn't we think of that before? If *we* can leave Earth and roam the Universe, why couldn't my brothers and sister? Maybe God had otherworldly plans for them like He had for me. Maybe they each have their own 'Arëk' somewhere! I've been so determined to find them on Earth, I didn't think to look anywhere else."

I asked, "So, where should we look first? We should make a list of places and check them off one by one until we find the siblings. Someone will know them if they're out in the Universe. Too bad we don't have recent pictures of them."

"Yeah, that would be helpful. But we'll find them. If you could find me on Fasi, we can find my sister and brothers wherever they are. We'll get started tomorrow unless you have more important plans with some *other* best friend," she said jokingly.

"Well, I did have a hot dog eating contest with Scooby Doo and Shaggy, but I suppose I could cancel," I joked.

She shook her head and bumped my arm.

"Oh, wait! Is tomorrow the fifteenth? Tomorrow is the basketball tournament on Rondo! The one we signed up for like a month ago!" she said.

"Dude, is it here already? I'm glad you remembered! It would suck to miss that one!" I said.

"Totally! We'll start our investigation in a couple of days. Let's stop by my house first to let Mom and Dad know we're going to be gone for a day."

"Good idea. It will be cool to shoot some baskets with Hoops. He's playing in this tourney, right?"

"As far as I know. I think he's on our roster," Chelsey said.

"I hope so. He's so funny. I love hanging out with him," I said as we both stood up to leave.

"Yeah, Hoops is a blast! Let's head to the house, buddy."

Axl interrupts the story to question if the "Hoops" Chelsey and I were discussing is the same celebrity "Hoops" I mentioned while telling him about planet Rondo yesterday.

Yeah, dude, he's a friend of ours. I'll tell you in a few how we met him. It's a cool story.

So, anyhoo, moments later, Chelsey and I were in her backyard, walking toward the door. When we walked in, the aroma of homemade lasagna filled the house.

"Duuude! I love when Mom cooks Italian," I said breathing in the smell of garlic and sauce.

"Kids?" Gracie asked as she walked through the house.

"Yes, ma'am," Chelsey answered.

"I've got lasagna in the oven. About half an hour until supper," she announced.

"Why are you cooking supper so early? It's only 4:00 pm," Chelsey said.

"Your dad and I are going to a pee-wee football game. We promised Kai, from church, we'd go watch him play football tonight and again tomorrow. It's such a hoot to watch five-year-olds play sports," Gracie said.

"Cool! Arëk and I are playing in a basketball tournament in a city called Jume, on Rondo tomorrow. We just wanted you to know where we were so you wouldn't get worried. We're planning to go on over there tonight so we can hang out with some friends."

I quickly chimed in, "We're staying for lasagna first, though, right?"

Chelsey shook her head and said, "Yes, we're staying for lasagna, guido."

"Yesss!"

Axl says, "Yum!"

"Sounds like fun," Gracie said.

"Rondo is a blast, Mom! You should brush up on your old high school basketball skills and let us take you and Dad sometime."

Chelsey picked a cherry tomato out of the salad Gracie sat on the table.

"My skills aren't *totally* ancient," she said, throwing a kitchen towel at Chelsey's face.

We all laughed.

"Let's set the table, Arëk," Chelsey said, tossing the towel on the counter.

16

Hoops With Hoops

When we arrived in Jume, the whole city was buzzing with excitement about the tournament. It was a much bigger deal than we realized. When we signed up, we thought it was going to be a small group of teams playing for fun.

We were wildly mistaken, dude. We unknowingly signed up to play in a weekend-long tournament with teams from all over the planet. The winner had the choice of either season tickets to the San Antonio Spurs home games or season tickets to the Golden State Warriors home games. The coolest thing, though, was all the participating teams were a mixture of regular folks and professional players! Of course, you didn't get to pick which pros you got to have on your team, but who cares! This tournament promised to be epic!

Axl says, "Whoa! Pros? That's awesome!"

We checked in and looked at the roster to see what team we were playing on. Hoops was on our team, as well as a couple of other people we knew, a few we didn't, and three pros. It was going to be super fun!

Chelsey asked, "I wonder if Hoops is sportscasting tonight or if he's off?"

"I don't know, let's ask around," I answered.

We walked around the arena until we ran into someone we knew.

"Hey, Alu," Chelsey and I said in unison.

"What's up, guys?" she responded. "I saw your names on the roster. It's going to be stellar!"

"Most definitely! Hey, so have you seen Hoops anywhere?" I asked.

"You ask as if you're buds with him or something," she said, laughing.

"We are, actually," I said.

"What? You're lying! Are you really? How? Can you introduce me to him? Think I can get his autograph?" she asked with hopefulness and excitement.

Chelsey and I laughed, remembering when I used to sound the same way about meeting Hoops. He's not only my friend now, but also my long-time hero. We met him a couple of years ago, and it was one of the best days of my life. I'll never forget it.

(Thinking back)

Two years ago, Chelsey and I were chillin' with Spoink and Weasel on Schmec.

Spoink asked, "So, Arĕk, did I tell you Hoops is coming here to promote a new basketball camp for a tiny planet called Konk?"

"Here, where?" I asked.

"Here, Schmec! In like two weeks!" he answered.

"No freakin' way, dude!" I said with excitement.

"Way! He's going to be at the Centennial Music Celebration in Yade. Apparently, there are going to be loads of bands, some celebrities, and miscellaneous acts there to draw a big crowd. It's been advertised all around the galaxy for like a month. I wanted to make sure you knew," Spoink said.

"We are so there," I said, fist bumping Chelsey.

Meeting Hoops was on the top five of my bucket list. This was the perfect opportunity to shake hands with my favorite celebrity! It would also be the longest two weeks of waiting in my life! Waiting is not my thing, brah.

Axl says, "Yeah, mine either."

When the day of the Music Celebration finally arrived, Chelsey and I were there with a Sharpie marker and basketball in hand. We walked down the busy streets where the celebration was underway. We looked for a big, enthusiastic crowd holding up pens and photos for the famous sportscaster to sign. We saw bands, booths, and a three-year-old prodigy from Hootie playing the drums, but nothing promoting Hoops or ESPNU. My enthusiasm was starting to plummet.

My bestie wasn't about to let discouragement get the best of me, though. We stopped at one of the booths and asked a lady whose face was painted to look like a fish if she knew where we would find Hoops. She was clearly not a sports enthusiast and didn't know who we were talking about. Weirdo. So, she asked one of the guys in her troop, who said he heard Hoops arrived but then canceled before they set up the stage. I thought for sure my ears would start bleeding at the news! I was crushed! Chelsey, still determined, asked the man if he knew where the ESPNU crew *would have* set up had they not canceled. He pointed in the direction.

"Come on, Arëk," my BFF said as she grabbed my hand.

"What's the point? They aren't even here anymore," I said with my head hung low.

"Oh, just come on," she insisted and pulled me to catch up with her.

We walked down the people-packed street, pushing our way through painted faces and colorful costumes. Personally, all I wanted to do was go to Chelsey's house, sulk on the couch, and cry into a gallon of butter pecan ice cream. But my buddy was determined to make sure I had a good day.

We ran into a girl we knew from planet Harley, who was at the music celebration with her family. She and Chelsey saw each other at the same time. They ran up to each other, hugged, and talked a hundred miles per hour in shrilling, high-pitched voices. They caught each other up on EVERY SINGLE THING in their lives in thirty seconds. It's quite a skill. The female species is unquestionably superior. Am I right, brah?

Axl nods in agreement.

I stood there watching until Sung's dad chimed in and said, "How do they do that?"

I laughed and shrugged my shoulders. He introduced himself as Jake.

"Hi, Jake, nice to meet you, I'm Arëk."

"So, this is quite a Music Celebration, huh?" he said, trying to make polite conversation.

"Yes sir, it is," I replied. "Have you seen the little kid from Hootie who plays the dru...," I started, but was interrupted when Chelsey grabbed my hand.

"We have to go! Hi, Mr. Yuve! Have fun!" Chelsey said.

"What in the world?" I asked as I tripped beside Chelsey, trying to keep up with her.

"Just come on," she said as her jog turned into a run.

"Where are we going?" I asked.

"You'll see," she answered.

We ran through the streets of the Music Celebration until we were on the outside of it, running up a hill. When we reached the top of the hill, she slowed us down to a stop. I was breathing so hard I had to bend over and rest my hands on my knees.

"What has gotten into you?" I asked with ragged breath.

"Look," she said, pointing down the road.

I stood up and saw a huge caravan of floating buses driving away from us about two miles down the road.

"I don't get it. What are we looking at?" I asked.

"It's Hoops, you big booger! Sung told me she saw them leaving the Music Celebration about fifteen minutes ago. It's them!" she shouted.

"WHAT?" I exclaimed. "What are we going to do?"

"We're going to stop their caravan!" she said with a "we can do it" smile.

Axl sits up in the hammock with anticipation.

My eyes brightened, and a smile stretched across my surprised face.

"Let's do it, bestie!"

She said, "I'll race you!"

The happiness I felt totally buried the sadness from minutes before. My best friend was not going to let Hoops leave town without meeting her buddy first. She's the best, brah, I'm telling you!

We sprinted down the road chasing after a celebrity who was off-limits to the public. Especially crazy people like us. At first, it didn't look hopeful since the floating buses were driving faster than we could run. But once they saw us running behind them, they slowed down and stopped. When we finally approached the caravan, we were so out of breath neither of us could speak a word. The driver of the lead bus stepped out and walked toward us. Chelsey tried to talk but still couldn't. She just held up a finger, silently asking him to be patient and let us catch our breath.

He smiled, shook his head, and said, "Take your time. You ran a long way! We've been watching you since you made it over the hill."

In between harsh breaths, Chelsey asked, "You watched us running the whole time and didn't stop?"

He laughed and said, "We were making bets to see how long you'd follow us before you gave up and turned back. I lost fifty bucks and my Jordan jersey!"

We stood upright as our pulses began to slow down.

I asked, "Who won the bet?"

"Hoops!" he answered.

My eyes must have grown to the size of dinner plates when he said the name. And then to hear he was rooting for us!

"So, what made you stop?" Chelsey asked.

"Hoops said your stellar determination deserves attention and an audience," he replied.

"Well, my bestie is his biggest fan, and when we were told he left the Music Celebration, Arëk was super bummed out. We've been looking forward to meeting Hoops since we found out he was scheduled to be here."

"I guess you'd like to meet him then, huh?" the man asked with a smile on his face.

"YES, WE WOULD!" I blurted out.

I could barely contain myself.

Axl laughs.

"Come on," he said, motioning toward the caravan.

"I can't believe this! Thank you, Chelsey! This is the most awesome thing you've ever done for me!"

"I love you, Arëk. Besides, I wasn't going to let some clown take your sunshine away."

She bumped my shoulder with hers.

"*You're* my sunshine, bestie," I replied, "and *don't* call my hero a clown."

It made her smile.

"Alright, guys, hang on, let me get him," the man said as we approached the second bus.

My heart was about to burst out of my chest!

The man opened the door, and out stepped my hero. He looked just like he did on the big screen.

"Hi! You two are quite the runners," Hoops said as he held his hand out to meet me and Chelsey.

"It is so amazing to meet you! I have dreamed about this moment for years," I said as I shook his hand, sounding like a psycho stalker.

Not my coolest moment.

Axl laughs and makes a heart symbol with his fingers. I push him, and he falls back on the hammock laughing.

"Hi, I'm Chelsey, and this is my best friend, Arëk."

"Pleasure!" Hoops responded.

"So, what happened at the Music Celebration? Why did you leave?" Chelsey asked, cutting right to the chase, as usual.

"As soon as we arrived, we were sent a message about the basketball camp we were going to be promoting. It was suddenly canceled. Apparently, the coach and his team, who were scheduled to coach the kids at the camp, bailed at the last minute. And since we have a gig tomorrow morning on Fluni, we thought we'd go ahead and pack up and get a head start. We didn't realize anyone saw us since we left as soon as we arrived. Someone was supposed to announce the show's cancellation at the Music Celebration," Hoops answered.

"Well, it makes sense, I guess. But since you *are* still on Schmec and have officially met your biggest fan, would you consider hanging out for a little while? It would make my friend's entire life," Chelsey asked as if I weren't standing right there being talked about.

I stood there praying on the inside, "Please God, please God, please God, make them stay!"

Hoops chuckled and looked at his ten-member crew, who had all gotten out of the buses by then.

"What do you think, guys? Do you want to hang out for a bit with these two track stars?"

One of the guys piped up and asked, "Do either of you play basketball?"

"Well, of course!" Chelsey replied. "What respectable human or alien doesn't?"

Everyone laughed at her quick wit.

"As a matter of fact, we happen to know of an outdoor court nearby if anyone's up for a challenge," she offered.

"A challenge, you say!" answered the man who initiated the conversation. "Are you saying you think you can beat the great Dunk?" clearly referring to himself.

"Bring it on, Dunky!" she said.

All the guys oohed and laughed.

"Two on two to start?" he asked.

"Let's do it!" she answered.

"Arëk, do you play, too?" Hoops asked.

"Heck yeah! I think you and I should take on my bragging bestie and the great Dunk," I responded.

"Game on!" He answered and gave me a high five.

My life improved a zillion percent, dude. I was stoked!

Axl laughs at my corniness.

"Alright, ladies and gents, it looks like we've got a game! Hop in, and we'll get the posse turned around. Arëk, you can get in with Hoops, and Chelsey, you can come up here and help me drive this monster," the man said.

It was super cool riding in the Universe's version of a tour bus. I sat opposite Hoops, and he immediately pulled out his phone.

"Do you selfie much?" he asked me, smiling.

"Are you kidding?" I asked sarcastically. "Have you met the cartoon character I call my best friend? I think we hold the record on both of our planets for the stupidest selfies!"

We both laughed.

"You two are nuts! This is going to be a fun day. Alright, Arëk, say cheeeese," my hero said.

He clicked the camera repeatedly as we made one goofy facial expression after another. I loved this guy, dude! No wonder he's my hero! He's stinkin' awesome! I'll introduce him to you, Axl. You'll love him, too!

Axl says, "Cool!" Fist bump.

"Hey, Arëk, what's your number so I can text the pics to you?" Hoops asked as if we'd been friends forever.

This day can't possibly be real, I thought to myself. But I didn't care if it was real or a dream. I was having the most epic day of my life!

After a few minutes, Chelsey directed the driver to the outdoor basketball court at one of the local parks. It was outside of town, so we didn't figure we'd be bothered, especially with the Music Celebration going on.

Basketballs came out of every bus in the convoy. These guys were serious! Of course, they were already dressed in shorts, jerseys, and basketball shoes. They were always prepared to scrimmage. Chelsey and I thought we might have to play barefoot since all we ever wore were flip-flops, but a couple of the guys had extra shoes on their bus.

We agreed to warm up before the big game. It was fun hanging out with Hoops and his crew. If you didn't know who he was, you would never know he was a celebrity. He's completely down to Earth, as humans say. Just a regular guy who made it big. It's super inspiring, brah.

When Hoops and I teamed up against Chelsey and Dunk, I didn't know what to expect. I figured Hoops' crew would be more experienced than my bestie and me. Surprisingly, our skills turned out to be about equal. What a relief! It would've been embarrassing to have been creamed after Chelsey made us sound like All-Stars.

Axl chuckles.

We were having so much fun we didn't notice the group of kids who had gathered around the court to watch us play. It wasn't until one of them shouted, "Shoot it, Hoops!" did we realize we had cheering sections. Hoops made sure to acknowledge those kids. After he shot the ball and made it, he ran over to fist bump the little boy who cheered him on. I'll bet his attention made that kid's life.

In the end, Chelsey and Dunk beat me and Hoops by two points. No doubt they cheated. Not really. It was a close game all the way through.

When we sat down to rest and rehydrate, I asked Hoops if he ever missed Earth. He said he didn't have any memories about his life on Earth. I assumed it was because he was so young. He didn't seem interested in talking about himself, so I filled his ears with adventures of me and Chelsey. I kept him laughing the whole time.

Finally, the day ended, and it was time to say goodbye to our new friends. They would leave for Fluni, and we would carry on with our daily lives. As much as it sucked for the afternoon to end, we walked them to their caravan to see them off.

Hoops said, "Hey, Arëk! I know we're all crazy busy, but we should catch up from time to time. Today was so fun! I would love for you and Chelsey to come to Rondo! You guys made me feel *normal* today. It was a nice change from my insane schedule."

I said, "Yeah, dude, for sure! It would be awesome!"

Chelsey told the crew goodbye and then hugged Hoops.

"I hope we'll see you again. This was so much fun! And you really made my bestie's day."

Hoops replied, "I had a blast today! I'm glad you two goofballs chased us down! You're totally ridiculous and weird (he bumped Chelsey's arm) but real. Real friends are rare these days. I was just telling Arëk, I want you guys to come to Rondo so we can hang out again."

"We would love to!" she said.

"Alright, chief, got to get this show on the road," the driver said, addressing Hoops.

"Coming, bro," he answered.

"Text me pics of your adventures," Hoops said as he climbed on the bus and stuck his head out the window to wave.

"We will!" Chelsey replied, giving shaka in return.

"See you, Hoops," I shouted and gave shaka as the caravan pulled away.

"This has been the best day EVER!" I shouted and grabbed my buddy into a big hug.

"It was epic, wasn't it?" she asked, smiling.

"Epic doesn't describe it! Thank you, Chelsey, you are the best friend God could ever have given me."

"Right back at you, Arëk," she responded.

And there you have it, brah. That's how we became friends with the legendary Hoops. We've seen him at his shows since then and played lots of basketball. We have more fun every time we get together.

The weekend basketball tournament I started telling you about produced unforgettable memories that Chelsey and I will brag about forever! But first, back to where we left off with Alu.

"…Think I can get his autograph?" Alu asked excitedly.

"I bet we can make it happen sometime this weekend, Alu. But first, we need to find him. Do you know if he's sportscasting tonight or if he's mingling in the arena?" Chelsey asked.

"I saw some of his crew a little while ago, but I didn't see Hoops, sorry," she said.

"No biggie, we'll look around. So, we'll catch you tomorrow, yeah?" I asked.

"Yeah, for sure! I can't wait to play with actual pros," she said.

"I know, right?" Chelsey exclaimed. "Well, we're going to check it all out. See you later, Alu!"

"Laters!" she said, waving, and we gave shaka in return.

"Look at all these people, bestie," I said.

"I know, it's crazy! I don't think I've ever seen Jume this packed!"

"It's going to make it hard to find Hoops, for sure," I said, shaking my head.

"Or *NOT*!" a voice came from behind, followed by a group bear hug.

"Hey!" Chelsey said happily.

"Hoops!" I said and offered a fist bump.

He said, "I saw you guys signing in a little bit ago. I was caught in a crowd and couldn't get over to you before you left the gym."

"Did you see our roster?" I asked.

"Yeah! Steph Curry! Mind-blowing!" he exclaimed.

"He's my favorite! Love him!" Chelsey said.

"And Kawhi Leonard? And Rajon Rondo, too?" I added excitedly.

Axl's mouth fell wide open.

"I know, right? It's going to be the tournament of tournaments! I've met all the pros lots of times, but I've never played ball with them. This is going to be quite a weekend to remember! I'll make sure my staff gets tons of great pics with the three of us and the pros," Hoops said.

"Awesome!" we said in unison.

"So, you guys are staying at my house, right?" Hoops asked.

"Are you sure?" Chelsey asked. "We wouldn't want to impose!"

"I wouldn't let you stay anywhere else while you're on my home court! I have plenty of room. Are you hungry?" he asked.

"No, actually. Chelsey's mom cooked homemade lasagna before we left. It was so good, dude!" I responded.

"Well, that explains your vampire-repellant breath!" he said, pushing my arm.

Chelsey had a good belly laugh at my expense.

Axl laughs, too.

"Ha-ha, very funny!" I said.

"So, show us your hut," Chelsey said.

"Let's go!" Hoops answered.

We rode with Hoops in his private floating car. We expected his house to be an out-of-this-world mansion for the rich and famous. We were quite surprised. Unlike most celebrities, Hoops lived modestly in an average-sized house in a regular neighborhood. In fact, you could almost fit his house inside Chelsey's house twice! He isn't showy or glamorous, brah. He's regular, like us.

"Great house!" Chelsey said as we walked in.

"Yeah, this is awesome, dude!" I exclaimed.

"Thanks! It's not fancy, but it's plenty for me. There are two guest rooms. Take your pick," Hoops motioned toward the hall with guest bedrooms.

"Thanks again for inviting us to stay here," Chelsey said.

"Of course!" he answered. "Why don't you guys get comfy, and we'll meet back in the living room. I'll conjure up something to snack on."

"Sounds good," Chelsey answered. "Oh, hey! You should make us some of those amazing smoothies you bragged about a few months ago. We'll see if they compare to our master smoothies at home.

"Yeah, cool! I'll get it started!" he said.

"You got popcorn?" I yelled from my guest room.

"Yep! I'll get it popping!" he yelled back.

It was such a fun night, dude! The three of us laughed, told stories, and played a side-splitting game of Pictionary. My bestie can draw the world's most versatile, comedic stick people you've ever seen! It's quite an impressive gift, let me tell you!

Hoops enjoyed our company as much as we enjoyed his. I think he needed to feel like a regular guy with regular friends who didn't want anything from him. He needed to laugh and let loose. Chelsey and I were just the friends he needed. We knew he was funny, too, but we really hadn't spent this kind of time with him before. We discovered just how hilarious he is! We all had each other crying with laughter. It was a blast, dude!

Axl comments that friends like that are few and far between. That's absolutely true.

Dragging our sleepy butts out of bed the next morning was rough, however. Chelsey, Hoops, and I realized we stayed up way too late the night before. But it was totally worth it. We'd just have to play basketball with crusty sleep boogies in our eyes.

"You wouldn't by chance have a Starbucks handy, would you, Hoops, old buddy, old pal?" my bestie asked out of sleepy desperation.

"As a matter of fact, no. But I can make you a breakfast juicy known to knock the butt hair off a baboon! It'll wake you right up! This planet grows some outrageously potent fruit!"

"Baboons don't have hair on their butts," I yawned.

"Exactly!" Hoops responded, pointing his finger at me.

"That makes no sense at all, dude, but whatever floats your canoe," I said sleepily.

"Your juice thing sounds disgusting. I'll try it, though, if it'll give me a boost. I feel like a zombie this morning!" Chelsey yawned.

Hoops blended up the gnarliest-tasting concoction. But as he promised, it woke us right up. It made me question how much crack he put in it.

Axl and I both laugh.

We were showered, dressed, and ready to play ball in no time.

These shenanigans happened all three nights and days of the tournament. Staying up late, laughing, karaoke, games, amateur gymnastics, and takeout food. Followed by getting up early, enduring Hoops' revolting and questionably legal breakfast fruit juicy known to knock the butt hair off a baboon, and hours of ruthless basketball.

And now, drumroll, please…the winner of the tournament, by a very lucky, miraculous basket at the buzzer...Team Arëk and friends!

Axl says, "No way!"

Yep, FIRST PLACE, dude! We were awesome! Ok, truth be told, Rajon, Stephen, and Kawhi were awesome, and we were desperately mediocre, but it was a blast! Best weekend ever!

Axl comments on how cool it must have been.

17

Distracting The Folks

After a fun-filled weekend with Hoops, our spirits were so high we felt like we could tackle anything! It was time for another exciting round of sibling search.

We decided it would be more productive to keep Gracie and Micah unaware of our investigation. We were certain they would want to help. And as nice a gesture as it would be, it would most certainly wreck our plans. So, we prepared our strategy in secret. We composed a long list of planets we'd explored and some we hadn't.

Once our operation was all ironed out, we decided to make a separate plan for the folks. We needed to ensure our mission would be void of any interruptions. We'd have to come up with a detour from Gracie's and Micah's regular routines so they wouldn't notice us being gone for days at a time. A "well-deserved vacation," we'd call it.

We knew it would have to be a smart plan. One which would ensure so much fun for the parents, they wouldn't spend a single moment wondering about Chelsey and me. The trip also needed to be semi-inexpensive since Chelsey would be robbing her savings account to fund this plan.

For days, we Googled mainland destinations like Las Vegas, Colorado, and tourist towns on the East Coast. But no matter how great our ideas were, Gracie and Micah would never fall for it. They knew us too well. A paid vacation off the islands out of the blue? From their daughter, who is the penny-pinchingest person they know? Clearly suspicious.

We had to come up with a believable scheme. One which would require serious brainstorming. We were smart and creative. We could pull something brilliant out of the hat, right? We always did. So, why did nothing come to mind? Why weren't our wheels turning? Why did we hear a flat line? Beeeeeeeeep.

Then, as if lightning struck my little brain, I had it, dude! We would finally talk the parents into visiting another planet! We'd been trying since we first told them about it so it wouldn't be a random or suspicious idea. Of course, our argument would have to be more convincing than all our prior attempts. My bestie and I felt the sparks of genius bursting into bright, hot flames! Oh, yeah, baby!

The Master Plan…. Bwa-ha-ha-haaaa!

Axl chuckles.

Objective #1, Step 1: Talk the parents, code name "chickens," into the plan.

Objective # 1, Step 2: Put Objective #1 on the back burner because we have no idea how in the world, we're going to be able to talk the chickens into it. Better start with Objective #2.

Axl laughs at the code name "chickens."

Objective #2: Make sure it's a good time for the chickens to take a trip, i.e., no book signings, conventions, classes, etc.

Objective #3, Step 1: Decide where we will send the chickens in case a miracle happens and they say yes.

Note: This vacation must be a guaranteed good time, or it could blow up in our faces. The chickens must have a great experience on their first trip off Earth. Otherwise, they might want to come home early or, worse, never want to go back out to space. We might need the chickens out of our hair again someday, so we must make sure our plan is airtight.

Objective #3, Step 2: Talk to friends on different planets to find out where the best tourist spots are. Also, if there is anything exciting happening anywhere, such as live entertainment, scenic tours, etc. You know, things that would interest the chickens.

Note: Remember, this must be a fun-filled, memorable, "want-to-go-back" kind of vacation. We can't screw this up!

Objective #3, Step 3: Once the destination is decided, we'll tell the chickens we'll personally escort them to the planet. We'll stay with them until they feel completely comfortable. Then, at the end of the vacation, we'll personally pick them up and bring them back to their beautiful island home.

Objective #3, Step 4: Have our friends, i.e., specially appointed tour guides, waiting to greet the chickens first thing. The chickens will be assured they have twenty-four-hour support for anything they might need after Chelsey and I have exited the scene. This will increase the chickens' confidence that everything will be ok during their first otherworldly vacation.

Objective #1, Take 2: Talk the chickens into the plan.

Objective #1, Take 3: Still no workable strategy. Crap!

Objective #1, Take 4: Beg and plead. Possibly make total fools of ourselves. Force ugly crying. Nope, no good, the chickens won't fall for it.

Axl laughs.

Objective #1, Take 5: THINK! THINK! THINK! What is a good motivator for the chickens? What would ignite an interest strong enough to get them to leave the only planet they believe has people on it, regardless of pictures, proof, and ME? What would it be, what would it be, what would it… BINGO! My bestie is a mastermind! Ha-haaa!

Objective #1, Take 6: Here's how it went down, with a few minor adjustments and rearranging of the Objectives.

Chelsey and I made several quick trips to our ten favorite planets. We talked to friends and friends of friends to get the scoop on the happenings around the Universe. After much inquiry, the three most favorable vacation destinations for the chickens were relaxing Cozy, exciting Zooch, and extraordinary Laya. Zooch won the survey, with Cozy coming in a close second. Destination decided. Objective accomplished, brah. High five!

Axl and I high five.

Next, we talked to several guys we know on Zooch to get all the details about the huge festival the city of Brint would be hosting in two weeks. According to our informants, this festival was held every couple of years, and it was outrageously entertaining! "Everyone comes to the Brint Festival!" they said. There would be people visiting from all over the Universe to enjoy live bands, theater, food, games, music, contests, prizes, and celebrities. Heck yeah! Schedule in hand. Objective accomplished, brah. High five!

Axl and I high five.

Tour guides were next on the Objective list. We contacted a couple of our friends who we knew would be happy to participate in the plan. Bones and Smoot, two bodacious Zoochians who came back to Earth with us ten years ago. Chelsey taught them how to surf. Since then, they've spent more time on the Pacific waves with us than they have on their own planet. Cool dudes. They were stoked to play the part of vacation chaperones for the chickens. Tour guides hired. Objective accomplished, brah. High five!

Axl and I high five.

Finally, the hard part. Talking to the chickens.

Dude, I can't tell you how many hours my BFF and I spent devising our grand scheme to get her parents off the planet. We didn't have a lot of time since the Brint Festival was only two weeks away. For two people who always had stellar ideas, Chelsey and I continued to come up with nothing. We were beyond frustrated. Then, something super cool happened while Chelsey and I chilled on the couch eating string cheese. Apparently, string cheese has magical powers.

Axl says he loves string cheese.

Chelsey said, "Arëk! I just thought of something!"

"What?" I responded.

"Come with me," she said, jumping up from the couch.

We quickly walked down the long hallway leading to her mother's office, a.k.a. outrageously awesome chamber of totally cool vibes. Dude, I love this room so much! One whole wall is a split sliding window facing the ocean. It opens to a gorgeous wooden balcony with a small table, chairs, and a hammock. The balcony is partially shaded by a huge palm tree. Gracie writes her novels inside and reads outside. It's dreamy.

In one corner of the office, stands an ancient surfboard given to her by a hundred and five-year-old native Hawaiian man just before his death. It was his grandfather's board and the one he, himself, learned to surf on. Gracie and the old man became friends when she lovingly financed the rebuilding of his little house after an unfortunate fire. She didn't even know him at the time. She just wanted to bless him.

Axl is wowed!

Yeah, dude, Chelsey's parents love to help people. They're awesome.

In the opposite corner, stands another surfboard, only much smaller. It's pink and white with a Polynesian tribal turtle painted in the middle. The board's most eye-catching feature, however, is a large missing chunk in the shape of a shark's mouth. The jagged edges remind Gracie of God's mercy the day her little Chelsey was attacked by a Tiger Shark. She suffered some gnarly wounds, but God kept her alive. The shark got away but not without a major beat down from a teenage boy who happened to be sitting on his board nearby. He swam to her and punched the shark in the face until it left Chelsey alone. I still thank God for the brave kid who put his own life in danger for my bestie. He's a hero, brah.

Axl shakes his head and says he's so glad she survived. I clear my throat, wipe my eyes, and continue.

Gracie is also a collector of fine crayon and Sharpie art. Her office walls display at least twenty framed drawings by her imaginative young children, from forever ago. The colorful masterpieces exhibit various activities illustrated by stick people. Represented are Gracie and Micah, Lindymom and Pipe (Gracie's Mom and Stepdad), Granddad and Grandma (Gracie's Dad and Stepmom), and Mam and Pap (Gracie's grandparents on her mom's side). Also featured are school friends, houses, sunshine, water, dogs, surfboards, and corndogs. Each piece is worth more than the entire world's fortunes in this proud mama's eyes.

The floor of Gracie's office was custom-made to look like glassy blue water. It is incredibly lifelike! When you first open the tall, frosted doors and take a step inside, it looks like you're going to fall into the water! Even though I've been in her office a hundred times, brah, it still freaks me out!

Axl laughs at the visual.

The wall behind Gracie's custom-made desk is mostly inset shelves showcasing more of her favorite things. The top couple of shelves display all her writing awards, including her Pulitzer Prize, which she cried over for days.

Other shelves contain framed photos of Gracie with famous people, including Keanu Reeves, taken during the making of *Point Break* on Oahu. "I hope we meet again" is written by Keanu on the back of the photo.

There's a photo of Gracie and several of her high school girlfriends with Leonardo DiCaprio giving shaka in Times Square during a spring break trip to NYC.

There are two separate photos of Gracie and the members of Aerosmith. One of them is backstage after a rocking concert in New Orleans. The other is *on* stage with the band in Miami when Steven Tyler pulled her up there to sing "Angel" with him. She said Steven remembered her name from when she met them backstage a few years before. He introduced her to the audience as "his friend, Gracie, from Oahu!" She was totally shocked he remembered her.

Axl is in awe! "She got to sing with the band? I love Aerosmith!"

Me, too, dude!

Gracie, Chelsey, and I took a super cool photo with Dwayne "The Rock" Johnson and our surfboards on Ehukai Beach. He was here surfing with some friends. Chelsey and I got to surf with him, too. That guy is a blast to hang out with!

Finally, there is a photo of Gracie, Micah, and Robert Downey Jr. while dining at Hoku's at The Kahala Hotel and Resort in Honolulu. Gracie runs into celebrities everywhere she goes, it seems.

Axl is totally wowed.

There is one shelf near the middle of the wall behind Gracie's chair that is mostly bare, minus four precious treasures. One is a misshapen clay bowl, finger-painted with every color by three-year-old Lexi. She made it on "I Love My Mom" day at preschool. The bowl is full of shells and rocks gathered by Lexi and Gracie during a Saturday walk on the beach.

Axl tears up a little. I always do.

Next to the colorful bowl is a coconut. It has carved-out and painted facial features, a black beard, big white teeth, a red bandana tied around the top, and a patch glued over one eye. This crazy little gem is Tripp's coconut pirate. Arg, maties! Micah did the carving to avoid a potential visit to the emergency room. Then five-year-old Tripp did all the painting and gluing by himself. "Captain Shark Breath" guards the other treasures on the shelf.

Axl tears up again and chuckles at the name.

Also, on this shelf stands a picture frame made of colorful sea glass. Each piece was picked specially by Chelsey and Gracie one morning after a storm. There were always fun things to find on the beach just after a storm. Chelsey, with the help of her third-grade teacher, Mrs. Yan, carefully glued the sea glass pieces together until they formed a heart. After the glue dried, Chelsey and Mrs. Yan placed Chelsey's favorite picture of her and her mother inside the frame. Mrs. Yan made the back and the stand for the frame out of cardboard from a box flap in her classroom storage closet.

Axl says these are the sweetest things he's ever heard of.

The fourth creation on the shelf is what Chelsey had on her mind when she jumped off the couch and ordered me to follow her down the hallway. When we entered Gracie's office, she walked directly to the shelves. She pulled a plain, 1' x 1' square wooden box off the shelf. She carefully set it on the desk. The unvarnished lid displayed the wood-burned words, "Austin loves Mama" in the script of a ten-year-old boy. This box took Austin three weekends to make secretly in the garage with Micah. He wanted it to be the best surprise ever for his mom's birthday. And it was.

Axl's eyes tear up again. Mine, too.

"What is it?" I asked.

"This is Mom's special occasion box. Austin made it for her birthday just three weeks before the crash."

"Oh, wow, cool! And sad! So, what are we doing with it?" I asked.

"You'll see."

She unhooked the simple latch and opened the lid. Inside were precious keepsakes. She pulled out concert and movie tickets, love letters from Micah, and Mam's scrumptious fresh apple cake recipe. Then came all four of her children's plastic hospital bracelets from the day they were born. There was a coffee shop receipt with "Delicious cup of coffee with my beautiful Gracie" written on the back in Lindymom's handwriting.

Next came a photo of Austin, Tripp, and Lexi soaking wet on the beach, giving shaka, a heart-shaped rock, and a photo of Gracie with an old friend from college who passed away. There was a Cherry Diet Coke lid, a peanut M&M's wrapper made into an origami swan, and Chelsey's first report card.

She pulled out Grandad's dog tags, Gracie's high school class ring, and backstage passes to a Def Leppard/Poison concert. Also in the box was Pap's favorite guitar pick, given to him by Roy Rogers, and many other wonderful mementos from her life.

The one Chelsey hoped to find, however, was a small torn-off corner of a blue piece of paper. After carefully removing piece by piece of her mom's sacred treasures, she found it. Her eyes lit up, and a big white smile stretched across her tanned face.

"This is it, Arëk!"

"What is it?" I asked.

"Look!"

She held up the little piece of paper, showing me a date with a heart drawn around it.

I shrugged my shoulders and shook my head.

"It's the date of my parents' first date!" she informed. "Two weeks from now!"

"Okay?" I said, shrugging.

"It's the anniversary of their beginning! Get it?"

I shrugged again.

"Seriously, Arëk? You're such a dude! Our little vacation plan for them is now an *anniversary* vacation plan!"

"Oooooohhhhhhh!" I finally caught on.

Axl laughs.

"This is totally a God thing! It has to be! It's perfect!" she exclaimed with her fists punching the air above her head.

Because God likes to do cool stuff for us, both parents were able to take vacation time. They were excited to see what Chelsey and I had planned. We assured them it would be the best expense-free vacation they'd ever experienced.

We invited them to join us for their favorite home-cooked TexMex-style tacos at the dining room table.

"So, what's this all about, kids?" Gracie asked while loading her taco shell.

"Well, we want to do something special for you and Dad *on your anniversary*," Chelsey answered.

"But honey, our wedding anniversary isn't for another five months," Micah said, passing the salsa.

"Oh, I know. This isn't for your *wedding* anniversary. It's for your *beginning* anniversary," Chelsey said.

Gracie and Micah looked at each other and then back at their daughter with confusion.

"Your first date anniversary. The beginning of your love and your life together, on Lei Day."

They giggled and looked sweetly into each other's eyes and then kissed.

"It was a wonderful beginning, wasn't it, babe?" Gracie asked Micah.

"Yes, it was! You became my forever sweetheart that day," Micah told Gracie and took her hand in his.

"Your beautiful first date is what Arëk and I want to help you celebrate," Chelsey said.

"Well, then, where are we going, Angelfish?" Gracie asked. "Arëk, pass me the guacamole, please."

"Well, it's a city you've never been to before. It's called Brint. They're having an epic festival there! Kind of like Lei Day. You'll love it! We've even arranged tour guides for you and reserved a sweet little private cottage for you to stay at. It has a full kitchen and even a hot tub!"

"It sounds wonderful, sugar!" Micah responded. "This is so thoughtful of you both! Cheese, please, sweet girl."

"It's our pleasure," Chelsey said looking at me with a wink, handing her dad the bowl of cheese.

"You'll need to pack for warm but not hot weather. Pack swimsuits, and don't forget your phone chargers. You'll want to take lots of pictures," Chelsey said.

"So, is it safe to assume Brint is on the mainland since Hawaii doesn't have a city named Brint?" Micah asked just before taking a huge bite of his taco.

"It's definitely not on the islands," I answered.

"So, we'll need to pack a carry-on bag for the plane then," Gracie added. "These tacos are incredible!"

"Uhh, actually, you won't be flying, per se," Chelsey said.

Her parents stopped chewing and looked at us with tilted heads.

"Brint is on Zooch," Chelsey said, closing her eyes tight and waiting for their response.

"Zooch," Micah stated with a full mouth. "As in the *planet* Zooch you've talked about?"

Axl says, "Uh oh!"

"Yes, sir," Chelsey answered.

"Chelsey, we've been through this a thousand times," Gracie answered sternly.

"Mom, Dad, listen! Please! I promise to stop bugging you about it if you'll just go this one time. Please! You'll love it so much!" their daughter insisted.

"No. And stop asking," Micah said as he took another bite of his taco.

"We'll go with you! You won't be on your own! You will have such a good time!" Chelsey pleaded.

Both parents exhaled heavy sighs.

"Should we just try it?" Gracie asked her husband, then gave us both an irritated look.

Micah shook his head no and asked his wife, "Are you serious?"

Gracie shrugged and said, "She won't shut up about it until we go. You know she wouldn't take us anywhere unsafe."

Micah let out another long sigh and looked at Chesley for about five forever-long seconds.

"Alright, fine. But the second we want to leave and come home, you are to bring us home immediately! No questions asked! Do you understand, kid?" he demanded.

Chelsey and I jumped out of our chairs and unleashed a happy dance! We ran around the table, grabbed her parents, and hugged them. They finally smiled and halfheartedly acted happy about it. Micah looked at his daughter as she returned to her chair. The excitement on Chelsey's face was more than he could stand. He loved her face, especially when it was so happy.

"It's going to be great!" Chelsey said as she took a monster bite.

Gracie and Micah smiled at each other, both happy to see their daughter so elated.

Micah said, "Someone, please hand me Arëk's delicious taco meat. I can't get enough of this stuff! Good job to both of you!"

"Mmm-hmm!" Gracie agreed with a mouth full of food.

We ate until we were stuffed, and then Gracie and Micah headed to the living room to rest their full bellies. Tacos are always a good choice! Chelsey and I quickly cleaned the kitchen and then joined them.

"So, when is this fiasco happening?" Micah asked.

"In two weeks," Chelsey answered.

"Two weeks. Plenty of time to come up with fifty excuses not to go," Micah said jokingly.

"Very funny, Dad. You and Mom are going to have so much fun there!"

"I hope you're right," Gracie said with a trusting smile.

We sat in the living room for a while longer. We talked about the rain, how awesome the waves were on the North Shore earlier, and some of the things they'd do on Zooch. Then Gracie got up to let the dogs out, and Micah decided it was his bedtime. Chelsey and I hugged them goodnight and headed back to her room.

Once the folks were out of earshot, Chelsey grabbed my arms and jumped us both up and down.

"I'm so excited, Arëk! THEY'RE FINALLY GOING! Thank you, Jesus!" she said in a shouting whisper.

I love my best friend, dude. She's so goofy!

Axl says he can't wait to meet her.

The next two weeks were torture for my buddy! Do you know how many smoothies, surfing expeditions, and concerts it took to entertain her for two whole weeks? It was exhausting, brah!

Axl chuckles.

So, at about 9:00 a.m. on the morning of the vacation, Gracie and Micah entered the living room toting luggage. Chelsey and I had already eaten our Cheerios and were finishing off our second latte. We'd been up and waiting for three hours already.

"Can we eat something first?" Micah asked, stalling.

"There's food there," Chelsey answered.

Micah sarcastically raised his eyebrows and looked over at his wife.

"I guess we'll be eating breakfast *there*," she responded. "Can we at least have a latte to get us started?"

"Ugh! I guess!" Chelsey answered.

Two lattes and forty-five minutes later…

"Ok, so this is how it works. Arëk and I will transport you to Brint. It is very important you *only* think about Brint until we get there. It'll only take about six seconds. Got it?" Chelsey instructed her parents.

"Got it!" they both answered.

"Are you sure? You can *only* think about Brint until we arrive," Chelsey reiterated.

"Yes, got it! *Only* think about Brint. How hard can it be?" Micah said, rolling his eyes at how crazy this whole thing seemed.

Chelsey and I looked at each other, wondering if this was a good idea after all.

"Ok, close your eyes and remember, *only* think about Brint," she said softly.

We grabbed their luggage, held their hands, closed our eyes, and in just a few short seconds, we stood firmly on the planet of Zooch.

"Whew!" Chelsey and I said to each other as soon as we saw all four of us standing there.

"Ok, guys, you can open your eyes now. We're here!" Chelsey told her parents.

I wish I'd recorded Gracie and Micah as they opened their eyes. Dude, it was epic!

Axl and I both laugh.

"Ooohhh my goshhhh, it's *real*!" Gracie exclaimed in wonderment and fear.

Micah couldn't speak. He turned slowly in circles with his mouth hanging open. His brain couldn't wrap around the amazing otherworldly surroundings and people.

"What is *that*?" Micah asked, then quickly moved behind me.

Axl and I laugh again.

"It's ok, Dad, those are Zoochians," Chelsey answered. "You look as much like an alien to them in your human form as they do to you in theirs. It's ok, they're just like us."

"Hey, there's Smoot!" I said, waving at our friend who was strolling our way.

"Dude!" Smoot said as he approached us. "Are these the Wicks?"

"Hey, buddy!" Chelsey answered and gave our friend a hug. "Where's Bones?"

"He's right behind me. He's paying for our yubls. Wow, toots, is this your mom?" he asked, clearly checking Gracie out.

"Yes, Smoot, meet Gracie and Micah Wick, my awesome parents."

Gracie and Micah were still trying to determine if they were dreaming or not. Their minds tried to make sense of the two-headed alien with multiple arms and legs and one giant eye on each head standing in front of them. And it was speaking *English*. After a few seconds, Gracie slowly extended her hand to meet this *person thing*. Her eyes were as big as *flying saucers*. Ha-ha! See what I did there? Oh, come on, Axl, it was funny, dude! *Flying saucers*? Aliens?

Axl fake laughs and punches my arm. Tough crowd.

Chelsey laughed.

"Hey Smoot, can you guys do 'human' until my parents get used to seeing other species? First time off Earth, remember?"

"Oh, yeah, totally!" he answered.

In a blink, he appeared as a human with a stellar tan, blonde ponytail, shark tattoo on his forearm, cargo shorts, tank top, and flip flops.

I thought Micah was going to fall out! It was AWESOME!

Axl and I laugh.

"There you go, guys! Better?" Chelsey asked, wrapping her arms around both of her parents for comfort. "So, Mom, Dad, meet our friend, Smoot. He lives here on Zooch but spends more time on Oahu than he does here."

Gracie and Micah stood there staring at Smoot in disbelief for several seconds.

"Oh, and here comes Bones! Dude! Come meet my folks!" she shouted, then mouthed, "Do human!"

Bones caught on right away, and in a second, he approached us in human form.

"Bones, Smoot, meet Gracie and Micah! Mom and Dad, meet your tour guides, Bones and Smoot!" Chelsey said.

"It's a pleasure!" Bones said, holding out his hand.

Finally, Chelsey's parents rejoined the living and responded, "Good to meet you boys, too."

Everyone shook hands and attempted small talk until I suggested we take the folks to the cottage to settle in.

"Great idea! We can sit down and give Mom and Dad a chance to take it all in," Chelsey agreed.

"We'll get your bags," said Smoot and Bones.

So, I've got to tell you, brah, Gracie's and Micah's initiation to another planet was much more emotional and involved than I had pictured in my mind. Like an idiot, I assumed it would be easy for Chelsey's parents to adjust to the Universe once they left Earth. They deal with sharks and hurricanes, so why wouldn't this be a piece of cake? I was way wrong, dude. It wasn't easy. Not for the first couple of hours, anyway. I thought we were going to have to call in Dr. Phil.

Axl chuckles.

After a short ride in a floating taxi to the cottage, the guys and I took the luggage inside. Chelsey escorted her parents to sit on the couch in the living room.

"Mom, Dad, are you ok?" she asked.

"Chelsey, I don't know about this," Gracie answered, taking hold of her daughter's hand.

"This might be a little too much for us, baby," Micah added.

"Let's just hang out here for a little bit. I promise you'll love this place once your nerves calm down."

Chelsey hugged her mom and then kissed her dad on the cheek.

"Your luggage is in the bedroom, Mr. and Mrs. Wick," Bones said as the three of us walked into the living room.

Gracie and Micah both gasped when they saw Bones and Smoot.

"Hey, Arëk, can you get us some bottled water from the kitchen?" Chelsey asked, hoping it might calm the parents.

"Oh, yeah, of course!"

Smoot said, "Mr. and Mrs. Wick, I know this is difficult for you, being your first time off Earth. It must be scary seeing people from other worlds all around you. But I promise we're all just like you. We just look different. If it'll make you feel more comfortable, Bones and I will stay in human form while you're here with us."

"Yeah, no problem at all," Bones agreed. "We want you to have a great time on Zooch. It's a wonderful planet, and our people are some of the best you'll ever know. We can even show you how to change your appearance to look like the Zoochians!"

"Can *you* change your appearance, too?" Gracie asked her daughter apprehensively.

"Of course! Remember, Mom? Arëk and I have been telling you and Dad about it for a long time. Everyone can look like other species! Even you guys can!"

Micah and Gracie looked across their daughter at each other. They've been married for so long that some conversations don't require words. Their silent conversation basically went like this:

"ARE WE DREAMING?" Micah to Gracie.

"WE HAVE TO BE! THIS IS *NUTS*!" Gracie to Micah.

"HOW DID WE LET CHELSEY TALK US INTO THIS?" Micah to Gracie.

"I HAVE NO IDEA! LET'S GROUND HER!" Gracie to Micah.

Axl laughs out loud!

"FOR HOW LONG? FOREVER?" Micah to Gracie.

"LONGER!" Gracie to Micah.

"AGREED!" Micah to Gracie.

"SO, WHAT DO WE DO NOW?" Gracie to Micah.

"DO WE HAVE A CHOICE?" Micah to Gracie.

"NO, I GUESS NOT. SO, WE'LL MAKE THE BEST OF IT THEN?" Gracie to Micah.

"YES. WE'LL GROUND HER FOREVER WHEN WE GET HOME!" Micah to Gracie.

"GOOD PLAN! BREAK ON THREE! ONE, TWO," Gracie to Micah.

"THREE!" Micah to Gracie.

Axl is rolling!

"Bones and Smoot have been some of our closest friends for years," Chelsey started. "They're just like me and Arëk. In fact, I'm sure they'll both be grounded and stuck with extra chores by the time your vacation is over!"

We all laughed, even Gracie and Micah. We hoped it was a good sign.

I walked across the living room with water bottles for the folks.

"You know, it's weird, but you boys actually look familiar to me," Micah said.

"You've probably seen us in Haleiwa or on the North Shore," Smoot answered.

"Yeah, we're there all the time," Bones added.

"The North Shore has the best waves!" Smoot said.

"No, wait, I know where I've seen you before. You guys were at the luau for the Pika wedding. We're close friends with Ben and Tia," Micah said.

"Oh, yeah, dude! I mean, Mr. Wick. Ben surfs with us all the time! He's been to Zooch a couple of times, too. Now you'll have something else in common!" Bones said.

"Are you kidding me? Ben's been here?" Micah responded with surprise.

"Small *Universe*, huh?" I said, bumping Micah's arm.

He kind of smiled.

Gracie looked at Chelsey and then at her husband.

"You ready to give this Zooch thing a try, babe?"

Micah smiled and exhaled a sharp breath.

"You know what, baby? It's our beginning anniversary. Let's do it. If we don't like it, we can go home, right guys?" addressing me and Chelsey.

"Yes, sir!" Chelsey answered.

"Alright, so, what's on the agenda, tour guides?" Micah asked Bones and Smoot, trying to sound confident.

My bestie and I smiled at each other. Parent vacation initiated. High five, brah!

Axl and I high five.

Gracie and Micah were surprised to find life on another planet wasn't terribly different from Earth. We hung out with them and took them on a tour of Brint so they could become familiar with our friends and the local scene. Chelsey offered to stay the night, to make sure her parents were ok in this strange place, but they declined her offer.

"You kids go on and do your thing. Your dad and I will be fine. We've got these two hooligans to keep an eye on us and make sure we don't get into too much trouble," Gracie told her daughter while winking at Smoot and Bones.

"We'll take excellent care of your folks, dude, don't worry," Smoot said.

"I know you will. Because if you don't, I know where all the hungry sharks live!" she answered playfully. "No, but seriously, I do. And I will feed you to them."

She was suddenly serious and scary.

"And on that fun note," I said, addressing Gracie and Micah, "you guys are going to have a blast! Zooch is right up your alley. You'll see!"

"We're counting on it!" Micah said.

They hugged me and Chelsey then scooted us on our way.

"Go have fun!" Gracie shouted as they walked away.

Operation sibling search, here we come!

18

Operation Sibling Search

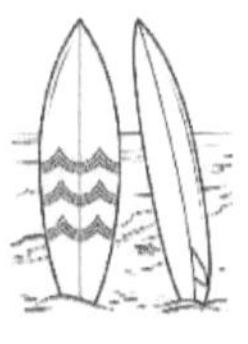 The first few days of the sibling search were unprofitable, at best. Your galaxy provided zero results.

My galaxy was next, with Laya first on the list of hopeful possibilities. For hours we asked one Layan after another the usual questions of our inquiry. None of them remembered any humans named Lexi, Austin, or Tripp who may have visited or moved to Laya over the past couple of decades.

Then, just before we gave up on Laya, we were blessed with a bit of good fortune. We met a super friendly lady named Suki, who worked in the Welcoming Center of her region. She told us she didn't remember any Austins or Lexis from Earth. But strangely enough, she did remember several Tripps.

One was a youth pastor from a little village in Indonesia who brought a group of kids on a mission voyage. Another Tripp was a repeat tourist from Rio de Janeiro, Brazil. Another was a medical scientist originally from a small Earth Island Suki couldn't remember the name of. And the last Tripp she remembered was a hairstylist from San Francisco, California.

My bestie and I knew exactly where to start.

Chelsey exclaimed, "Wow, that's awesome! Let's start with the island guy, Suki. Then, the American. Will you describe them for us?"

"Of course. The islander Tripp, the medical scientist, had light-colored hair and big brown eyes. He smiled the whole time he was here. He had a glowing joy about him. Like you," she said to Chelsey with a warm smile. "The Tripp from California had black hair and green eyes. He was lost. He just stopped for directions to Kooma."

"I think we should focus on the light-haired, brown-eyed guy. He has similar features as yours and your parents," I told Chelsey.

Chelsey agreed and then asked Suki, "Can you tell us anything more about "island" Tripp?"

She told us about the human medical scientist who visited their planet about a year back. He was looking for something specific, the root of a rare flower.

"We weren't much help to him because our planet doesn't grow flowers like he described. But we loved having him here. Island Tripp was very friendly and fun. He stayed a week with us to help a Tyrannosaurus Rex who had a tree stuck up its nose! It couldn't stop sneezing!"

Suki laughed at the memory.

"Tripp knew exactly what to do. With the help of about four hundred Layans, he plugged the big guy's other nostril with a huge rock. Then, they tickled its nose with the tail feathers of a Cutu bird. When the Tyrannosaurus Rex sneezed again, the pressure in its sinuses shot the tree, the rock, and a couple hundred Layans across the sky!"

Suki laughed out loud, holding her stomach. She had an awesome laugh, brah! Like a cross between a goat and a donkey!

Axl laughs at the description.

"I don't think I've ever laughed so hard in all my centuries!" she said.

I laughed with her. Because the story was funny, but her laugh made it even funnier!

I try to imitate Suki's laugh and it makes Axl laugh, too.

She added, "When we finally found the flying Layans, they were scattered about in trees, on roofs, and in lakes! It was the talk of the planet for a long time!"

I laughed with her some more.

"I would love to have seen that!" I said.

"Oh, and you should have seen the funny look on the dinosaur's face each time it sneezed before the big tree sneeze. It would close one eye, look around with the other one, quickly tap its foot numerous times, and then release two or three sneezes, one right after the other. It rattled the whole planet! Sometimes, its nose would make a whistling sound before a sneeze, and the dinosaur couldn't figure out where it was coming from. It was like watching a giant confused puppy!"

Suki had me rolling, dude! Chelsey seemed to be in another world all by herself.

She said quietly, "A medical scientist. I wonder if my brother is a medical scientist?"

I saw the excitement on my best friend's face, which made my heart smile. On another note, I found it a bit unfortunate she didn't hear one single word about the whole *sneezing dinosaur* thing. That was the *ONLY* thing I heard, dude! And Suki's contagious laugh!

Axl and I laugh again at the hilarious image.

"Thank you so much, Suki," Chelsey said, touching her arm.

She smiled and replied, "I am glad to help. I am hopeful you will find your siblings. God be with you both."

We crossed Laya off the list along with about ten other planets and stopped to think.

"Arëk, can you think of any other planets, possibly interesting to a medical scientist? Or useful in the *roots of rare flowers* department?"

Beginning to laugh again, I said, "I can't stop thinking about the T-Rex!"

Dude, it was the funniest thing I'd ever heard! Chelsey looked at me like I was high.

Axl and I laugh, imitating Suki's laugh together.

"Are you done, funny pants?" she asked, clearly not amused.

I was still trying to get myself together, dude.

I said, in between laughs, "Oh, yeah, roots. Maybe Rica?"

"*Rica*? Where's Rica? We've never been to that planet," Chelsey said with wonder in her eyes.

Brah, I'm telling you, I could not get my crap together after the T-Rex thing! You know how you get tickled, and then everything is hilarious? Yeah, I was worthless, dude!

Axl laughs, knowing exactly what I'm talking about.

"Rica is a tiny planet (laughing) about twelve galaxies from here. (deep breath) And it's not occupied by beings (trying to pull myself together). But its vegetation is unusual and renowned (doing better now). I've never been there but I studied it in school a long time ago. Anyhoo, it's an option we haven't covered yet."

I wiped my face with my tank top, trying to remove the smile I couldn't get rid of.

"Well, let's go!" she responded. "And knock it off!

She was annoyed at my delirium. That made it even funnier. I laughed again with my face inside my shirt.

Axl laughs.

When we got to Rica, it was barren of any species except vegetation. It didn't take long to search the entire planet. Unfortunately, we were disappointed with the results. No brother, no medical scientist, no sign that anyone had been there.

Next on our list was planet Int. No siblings. Then we went to planet Kimpab. Nothing. Planet Hunji. Nada. Planet Skuup. Zip. I was getting tired, and Chelsey was getting really bummed out.

I said, "Let's go back to Zooch for a little while. We can have yubls and share some stinky fries with lots of goopy stuff."

FYI, a yubl is like a smoothie, only better. And stinky fries are called stinky fries because they smell like feet. Oddly, they taste oh, so good! Stinky goodness. And the goopy stuff is kind of like melted cheese but with mystery chunks. We've never had the nerve to ask what it is, but it tastes amazing.

I continued, "It'll make us feel better and we can rest a while before we start again. What do you say?"

She looked at me with a tired, discouraged expression and said, "I don't care, whatever you want to do. But I don't want to run into my parents. They'll know something's up. I'm not their little ray of sunshine today."

"You know what would cheer *me* up? Seeing that sneezing dinosaur!"

I cracked myself up again.

Chelsey looked at me like I had ten heads.

"What stupid thing are you talking about, Arëk?" she asked, not really interested.

"We are going back to Laya after we find your brothers and sister. You missed out on the funniest story ever, dude! It would be criminal for me to let you live the rest of your life without knowing about the sneezing T-Rex. Crim-in-al!" I answered with a laughing smile.

She gave me an unenthusiastic thumbs up.

"T-Rex. Got it."

She'll think it's funny when she's in a better mood. I'll try again later, I thought to myself.

We stayed in Brint for a couple of hours, hanging out at the Mima Café. I pulled out the list and laid it on the table. About then, a Zoochian we know named Fot walked up to our table. He's always happy to see us, mostly because he's stupidly in love with Chelsey.

He noticed she was a bit gloomy.

In his best "surfer" accent, which he learned from terrible B-rated movies solely to try to impress Chelsey, he asked, "Hey, Chelsey, hey, Arëk, what are you two water monkeys doing here? Checking up on the parents? I saw them with Smoot and Bones earlier. Hey, are you ok, Chels? You look crazy sad. But still totally beautiful, though."

You could almost see bubble hearts floating out of his heads. Barf.

Axl chuckles.

"Dude, bring it down a notch! Sheesh! And, no, we're not checking up on the parents. We're on a serious mission to find Chelsey's brothers and sister. But we've only had a smidge of luck so far. We talked to someone on Laya who said she'd met a human medical scientist with one of Chelsey's brother's names. The problem is, we don't really know what we're looking for. So, we've been looking for *that* guy, hoping *maybe...*"

"Have you looked on Smithers, brah?" Fot asked.

I shook my head no.

"Why haven't you looked on Smithers? That's where all the smarty types hang out and do smarter-than-everyone-else-stuff. Maybe they'd at least know who you're talking about," he suggested.

"*Smithers*," I thought, then looked at Chelsey with a "DUH!" face. "Why didn't I think of Smithers? Chelsey, my friend, we're going to Smithers, let's go! Thanks, Fot, you're a genius," I said, rubbing both of his bald heads at the same time.

He smiled and promised to keep an eye on the parents. Just as we disappeared, he put his hand over his heart. He sighed aloud and said, "It hurts so much to love her."

Fot is just one of our friends who is or has been "in love" with Chelsey. My bestie has a fan club. She's a hottie. What can she say?

Axl says again that he can't wait to meet her.

19

Fingers Crossed

The Smitherines were mostly unhelpful. They're clearly allergic to people with "average" intelligence. They must be afraid it's contagious.

Axl judgingly says, "Ugh!"

After about an hour of being shooed away like we had rabies, we finally found a Smitherine named Stein, who agreed to speak to us. In the shadows and with a frosty attitude mind you, but at least he was willing to hear us out.

He led us into a lecture room and closed the door. With crossed arms and smug insolence, he asked, "Well? What can I help you with so you can be on your way?"

We asked Stein if he knew a human medical scientist named Tripp. We gave him the Layan's description. He said he did a scientific lab study with a human named Tripp last semester. Tripp was known on every university campus all over the planet as "Dr. T."

This "Dr. T" had an exceptional gift for concocting cures for incurable diseases. His cures have saved hundreds of thousands of lives on several planets. Stein said Dr. T. is determined to find the root of a rare flower rumored to grow on a planet only brave souls dare to venture. He *knows* this root will be the final component missing in his research for the cure of several incurable diseases specific to Earth. Stein said Dr. T is brilliant.

Chelsey interrupted, "So, in the time you spent with him, did he ever mention his Earth family?"

"I don't recall. We didn't associate on a social level, only academically. There's no time for fraternizing in the intellectual world. Obviously," he said, examining us like we were germs, "you would know nothing about... the intellectual world."

Cancelling his insult, I firmly said, "Yeah, that's enough of that. Do you know where Tripp might be now?"

"What's with all the questions?" he asked rudely.

Chelsey said, "We think this 'Dr. T.' might be my brother."

"*Might* be?" he asked snottily. "You don't know who your own family members are? What, are you an orphan or something? Revolting."

He snickered at her, clearly drowning in the stupidity of the two imbeciles standing in front of him. WHAT. A. JERK.

Axl says he already can't stand this guy.

Chelsey and I looked at each other, completely irritated with Stein. Chelsey reached out and grabbed him by his barf-green sweater vest. She forcefully pulled him down to where they were nose to nose. Then, in a quiet, menacing voice, she continued where she left off.

"Listen here, *Stein*, you're going to be nice. I've had kind of a bad day, and I'm not in the mood for your arrogant, snotty, superior attitude. I'm not asking for a blood sample, or your first-grade science fair trophy, or your favorite planet-saving discovery! All I'm asking for is a little *help*! IS A LITTLE HELP TOO MUCH TO ASK OF YOU, *STEIN?*"

By the time she finished, she was yelling. Her face was red, and she was breathing in hard ragged breaths. I was a little scared, and Stein was crying. This all happened in about thirty seconds. My friend turned from Dr. Jekyll to Mr. Hyde in no time flat.

Stein had a sudden desire to be Mr. Helpy Helperton. And to pee himself.

Axl laughs.

I tried to pry her white-knuckled hands from his stretched-out sweater vest. She was a bit beside herself.

I said, "Let go, psycho!"

Axl laughs again.

I looked up at Stein and said, "She's just a little stressed."

"I SAID... LET... *GOOO*!" I shouted and finally pulled my maniac bestie off him.

He stumbled backwards onto a chair.

I held up one finger and said, "Give us a second, will you?"

I put my arms around my best friend. I could feel her crying on my chest.

I said, "Buddy, it's ok. Stein's going to help us. We'll find your brother. Just breathe and calm down, ok? You're acting like a nutjob."

Axl laughs again.

She looked around me at poor Stein, sitting nervously in the chair. He was trying to catch his breath while watching for sudden moves. He jumped when he noticed her peeking around at him. It made her laugh a little, and she suddenly felt guilty about her behavior.

She put her face on my shoulder and said, "You're right, I'm sorry."

"You going to be nice now?" I asked quietly.

"Yes, I'm going to be nice now," she answered sarcastically with a scrunched-up face.

We sat down in the chairs opposite Stein.

Chelsey said, "I'm sorry, I really am. The thing is, I've known almost my whole life that I have a sister and two brothers who I've never met. My search for them has been unfruitful, minus the mention of someone named Tripp today. I don't know if the Tripp you know is one of my brothers or not. But it's worth finding out if I can get some help!"

Stein's expression started to soften as Chelsey told her story.

"Is there anything else you can tell us, Stein?" she pleaded.

"He still lives on Smithers. In the next sector," he answered.

Axl happily says, "Yes!"

Smithers doesn't have towns, villages, or cities. The planet is like one big city, with square sections or "sectors" separated only by giant trees. It's quite beautiful, actually. Very artsy and cleverly planned from an aerial view.

Chelsey's eyes grew large, and her mouth became a big smile. She grabbed my hand and squeezed it until sharp pain swallowed it.

"He's *here*? Can you take us to him?" she asked, barely breathing.

I said, "Chels, my hand?"

She looked down and saw the squished purple hand inside hers.

She said, "Oh! Sorry, Arëk!"

I smiled at her, accepting her apology.

Stein said, "I can't promise Dr. T. is here now. He often travels to other planets and galaxies for research purposes. I will take you to his house on one condition. I want a guarantee for my safety in the event he's not there. No violence, agreed?"

He looked at Chelsey with sternness as he smoothed down the stretched-out threads of his ugly sweater vest.

Axl laughs.

"I promise," she said nicely.

She looked at me and rolled her eyes.

"Weenie," she whispered.

Smithers is a charming planet, minus the snooty better-than everyone-else attitudes of the people who inhabit it. It's green with vegetation and decorated with originally designed architecture. Chelsey and I took in the sights as we rode in Stein's self-designed car, a floating frame with an invisible shell.

After about thirty minutes, we arrived at Dr. T's house.

20

Tripp

When we arrived, Chelsey took my hand to ease her nerves as we followed Stein to the door. He knocked several times. Finally, the light-haired, brown-eyed scientist Suki described, opened the door. Chelsey studied him like a specimen under a microscope.

"Greetings, Dr. T.!" Stein said.

"Hey, Stein! Been a long time, what's up?" he responded, surprised to see Stein.

"I would like to introduce you to Chelsey and Arëk," he replied.

He stepped aside allowing us to be seen.

"They have some questions for you which I think you might find *interesting*."

He looked at Tripp like, "You'd better sit down for this."

"Yeah, sure! Come in!" he said.

He opened the door wide and gestured with his arm.

Stein said, "I can't stay, Dr. T. Is it alright if I leave these two here with you?"

Then he leaned into Tripp's ear and whispered an insulting snicker.

"The Schmecum is harmless, I'm sure, but watch out for the other one. Although she is just a mere human, she's clearly crazy."

"*I'm* a mere human, Stein, remember?" he said with a slight harshness. "I'm sure I will be perfectly safe, thank you."

"Yes, of course, Dr. T., my sincere apologies!" he said.

Then Stein, who has no sense of humor whatsoever, tried to make light of his mistake.

"Of course, I was joking about the 'human' comment. You'll forgive my humor, I'm sure!" he said backing up until he was out the door.

Tripp shut it behind him without responding to his clumsy apology.

We walked through the tall front doors into an entryway. Each side was lined with giant plants nearly reaching the top of the ceiling. Past the jungle was a massive living area with windows for walls. The view of the landscape and trees outside was gorgeous!

The living area was decorated with a variety of cool stuff. There were life-size black and white photos of what looked like a tropical rain forest. And huge oddly shaped pottery in the corners of the room. There was also a totally chill water fountain on one wall that made me want to pee.

Axl chuckles.

But of all the extra cool stuff in there, my favorite was a huge, 5' x 5' wooden sculpture. It was intricately carved into a beautiful weeping warrior from some ancient time. He was created on his knees, bent over with his face in his hands, crying his heart out. It was like nothing I had ever seen before. In fact, I caught myself wanting to hug him and let him know everything would be ok. He was ultra-intense, dude. I officially named him Sad Wooden Dude.

Axl says, "Sad Wooden Dude could use an awesome smoothie." Love this guy.

To the left of the living area, in the same open space, were the kitchen and dining area. This section also had windows for walls. There's even a remote control that can tint or black them out. Cool, right? I was super impressed, brah! And those were just the rooms we could see! It's so cool, dude!

After watching us scope out his place, Tripp sat up on the edge of his chair and started the conversation.

"So, what can I do for you?"

He gestured with his hand for us to sit on the furniture opposite him.

After sitting down, Chelsey asked, "Tripp, would it be too bold to ask you some personal questions about your life on Earth?"

"There's not much to tell, but you're welcome to ask," he said curiously.

Chelsey took a deep breath and looked at me for encouragement. I nodded and smiled at her.

She asked, "Do you, by chance, have siblings on Earth? A brother named Austin and a sister named Lexi?"

He looked at her with surprise and asked, "And *who* are you again?"

"Tripp, I think you might be my brother." He raised his eyebrows and started to say something, but she continued, "Please just hear me out."

"Ok, I'm listening," he answered with a bit of trepidation.

She took another deep breath.

"When I was a little girl, Jesus told me I had a sister named Lexi and two brothers named Austin and Tripp. They were gone before I was born because of a tragic plane crash into the ocean. My parents never discussed the event with me because it was too painful for them. Little did they know, I'd known for some time.

"Recently, I told them I knew about the plane crash but didn't have any details. It was very emotional for them, but they finally shared the whole story with me. Since then, Arëk and I have been searching diligently for my brothers and sister. Only today did we run into a hopeful possibility of finding one of them.

"We spoke with a Layan named Suki who remembered someone named Tripp, with an accurate description of you. She also described a couple of other Tripps she'd met, who didn't fit the profile.

"With the information Suki provided, we searched several planets we thought might lead us to more clues. But we didn't find anything and got discouraged.

"Arëk and I decided to take a break and regroup on Zooch. During our rest, we talked to our friend, Fot. We told him about our mission to find my siblings. After hearing the description of the man Suki spoke of, Fot suggested looking on Smithers. That's how we met Stein. After a little *persuasion*, he told us about you then brought us here to meet you."

Dude, I couldn't stop looking at Tripp. His expressions were comical! His mouth was hanging open, his head was tilted, his eyes were wide open, and it didn't look like he was breathing. I was very interested to see what would happen next.

Tripp finally took a deep breath, exhaled, then took his time to speak. It seemed like forever before he finally said, "Umm, wow!"

We waited for more. He stared at the floor, then looked at me, then at Chelsey.

Finally, he said, "I do, or *did*, have a brother named Austin and a sister named Lexi. And I do remember my mom being pregnant with a baby girl just before the trip from Hawaii to Texas."

Chelsey's eyes quickly filled with heavy tears.

Chelsey looked at her brother as tears dripped off her chin. I put my arm around her shoulder and wiped a tear off my face.

Axl smiles.

Tripp continued, "I don't know what to say, really. I haven't seen Lexi or Austin since the day of the crash. And I made myself forget about you a long time ago because I didn't think I'd ever meet you."

He studied Chelsey and said, "You do resemble us."

His eyes filled with tears and his chin started to quiver. He looked down toward the floor and a tear dropped onto his bare foot.

He softly asked, "How are they, Mom and Dad?"

Axl's eyes tear up.

Chelsey and I looked at each other, realizing we had found her brother! This was really happening! Our emotions wrestled between happiness, freaking out, and being overwhelmed. Each with its own bucket of tears.

We held hands tightly while Chelsey pulled herself together enough to respond to Tripp's question.

"They're good. But why haven't you been back?" Chelsey asked, chin quivering.

Tripp took a deep breath, then answered, "When the plane hit the water, it was pure chaos. People who were still conscious were panicking and screaming. They were trying to get free of their safety belts to help or find their family members. Water quickly filled the cabin. The plane was sinking. It was terrifying!

"The three of us kids sat in the seats across the aisle from Mom and Dad. They were both knocked out cold at impact. I remember seeing blood from a gash on Dad's head mixing with the water. Mom was bleeding, too, but I couldn't tell from where.

"I never felt more alert in my life than at that moment! I was so scared, fighting to hold my breath as the water quickly rose. Then someone who looked about my age unlocked my safety belt, then Mom's and Dad's. It was then that I realized Lexi and Austin weren't there. The kid who unlocked our belts pulled me and our parents from the sinking plane to the surface. He made sure Mom and Dad were with the survivors. I looked for Austin and Lexi but didn't see them.

"The next thing I knew, the rescuer said, 'Hold on, Tripp!'

"Seconds later I was in a strange place. The kid who saved my life carried me on his back into a white stone building. I was laid on a bed and my wounds were nursed back to health by an alien species. I remember the confusion and wondering where I was. But even at six years old, I wasn't afraid. It felt like I was in a dream.

"After a short while, a smaller version of the alien species taking care of me walked into the room with a big smile on his face."

"Tripp!" the small alien shouted happily. I slowly sat up as he hopped onto the end of the bed facing me. Before I could say anything, he said, 'I'm so happy you're ok! I was afraid I didn't get there in time! It was scary! Planes are a lot bigger than I thought they'd be!'

"He seemed genuinely excited to see me. I had no idea what was going on. He just kept talking and talking. I was too jet-lagged to stop him.

"Then the alien said, 'I know this will sound weird to you but you're not on planet Earth right now.'

"As if the metallic-blue, slick-skinned alien with gills, webbed feet, and a long thick tail, sitting across from me talking my head off wasn't the first clue!"

We all laughed.

Axl laughs, too.

Chelsey's brother is funny, dude.

Tripp said, "I had an incredible desire to touch his weird skin, but I didn't dare. I thought it might be contagious."

We all laughed again.

Axl laughs.

"The little alien said, 'I'm hoping you haven't been off your planet before because I want to be your first best friend from another planet.'

"His smile stretched wider across his oddly shaped face with every fast sentence. It was the biggest smile with the greatest number of teeth I had ever seen."

Chelsey and I laughed.

Axl laughs and says, "He is funny!"

"The alien said, 'My planet is called Ustak. I've known about you for a long time. God told me all about you. He said one day, I would save you from a crazy plane crash in the Pacific Ocean on Earth.

Then we'd be best buddies forever once we finally met. I think you'll like it here. Oh, I'm Tate, by the way.'

"The strange little guy held out his webbed hand like humans do when introducing themselves. He quickly realized that when I didn't return the gesture, I was uncertain of who and what he was in his native appearance. He immediately closed his eyes, and within a split second, he became the curly, black-haired, brown-eyed, dark-skinned human boy who rescued me from the plane crash.

"He said, 'Better?' Then smiled and stretched out his hand.

"I couldn't believe my eyes again! I gasped, jumped out of the bed, fell to the floor, and peeked slowly over the mattress at the alien-turned-black kid who saved me. I slowly stood up and reluctantly held out my hand. We shook one big up-and-down shake. Tate seemed very satisfied as if our handshake solidified a forever-long friendship. I finally found my voice and asked him where my mom and dad and my brother and sister were.

"Tate said, 'I'm not sure. I didn't see your brother and sister on the plane, but your parents were with some other passengers when we left.'

"I asked him if they were dead because I remembered they were bleeding. Before he could answer me, I broke down and cried my heart out. Tate crawled across the bed and hugged me as a forever best friend would do. I cried on his shoulder until I had no more tears.

"Tate said, 'Jesus will take care of them, Tripp, on Earth or in Heaven, I promise.'

"That was the last time I mentioned Mom and Dad or Austin and Lexi for several years. I couldn't talk about them without it breaking my heart. So, I buried my life on Earth."

Chelsey wiped a tear off her face.

He continued, "Time was so weird on Ustak. The days seemed longer than normal, but it was the happiest place I'd ever been. It had a healing power about it, making my sadness and worry disappear. Oh, and scars, too! After a few days at the clinic, I noticed the scar on my arm from a bad bike wreck about a year before was completely gone! It had been a big, thick purple scar almost the length of my forearm! And suddenly, my skin was smooth and perfect! So, I started looking for other little random scars, and they were all gone, too! I asked Tate where my scars went. I didn't understand what was happening. Tate laughed with delight at my wonder of such a 'magical' place that makes boo-boos disappear.

"Tate said, 'My planet is one of the healing planets. Isn't it cool? There are zillions of planets, galaxies, and solar systems out here in space. God made each one of them special!'

"Tate explained a lot of things to me over the next few weeks, including how the whole shapeshifting from native to some other thing works. I look super awesome as a blue fish guy, if I do say so myself. *Lots*... of teeth."

Chelsey and I laughed.

Axl laughs, too. He likes Tripp's sense of humor.

Tripp continued, "I hope I answered your original question about why I never went back. As much as I wanted you all to be alive, I couldn't get the image of Mom and Dad in the sinking plane out of my head. I couldn't bear to go back to Earth to visit graves.

"I let Ustak become my new home. I went to school there with Tate, who is still my best friend. After I graduated from school, I moved to Smithers to study chemistry. It was here that God started giving me formulas and solutions for the cures of several planets' fatal diseases. I'm currently looking for a root I believe will be the cure for human diseases like Alzheimer's and various cancers.

"God has blessed my life, and I'm happy out here in this galaxy. I have to say, though, I'm very excited to meet my little sister! It makes me wonder about Austin and Lexi!"

"Their bodies were never recovered from the plane crash," Chelsey said with sadness.

Tripp looked up at his sister and said, "What? What do you mean?"

"Well, neither was yours," she said with a smile. "And since we found you out here, I'm hopeful we'll find them, too."

"What would our parents do if they found out we're Universe travelers?" Tripp said, laughing at the thought.

"Oh, they know," she said matter-of-factly.

Tripp's eyes widened, and his jaw dropped. He jumped to the edge of his seat with joy.

"*Our* parents? No way! I know I was pretty young when I left, but I remember them being super overprotective parents! I can't believe they're cool with you flittering around space! I totally wish I'd gone back to Earth now!" he exclaimed.

We all laughed at his cheeriness about the whole thing.

"In fact," she interjected, "they've met Arëk."

"And they *love* me!" I added.

"You want to hear the craziest part? Our parents, Gracie and Micah Wick, are at this very moment vacationing on Zooch!" Chelsey said with a sheepish grin.

"*WHAT?*" Tripp shouted with a high-pitched voice.

"Yep, Arëk and I sent them on vacation for a couple of weeks to get them out of our hair while we look for you guys," she said.

Tripp sat on the edge of his seat, shaking his head in disbelief.

"Wow," he said, taking it all in. "I don't know what to say or what to do. Since I know they're still alive, I should go back to see them, right? Or should I leave it alone? What's the right thing to do?"

"Without question, you should go back to see them. But it would probably be best if I talked to them first. We don't want either of them having a heart attack when they see you," Chelsey said, smiling.

"Right! So, you let me know what the plan is, and we'll make it happen," Tripp said.

"I can't believe we finally found you!" Chelsey said with excitement. "Hey, do you want to join Arëk and me in our quest to find Austin and Lexi?"

"I would love to, I really would, but I'm so close to finishing this formula. All I'm missing is that crazy root. I know I'm going to find it soon. I feel like it's right under my nose. I'll pray that God will lead you to our brother and sister. And you better bring them to me ASAP when you do!" Tripp said happily.

"Have you looked on Rica for your root?" I piped in.

"I've never heard of Rica. What's special about it?" he asked.

"Rica is a tiny little planet about six galaxies from here and is only inhabited by vegetation. We stopped there looking for you. You should check it out," I said.

Tripp's face lit up like the Griswold's house on Christmas.

"I'll leave right away! I'll have to get my things together. Thank you, Arëk! Let's hope for the best!" he said.

"We're going to get back to work ourselves. I'm super hopeful now! Keep in touch with me, big brother," Chelsey said.

"You better believe it!"

He hugged his little sister tightly.

"Oh, and someday I want to hear everything about Sad Wooden Dude! He's awesome!" I said.

"For sure! It's a great story!" Tripp said.

"Ok, we'll catch you later!" Chelsey said.

Shaka all around, then we were gone.

What a major relief, brah! We'd found one of Chelsey's siblings! One down, two to go! But first, we thought we'd go home and rest.

Axl says, "No doubt!"

21

Back On Oahu

Chelsey had gone about a week without surfing the Pacific waves. Not more than a couple of days go by in a normal week without her cruising the board. She was craving it. As soon as we got to the house, we loaded up the Jeep with boards, dogs, and monkey and headed to the beach.

I love surfing, dude. There's nothing like catching the perfect wave.

You should see Charlie, Poot, and Booger surf. They love the ocean. It's so entertaining to watch them.

After a whole day of fun in the water, we were worn out. We lay on our lounge chairs and let the late afternoon sun dry our skin. The pets crashed out on the beach next to us.

"I wonder what the folks are up to," Chelsey said. "They must be having a lot of fun since we haven't been called in by Bones and Smoot to rescue them."

"That's what we wanted, right? To make sure they have a blast so we can investigate without interruption?" I asked.

"I know, I just miss them a little. I hope they're having a good time experiencing the Universe. I kind of wish we were the ones showing them everything instead of our friends."

"Don't worry, buddy, we'll get to take them to lots of places since they're finally cool with leaving Earth," I comforted.

"I know. I just feel a little regretful. Their very first time, we dumped them off and left. I've dreamed all my life of taking them on their first trip off Earth. And because of our grand expedition, I'm not the one who gets to see their first reactions to all the wonders of another world."

"Dude, don't guilt yourself. You're the most selfless person I've ever known. Besides, you'll be glad we made this decision when you tell your parents about finding Tripp. And who knows, maybe Austin and Lexi soon, too," I said.

"You're right, Arëk. I can't wait to tell Mom and Dad about Tripp!"

"I can't wait to see the looks on their faces! Your parents are hilarious when they're in shock!" I said.

We laughed.

"We should continue with our search for Austin and Lexi in the next day or two. I'm excited to tackle another trip. Where do you think we should start next, buddy?" Chelsey asked.

"Good question. We haven't run into anybody so far who can remember any humans named Austin or Lexi on their planets. We'll start over with a new list," I answered.

"Sounds good."

Then, with an ornery expression on her tanned face, she added, "By the way, I saw you totally biff it in that big wave earlier. It was gnarly! I think I heard Poot laughing at you."

"What? What are you talking about? Biffed it! I didn't... Ok, I did, but it wasn't *that* major, drama mama!" I said, pushing her shoulder.

She started to laugh.

"Dude! You are such a terrible liar!"

"Ok, fine, it was kind of major," I agreed.

"Kind of?"

"Alright, so the wave tried to kill me! It body-slammed me over and over for like five minutes! Are you happy now?" I said, smacking her with my flip-flop.

Axl's laughing at me.

Chelsey laughed a good belly laugh.

"What happened out there? When you came up for air, your eyes were bigger than your head! You tried to out-swim the next wave, and it smashed you! Why didn't you think yourself out of the water, goofball?"

"My thinker was soaking wet! Ha-ha!" I said.

Axl laughs.

We had a good laugh at my expense. Chelsey and I laugh at each other all the time. And I've noticed you have no trouble laughing at me either, Axl!

I push Axl off the lounge chair. He laughs again.

22

Check On The Folks

After sleeping in late the next morning, we felt energized and ready to face the next challenge. Chelsey was really missing her folks. We decided we'd peek in on their vacation to make sure they were still having a good time.

It didn't take us long to figure out where to find Gracie and Micah. Brint was hosting the beloved Zooch festival, and everyone was there. We walked through the large crowds, talked to a couple of friends, and even ran into a few human celebrities. We got autographs we probably never would have gotten on Earth from Michael Pena, Jim Carrey, who is from planet Hootie, and Bruno Mars, who was performing in Brint's largest park. We've seen him three times on Earth! Super cool dude!

We also ran into our friend, Doo, who was visiting from planet Shaz for the festivities. We asked him if he'd seen Chelsey's parents around anywhere. He was happy to see us and punched Chelsey's arm.

She said, "What the hey, dude?"

"I didn't know Gracie Wick was your mother! The author, Gracie Wick, from Earth! She's a celebrity on Shaz! Everyone there has read all her books. We can't wait till the next one comes out next summer! I just got her autograph and took a selfie with her like an hour ago. Your mom is smokin' hot! What happened to *you*?" he joked.

He tried to duck but wasn't quick enough. Chelsey grabbed his backpack and punched him in the shoulder. I laughed.

Axl laughs, too.

She laughed and said, "I bet Mom was shocked to find out she's a famous author across the Universe! She's never been off Earth until this week!"

Doo replied, "Dude! I couldn't believe it was her when I saw her! She is so nice. I'm crushing hard on your mom!"

"Shut your mouth, psycho!" Chelsey laughed and pushed Doo playfully.

He said, "When she was signing my book, which I luckily happened to have in my backpack, she started bragging about her daughter and her daughter's bud. She said they recently introduced her to the Universe. After only a few minutes, I asked, 'Your daughter wouldn't happen to be Chelsey, would she?' She got so excited and grabbed me and hugged me and said, 'You know my Chelsey and Arëk?' And she went on and on, bragging about how wonderful you are."

"Yep, sounds just like my mother," Chelsey said, smiling with pride.

We told Doo about our "find the siblings" mission and that we brought the parents to Zooch to get them out of our hair for a couple of weeks. He understood and was amused at our slyness. The three of us hung out and walked around the festival until we spotted one of the parents.

Micah was walking out of a flower shop with a huge, colorful bouquet of assorted daisy-like flowers for Gracie. Daisies have always been her favorite, but these topped any daisies he had ever given her before! The flowers on Zooch are extraordinary! Good thing to remember if you ever want to get your girl out-of-this-world flowers, brah.

Axl nods his head and thanks me for the advice.

We called Micah's name. When he turned around, he was happy to see us. He hugged us as best as he could with the flowers in his arms. He also recognized Doo from the book signing session earlier and patted him on the back. He called him his wife's biggest fan. Chelsey asked her dad where her mom was. He told her Gracie was reserving a table at an outdoor café just up the way. Of course, he invited the three of us to join them. Doo appreciated the invite but declined and said he'd catch us later.

As always, Gracie expressed loving gratitude when Micah presented her with beautiful flowers. But when she saw *these* flowers, she was speechless! She couldn't believe how incredibly gorgeous they were! And, as per usual, Gracie fell deeply in love with Micah again. Those two know how to keep the fire burning, brah!

Once the flower surprise subsided, Gracie noticed Chelsey and me standing there. She jumped up to hug us and started talking a hundred miles an hour about their vacation.

Gracie told us about their fun experiences and all the amazing people they had met. She was extra stoked about meeting Mark Wahlberg, who she described as "totally down to Earth and hot as molten lava." He has always been one of her celebrity crushes.

Axl laughs at the molten lava comment.

Mark and his family were in Brint for the festival. He saw her signing her novel for Doo and walked over to ask about it.

Apparently, he likes books. Once the shock wore off that Mark Wahlberg was speaking to her, she gave him a synopsis of her book. He said he would like to read it and asked her to autograph one for him when she got home. He dug in his jeans pocket for a restaurant receipt and asked if she had a pen. Gracie showed us the back of the receipt with his mailing address written in his handwriting. Then she kissed it and gently put it back in her purse. Micah rolled his eyes. Chelsey and I laughed.

There were also about seventeen photos on her phone of her and Mark Wahlberg. Her favorite one will be framed and sitting on the celebrity photo shelf in her office in about a week. We laughed as Chelsey poked fun at her dad about his new competition. He just shook his head at us.

"Brats," he said.

Axl chuckles.

"We heard Keanu Reeves is here somewhere, too! I'm hoping to run into him. Do you think he'll remember me? We met during the filming of Point Break a long time ago," Gracie reminded us for the thousandth time.

"Oh, I'm sure he will, Mom," Chelsey said, looking at Micah and me with a *yeah, right* look.

"You never know, babe. You're unforgettable," Micah said just before he kissed her hand.

Chelsey and I smiled at each other.

We tried several times to tell Gracie and Micah of our success in finding Tripp. But they continuously interrupted us with their excitement about the fun they were having on their vacation. We heard all about Zooch as if we hadn't been there a thousand times. We listened with delight. It was fun seeing them so happy.

Micah asked if we were staying in Brint. We decided we would, for one night. Besides, we thought it might give us the right opportunity to tell them about finding Tripp.

Chelsey mentioned we ran into Doo, "her mom's biggest fan." Gracie's eyes lit up like fireworks, and she said, "Can you believe my books are being read across the Universe? How is that possible?"

I said, "Remember, we told you guys that people from other planets visit Earth. Some even live on Earth. Apparently, someone read your books and took them back to their home planet. Your name was spread around the Universe!"

She laughed and said, "Too bad I'm not this popular on my own planet!"

"Seriously? You're one of Earth's best-selling authors!" Chelsey jabbed jokingly.

"I'm just saying, maybe I should start my next book sale on Zooch first! Just to see how it goes," she said with excitement.

"Might not be a bad idea!" Micah replied.

"Sounds to me like someone is digging this whole Universe thing," I said and wiggled my eyebrows.

"You kids were right. This place is amazing, and so are all these people," Gracie said.

"We feel right at home, as weird as it sounds," Micah added.

"See, we told you! There are so many planets Arëk and I want to take you to," Chelsey said.

"We're all in, baby cakes!" Micah said, hugging his daughter.

After snacking on some delicious food, the four of us wandered off into the festival, taking in all the sights. Chelsey and I had so much fun watching her parents interact with people of different species. You'd never know it was their first time on another planet.

We decided it wasn't the right time to talk to them about Tripp. Their vacation needed to be about them.

After several hours of festival fun, we bid the parents goodnight and left them with some friends they made from planet Harley. Chelsey and I crashed at the cottage with great anticipation of success the next day.

23

Stoner Dude

Dude, I wish I could tell you we found Austin and Lexi the next day. Unfortunately, not even close. Chelsey and I searched the Universe for *months* until we were completely worn out and more than a little discouraged. We discussed the possibility we might *not* find them. After all, we were searching blindly in a Universe reaching farther than anyone can imagine, and with no clues to lead us in any direction. We decided to give it a break.

We did see Tripp several times within the next few months. It's cool how much Chelsey and Tripp have in common, including personality traits. They're both crazy, in my opinion.

It hadn't worked out for Tripp to return to Earth to see the parents, with his root search taking up all his time. Poor guy was not having the success he had hoped for. He was determined, though, so he would indeed find the master ingredient he was in search of.

We also hadn't told Gracie and Micah we had found Tripp after all those months. He was on a serious mission requiring zero interruptions. Finding the cure for life-robbing diseases was very important to him. The parents would have to wait a little longer. It's not like they knew they were missing anything anyway.

In our random travels, we also met a really cool dude from Talendar. He was the equivalent of Earth's stoner hippy flower child. We nicknamed him Stoney. It seemed fitting. He was way out there, but he had some prevalent information we were able to tell Tripp about. Stoney was well-versed in herbal plants, if you know what I mean. He gave us a list of planets in his galaxy inhabited only by vegetation. Apparently, some of the vegetation makes you feel *really* groovy! We couldn't get to Tripp fast enough! We hoped it was the information he had been waiting for.

Dude, are you hungry? My pancakes are gone!

Axl suggests Garcia's again.

Garcia's is never a bad idea, brah! Let's go eat some Mexican food. Then we'll come back to the beach, and I'll tell you more about the search for Austin and Lexi.

24

Update On Fasi

You know what, Axl? You haven't told me much about you. Who are you, dude? What did you come to Hawaii to escape from?

Axl says his story isn't nearly as interesting as mine, then tries to change the subject.

No, seriously, brah. I'm super stoked to meet you and hang out. But you've got to tell me *something* about yourself.

Axl tells me his life is unsatisfying, and he wants a change. Then he tells me he might not get back on the plane in a few weeks!

Dude! That would be awesome! Leave it all behind and stay here! Your life will improve a hundred percent! Guaranteed!

Axl says he's seriously considering it.

We make a toast with chips and guac to Axl's new and improved life.

An hour later, we are miserable after gorging on Garcia's again.

Dude, I am so stuffed! Why do I do that to myself?

Axl comments about how we ate our weight in chips and salsa.

I do it every time, dude! It's so good I can't stop, but I hate myself now! UGH! Nap on the beach, then story time, brah? There are some umbrellas over there. Let's sleep these enchiladas off!

Axl agrees wholeheartedly.

Two hours later, we wake up to the sound of laughing kids filling our belly buttons with sand.

Get out of here, you little monsters!

Axl wipes sand off his belly.

We need H2O. I'll be right back, brah, hang tight.

I walk to the smoothie shack up the beach and buy a couple of bottles of cold water. Axl is happy to see it and gulps it down in seconds. He suggests we take a swim before getting back to the story. I'm always up for a swim.

After some time in the water and introducing Axl to some locals, we drip all the way back to the lounge chairs. I hand my friend an extra towel from my backpack, and I pull one out for myself. We dry off as best as we can, then take our comfy positions in the lounge chairs for some more awesome adventure telling.

Chelsey and I went back to Fasi about a year after their big life change. In case you're interested, Fasi is a completely different planet these days. You wouldn't believe the changes they've made in all their cities!

They built hotels and B & B's. There are now theaters for plays, stadiums for concerts and events, and hundreds of awesome restaurants. They've adopted some Earth brands, as well. There's a Starbucks on almost every corner, and they've got some of the most impressive shopping malls in their galaxy.

The soldiers have become regular citizens. That's been quite an adjustment since war and killing were their main skill sets.

Axl laughs.

Now, they work regular jobs, wear normal clothes, play sports, and go to church on Sundays. They even started dating people on other planets, brah. Big stuff for them!

Axl says, "Good for them!"

The elders have learned to relax. They now let day-to-day things fall into place instead of controlling every second of everyone's lives. They're enjoying a more stress-free existence.

God blesses the Fasians like crazy these days, brah. Their renewed relationship with Him is such a great example of God's mercy and grace. Because if He can forgive and love *them*, anyone has a chance to make it right with God. The Fasians are proud of their new way of life. Chelsey and I are proud of them, too.

We actually took Chelsey's parents there.

Axl says, "Whoa! Even after the kidnapping thing?"

Yeah, dude, it was gutsy! It took some serious convincing to get Gracie and Micah to go to Fasi. All they could think about was the day Chelsey and I returned home after being missing for three days. The words "kidnapped" and "monsters" blared like neon signs in their minds.

So, our little outing with the parents to Fasi started out a little jaded. Fortunately, the Fasians took it in stride and didn't take offense. No doubt they were used to the occasional judgement from other planet beings, having been so terrible to everyone previously.

We decided to rip the band-aid right off and introduced Gracie and Micah to several of the elders and soldiers. The enormous men knelt in front of Chelsey's parents and apologized for kidnapping their daughter and causing them heartache. Gracie and Micah forgave them, then made a joke about the event to ease the Fasians' embarrassment. Chelsey's parents fell in love with the monsters who became gentle giants.

The trip to Fasi was Gracie's and Micah's first weekend off the Earth in several months. They seemed to adapt easily to every planet in their travels. After their first outer-worldly vacation, you couldn't keep them on Earth! Once they went to Zooch for the first time, they were itching to see what else was out there.

Out of the handful of planets the parents had experienced, Zooch was still their favorite. Maybe because it was their first, I don't know. They'd been there twice already, which is why we knew it would work to send them there again.

My bestie and I were ready to resume our attempt at finding Chelsey's brother and sister after a year-long sabbatical. And it was perfect timing.

It was the time of year when the folks got the vacation bug and were chomping at the bit to go somewhere for an extended stay. Leave it to Chelsey and Arëk, travel agents extraordinaire! We thought two or three weeks seemed a reasonable amount of time for a fun-filled trip and an opportunity for us to work. Once the subject of a Zooch vacation was on the table, the parents started vamping out their entertainment schedule. The plan was a go! One week until take off!

25

M.I.A.

Gracie and Micah loved traveling the Universe. However, they were never hip to the idea of learning how to transport without assistance. Every trip up until now still had training wheels. I think maybe they were afraid of winding up in some strange place they didn't intend to go to or couldn't transport back from. Totally understandable.

This time, however, was surprisingly different.

Just before departure, Chelsey's mom announced, "Your dad and I have decided to transport ourselves to Zooch without help. We want to prove to ourselves that we can do it successfully. The only favor we ask is that you make sure we made it safely."

"Yay!" Chelsey shouted with her arms opened wide for a group hug. "I am so proud of you guys!"

"We're still a little nervous but how else are we going to beat the fear, right?" Micah said, obviously a wreck at the thought of getting lost in space.

"We'll be right behind you, I promise. Don't worry, you'll be fine. Piece of cake! We've done it together lots of times," Chelsey said with complete confidence.

"So, let's do it!" Gracie said.

"Think we should pray first? It would make me feel better about the whole thing," Micah said.

"You can't go wrong with prayer," Chelsey responded. "Go ahead, Dad."

We all joined hands in a circle, and Micah began, "Jesus, we love You, and we are so grateful for all the many blessings You have poured into our lives. Thank You for this family and for our kids, wherever they may be. Please keep them safe and in Your special way let them know we love them, we miss them, and we hope to be reunited one day."

Chelsey squeezed my hand, thinking about Tripp.

Micah continued, "Thank You, God, for Chelsey and Arëk. They mean so much to us. Thank You for bringing the gift of Universe travel into our lives and for using our kids to teach us. Please be with us on this vacation and help us to get to Zooch safely. Ease our nerves and help us to put our trust in You. In the name of Jesus, we pray. Amen."

The rest of us said, "Amen."

Gracie and Micah took a deep breath and grabbed their luggage. They closed their eyes and disappeared. Chelsey and I looked at each other and smiled.

"Let's go," I said to my bestie, and we were off.

When we arrived in Rew, the parents' Zoochian destination choice, we looked around for Gracie and Micah. We didn't see them. I told

Chelsey we probably just transported to a different area of Rew than they did. No problem.

We walked around some of the touristy spots we expected to find the parents, but we still didn't see them. After about fifteen minutes, Chelsey started to get worried.

She asked, "Where do you think they are, Arëk? We've got to find them."

"Try Gracie's cell phone," I suggested, knowing AT&T didn't have Universal service.

Chelsey called her mom's phone, although she knew the same thing. No answer.

My thoughts rushed back to when Chelsey went missing, and I found her kidnapped on Fasi. Not a good feeling in my guts.

Then, from a distance, we heard, "Chelsey! Arëk!"

It was Gracie.

We ran to meet her. When we reached her, she grabbed Chelsey in panic.

Chelsey asked, "Mom, what's wrong? Where's Dad? Where have you been?"

Gracie was crying in gasps.

"I don't know! I don't know what to do! Your dad didn't make it!" Gracie cried.

"What? What do you mean he didn't make it?" Chelsey shouted in shock.

"He didn't arrive with me! When I opened my eyes after your dad and I transported ourselves off Earth, I was standing in Rew alone! I waited for a few minutes and then tried several times to go back to the house, but I couldn't get there. I was lost! I ended up somewhere where there were freaking *dinosaurs* everywhere! *DINOSAURS!* *REAL* ONES! Then one of the little people there helped me get back here but your dad still wasn't here! I don't know what to do!" Gracie sobbed.

She wept like a scared child as Chelsey and I pulled her close to comfort her.

Knowing she'd seen the dinosaurs, I couldn't wait to tell her about the sneezing T-Rex! But not right now, obviously.

Axl laughs and shakes his head.

"First of all," Chelsey started, "you couldn't have run into better people than the Layans. Laya is where you saw the dinosaurs. *Our* dinosaurs, but that's another story for another day.

"We'll find Dad, don't worry. We'll all be back together before you know it. Then, you guys can start enjoying your vacation. Please stop crying, Mom, I promise Arëk and I will find him."

"Without a doubt!" I said, putting my arm around her shoulder.

"Arëk, let's take Mom to Mr. and Mrs. Raan's house. Mom, you'll love them. They're from Earth. They moved here from Savannah, Georgia, a long time ago. They've been looking forward to meeting you and Dad for years. You'll be safe and comfortable there until we come back with Dad," Chelsey said.

Gracie took comfort in knowing Chelsey and I knew the Universe like the back of our hands. Some of it, anyway. She agreed with our instructions.

It only took us seconds to arrive at the Raan's house. Mr. Raan opened the door wearing his usual Jimmy Buffet-style shirt and khaki cargo shorts.

He threw his arms up in the air and, with a thick southern drawl, said, "Well, I'll be a monkey's uncle! Look who it is! Ellie, sugar, look who's here! It's Chelsey and Arëk! And they brought somebody with 'em! Come to the door, precious, and say hello! Y'all come on in here and make yourselves at home. Ellie just made some homemade Georgia peach tea! Have a seat," he said as he hugged us all, including Gracie.

"I'm comin', darlin'! Hang on just a minute. I can't come out half-done!" Mrs. Raan shouted in the same southern accent from several rooms away. "Chelsey, honey, what in the world are you doing here, anyway? I'll be right there!"

"It's wonderful to see you two again, but we're in a hurry. We need your help," Chelsey said.

Mrs. Raan rushed into the living room in her colorful flowered Mumu and freshly painted nails. She blew on them in between words.

"Hello, gorgeous girl! How in the world are you? Arëk, hon, you're just as darlin' as ever!"

She hugged us, trying not to touch us with her wet nails.

Mr. Raan interrupted, "What's the trouble, sugar? We'll help in any way we can."

Mrs. Rann readily nodded her head in agreement.

"This is my mother, Gracie. We have a family emergency, and we need to leave her in a safe place while Arëk and I go solve the problem. You guys were the first people I thought of. Will you please take care of my mom for a little while? We shouldn't be gone long. Mom can share the details while we're gone," Chelsey explained.

"Well, of course, darlin'! You don't even need to ask! Gracie, hon, please make our home your own. Ellie's got homemade fried chicken and mashed taters just dyin' to be eaten. You got here just in time!" Mr. Raan said with a good ol' boy smile.

"Don't forget about my pretty peach cobbler sittin' on the counter over there, honey!" Mrs. Raan said with pride over her sweet-tasting masterpiece.

Gracie smiled at the hospitality of her wonderful hosts.

"Mom, you're in good company. And these are some praying folks, let me tell you! Promise me you will relax and not worry. Everything will be fine. Before you finish the prize-winning peach cobbler, we'll be back with Dad, and we'll laugh about the whole thing," Chelsey said.

"I love you, Chelsey," Gracie said, "please be careful and come back to me. Arëk, don't you let anything happen to my Angelfish."

"Are you kidding me? Chelsey's the boss. I'm just the cool and extremely handsome sidekick who's lucky enough to tag along," I said, trying to make her smile.

Chelsey rolled her eyes and said, "Really?" Then she addressed her mother, "Mom, we will be fine. Promise. Relax. Eat. Once you get to know these two people, you'll fall in love with them. Enjoy yourself, please. We'll be back shortly."

Chelsey winked at her mom and smiled.

"Chelsey, Arëk, you two best be on your way and safely," Mr. Raan said. "We'll be prayin'. Remember, when you've got God Almighty on your side, you can't lose. Now y'all get back here real soon so you can eat some of Mrs. Raan's fine home cookin'!"

"Yes, sir! And thank you again," Chelsey answered.

We hugged Gracie tight, and then we were out the door.

"Ok, Arëk, where do we start? Dad could be anywhere," Chelsey said.

"Yeah, especially as nervous as your dad was before they left. There's no telling where he transported to."

"I know!" Chelsey agreed.

"I think the best thing to do is to gather a search team and split up. I know Fot and Doo will help, and we'll grab some others along the way," I said.

"Good idea, buddy," Chelsey responded, and we were off to find our friends.

Doo was super excited to play a part in the parent rescue, being Gracie's biggest fan and all. He had a celebrity crush on her, so getting to be a hero in her life would be a historical marker in his! He made us promise we would take him to see Gracie after Micah was found.

Fot turned out to be our most useful resource. Again, a girl crush helped save the day. I was super impressed at how focused he remained on the mission with Chelsey in the same atmosphere.

Axl chuckles.

When we located Fot, he was hanging out with some friends who immediately volunteered to help when they heard our predicament. They knew some other guys who they could recruit as well. We ended up with twenty-four people from Zooch alone! We made a list of places to divide amongst everyone and agreed to add people on each planet to our search team until we found Micah. We would meet back at Doo's house, on Shaz, every hour to check in until someone showed up with Chelsey's dad.

At first, time seemed to stand still, regardless of how busy we were. Two check-ins at Doo's house with no rescue was nerve-racking for my bestie. But finally, some results. When we met at Doo's house for the third time, one of Fot's friends reported that he had found Micah. But he said Micah wouldn't leave with him. He was petrified and insisted someone bring Chelsey and me to him. We all went together to rescue Micah on a planet Chelsey and I had never even heard of! It looked a lot like Oahu.

When we arrived, Micah grabbed us and hugged us so hard I felt like he was going to break us in half! We thought it would be best to get him to Zooch in the comfort of his wife before we asked him a bunch of questions. We took Chelsey's dad to the Raan's house. You should have seen the surprise on Mr. Raan's face when he opened the door and saw about fifty people of various species standing on his front lawn.

He turned to face the inside of the house and said, "Precious, you better fry up some more chicken. We've got a herd out here, and they all look hungry!"

We all rubbed our bellies and laughed.

Mrs. Raan came to the door and saw the yard full of people. She clapped her hands with joy and said, "We've got foldin' tables in the back! You kids go fetch 'em and set 'em up in the yard. I'm goin' to fry some more chicken, and we're goin' to have an old-fashioned Georgia picnic! Y'all want peach tea or lemonade?"

Gracie squeezed by Mrs. Raan in hopes of seeing her brave daughter and her husband. As she had prayed, there we all stood, in front of the crowd. Gracie ran to Micah. Neither of them could even speak. They just cried, hugged, and cried some more. It was a wonderful and grateful reunion.

We decided food before the long story would be best. Micah helped the search team set up tables, and Gracie helped Mrs. Raan in the kitchen. Chelsey and I flopped down on the couch to catch our breath for a minute.

We overheard Chelsey's mom and Mrs. Raan praising Jesus together while clanging pans and glass bowls. Gracie happily chopped potatoes as fast as Mrs. Raan could hand them over to her. She was grateful to be back in the company of her family.

I knew it was driving Gracie nuts to wait to hear Micah's story about what happened to him earlier. We were more than curious ourselves.

Chelsey and I stepped outside to help our friends set up tables and chairs. They had it all finished and were scattered all over the yard. Some of the search team sat at tables and others laid on the Raan's manicured lawn. Everyone enjoyed themselves. Chelsey and I found Doo sitting with some of his friends. They were from planet Rondo. Totally cool dudes. Like normal Rondoans, they had basketball on the brain. A couple of them were discussing sad retirements and the best moments. Others debated about whether the Spurs or the Warriors would win the NBA Championship.

One of the Rondoans was telling stories about my personal hero and friend, "Hoops." We learned something about him we didn't know. He was born on Earth and started his career on Rondo, which we knew. But he grew up on some planet called Roiva, which no one in the group had ever been to. Chelsey and I had never even heard of the planet until then. It was somewhere on the other side of a wormhole none of us had ever seen or learned about. The dude telling the story was kind of proud that he knew something about Hoops the rest of us didn't know. Chelsey and I still knew Hoops better than anyone in the group, but I didn't want to brag.

Axl smiles and settles back on the hammock.

The door opened, and Mrs. Raan shouted, "Lunch is ready!"

Mr. Rann jumped in, "Let's get this food blessed so you kids can eat!"

Everyone shook their heads in agreement with happy faces.

Mr. Raan prayed, "Lord, You are just so amazin' to us, and we want to thank You. You have helped us out today, and we are unmeasurably grateful. Thank You for bringin' Micah home to us safely and for all these volunteers who helped get him here. Thank You for our new friends, Lord. I also want to thank You for this wonderful food we are about to share with them, and we ask You to bless it and nourish our bodies with it. In the name of our Lord and Savior, Jesus Christ. Amen!"

Amens were shouted all over the yard then Mrs. Raan yelled, "Come fill your plates, babies! Make a line, and don't push and shove! There's gobs of food for everyone! We've got my famous fried chicken, tater salad, homemade buttery bread that'll melt in your mouth, and my prize-winnin' Georgia peach cobbler! Come and get it!"

Everyone was on their feet and in a line down the sidewalk in seconds! You could smell fried chicken all the way out in the yard. Chelsey's mom can cook some mean fried chicken, but the smell of Mrs. Raan's fried chicken took home the blue ribbon! Don't tell Gracie I said that!

Axl buttons his lips.

We insisted Chelsey's parents get their food first, then the rest of us filed in. Mr. and Mrs. Raan served everyone. They stacked chicken, potato salad, and homemade bread on everyone's plates until they were heavy. We each walked away with ridiculous amounts of food.

Mrs. Raan said, "Now grab some tea or lemonade, young 'ins, and go find a seat in the yard."

I've got to tell you, dude, it was one of the funnest times I've ever had! New friends, amazing food, crazy memories, lots of laughs, and all on a super cool planet. Awesome day!

By the time some of the crew had gone back for seconds, plus cobbler, we were stuffed! Mr. Raan told everyone to feel welcome to take a "fat nap" on the plush grass. Apparently, a "fat nap" is the kind of nap you take after you eat a big meal and your belly is full and fat. At least half of the search team took him seriously and crashed out in the warm breeze on the lawn. Chelsey and I lay in the grass, watched the clouds, and talked.

"Well, this has been quite an eventful day!" I said.

"Yeah, no kidding!" Chelsey responded. "I didn't expect this to happen at all! I still wonder what happened to Dad."

"We'll ask him after the excitement wears off and everyone goes home. I'm sure he doesn't want to talk about it in front of all these people."

"I'm just glad he's ok. He was terrified when we got to him. I hope this experience doesn't ruin Mom's and Dad's plans for future space travel," Chelsey said with a little concern.

"I think once Micah has a chance to talk about it, followed by a good night's sleep, they'll be fine. They'll start having fun here in Rew, and they'll be glad they came. Today will just be a story they can tell their friends."

"I'm sure you're right," Chelsey said with a slight smile.

"So, fat nap? I'm pooped," I said as I yawned.

"Me, too," she answered.

But neither of us napped. We both lay in the grass, watching the clouds, thinking about Micah getting lost.

26

Explanation Of Transport Gone Wrong

After waking up from their "fat naps," our new friends told Chelsey and me goodbye. We all promised to hang out again someday. Once they were gone, Chelsey and I strolled inside to hang out with the parents and the Raans.

The grownups sat in the living room drinking tea and lemonade. Gracie and Micah motioned for us to come to sit with them. Chelsey sat between her parents, and I sat on the other side of Micah. Gracie put both of her arms around her daughter and squeezed her.

Mr. Raan said, "You folks sure do have some good kids here."

"Yes, sir, we do," Micah agreed and kissed his daughter on the head. "She is one brave girl. We're sure proud of her. And you, too, Arëk," he said, rubbing the top of my head.

Micah and Chelsey both love to make my hair look crazy.

I catch Axl looking at my hair.

Don't even think about it, dude.

I slap his hand away, and he laughs.

"I don't know what we'd have done without you kids and your friends today," Gracie said.

"So, what happened, anyway?" Chelsey asked her dad.

"It was really my fault," Micah admitted.

"How? What went wrong? You guys know how to transport now," his daughter interjected.

He explained, "Well, you know what the Bible says about faith vs. fear and doubt? Well, when your mother and I agreed we would transport without your help this morning, my fear apparently won the battle over my faith. That's when I suggested we pray, but I still didn't let go of my fear. When Mom and I joined hands initially, Rew was on my mind. But when we closed our eyes, I was suddenly afraid to leave Haleiwa. By then, it was too late. We had already left Earth. I got detoured when my mind switched back and forth from Zooch to Earth.

"When I opened my eyes, I thought I was still on Oahu. It looked like it, until I saw a crazy-looking species coming out of the trees with sharp spears! That's when I realized your mom was gone! I didn't know what to do. And it didn't help matters that the natives didn't speak English and they seemed hostile."

"Why didn't you try to transport off their planet?" Chelsey asked.

Micah continued, "Besides being petrified, I had already messed up my first attempt at transporting. I didn't want to end up somewhere worse! So, I stayed put until I could come up with a good idea or until you two rescued me.

"Then your friends showed up out of nowhere looking for me, and I was so relieved! They told me there were tons of people searching for me, and whoever found me was supposed to take me to you."

"So, why didn't you leave with them? Why did you insist on them coming to get us first?" Chelsey asked.

"I don't know. I guess I was just too scared to move!" Micah answered with sudden embarrassment at the thought.

I looked at him with raised eyebrows.

With a mouth full of sarcasm, I said, "*WHAT?* You mean to tell me that my mentor, the tough and rugged Texas outlaw, was afraid of a few little *aliens*?"

"THEY HAD SPEARS!" Micah exclaimed. "AND THEY WEREN'T LITTLE! And I'm not an outlaw, doofus."

Everyone laughed at Micah's self-defense.

Axl laughs, too.

"Dad! The guys told us the natives had small *sticks*! The harmless kind! The digging in the sand for food kind!" Chelsey laughed.

Everyone continued laughing and teasing.

Micah admitted, "Well, they looked like scary sharp spears at the time!"

"I bet you screamed like a little girl!" I jousted.

"So, what! They were *SCARY!*" he responded with a high-pitched voice.

"Babe! You screamed like a little girl? You probably terrified those little people!" Gracie said, laughing.

Micah took off his flip-flop and gently swatted Gracie and Chelsey, then took a swat at me.

"I'm telling you guys, they were *scary*!" Micah said, realizing how silly it sounded.

Gracie and Chelsey dodged the shoe and laughed even harder. We all did. Mr. Raan laughed so hard he wiped a tear from his cheek.

"The important thing, honey, is you're back here where you belong," Gracie said, wiping tears of laughter out of her eyes.

"Are you alright, though, Dad? All kidding aside?" Chelsey asked him, scooping his big hand in hers.

"I'm tired, and I need a good night's sleep. But I think I'm good. I know one thing for sure. I will put my complete faith in God from now on. No more fear, especially when transporting!"

"I'm just glad you didn't drag me along with you!" Gracie said, wiping imaginary relief off her forehead.

"Ha-ha, very funny, toots. Next time, it will be successful. I have faith it will be," he responded confidently.

"That's my guy. I love you, honey," Gracie said.

She reached around Chelsey to stroke his cheek.

"What a relief! Chelsey and I were hoping this experience wouldn't ruin any further traveling adventures," I said.

"No way! We love this Universe traveling business! Besides, what a shame it would be to let fear take it from us. No stinkin' way!" Micah said.

"I tell you what," Mr. Raan interrupted, "when Ellie and I first learned of space travel, we jumped on it like a June bug on a light bulb! Our mailman there in Savannah told us about it. We thought he was jokin' with us at first. Until he told us about his experience, and how you do it. Curiosity got the best of us, so we had him show us. We brought him into the house, and he took us through the steps. Before we knew it, POOF! We were on Zooch! On our first day, we saw Elvis in concert! He'd been dead for twenty years! We couldn't believe it!"

"Have you seen Michael Jackson perform? His is the concert to see!" I said, interrupting Mr. Raan.

"No, Arëk, he's not quite our speed, but I've heard good things!" Mr. Raan answered.

Gracie mouthed to Micah, "Michael Jackson's alive?"

Micah shrugged, wondering the same thing.

"So, let me tell you, kids, Universe travel is the *thing*! It didn't take us long to decide where we would move once I retired from the Army. Ellie June told me she was done with base livin' and military schedules. She told me I had a choice to move her to Zooch or wave goodbye!"

Mrs. Raan nodded her head in agreement.

"You better believe it, babies. Once I laid eyes on this beautiful planet, I couldn't wait for Bob's retirement! We were packed and ready to go the same day. We've visited bunches of planets, but Zooch won this southern belle's heart."

"I know exactly what you mean. Since Chelsey and Arëk introduced us to other planets and space travel, we just can't get enough. I don't know about moving off Earth, but leaving it occasionally is wonderful! We're so glad our kids talked us into it. And now we have human friends on Zooch! You two are such a pleasure!" Gracie said.

"Well, thank you, darlin', you are just as cute as a button! We've heard about you and Micah for years! We're just so excited to finally have you in our home. You are welcome anytime. In fact, why don't you just unpack your things and consider this your home away from home durin' your little vacation? We'd love to have you! We have bookoos of room! This house is entirely too big for just the two of us, but we fell in love with it at first sight! There are four bedrooms and three extra bathrooms. Make yourselves at home with the Raans!" Ellie said.

Chelsey's parents looked at each other and agreed it was a marvelous idea.

"Mahalo, Ellie!" Gracie said.

"This is so nice, Bob! Thank you! You two are one of a kind!" Micah said, and Gracie agreed.

"Babe, will you help me get our bags? They're over by the door," Gracie said.

Chelsey and I had stayed at the Raan's house many times over the years, so we knew how to make ourselves at home. We raided the fridge, kicked off our flip-flops, and gave ourselves a tour around the house.

We love the Raans. They're just like family. In fact, they'd been Chelsey's self-adopted grandparents for half her life. They knew all about the plane crash when she was in her mom's womb. They knew about her missing siblings, about her traumatic shark attack when she was a little girl, and so much more. They knew some things about Chelsey's life before I did. I'll admit, that made me a little jealous. But she had her reasons to talk to them about stuff first.

After Chelsey's parents unpacked and settled in, we all rejoined in the living room for a short while before bedtime. The Raans asked them how they planned to spend their time in Rew or if they had anything special on their agenda. Gracie and Micah looked at each other and shook their heads no. They were just excited to play it by ear and see where each day took them.

The Raans promised not to interfere with their vacation. They didn't want Gracie and Micah to feel obligated to spend time with them since they'd be staying at their house. But they offered to take Chelsey's parents on any tours or to other planets if they wished. The folks were grateful and said they'd keep it in mind.

In no time, everyone was yawning, so we decided to call it a night. Gracie and Micah stood up and stretched. They hugged the Raans and thanked them again for their wonderful hospitality before heading to their room.

Chelsey and I thanked them for taking care of Gracie while we looked for Micah. They hugged us both together in a group squeeze and kissed our foreheads.

"We're grateful we could help. Your parents are jewels. Thank you for bringin' 'em to us," Mrs. Raan said and hugged us again.

"You know where your rooms are," Mr. Raan said. "We'll see you in the mornin'."

"Bacon, biscuits, and gravy sound ok for breakfast?" Mrs. Raan asked with a smile, already knowing the answer.

Chelsey and I looked at each other and smiled.

My bestie said, "Oh, yes, ma'am, it sounds wonderful, as always! Do you have any homemade plum jelly, like last time?"

"Well, of course, we do, are you kiddin'? We stay stocked up on fresh jelly, just for you, my love," Mrs. Raan said, hugging Chelsey extra tight.

"I think I'll just have Fruit Loops," I said, expecting to be smacked.

Mrs. Raan spanked my butt and said, "I oughta wash your mouth out with soap, mister!"

We all laughed.

Axl laughs, too. He says that sounds like his grandmother.

"Goodnight, babies," she added.

"Goodnight, guys. We love you," Chelsey said as we turned to walk down the hall.

"We love you too, honey. Sleep tight," Mrs. Raan said.

Mr. Raan waved and smiled.

"I love those kids. They're like our own," he said to his wife as they watched us walk sleepily to our rooms.

"They're the grandkids we never got to have. And now we have kids *and* grandkids since Gracie and Micah entered our lives. What a blessin'! Thank you, Jesus!" Mrs. Raan said.

"Yes, indeed!" Mr. Raan agreed.

27

New Friends

On the second day in Rew, Chelsey and I agreed to join her parents for a couple of hours before we took off on our mission. The four of us decided to check out a talent competition at the outdoor music festivities.

Gracie entered herself and Chelsey in a dance contest, and they won! Those two girls have got some crazy moves, thanks to all the cultural island dancing they've done for so many years! Not many of the Zoochians are familiar with hula hips but they loved it, even without grass skirts. I was the loud and proud cheering section on the front row.

During the dance contest, Micah made friends with a Flunian couple who were sitting at the next table. They were also vacationing in Rew. Fluni is known for its unusually long-named residents. So, as humans tend to do, Chelsey's dad gave his new friends nicknames to make communication easier. Dracumoteroto and Mandarumku Yul became Dracula and Mandy. Thank you, Micah! Right, brah?

"Good Lord! Those names are awful!" Axl jokes.

After proudly accepting their dance trophy, Gracie, Chelsey, and I joined Micah and his new friends. They all applauded and whistled as we walked up to the table.

Micah introduced us to Mandy and Dracula. Chelsey and I shook hands with his new friends and told them how nice it was to meet them, especially Dracula. Because how often do you get to meet someone named Dracula?

Axl chuckles and agrees.

After that, we decided it was a good time for us to split. We hugged the parents and wished them a fantastic vacation. Then, after giving shaka, we took off.

In celebration of their new acquaintance, the four new amigos ordered bimys, one of Zooch's amazing fruit drinks. They sat at the table of the little outdoor café all morning, through lunch, and into the afternoon.

The Wick/Yul friendship was a hit! They laughed, told stories, and became old friends in one day. They all shared the same goofy sense of humor, and they liked many of the same things. Plus, with the couples living on different planets, there was constantly something interesting to talk about.

After several hours of great food and bottomless bimys, the four decided to check out the music festivities in the park. The new friends were delighted by entertainers and costumes in every direction. Music was in the air, along with confetti and balloons. The energy was exciting and fun! Chelsey's folks and their new friends stopped to watch an acrobatic act and ran into Gint, one of the search team members from the day before.

"Hey, Mr. and Mrs. Wick!" she said. "How are you doing?" now directing her attention to Micah.

"I'm good, thanks to you and your friends," he said as he patted Gint's arm.

"We were happy to help! So, are you all enjoying the festivity fun?" she asked, changing the subject.

"Yeah, it's exciting!" Gracie said. "Oh, hey, these are our new friends, Mandy and Dracula. They're from Fluni."

"Dracula, huh?" she giggled. "Pleasure! I'm Gint!" she said, shaking hands with them both. "I have some really good friends from Fluni."

"Oh, wow, cool! What region?" Mandy asked.

"Requa," Gint answered.

"That's where we live! Maybe we'll see you there sometime!"

"I'll look for you!" Gint said as she waved at someone she recognized in the park. "Are you going to the big concert tonight? Rumor has it TobyMac will make a surprise appearance and is supposed to sing with a couple of the local bands! It's going to be stellar!"

"We didn't know about the concert, but it sounds fun! What do you guys think?" Gracie asked the gang.

"Yeah, I'd love to see TobyMac in concert!" Mandy said.

"Well, then, maybe we'll see you there! Thanks for telling us about it!" Gracie said.

"You're welcome! Catch you later!" Gint said, and she jogged off to meet her friends.

"The concert is going to be *soooo* good!" Mandy said, gripping Gracie's arms. "TobyMac was supposed to perform on Fluni a couple of years ago, but something happened, and they had to cancel. We were so bummed out!"

"Well, it looks like you're getting your chance now!" Gracie said.

"It sounds like we're going to a concert, Drac," Micah told his new friend.

"Cool!" Dracula responded, going along with what everyone else wanted to do.

The group walked down the people-covered street next to the park. Musicians were playing instruments, and actors were putting on musical skits. They enjoyed all the festivities, but just as much, they enjoyed the perfect weather and the company of their new friends. Although the vacation started out kind of rough, it was already turning out to be the best one any of them had ever taken.

They noticed a large gathering up ahead and decided to see what was going on. They made their way through the crowd and saw the best act they had seen yet. It was human twin boys, about five years old. Based on their accent, it wasn't hard to determine they were Jamaican. One played steel drums, and the other played a small guitar. They sang Michael Franti's feel-good song, "The Sound of Sunshine."

Besides the Raans and a few celebrities on their first trip, Chelsey's parents hadn't seen humans on Zooch. So, it surprised them to see two young boys from the Caribbean performing at a festival! But even more surprising was the little white dog with black spots howling in tune with their song! She was the first animal Chelsey's parents had ever seen on any planet other than Earth. Well, besides Gracie's brief encounter with the dinosaurs on Laya.

The couples watched the boys perform several songs, and they even danced to a song or two. When the boys took a short break, Gracie made her way over to them. She congratulated them on a dynamic performance and then asked the question that had driven her nuts for the last half hour.

"I've got to know, how did your dog come along with you to Zooch? I didn't know animals could transport," she said.

One of the boys motioned to Gracie to bend down so he could tell her a secret.

He cupped her ear with his little hands and said, "We don't know how she did it. She's the only animal we've ever seen transport off Earth, too!"

The other boy whispered, "She's not even our dog, but don't tell her. She followed us home two nights ago. She was on the beach where we were playing near our house. When we sang, she sang with us like she knew the songs. Then, when we were getting ready to transport to Zooch, she stood next to us and closed her eyes. The next thing we knew, she was here with us!"

"Incredible!" Gracie responded. "I wonder how she did it!"

"I don't know," the first boy said, "but we can't keep her when we go back home in a few days. Our guardians don't allow pets."

Gracie's eyes brightened up, and she turned around to look at Micah, who was standing behind her and heard the entire conversation.

"What do you think? Can we adopt her?"

"How did I know you'd ask?" Micah asked with a big smile on his face.

"She needs a home, and we can give her a good one. Besides, it will make Chelsey really happy and Charlie, too! Charlie needs a dog more her size to play with! Booger loves to play with her but he's so big and rough," Gracie stated, trying to convince her husband it was an excellent idea.

"You know I'm not going to deny an animal a loving home. Of course, we can take her home. But where will we keep her until we leave? We've still got our entire two weeks of vacation ahead of us," Micah said.

"I wonder if the Raans would mind letting her stay in their backyard. I think I'll ask. If it's not ok, then I'll figure something else out," Gracie said.

Gracie turned back to the boys and said, "I'll take her and give her a wonderful home. Sound good?"

The boys both hugged her and thanked her.

One of them said, "We were so worried about what might happen to her. Thank you so much. We call her Friday because we met her on a Friday."

"Friday. I love it!"

The boys' faces lit up when Gracie agreed with them.

"Come here, Friday!" she called to the happy little dog and held out her hands.

Friday came right over to her and let Gracie love on her.

"Hi, Friday, I'm going to take you home with me. You and I are going to surprise my daughter, Chelsey. She is going to love you, and spoil you, and probably teach you how to surf. You'll love it!"

Friday licked Gracie's face as if she understood every word.

Gracie asked the twins, "Will it be ok if Friday hangs out with you while I go talk to the people we're staying with? I need to make sure she can stay at their house until we go back home."

"Yes! We'll be right here until it starts getting dark. Then, we'll walk to our uncle's house, five streets down," one boy answered.

"I'll be back shortly, ok?" Gracie assured them.

The boys nodded and went back to their instruments to begin another song.

"Y'all want to meet some fine Georgia folks?" Gracie asked Mandy and Dracula.

"Of course!" Mandy said, and Dracula agreed.

They overheard the conversation between Gracie and Micah regarding Friday, so they knew what was up.

The four of them took a floating taxi ride to the Raans house, where they found Mrs. Raan on all fours in the flower garden. She was singing her little southern heart out.

"What a mighty God we serrrrrrve… What a mighty God we serrrrrrve…Angels bow before Him. Heaven and Earth adore Him…What a mighty God we serrrrrrve…," she sang.

Axl laughs at my attempt to sing and suggests I don't try to go professional. Axl's a punk.

Gracie had to say Mrs. Raan's name three times before she finally heard her calling from across the yard.

"Well, hello, kids!" she said, waving her dirt-covered glove.

"Hi, Ellie! Can we come over?" Gracie asked.

"Well, of course! Get over here and give me a hug! Who are these cutie pies?" she asked, referring to Mandy and Dracula.

"Ellie, we'd like you to meet our new friends, Mandy and Dracula. They're from Fluni," Gracie said.

"Dracula? Are you kiddin' me?" Ellie tilted her big southern hair-sprayed updo.

"Nope, not kidding. His name is Dracula," Micah answered proudly. "Named him myself!"

Axl laughs.

Micah loved his awesome nickname for his friend.

Dracula shook his head with a big smile and said, "My name is actually Dracumoteroto, but you can call me Drac."

"*Dracula*!" Micah said under his breath, where everyone could hear.

Dracula and the girls chuckled and shook their heads.

Ellie said, "Well, Drac and Mandy, welcome, welcome, welcome! It's so nice to meet y'all! Let's go inside for some fresh brewed sweet tea and my prize winnin'..."

"... peach cobbler!" Gracie and Micah lip-synced along with Mrs. Raan.

They all laughed.

Axl says he should've known.

"Smart alecks!" she said, slapping Micah on the shoulder with her dirty glove.

He pulled her into a hug, laughing.

"Brat!" she added, as they started their trek across the huge lawn.

Mandy and Dracula told Mrs. Raan what a pleasure it was to meet her. They already knew they were going to love her.

She grabbed Mandy's hand on one side and Dracula's on the other and said, "See, darlins', we're already friends."

Mandy looked over at Gracie and smiled.

Once they reached the front of the house, Micah pushed the door open.

Mrs. Raan hollered, "Bob, honey? Where you at, love? We've got company!"

Seconds later, Mr. Raan walked from the back of the house.

He said, "Well, looky here!"

He hugged Gracie and patted Micah on the back.

"Oh, we have new ones! I'm Bob Raan, and who might you be, pretty little lady?"

"I'm Mandy, and this is my husband, Drac," Mandy answered.

"*Dracula*!" Micah coughed into his fist.

Axl laughs and says he can't wait to meet Micah.

Dracula shook his head and chuckled.

"Well, Mandy and Drac, welcome to our home!" Mr. Raan said hugging Mandy and patting Dracula on the shoulder. "What can I get you youngins' to drink? Tea, lemonade, or bottled water? Or I bet we could even whoop up a pot of coffee."

"Unsweet tea sounds good to me," Gracie said.

Both of the Raans stopped and looked at her with shock, confusion, and maybe even a little southern disappointment. Possibly disgust. It's hard to tell sometimes with southerners.

"*UN*sweet?" Mrs. Raan asked with a scrunched-up face, stressing the "un."

"Yes, ma'am, if it's ok," Gracie replied timidly as if she were in trouble.

The Raans looked at each other like they had never heard of *UN*sweet tea before.

"Well, alright, if you *insist*," Mrs. Raan continued shaking her head in disbelief.

"And what about the rest of you *normal* kids," Mr. Raan asked then looked back at Gracie with a wink.

"I oughta tell your mama on you. *UN*sweet tea. Who ever heard of such a thing? And I thought you were American," Mrs. Raan mumbled under her breath, making sure Gracie could hear her. "I oughta spank your little hiney!"

Gracie had the sudden urge to sweeten her iced tea. But she stood her ground.

Axl laughs.

"Just water for me," Micah replied.

"The same for me," from Dracula.

"I'll have some of your sweet tea, Ellie," Mandy said, although she preferred unsweet tea.

Dracula coughed the words, "Brown-noser!"

Everyone laughed.

The girls helped Mrs. Raan deliver the drinks to the living room, where the guys were already sitting comfortably.

Mandy and Dracula enjoyed the hilarity of the Raan's humor. Bob and Ellie enjoyed hearing about the exciting day Chelsey's parents and friends were having.

After a while, Mandy looked at her watch and said, "We've only got three hours until the concert. Shouldn't we take care of the 'Friday' business soon, so we don't end up with crappy seats?"

"Oh, wow, I didn't realize what time it was!" Micah responded. "Babe, wasn't there something you needed to talk to Bob and Ellie about before we go?" he hinted to Gracie, reminding her of the reason they were all there.

"Oh, yes! Thank you, babe," and she turned to the Raans. "I have a favor to ask the two of you but if it is not feasible, it's perfectly ok."

They both nodded their heads and smiled.

Gracie continued, "First, let me ask you, have you ever seen a dog on any planet other than Earth?"

They looked at each other and shook their heads no.

Mr. Raan said, "We've heard rumors about *dinosaurs* (air quotes) on a planet far away from here, but I don't know of any other animals. Do you, punkin?"

"No, but it sure would be nice, though. We used to have the most precious little French Bulldog named Tulip. Sure miss our little girl," Mrs. Raan said as she thought back to good memories.

"Well, the reason I ask, is earlier today we saw a dog in the park with twin Jamaican boys," Gracie said.

The Raans looked at each other, then back at Gracie, and laughed as if she were joking with them.

"I know it sounds silly, but I'm serious. We all saw the dog, and I talked to the boys about her. They told me how she got here. But they can't keep her. I told them I'd adopt her, but I need a place for her to stay until we go home in two weeks. I was wondering if we could keep her in your backyard until we leave for Hawaii. We'll supply her food and keep the yard clean, I promise," Gracie said.

"You sure you saw a dog, sugar plum? You know, some of the planet species are a little unrecognizable as people sometimes.

Maybe what you thought was a dog was a little person from another galaxy. There are a lot of folks out there," Mr. Raan said, trying to make sense of the subject.

"She is a dog, I assure you. My guess is a Pointer mix of some flavor. So, what do you say? Can I keep her here for a couple of weeks?" Gracie asked.

"Well, of course, you can keep her here, honey, we'd do anything for you kids. We love y'all!" Mrs. Raan said, and Mr. Raan quickly agreed. "Bring her on over so you can get to your concert. We'll take care of her while you're gone. Happy to do it. Besides, it'll be wonderful to enjoy the company of a little critter around here. It's been a long time since we've even seen one."

Mr. Raan winked at Mrs. Raan as if to say, "I'll believe it's a dog when we see it!" She winked back in agreement. It was one of those silent conversations, like the ones Gracie and Micah have.

"Ok, then, if you're sure, we'll go get her and bring her back here," Gracie said, full of excitement. "Oh, her name is Friday, by the way. The twin boys gave her the name because they met her on a Friday. Isn't it sweet?"

"Well, go get her! Hurry up!" Mrs. Raan said. "We're excited to meet her! And bring those twins, too, if they want to come. We'd be happy to fill them full of…"

"PEACH COBBLER!" everyone shouted out together, then had a good belly laugh.

Axl says "peach cobbler" with me and laughs, too.

Mr. and Mrs. Raan laughed along with them. Ellie jovially spanked each of them with her sandal before pushing them out the door.

"Bring the kids!" the Raans yelled as the group floated down the street in the taxi.

Wide smiles stretched across the faces of the Jamaican twins when they saw Gracie and the gang walking down the street toward them. They had just finished performing for the day and ran to meet the group.

Gracie and Mandy held their arms out for hugs. Apparently, hugging is an automatic reflex for the female species. The boys ran past Micah and Dracula to wrap their skinny little arms around the girls. They soaked up the warmth of motherly affection.

The boys' embrace reminded Gracie of what one of them said earlier about having "guardians" back home.

She knelt, and asked them, "Do you live with your parents in Jamaica? Your mother and father?"

The guys knew this could get lengthy, so they went to play with Friday.

"No, our parents died last year in a car accident," one boy said with sadness in his voice. "We had to move out of our house to live with Mama Sue and Papa James. They have other children living at their house, too. Thirteen, I think. They are foster parents."

"I see. And you said you have an uncle here in Rew?" Gracie asked.

"Yes. Well, kind of. He is not our real uncle. He was a friend of our father, but we always called him uncle. He is nice. He invites us to Rew because he knows we like it here," the other boy said.

"You know what? We don't know each other's names! How can we be friends if we don't know each other's names?" Gracie said with childish energy.

The twin boys' eyes lit up with exhilaration, hearing someone was so interested in knowing them.

"My name is Elijah, and my brother is Isaac," the more vocal one spoke up.

"Good Bible names!" Mandy said, and Gracie agreed. "My name is Mandy."

"And my name is Gracie. Those guys over there are our husbands, Micah and Drac. You can meet them in a minute."

"Let me ask you boys another question. Have you boys ever eaten homemade peach cobbler?" They shook their heads no. "Well, we have some good friends named Ellie and Bob, who would love to meet you! Ellie makes the world's BEST peach cobbler! It is so good it will make your tummy smile!" Gracie said as she lightly tickled each of their stomachs.

"They want to meet *us*?" Elijah giggled.

"Are you kidding?" Mandy jumped in. "When we told them about you boys, they couldn't wait to meet you!"

Their eyes and smiles grew larger.

Isaac said, "Really? Can we go meet them now?"

"Absolutely! Tell you what. Mandy and I will go get Friday and the hubbies, and we'll all go together! Does that sound ok?" Gracie asked.

"It sounds great!" they both said, jumping up and down. "Can we bring our music?" referring to their instruments.

"Of course!" Gracie answered.

Mandy and Gracie gathered the twins, the husbands, and Friday. The group hopped in the floating taxi and headed to the Raan's house. The boys held Gracie's hands the whole way, nervous and excited all at the same time.

When the group arrived, the Raans were anxiously looking for them. The front door swung open, and they came running down the sidewalk.

"Oh, my goodness, look at these precious babies! Oh, I must have hugs! Give me lots of big hugs!" Mrs. Raan said, grabbing Isaac and Elijah.

They hugged her back, looking up at Gracie with grateful, big, toothy smiles.

Mrs. Raan released them and said, "Bob, they weren't kiddin'! Look at these boys! Aren't they the most precious children you have ever seen?"

"Indeed, they are!" Bob replied as he knelt to meet them. "My name is Bob, and this is my wife, Ellie. We are very happy to have you here. Do you want to come inside?"

"Is that where the peach," Elijah looked back to Gracie for help.

"Cobbler," she whispered.

"... cobbler, is?" he finished.

"Why, yes, it is, young man. Would you like to try some?" Mr. Raan asked.

"Yes, sir, if it's alright," Elijah answered.

"You better believe it! Let's go inside, shall we?" Mr. Raan said.

"We'll take Friday to the backyard," Micah commented.

Seeing Friday for the first time since we arrived, Mrs. Raan said, "Well, my great goodness, she really is a dog!"

Axl laughs.

"Well, I'll be!" Mr. Raan exclaimed, bending down to pet the white spotted dog.

"We'll get these boys fed, and then we'll all go out back and play with her," he added.

Micah and Dracula ran and played with Friday all the way to the backyard. She was such a fun little dog, and full of energy. The guys hung out with Friday so she wouldn't be afraid in a strange place, and the girls helped the Raans make Isaac and Elijah comfortable.

Mrs. Raan asked the twins if they had eaten lunch before she served heaping bowls of cobbler.

Elijah replied, "No, ma'am, we haven't had food since yesterday. Or was it the other day?"

"What? Well, I guess you must be hungry, then, aren't you? Let's get some solid food in your bellies, and then we'll eat some cobbler, ok?" she responded.

"Ok," they both agreed.

"Do you like fried chicken and tater salad? We have leftovers from our big picnic yesterday," Ellie said.

"We like chicken! Chicken tastes good!" one boy said with excitement, and the other eagerly agreed.

"Well, you're about to have the best chicken you've ever had right here in Mrs. Raan's kitchen!" Mr. Raan said.

The twins clapped and smiled.

"Bob, why don't you take the boys to wash up while we ladies fix a late lunch for them," Mrs. Raan asked.

"You bet! Let's go, boys! I'll show you around the house while we're at it!" Mr. Raan said.

The three of them left the kitchen.

"Ok," Mrs. Raan started, "so, what's their story? I sense their lives aren't as peachy as my cobbler."

Gracie and Mandy took turns telling what little information the twins had told them. They mentioned the parents dying in a car crash, and they now live in foster care with thirteen other children.

"I don't like it, not at all!" Mrs. Raan responded, with tears in her big blue eyes. "No, sir, not at all. Those boys need a proper home."

Gracie and Mandy were as unhappy about the boys' situation as Mrs. Raan. It was heartbreaking to the girls. They were happy the Raans invited the kids to come to their house to at least feed them and show them some love. Gracie mentioned the father's friend who lives in Rew and who invites them to come there occasionally.

Mrs. Raan said, "What's the deal with him? If he's such a good family friend, why hasn't he adopted them or helped them or somethin'?" she trailed off as tears fell from her chin.

Mandy wrapped her arm around Mrs. Raan in comfort.

Gracie commented, "Well, we don't really know enough about him to want him to adopt them, but these kids do need a healthy and permanent home. Mandy, you work with similar situations on Fluni. Do you think we could do some research together to find out what their options are?"

"Oh, absolutely! I know someone who can get a list of families on Earth who are looking to adopt young children. The problem is many people want to adopt babies, not five-year-old twin boys."

"Does it have to be a family on Earth? Isn't there some way people livin' on other planets can adopt Earth kids?" Mrs. Raan asked out of desperation.

"Interplanetary adoptions are not as common. I'm not saying it can't be done, but I'm not familiar with any of those cases," Mandy said.

They could hear Bob and the boys coming, so they ended the conversation.

"Ok, the boys are all washed up and ready to eat some chicken and tater salad!" Mr. Raan said excitedly with his arms raised high in the air.

The boys raised their arms, imitating Mr. Raan, and said, "YAAAY!"

"Alright, y'all, come sit down at the table in the dinin' room. Bob, would you please bless the food?" Mrs. Raan asked.

"Yes, ma'am! Everyone join hands. Dear Heavenly Father, I feel so blessed at this moment," Mr. Raan prayed as tears filled his closed eyes. "Thank You for bringin' these precious boys into our home and into our lives. Thank You for allowin' us the honor of fillin' their bellies and showin' them Your love. I ask that You pour out big special blessins' on Elijah and Isaac every day of their lives. Please bless this fine chicken, Lord, which my beautiful bride prepared for them. We love you with all we are. In Jesus' name, amen."

"Amen!" everyone said.

"Ok, dig in!" Mrs. Raan said.

"Elijah and Isaac, darlins,' would you mind sittin' here without us for just a minute? I'd like to have a quick conversation with Bob and the girls," Mrs. Raan said.

The twins readily nodded as they took big bites of chicken.

Mrs. Raan took Mandy and Gracie each by the arm and led them and Mr. Raan into a windowed sitting room on the other side of the living area.

Once they all sat down, she said, "Bob, would you be opposed to us askin' the boys if they'd like to stay the night so we can spend some more time with them? My heart just breaks for those two boys," she said as she began to cry.

"We filled Ellie in on as much as we know about them and their situation," Gracie told Bob. "It's not great. They're foster children in a home with way too many kids. My guess is it's a severely poor area of Jamaica. They need baths, better food than what they've been eating, based on how they look, and they need love and attention. These boys seem to be fending for themselves."

Bob inhaled deeply and exhaled slowly.

Then he began, "There's a story Chelsey knows about us, and we will now tell you because we believe you kids are truly our friends. Ellie and I had kids once, a long time ago, a boy and a girl. We had a wonderful family. We spent tons of time together, more than families do nowadays. We gave the kids everything they wanted when we could afford it. But more than anything, we loved them and made sure they knew it every day of their lives. Their names were," he swallowed hard and covered his eyes with his hands as he began to weep. "Luke and Tess. He was nine, and she was seven."

He began to cry harder, and Gracie moved to sit next to him to comfort him. Mandy held Mrs. Raan close to her as she cried with him.

"They were just babies!" he cried.

Gracie rubbed his back and asked, "What happened, Bob?"

"Cancer. The same kind. It took them both within the same year."

Axl wipes a tear away.

"Oh, no, I am so sorry," Gracie and Mandy both said with the deepest sympathy.

"By the time we discovered it, it was too late for treatment. Technology back then wasn't what it is now. Luckily, it took them quickly and without much pain. We thank God for that," Bob said, wiping tears off his face. "Years went by, along with a lot of prayin' and counselin', before we could talk about them without breakin' down. It was a horrible tragedy. No one should die so young. Especially like that."

He reached over to take a tissue from the box on the coffee table and blew his nose.

"After we were somewhat healed, years later, God began to speak to us about a second chance. We told Him we didn't want to have any other children. As a matter of fact, I had a vasectomy to prevent it. Our hearts only had enough room for Luke and Tess."

"God never let up, though," Ellie interjected. "He kept talkin' to us about a second chance. We argued and argued with Him until finally, He became silent about it. We were relieved, to tell you the truth. It was the only time we *didn't* want to hear from God."

"Then, strangely enough, about a year ago, out of the blue, God started in again about a second chance. We thought, Lord, who do you think we are, Abraham and Sarah? And then He didn't mention it again until today, this mornin' while Ellie and I were drinkin' our coffee on the patio out back. You kids were still asleep. It made no sense at all until y'all came in to ask about Friday, and you mentioned the twins from Jamaica. Somethin' lit up inside me, and I knew we were supposed to meet those boys," Bob said.

"I did, too," Ellie interrupted. "And when I saw them, I knew what God was talkin' about. And I want to do what needs to be done to have a second chance now."

Bob stood up and took Ellie's hands and pulled her up. He hugged her, and they both cried. Mandy and Gracie looked at each other, and they cried, too. What a privilege to be sitting in the same room where God's divine plan was unfolding.

"So, to answer your question, Ellie, yes, I want Elijah and Isaac to stay the night with us. And a thousand nights after!" Mr. Raan said as he proudly looked his wife in the eyes.

Ellie hugged Bob again and said, "Thank you, God, for bein' patient with us all these years. And thank you for Gracie and Mandy and their husbands. Please guide us in the right direction so we can adopt these two boys and give them the home they so deserve."

"Amen," they all agreed.

"Well, I'm willing to bet Elijah and Isaac have eaten all the chicken and tater salad their little bellies can hold. Think it's time to bless those sweet boys with some peach cobbler if they have room for it?" Gracie asked.

"Yes, I do! Let's go feed *our* boys some cobbler, Mr. Raan," Ellie said to her husband, and they walked arm-in-arm to the kitchen.

"Whoooo's ready for cobbler?" Mrs. Raan dramatically asked as she entered the dining room with two heavy bowls of peach cobbler and vanilla ice cream.

"Me!" Elijah and Isaac both shouted.

The Raans sat with the boys while Gracie and Mandy went outside to see what the hubbies were up to.

"You guys were in there forever!" Micah said just before kissing Gracie.

"Oh, you're not going to believe *this*!" Gracie responded.

The two girls filled their husbands in on what had taken place. It was a heart-happy story for everyone. The couples decided to hang out in the backyard for a bit to give the Raans time to get to know the twins a little better before they took off to the concert. Gracie was also very happy to get to know Friday, the newest member of her ever-growing family. Friday is a cool dog, dude! She's one of my favorites. But don't tell the other pets.

Axl holds his hand up and shakes his head no.

After another half hour had passed, the Raans and the twins joined the group outside.

Mr. Raan said, "You kids better be gettin' on to your concert, shouldn't you?"

Chelsey's parents and friends looked around at each other, then Gracie said, "I feel kind of bad dropping off two kids and a dog and then leaving. It's like doing a drive-by."

"Don't you worry about a thing. We are so happy right now because of y'all. We're goin' to hang out in the yard and play with Friday for a while. Then, I think we might have us a jam session. I play a little guitar myself," Mr. Raan bragged to the boys.

Elijah smiled a big smile and said, "You do?"

"Oh, you better believe it! I was in a band when I was a young man. We were called The Black Cats, and, boy, could we draw a crowd back then. Those were the days," Mr. Raan said, enjoying a distant memory.

"You can be in *our* band!" Isaac told Mr. Raan.

"I'd like that very much. Thank you, Isaac," he graciously accepted.

"So, back to it! You kids be off! We'll be here when you come draggin' in tonight. The boys will be in Chelsey's room in case you feel the need to kiss them goodnight," Mr. Raan said with a smile.

"Alright then, let's be off, gang!" Micah said.

They petted Friday, hugged the Raans and the twins, and they loaded up in the floating taxi.

"TobyMac here we come!" they all shouted as they floated off.

28

Vacation Day 3

After sleeping in, because of a very fun and long concert, Chelsey's parents dragged themselves out of bed. They stumbled into the kitchen to find Mr. Raan setting steaming hot lattes on the table. Chelsey told him years back what a latte junky her mom was. So, he thought he'd start their day with a familiar favorite.

The oversized mugs, filled to the top with a delicious mixture of hot espresso, milk, and foam, were a welcomed sight for Gracie and Micah. To top it off, Mrs. Raan had outdone herself on a breakfast fit for royalty. She made homemade buttermilk biscuits, sausage gravy, bacon, pancakes, and eggs. Chelsey's parents didn't know where to start! They ate till they were stuffed.

They questioned the Raans as to why Elijah and Isaac weren't at the breakfast feast. Bob told them they were going to let the boys sleep until their little bodies woke them up. He said he asked Elijah and Isaac the night before what kind of beds they were used to sleeping in, and their answer broke his heart.

The boys told him they hadn't slept in a bed since their parents died. In the foster home they lived in, the oldest kids got to sleep in the beds, and the younger ones slept like sardines on the floor. Bob said he and Ellie stayed up for hours talking to God about the details of adoption. They were determined to give Elijah and Isaac a loving home and family. Micah and Gracie promised to do anything they could to help make it happen.

When Chelsey's parents finally got up from the breakfast table, they showered, got ready, and met back up with Mandy and Dracula. The four decided it would be fun to spend the entire vacation hanging out together.

Micah and Dracula hinted they wanted to do some guy stuff. The girls were happy with the request since they also hoped to spend some girl time. It worked out perfectly for all of them. They decided to split up and meet back together at sunset for a nice romantic candlelit dinner at a restaurant the Raans recommended. Gracie and Mandy kissed their husbands goodbye and wished them a fun-filled "guy stuff" day.

The guys began their day with a walk down the main street, where the festivities were still going strong. They stopped at a park where several young Zoochian boys were throwing their equivalent of a football to each other.

Dracula said, "Ah, youth. If only to have half of their energy again."

Micah shook his head in agreement and said, "No kidding, bro. Kids have no idea how easy their lives are at that age. Playing ball, hanging out with their buddies, and just having fun."

"I sure miss those days sometimes. I loved playing basketball and hearing my parents cheer me on at every game. Those were the glory days!" Dracula said.

"You better believe it was!" Micah responded, thinking back to his high school football days.

The guys discovered they had tons to talk about. They discussed their favorite teams and the latest sports victories on Earth. Dracula was a fan of several American football, soccer, and basketball teams. He and Mandy had been loud screamers at a few NBA and MLS Championships. They attended as many seasonal games as they could, too. It was so fun for Micah to know someone from across the Universe who could carry on enthusiastic conversations about Earth sports.

Dracula suddenly had a great idea. He told Micah about a planet called Ack. He said it's a "manly" planet, and they should check it out.

"Why not?" Micah asked. "You know the girls are going to be busy all day, shopping, and spa-ing, and whatever else girls do when they're together. Plus, they told us to have a good time. And they didn't specify which planet to have fun on!"

Dracula replied, "Well said! This is dude's day!"

"Let's do it! Lead the way, amigo!" Micah said with enthusiasm.

29

The Guys Explore Ack

When the guys arrived in the city of Nuch, Chelsey's dad was blown away. His first discovery was Ack's lack of gravity. Dracula failed to mention this little detail, accidentally on purpose, prior to the transport. He thought it would be comical to watch Micah's reaction. Micah had to concentrate hard to stay in one place without floating away! After bouts of hysterical laughter between the two friends, Chelsey's dad figured out how to control it.

Dracula was an experienced Universe traveler, so he knew all the coolest places to take first timers. He wanted to show Micah a memorable time in Nuch, so he made a mental list of fun things to do.

He decided to take Micah to a big lake, called Hongz, where the fish were huge, flying out of the water, floating in the air, and begging to be caught! It was irresistible for an outdoorsman! Micah couldn't believe it! The fish were shimmering with bright colors, and they were different shapes and sizes. Some were three feet long, while others were anywhere from seven to thirteen feet long. Some were skinny as a post, and some were fat like the Goodyear Blimp.

Micah asked, "Are we going to fish?"

Dracula said, "Heck yeah, we are, buddy! You're going to love this!"

The two men rented a small boat and fishing poles and bought bait at the local marina. Dracula taught Micah the basics of how to catch fish from the air, which he caught onto quickly.

Micah said, "You know, Gracie's grandmother, Mam, was an avid fisherwoman in her younger days. She claims that *real* fishermen make competitive bets."

Dracula said, "I'm listening."

"Mam says you bet on who will catch the first fish, the most fish, and the biggest fish. Of course, every smart fisherman bets on himself. So, you've got three cash pots, one for each category, and the winner of each category takes home the dough."

"I'm game! Name the amount!" Dracula said excitedly.

"Let's keep it simple. How about ten bucks per category?"

"Deal!" Dracula responded with a fist bump. "Let the games begin!"

Micah had no idea how much fun fishing could be until he fished with Dracula at Lake Hongz. As competitive as these two men were, it made the challenge even more exciting! Especially when the race to win involved pushing each other off the boat and throwing super slimy green bait at each other when one or the other was trying to reel in a big one.

They laughed the entire time and caught lots of fish! The photos they took to prove the experience are hilarious, brah! Both guys were soaked, covered in fish scales and they stunk to high heaven by the end of the adventure! Micah even ended up with a hook in the top of his ear from one of Dracula's wild casts.

Axl laughs.

How they would explain it to Gracie, they didn't know. What they did know was without pictures to prove this "big fish story," the girls would never believe them.

After the three-hour fishing quest, it was time for two things: paying up the bets and then finding a place to wash off. It turned out Dracula caught the first fish. And it was nothing short of hysterical when it pulled him up into the air, took him for a ride, then dumped him in the water! Micah caught the biggest fish, which tackled him in the boat and flopped all over him. Dracula laughed so hard he rolled off the boat!

Axl laughs and says, "That's awesome!"

The two amigos tied for the greatest number of fish, with a whopping combined total of eighteen brightly colored, multi-sized fish! Quite impressive and loads of fun! Mam would be proud, dude!

The next task was to find some clean water to wash up with. They hiked a short distance to a nearby waterfall, where they stripped down to their skivvies. They showered off under the falls and then floated around the clear water.

"You know, I never learned how to swim until I moved from Texas to Hawaii. Gracie insisted I learn since we live on the ocean," Micah said.

"I love the water! I've never been to an Earth ocean, though. I've always wanted to try surfing," Dracula replied.

"You've got to come to Hawaii, dude! If you like playing in the water, you'd totally dig surfing."

"I may take you up on that offer," Dracula replied.

"Come to Oahu and let Chelsey teach you. She's a master of the waves! She's won several major surfing competitions over the years. Personally, I think she's as good as any pro on the planet. You should see her out there. It's like she's a part of the ocean."

"It sounds like you're proud of your girl. Mandy and I will have to plan a trip to Hawaii. I'll sign up for lessons with Chelsey."

"Definitely, come see us! While you're there, you can watch Chelsey's dogs and monkey surf, too! It's very entertaining!" Micah commented.

"Are you serious?" Dracula asked.

"Yep! And there's an iguana now, too. It has an eye patch like a pirate. No doubt Chelsey will have him surfing, too!" Micah said, chuckling.

"It sounds like you've got a zoo at your house!"

Micah laughed in agreement.

"Mandy and I will have to get over there. It sounds like fun. I'd love to experience your ocean," Dracula said.

"There's nothing like it."

"Well," Dracula said, "Since we're all wrinkled and semi-clean, what do you say to a late lunch?"

30

Checking In With The Girls

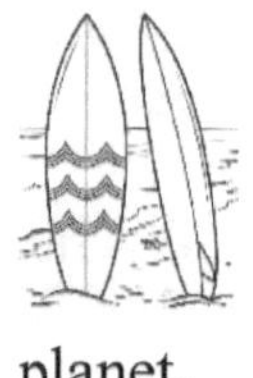 After sightseeing in Rew, Gracie and Mandy decided to pay a visit to beautiful Cozy for a late morning at the spa planet.

Upon their arrival, the girls were wowed with spectacular waterfalls, natural steaming springs, and beautiful flowers known across the Universe for their rejuvenating power. Mandy and Gracie were invited to be pampered like queens. They enjoyed massages, body wraps, facials, and mani-pedis. They even agreed to new colors and styles for their hair. By the time they left Cozy, Gracie and Mandy looked ten years younger, and they felt as refreshed as they appeared.

"Micah will think he's died and gone to Heaven when he sees me," Gracie said, laughing as she admired her new-found youth in the mirror. "I could get used to *this*!"

Mandy said, "Oh, girl, me too! We'll have to make this a regular thing!"

The girls laughed as they walked away from the salon.

"Now, let's go shopping!" Mandy said enthusiastically.

The two grasped hands and transported to planet Tumah.

Planet Tumah is a wealthy planet, and I'm talking *stupid* wealthy, brah! A foreigner might think only the richest could afford to vacation there. Or even to shop in the exquisite stores, malls, and boutiques scattered across the planet. However, such a theory would be far from the truth. Although the locals are blessed financially, they don't turn their noses up at less-than-loaded people. In fact, Tumahns are some of the friendliest, most humble folks you could ever meet. They'd give all their wealth away to help someone in need if the opportunity arose. It's probably why God blesses them so abundantly.

Axl says, "That makes sense."

The foreigner's erroneous notion I just mentioned is what Gracie thought when she and Mandy arrived in the village of Ci, Tumah's capital. She saw all its glitter and glamour and felt wildly out of place. Of course, after spending the whole morning on Cozy, the girls looked like they were *born* on Tumah! Mandy had been to Ci several times, so she knew all the most fabulous places to shop. And luckily for Gracie, the American dollar was worth bookoos on Tumah! Tumah commerce was a steal!

This planet has a similar government system to England. It has the equivalent of a Queen, only on Tumah, the title is called Vinga. And the Vinga, whose name is Isun, happened to be browsing at the same boutique where Gracie and Mandy were shopping.

Allow me to interject: the sociability of most planet leaders throughout the Universe is very different from the sociability of the national leaders of Earth. As you know, brah, Earth's presidents, kings, queens, etc., are on some weird level of celebrity status. They require around-the-clock security and are mostly unavailable and unapproachable to the common citizen. In contrast, the leaders from most of the other planets are sociable, friendly, available, and helpful to their citizens. They seem to be more concerned about their people than politics. Eww, sting! Moving on.

Axl half-smiles and says, "Sad but true."

As I previously mentioned, Isun, the Vinga of Tumah, was socializing and shopping in the same boutique where Gracie and Mandy were shopping. All eyes were on her as she cheerfully walked through the store, touching the fabrics, especially the softest pieces. She also honored the store owners by trying on their beautiful apparel.

This woman unquestionably stood out in the crowd of Tumahns and other planet beings. Partly because she was in human form. Yes, the Vinga of Tumah is human. That will be explained shortly, so stay tuned. She also stood out because she was so incredibly stunning! Isun had long golden waves of hair framing her perfect olive complexion. Her bright blue eyes were as big as the Pacific. And her smile had the power to turn the darkest day into pure sunshine. She was beautiful, graceful, and full of life. Isun was indeed the honorable Vinga of this planet, but under her title and crown, she was a vibrant girl whose heart was as free as the birds in the sky, and she didn't pretend to hide it.

Axl says he loves her already. Calm down, tiger!

Gracie and Mandy saw the back of Isun just before a group of employees rushed past them with a sparkly blue dress. Gracie asked a woman shopping near them what the emergency was. She said the Vinga was there. That made no sense to Gracie, of course, so she and Mandy continued to watch the excitement. After a few minutes, they heard a very elated woman announce, "She loves the dress!"

Moments later, a young woman exited the fitting room wearing the sparkly blue dress, custom-made just for her. She was exquisite! Gracie watched curiously, not knowing who this woman was but assuming she must be important. The people in the boutique clapped as she walked through the center of the room. She smiled at every person, spoke to them, lovingly touched them, and even laughed with a couple of women whom she clearly knew.

Then she threw her hands up and loudly asked, "Where's the music?"

An employee of the store quickly stepped into a room next to the checkout counter to turn the music volume up. Everyone, including this celebrity, cheered and began to dance right there in the store! Gracie figured this must be a regular occurrence, as carefree as everyone appeared. What a fun experience! Gracie watched this woman in the beautiful blue dress, who had the undivided attention of every person there.

And Axl's.

The Vinga noticed a little Pathubian girl admirably watching her, so she grabbed the little girl's hands. The two danced and sang aloud to the happy song playing. The little girl glowed with joy at such personal attention from the Vinga. As Gracie smiled at this unusual sight, she thought about Chelsey. That girl loves to dance and sing no matter where she is. It made Gracie miss her daughter and wonder what she and I were doing.

Her reminiscence was interrupted, however, when the dancing duo twirled right up to Gracie and Mandy. The Vinga placed the tiny hands of the little girl into Mandy's hands. That was her queue to continue dancing where she and the Vinga left off.

Then, unexpectedly, the elegant young woman in the shiny blue dress took Gracie for a spin. Gracie giggled at the surprise of it and happily played along. As she spun hand in hand with the Vinga of this wonderful planet, Gracie looked into the face of someone oddly... *familiar*. Like everyone else in the room, she was spellbound by Isun's beauty and grace. But there was something else drawing Gracie's attention to this woman.

Mandy noticed Gracie staring at the Vinga as they danced.

She said to the human lady dancing next to her, "Gracie has no idea who she is, does she?"

Mandy had seen Isun many times during previous visits, eating with the locals, visiting with tourists, and shopping at the boutiques. The Vinga was undeniably down-to-earth, or "down-to-Tumah," I should say.

The lady dancing next to Mandy replied, "No, I don't think so. She's wonderful, though. Who is she?"

Mandy looked at her with surprise.

"You don't know either?"

The lady shook her head no.

"She's Isun, the Vinga of Tumah. She's the queen here," Mandy said.

"What? Are you kidding me? And she's out in public? Is she crazy? She could get kidnapped! Or shot!" the lady exclaimed.

Mandy laughed and said, "Oh, don't worry. Tumah is different from Earth. Isun is always with her people. She loves them so much, and they all love her. I met her some time ago when my husband and I were visiting. She's very sweet and fun. She gave me this ring I never take off. She actually made it herself with the jewels found in the Wuvet River flowing just outside the village near here. It's my favorite piece of jewelry."

Mandy held out her hand to show off the colorful ring.

"I want a ring like that," the lady said with jovial envy.

Mandy smiled and winked at the lady, then said, "You shouldn't leave without one."

The lady smiled and answered, "I might leave with *two*!"

Mandy lightly bumped her shoulder and smiled back.

The two turned their attention back to Gracie and Isun.

Mandy asked the lady, "Is it me, or do the Vinga and Gracie favor a little?"

"Now that you mention it, they sure do. You know how they say we all have a twin somewhere," the lady commented.

"Who says that?" Mandy asked, clearly never having heard the cliche before.

"I guess it's an Earth thing!" the woman answered.

They both giggled.

Gracie had the strangest feeling in her gut telling her she knew this beautiful stranger from somewhere. But how?

After all, she was zillions of miles away from Earth. It's not likely she would run into someone from back home. Gracie didn't know why she knew this remarkable woman. Her *heart* knew her, and it wouldn't let go until she found out who this familiar person was.

When the happy song ended, Isun curtsied in front of Gracie and her adoring fans. Applause broke out inside and outside the boutique. She had drawn quite a crowd. It was clear to Gracie everyone knew and loved her.

Axl says he thinks he loves her, too. Chill, dude.

When the applause ended, the people resumed their shopping.

The stranger took Gracie's hands in hers and, with shortness of breath, said, "What a lovely experience! Thank you so much for humoring my silliness."

She finished with a giggle and fanned the heat from her face with her hands.

Gracie smiled and said, "It was a delight to dance with you. You are bookoos of fun! My name is Gracie, by the way."

Isun squeezed her hands and replied, "Welcome to Tumah, Gracie. My name is Isun. It is a pleasure to have you here."

But what Isun was really thinking as her heart began to thump like a bass drum in a high school band was, "Oh, my God, oh, my God, oh, my God! I can't believe it's her! I can't believe she's standing right in front of me! Is this really happening, God? Does she know who I am? Is it time, Lord? Ok, stay calm."

"Thank you, Isun. My new friend, Mandy, introduced me to Tumah. I *love* your planet. It's like a dream!" Gracie said enthusiastically.

"It always makes me happy when visitors express their love for our planet. We try to make it the most hospitable place you could ever visit," Isun said.

Then she took Mandy's hand and, with her cheerful smile, said, "My friend, Mandarumku. It's been a while since you've been here. I'm thrilled to see you again."

Mandy was pleasantly surprised and said, "Wow, I can't believe you remember me! You've made me feel very special! Thank you!"

Isun replied, "You left a special impression on my heart when you were here. I will never forget how the Lord opened such an amazing door for the two of us to meet and visit."

She looked at Gracie and asked, "Has Mandarumku told you how we met before?"

Gracie shook her head no to the question while trying not to crack up at the sound of Mandy's ridiculous name.

Axl laughs in agreement.

Mandy caught on to it right away and told Isun, "You can call me Mandy. It's the much shorter and easier nickname Gracie's husband gave me."

She bumped Gracie's shoulder and smiled at her.

"Please continue with your story," Gracie said, still smiling.

Isun picked up on the inside humor and went along with it.

"So, *Mandy* and her husband, stopped by Ci on their way to Samien several years ago for their anniversary. Mandy was shopping for a special dress to wear for the occasion. I happened to be across the street buying fruit when she and her husband walked out of the store. The couple immediately caught my eye. They looked so in love and happy. I didn't remember seeing either of them before, so I caught up with them to welcome them to Tumah. While we chatted, Mandy's husband noticed an elderly gentleman struggling to manage an arm full of flowers and a shopping bag. He rushed over to help him.

"Meanwhile, Mandy and I sat down on a bench next to the fruit stands. I suddenly felt a heaviness in my heart for her, and I heard the Lord speak to my spirit, as He often does. I knew right away that our meeting was no coincidence. I asked Mandy if she knew Jesus, and she said no. I began to tell her about my amazing Savior, His sacrifice, and His indescribable love for us. It wasn't but just a few minutes later, she asked Jesus to be her Savior, too.

"When her husband walked over to where we were sitting, Mandy and I both were crying and hugging. He was confused, poor thing. When he left her, she was fine. After a few minutes with me, she was crying."

Axl smiles.

The three women laughed as she continued, "After telling him what happened, he gave his life to Christ, too. It was a wonderful day for all of us. Afterwards, I took them to lunch at my favorite café, where we talked and laughed. It wasn't long before Dracumoteroto started to yawn after eating such a hearty meal. I suggested a nap for him at a relaxing place next to the water. He readily agreed. Mandy and I dropped him off to rest, and then she and I took a walk to the Wuvet River.

"I showed Mandy my favorite place in the river. God provided it with an eternal supply of magnificently colorful jewels and metals. It looks like a rainbow under the water.

"There is also a small cottage near the river where a wonderful elderly gentleman lives. If you take the jewels you pick from the river to him, he will help you make jewelry with them.

"I wanted Mandy to take a memento with her, so I made her a ring to remember our new friendship by. I noticed the ring when I handed you the little girl earlier. I'm so happy to see you wearing it, Mandy."

"I haven't taken it off since then. I love it so much," Mandy responded.

"What a wonderful story!" Gracie responded. "God is so awesome. Isn't it something how He always places people in the right place at the right time? I love that about Him."

"Oh, my goodness, yes, like today! It is a blessing and a pleasure to make your acquaintance, Gracie. You and Mandy are such beautiful and special ladies. I am certainly in the presence of queens!" Isun said with a genuine smile and a curtsy.

"Wow, that's quite a compliment coming from an *actual* queen!" Mandy exclaimed.

Gracie looked at Mandy and said, "Queen?"

"Yep! Your new friend is the Vinga of Tumah," Mandy announced.

"Say again?" Gracie asked, clearly not getting it.

"Let me explain it to you this way. When this lady welcomes you to her planet, she is literally welcoming you to *her* planet."

"Sooo, you're a queen, like Queen Elizabeth? Like with a crown and a castle and subjects, kind of queen?" Gracie asked, sounding a little skeptical.

Mandy interrupted, "Isun is the equivalent of a queen on Earth, only here they call her Vinga instead of Queen. She is the leader of the planet. The ruler of the joint."

Isun laughed at the last comment.

"Ok, sooo, what are you doing out here in public? Isn't this dangerous for you?" Gracie asked with concern, looking around for bad guys.

Isun laughed, "Don't worry, it is safe here. Yes, I am the Vinga, the ruler of Tumah, but I am appointed by God, not the people. It's not like it is on Earth. I may be in charge, but I'm still one of the peeps."

They all chuckled at the remark.

Axl smiles at the word "peeps," a word he uses quite often.

"Well, isn't *that* just the coolest thing ever? Earth could learn a few things from some of these other planets. I might just make some suggestions when I get back," Gracie said humorously.

"Have you ladies had lunch yet? My stomach's talking. There's a cozy little outdoor café down the street if you'd like to join me," the Vinga said.

"Food is exactly what we need," Gracie replied, and Mandy readily agreed.

Axl can't stop talking about Isun. He tries to dumb down his super crush on her by talking about how cool it is that Gracie and Mandy got to hang out with the queen. Riiight, brah.

31

Back To The Fellas

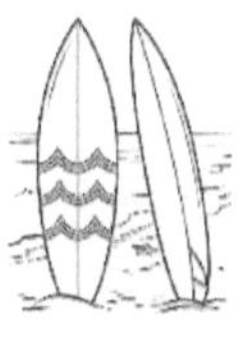 The guys were starving! Dracula took Micah to a famous grill where he had eaten many times.

As they were waiting to be seated, he said, "I bet you're a meat lover, being from Texas!"

"You better believe it!" Micah declared. "You can't beat a good medium-rare ribeye, homegrown on a ranch in West Texas!"

Dracula replied, "Buddy, you haven't eaten tasty meat until you've eaten meat at *this* grill!"

The big, burly guy behind the fire looked up at Dracula with a "that's right" smirk.

"What makes the meat here so special?" Micah asked. "And besides, I didn't think there were animals on other planets besides Earth. Well, besides Friday. I guess she blew that theory out of the water. So, disregard. I guess Ack is entitled to have animals, especially good-tasting cows."

He laughed at his own joke.

"You don't necessarily have to be a cow to be an amazing steak," Dracula responded.

"Blasphemy! Have you eaten steak on Earth? Like as in Texas beef?" Micah interjected with insulted beef pride.

"Yes, I have, and yes, it's good. Great, even. But I'm telling you, you have never tasted steak until you have tasted one of these. Trust me, brother," Dracula assured him.

Micah and Dracula sat down at the tall bar which wrapped around the big grill. After the server took their drink orders, one of the most enormous men Micah had ever seen walked up behind them and tapped Dracula on the shoulder.

Micah thought, "Dracula's going to die right here in front of me!"

Dracula turned around to a familiar face.

"Booka! What in the Universe are you doing here, you big ape?"

Dracula stood up and hugged the huge body in front of him.

"Booka, my good friend from Fasi, meet Micah, my new friend from Earth," he said.

Micah stood up and became the smallest he had ever felt.

The Fasian held out his ginormous hand.

In his mafia-sounding accent, he said, "Pleasure to meet you, Micah. What are you doing hanging around this punk?"

Micah replied, "The pleasure is all mine, Booka. I picked him up on the side of the road. I'm a sucker for a charity case."

They all laughed.

Micah added, "So, you're from Fasi, huh? I wonder if you know my daughter. She made quite a splash on Fasi a few years ago."

"Really! What's her name?"

"Chelsey Wick. And her buddy is a Schmecum named Arëk. You can't miss them. They're always together," Micah said with a smile.

"Oh, yes, I know Chelsey and Arëk! Chelsey's a legend on my planet! We'd all still be in big trouble if it weren't for her. And your people would either be slaves or ashes floating around space right now."

Dracula raised his eyebrows and said, "Whoa, details!"

"You know how a few years back, everyone was afraid to go to Fasi because it was so bad?" Booka reminded him.

"Yeah, I remember. But what does it have to do with Micah's daughter?" Dracula asked.

"Remember me telling you about the girl from Earth we almost killed on Fasi, but she led us back to God instead?"

Dracula's eyes widened, and he looked at Micah.

"That was Chelsey? *Your* Chelsey? How in the world?"

"Tell me about it, man! It was insanity to my ears when Chelsey and Arëk told us. Seriously, *unreal*! It was the same night we met Arëk for the first time and learned about other Universal people. We were also informed that Chelsey had been traveling the Universe all her life!" Micah said.

"All that at once, huh?" Dracula commented jokingly.

"And explained in five minutes!" Micah said, laughing.

"Your girl is extra special! She and Arëk have been over to see us several times since then. Chelsey is such a pleasure, and it is quite an honor to meet her father," Booka said.

"Thank you, Booka, I appreciate it," Micah answered, offering his hand for another handshake. "Why don't you join us? I'm about to prove to Dracula that Texas grows a better steak than Ack."

The giant laughed and bumped Dracula on the arm.

"We've heard those words before, haven't we!"

They both laughed as Booka sat on four stools next to Dracula.

Axl says, "Four stools?"

Yeah, dude, I'm telling you, Fasians are freakin' huge!

Micah told Booka that he and Gracie had visited Fasi once with Chelsey and me. Then Micah told him he was the biggest Fasian he had ever seen!

Booka laughed and said, "Hard to tell I was the runt of the litter when I was born, huh!"

"Yeah, I have a hard time believing that, my friend," Micah said.

"It's the truth, I swear it. My littermates were all much larger than me for many years. I surprised them when I had a growth spurt and outgrew them all by a large measure! It was a good vengeance for me after all the taunting for so long."

Finally, the victory-banging of the grill master's knives indicated his masterpiece was ready. The platters were delivered to the guys with huge slabs of juicy, mouthwatering meat hanging off the plates. The steaks were accompanied by seasoned roots and fresh veggies.

Still skeptical of what the non-cow meat was, Micah looked at Dracula and said, "You first!"

Dracula and Booka laughed and grabbed their knives.

The two men cut into their thick, perfectly prepared steaks and took the first bite. Pleasure didn't come close to describing the expressions on their faces. Micah looked at his friends and picked up his knife. He discovered the meat was the most tender he had ever cut into. With the first bite, Micah's taste buds burst with a brand-new, exciting level of deliciousness.

"What is this, Drac?" Micah asked as he stabbed his second bite of steak.

"First, you have to admit, *out loud*, it is better than any Texas steak you have ever tasted," Dracula joked.

"As hard as it is to lay down my Texas pride, I admit it. I have never tasted anything more delicious in all my life, in Texas or anywhere else! So, fess up! What is it?"

"It's dajan. By looking at one, you would never imagine it tasting so good. Believe me, humans have tried for decades to take them to Earth, but they can't transport them. I guess dajans are only meant to live on Ack. And there are plenty of them to last forever, too, thank God."

Micah said, with a mouth full of steak, "I love me some dajan, whatever it is! Gracie would never leave here if she could taste this! Dracula, my friend, you are, without question, a meat connoisseur. This is so good!"

"I knew you'd like it!" Dracula responded before he took another juicy bite.

Axl says he wants to try dajan.

I'll take you to Ack sometime, brah. You'll love it.

After the guys finished their delicious meal, Micah rubbed his full belly.

He said, "I could take a nap right now!"

Dracula and Booka agreed.

"I know the perfect place to kick back and let our food digest," Dracula said.

"Thick blue grass?" Booka asked, assuming he knew where they'd go.

"Thick blue grass," Dracula affirmed.

"Lead the way, tour guides," Micah said, patting his belly.

Dracula and Booka took Micah to a super cool place. The grass they referred to is cool and plush like Earth lawn grass but it's the strangest of blues. It's kind of like royal blue but with a shimmer. Running beside the grass is a brook, which turns into a river, which leads to a waterfall. The sound of the water is super relaxing.

The guys lay on their backs in the grass, looking at the sky.

Micah said, "Remember looking up at the sky as kids and finding shapes and characters in the clouds?"

Booka shook his head no and looked at Micah for an explanation.

Dracula piped in, "We don't have clouds on Fluni or Fasi. Our weather and moisture levels are comparatively odd next to Earth's or Ack's. I admit I enjoy the sky here. You'll have to show us how to find shapes in the clouds, though. It must be an Earth thing."

Booka made a conscious effort to find something familiar in the clouds.

It wasn't long before they dozed off to sleep.

Hey Axl, what do you say we take a break from the story for a surfing lesson? The waves are perfect!

Axl quickly sits up and says, "Heck yeah!"

Awesome, brah, let's surf!

32

A Big Wonderful Surprise

After lunch, Gracie and Mandy spent the rest of the afternoon hanging out with the Vinga of Tumah. Isun took them to some of her favorite places and introduced them to several locals.

Mandy insisted Gracie experience the jeweled river she enjoyed so much on her previous visit to Ci. She hoped to leave with another wonderful piece of jewelry from there. And she did.

The Wuvet River was more magnificent than Mandy remembered. The rich colors of the jewels under the water were a sight Gracie could never have imagined. Isun showed her how easy it was to reach into the water and scoop up a handful of red, blue, green, and many other colored rocks. These stones were worth more than most people could ever afford in their lifetime. There were all colors, sizes, and shapes. And they were all for the taking, courtesy of God, the generous Creator.

Mandy chose a large ruby red stone. It would become the centerpiece of her new favorite necklace. Gracie looked at many stones but favored the sapphire blue ones. They reminded her of her big, beautiful ocean back home in Hawaii.

Isun watched Gracie admire the blue stones as she held them up to the sun.

"Gracie, would you allow me the privilege of making you something special to remember me by?" Isun asked.

"I would be honored! Thank you, Isun."

Gracie sat on the grass next to the water. She watched Isun take a handful of stones to the cottage, where the elderly man met her at the door. He was thrilled to see his Vinga. He hugged her with the affection of a grandfather. Mandy was close behind Isun with the jewels soon to become her new favorite necklace. The gentleman hugged her, too, as if he had always known her. He called her "child." Gracie smiled at how sweetly he treated Mandy and Isun. She was falling in love with Tumah and all it represented.

It didn't take long for Mandy to come back wearing a gorgeous necklace. The braided silver chain the huge jewel hung from was the shiniest metal Gracie had ever seen. This necklace would certainly be the envy of everyone on Fluni.

Mandy sat next to Gracie to show off her new treasure. Neither of them could believe how beautiful it was! And it didn't cost a dime. Only precious time spent with their new friend, the Vinga of Tumah.

A few minutes later, Isun walked out of the cottage and over to the girls. She offered her hand to help Gracie stand so she could present her gift. The moment their eyes met, Gracie's filled with tears. She didn't understand why and didn't try to explain them away.

Isun opened her hand to expose the most spectacular blue stones Gracie had ever seen. They were intricately placed inside a lattice of shiny silver which formed a beautiful choker. Gracie removed the puka shell necklace she wore so Isun could fasten this lovely offering around her neck. Gracie didn't need a mirror to know how beautiful the choker looked on her. She was beyond grateful.

She hugged Isun tightly and said, "This is such a blessing, Isun. Thank you so much."

When the two released their embrace, Gracie told Isun, "I know this doesn't compare to the extravagant gift you just gave me, but I want you to have this."

Gracie opened her hand and stretched out the puka shell choker she'd worn before.

"My daughter, Chelsey, made this for me as a symbol of hope. She believes in the power of prayer and the love of God like no one else I have ever known. I have waited years for the answer to one specific prayer that I will never give up on. I would like for you to have this special token to remember me by."

Tears fell from Isun's big blue eyes as Gracie fastened the shells around her neck.

She said, "I could never forget you. This will forever be my most prized possession. Thank you."

Mandy was crying when she stood up next to the girls. She motioned for hugs all around.

Wiping tears from her face, Isun said, "I would love for you ladies to come to my house if you have time."

Mandy spoke up just as the rose-colored moon began to cover the sun.

"Isun, I hate to say it, but we should probably go. Our husbands will be wondering about us. We're supposed to meet them in Rew at sunset. What do you think, Gracie?"

Gracie replied, "I would never leave this place if I didn't have to, but Mandy's right. We should go check in with the guys. I had the most wonderful day. I hope it can be the first of many."

Gracie was disheartened that God had not revealed why her heart was drawn to Isun. She felt silly letting it bother her so much, but it did. In fact, hot tears welled up in her eyes, and she couldn't stop them.

"My heart would break if you didn't come back," Isun replied with the sweetest smile, holding back tears of her own.

"Don't worry, we will be back," Mandy responded.

"Soon!" Gracie added, wiping away another tear.

The girls all exchanged hugs then Mandy asked, "Are you ready, Gracie?"

Just before they closed their eyes to transport back to Zooch, Gracie abruptly stopped. She wasn't leaving without an answer.

"Isun, wait!" she said. "This might sound crazy, but I know you from before today. I don't know from where or when, but I know I know you."

Heavy tears dropped from Gracie's eyes.

"Please tell me who you are. I must know," she begged.

Mandy quickly comforted her friend.

"Gracie, are you ok?" she asked.

Gracie shook her head no and closed her eyes. Tears streamed down her cheeks.

Isun stepped close and wrapped her arms around her in a hug. Gracie sobbed on the beautiful woman's shoulder.

Isun spoke into Gracie's ear, "You *do* know me, and I know you. I've been waiting for this day for a long, long time."

She pulled away just far enough to look into Gracie's face. She smiled an identical smile to the person opposite her.

"It's me, Mama. Lexi," she said, crying.

Axl says he hoped it was her! Now he's crying, too.

Gracie lost her legs and melted to the ground. Mandy and Lexi each took an arm to ease her to the grass, then held her close to comfort her.

Gracie looked into Lexi's big blue eyes and sobbed.

"Oh, my Jesus! I've been trying to find you for so long. I thought you were lost or dead. I have so many things I've wanted to tell you all this time. Oh, my God, you're beautiful. My daughter! The Vinga of Tumah is my daughter! I *knew* I knew you! My heart knew you!"

Gracie held her daughter tightly.

Mandy cried with her friend. The moment almost seemed like a dream, like it couldn't really be happening.

"This is crazy!" Mandy said through her tears. "I didn't know you had other children besides Chelsey. Apparently, we still have a lot of getting to know each other to do!"

Gracie turned to look at her new friend and said, "I have two sons, too. They're also missing. But now I have a greater hope of finding them."

She looked into the face of her beautiful daughter.

"I can't believe you're really here."

"I can't believe *you're* really here!" Lexi said.

"Not to take away from this incredible moment, but how did a human become the Vinga of Tumah? It would never work like that on Fluni," Mandy said.

"Or on Earth," Gracie interjected, clearly forgetting that President Trump is a native of Pathub.

Lexi laughed and said, "Well, it's kind of a strange story."

Axl sits up to listen closer. I've discovered it drives him crazy when I go back and forth between what the guys are up to and what the girls are doing. Especially now that Isun is in the picture. He gets invested in whichever group I'm talking about, and then I switch back to the other one. What can I say? I'm a wascally wabbit! And...

Back to the guys.

Axl throws up his hands and says, "REALLY?"

33

Football On Ack

After about an hour, Booka woke up, yawned, and stretched his big arms. Dracula was next to wake from his slumber. Micah was still sleeping like a baby.

Dracula said loudly, "I wonder if Micah might be up for some football?"

Micah perked right up.

"What? Did you say something about football, or was I dreaming?"

"I was just wondering if you might want to catch a game," Dracula said.

"Heck yeah! I'm always up for a game!" Micah said, standing to his feet, then stretching. "When and where?"

"In about half an hour, about a mile from here. The Ackens are playing the Eos in a football scrimmage."

"How differently is football played on other planets?" Micah asked.

"You'll see. It's especially entertaining on Ack," Dracula answered.

"Football is the greatest sport no matter what planet it's on!" Booka added.

"One hundred percent! How much are the tickets? I'll buy," Micah said.

"We won't need tickets today. It's a free game for a charity event," Dracula responded. "I saw a flyer about it at the grill earlier."

When they arrived at the stadium, Micah was shocked at the size of the crowd.

"Wooowww!" he said with wide eyes and a huge smile. "This is unbelievable!"

Booka and Dracula led the way, and they all sat down. It was super crowded, and the fans were psyched! Micah didn't know what to expect, but he was excited to see the show.

Micah asked, "So, who are we cheering for, the Ackens or the Eos?"

"Well, by track record, the Ackens are likely to win. They are in a much stronger, more experienced league. But the Eos never give up trying to beat them. I guess they see it as good practice. They are such good sports, too. I like them, but they're just not as skilled," Dracula answered.

"In that case, I think I'll put my dollar on the Eos. You never know. They just might win! There's a first time for everything, right?" Micah said.

Booka smiled and said, "I've got friends on the Acken team. I'm sticking with my boys."

"I'd be happy to take your dollar, Micah! Go, Ackens!" Dracula shouted with confidence.

"Well, then, game on!" Micah said, and high fived each of them.

Axl says he always cheers for the underdog. Me, too, dude!

The stadium filled up to standing room only. The excitement was atomic! The crowd cheered as the Ackens and Eos entered the field, waving to their fans.

It was immediately evident why the Ackens had an overwhelming advantage over the Eos. They had four more legs a piece! It didn't seem fair to Micah, but Dracula assured him it was the Eos's choice to take on the challenge. It would seem like they were gluttons for punishment. But they truly believed they would beat their advantageous opponent one day. It would be the victory of victories. You've got to give them credit for their grit, brah.

When the game began, Micah was quickly reminded that anything not nailed down on Ack floated away. That was what Dracula hinted about when he said football on Ack was especially entertaining.

It was crazy watching the players jump high into the air to catch a ball, floating further and further into the atmosphere. Talk about a challenging sport, dude! No gravity football!

You can imagine what fun the guys had watching these talented athletes keep track of the ball. The three of them laughed and cheered from start to finish. They even caught t-shirts thrown by bench players as game souvenirs.

After the game ended, Micah thanked Dracula and Booka for showing him such a great time.

Dracula replied, "Oh, it's not over yet, buddy. I have a little surprise for you."

After the adventures Dracula had delivered so far, Micah was excited to see what was next.

Dracula said, "This way, bro!"

They led Micah out of the seating section down a long corridor past the concessions. The three men approached an oversized door with a sign stating, Home of the Ack Champions. Booka entered a code on the keypad next to the locker room door and swung it open.

All the Acken players were changing out of their uniforms and into their clothes. Ackens don't need showers after playing hard because they don't sweat. Weird, I know. Booka was buddies with one of the running backs and several of the other players, so he had an anytime free pass into the locker room to hang out.

Axl says, "Cool!"

With his loud, mafia-sounding accent, Booka got everyone's attention. "Yo, guys, ears open! I'd like to introduce you to a new friend of mine. This is Micah. He's visiting from Earth. He's a big football fan!"

"Booka!" the players shouted all over the room.

Micah was impressed at how laid back and cool the Acken team was. They all made their way over to welcome him to Ack.

"Who's your team on Earth?" one of the players asked him.

"The Kansas City Chiefs!" Micah answered with enthusiasm.

Axl agrees wholeheartedly.

"Patrick Mahomes is legit, bro!" the Acken quarterback said. "He and a few other Earth players come to play with us occasionally. They like the challenge."

"Mahomes has been to Ack? No way!" Micah exclaimed.

"Gravity or no gravity, the dude is a legend! Did you ever wear a uniform, Micah?" the quarterback asked.

"A long time ago, dude."

"You should buy a pair of cleats and come play with us in next month's scrimmage. There will be players from all over the Universe," a wide receiver added.

"It sounds like serious fun! You should do it, Micah!" Dracula interjected.

"I haven't thrown a ball in years," Micah said.

"Come to a practice session. We'll get you warmed up again. What is it humans say, it's like riding a bike?" the wide receiver asked.

"Or getting back on a horse, in Micah's case," Booka interjected. "Our boy is from Texas."

"I dated a gorgeous cowgirl from the Texas Panhandle a few years ago. She liked to rope me like a steer when I ran from her," a running back said, and everyone laughed. "Texas girls are the prettiest girls on Earth!"

"Let's go to Texas, boys!" the quarterback shouted.

The team all shouted and yee-hawed.

Axl says they make them pretty in Hawaii, too.

You're not wrong, brah!

So, back to the locker room.

Micah said, "So, regarding your football invitation. If Drac agrees to play, too, I'll do it. I don't want to be the only idiot on the field."

The players laughed.

Axl laughs, too.

"I'm in, buddy! Let's do this!" Dracula said and fist bumped his friend.

"Alright then! We're out here every day!" said the quarterback.

"We'll see about getting Patrick Mahomes to join us on scrimmage weekend! Maybe he can bring a few of his buddies, too," one player said. "We'll all hang out!"

"Oh, dude! That would rock!" Micah said.

"You about ready to go, bro?" Dracula asked.

Micah told the team, "Awesome meeting you guys!"

"See you at practice then?" the quarterback asked as he and Micah fist bumped.

"We'll be here!" he answered.

"Then you can tell us the story behind the fishhook in your ear!" a player in the back of the room shouted.

The players all laughed.

"Yeah, for sure, dude! I forgot it was there!" Micah said.

He touched his ear and laughed.

"See you soon, bros!" the quarterback said as Dracula, Booka, and Micah walked out the door.

Micah smiled in silence as they walked down the long hallway. Dracula was, without question, his new best bro!

Axl laughs and agrees. I can tell he's excited to hear what the guys do next. He's totally into the Ack experience.

So, remember how Lexi was about to tell Gracie her crazy story?

Axl's smile turns into a serious, frustrated face. I think he wants to punch me. HA!

34

Lexi's Intro To Tumah

Lexi began, "After the plane crashed into the ocean, someone pulled me out of the wreckage. A moment later I was here on Tumah. Of course, at eight years old, I was confused and disoriented. But I wasn't afraid. I thought I was dreaming.

"I remember looking all around me as I stood in the center of a beautiful garden with my rescuer. There was a waterfall that appeared to be five thousand miles high. It shimmered with colors. I felt so at home in this strange place. It was as if I had always been here. It was such a weird but warm feeling.

"There were people all around, but none of them looked human, including my rescuer. She didn't stick around long. She hugged me and said she'd see me later. Then she skipped away. A moment later, a beautiful woman of their species approached me. She asked if I would like to take a walk with her. Apparently, I didn't learn from my 'stranger danger' lessons. I immediately took her hand and trusted her not to take me to a basement deep in the woods."

All four women smiled.

Axl smiles, too.

"The woman and I walked to a nearby bench and sat down. She introduced herself as Vanise. She told me she had been anxiously awaiting my arrival. I wondered how she knew I was coming when I didn't even know I was coming. I said, 'My name is Lexi. Do you know where my mommy is?' I remember her smiling and then telling me she would explain where you were after she told me a story. I sat there with open ears. Vanise told me in the most comforting way possible about the plane crash, then assured me I would see my mom again. She also told me that Pime, the person who pulled me out of the plane, was her daughter. She said Pime was very excited to finally meet me after Jesus told her about me just after she was born. I thought, 'What baby talks to Jesus right after they're born? Good one, crazy lady.'"

Mandy laughed. Gracie raised her eyebrows thinking about Chelsey having the same conversation with Jesus concerning me.

"Then, Vanise told me the most important part. She said God had a very special plan for me, which was the reason I was brought to Tumah. Of course, it required an explanation of the Universe, planets, and people who don't look like humans.

"Next, Vanise told me she had some important things to teach me. She said I wouldn't understand it all right away, but she would help me over time. I trusted her as if I had trusted her all my life. Somehow, I knew everything would be ok, and I was where I was supposed to be. It was like God poured supernatural comfort and wisdom into me that day.

"Vanise took my hand as we sat on the bench. She told me she had a story to tell me that might make me happy and sad at the same time. As a preventative measure, she asked, 'What do you say we talk to Jesus first?' I nodded my head yes and closed my eyes. Vanise softly spoke a short prayer, asking God to guard my heart as she told the story. She asked Him to help me to accept His plan for me there. She also asked Him to help her to be the best guardian she could be to me, then she thanked Him for choosing her.

"When we opened our eyes, Vanise smiled at me with the love of a mother. What this beautiful lady would tell me next would indeed make me happy and sad at the same time. Heart happy and homesick sad."

Gracie's eyes began to fill with tears.

"Vanise said, 'About three years ago, I was planting flowers in the garden behind my house when I heard God speak to me. Most often, I hear His voice through nature. But this time, it was more than that. I heard Him tell me to go to the beautiful Hawaiian island of Oahu on Earth.'

"That's where I live! In Haleiwa! I said with excitement as I tugged on her hand.

"Vanise smiled, then with jovial eyes responded, 'Yes, I know!'

"She realized it was going to be harder to tell the story than she had anticipated.

"Vanice continued, 'When God told me to go there, I was a little puzzled. Pime and I vacationed on the island once before, but I didn't have a connection there. God said I would know the reason later. So, I went inside, packed my bag, and took Pime to stay with the neighbor. When I arrived on Oahu, I remembered why everyone loves Hawaii so much. It was so beautiful and fragrant.'

"I could tell Vanise was having a wonderful memory of Hawaii. As she described it, I could smell the ocean. I missed home and you, Mom, so much."

Tears dropped down Gracie's face.

"Vanise continued, 'I went to the house of a lady named Meleah. Pime and I stayed in her condo when we vacationed there before. She didn't seem surprised at all to see me. Meleah met me on the sidewalk with a big hug. She told me it was good to see me again and asked about Pime. She invited me inside, where I quickly filled her in on our lives. Afterwards, she reached into her pocket for a key ring with the keys to her condo and a car. The expression on my face must have been one of surprise. She laughed under her breath.

'Meleah told me she wasn't a religious person, but anyone would know the voice of God if they heard it. She said she clearly heard Him say I was coming. He asked her to prepare her condo and a car so I could drive to the beach.

'I told her it is just like God to do something like that. Meleah asked me to stop by before I left so I could tell her a little more about Him. She admitted she wasn't very receptive when I tried to introduce her to Him before. I told her I would love to tell her more about the love of God. She hugged me again, then shewed me off.

'I drove to the condo, which faced the water. It held so many wonderful memories for me and Pime. I got settled in and then asked God what He wanted me to do next. He told me to enjoy myself. He would reveal to me what He needed me to do at the right time.

'So, I drove to the beach with a towel and a book. I found a great spot, laid out my towel, and sat down. I read for a while, then decided to get into the water. It felt so warm and soothing.'

"I was right there inside her memory. I vividly remembered how the water felt and how much I loved to be in it. I had been in the water only hours before we left for our two-week stay in Texas. It was unnatural for me to be *out* of it! I thought about our family splashing each other, laughing, and having such a good time.

"I started to cry. I told Vanise I wanted to go home. She hugged me closely, with tears in her eyes. She knew I was homesick, and my family missed me, too. She assured me I would see you again as she wiped tears off my face. Once I'd settled down a bit, she picked up where she left off.

"Vanise said, 'After a little while at the beach, I drove back to the condo. I ate a bite while I talked to the Lord, then went to bed. The next morning, I woke up feeling very rested. With a grapefruit and a towel, I headed back down to the beach.

'The waves were beautiful and so powerful. In the water directly in front of me was a young family on surfboards. They all seemed to be having such a good time in the sun. After I watched them for a bit, I decided to take a stroll down the beach to see what else was going on.

'A few minutes later, the sound of laughing kids caught my attention from behind. The family I saw surfing a few minutes before had come in to dry off for a short time. The father played a game of chase with the two little boys. There was so much laughter it made me giggle.

'The little girl helped her mother lay a blanket out on the sand. She opened a cooler containing all the makings for a good family picnic. It looked like there was even something for their dogs. I was so entertained by this family's loving and comical interaction with each other. I decided to take a seat on the sand and observe.

'After the mom called everyone to eat, the girls passed out sandwiches. While the dad prayed over their meal, one of the dogs sneaked a slice of ham off Dad's plate. I couldn't help but laugh. After everyone was finished eating, the mom cleaned up the mess. The little girl took off after the dogs. And the dad and boys took a Frisbee down the beach a little way. What a happy family, I thought.'

"As Vanise described her memory, I pictured it in my eight-year-old mind. Then I realized it was also *my* memory! I told her my family had a picnic on the beach just like that. She smiled that motherly smile again.

"Vanise continued, 'It didn't take long after cleaning up the picnic mess that the mother realized the daughter was out of sight. I watched her hold her hand up to her forehead to shade her eyes from the sun. She looked right, then left, then turned in a complete circle. She seemed calm at first. She called out to her husband, asking if he knew where their daughter was. He clearly didn't because he did the same thing she had done. He shaded his eyes with his hand, looked all around, and shook his head no.'

Gracie is wiping tear after tear away at this point.

Axl says, "Oh, no!"

"Vanise continued, 'Then, one of the dogs started barking toward the water. He jumped in and started paddling as fast as his paws could go. Immediately, the mother screamed, 'NO!' She ran to the water, closely followed by her husband. I jumped to my feet, seeing what the parents and the dog had just discovered.

'A long distance out in the water was the same tiny little body I had seen earlier surfing like a pro. Now, it was floating on the waves. I ran to the shoreline, praying my heart out. It seemed to take forever for the parents to swim out to her. In fact, the dog made it to her first and started pulling her body toward the shore. The parents finally reached the little girl and the dog. Together, they swam with her as quickly as they could.'

Gracie was bawling!

Axl is wiping tears away, too.

"Vanise said, 'I met them about a hundred feet out in the water. I took her from the exhausted parents. They didn't argue about it. Clearly, they knew I was there to help. I laid the little body on the sand and listened for a heartbeat. There wasn't one. I saw the two brothers standing about ten feet away, both scared and crying. I wanted so badly to tell them everything was ok. I started performing CPR. Nothing seemed to help. The dad took over the CPR, but to no avail. The mother ran to a local business to call for help. Then, I suddenly felt a peace, which could only have been God. I asked the dad to let me pick her up. He was so distraught and exhausted that he nodded his head yes.'

Gracie is beside herself!

Axl says he can't imagine what she's feeling!

"Vanise continued, 'I knew at that moment this was the reason I was on Oahu. I held the tiny, lifeless body close to mine and began to pray out loud. 'God in Heaven, please breathe life back into this precious body in the mighty name of Jesus! Breathe life, Lord, please! In the name of Jesus, let this body live!' And I heard a whisper, 'Breathe into her!' I laid her back onto the sand. I took a deep breath and then breathed into her mouth. A second later, the little girl gasped for air. Her dad grabbed her and held her close. Her brothers joined their dad in a group hug. Tears of relief and joy were on every face.

Axl wipes away tears of relief.

'I started sobbing so hard I couldn't get myself together. Then, someone grabbed me and pulled me close to them. It was the little girl's mother.'

Gracie cupped her face, weeping tears of remembrance.

'She prayed over me until I gained my composure. When I opened my eyes, she thanked me with the most grateful heart. She said they might have lost their daughter without my help. I told her it was all God, not me.

'The sound of sirens was nearing. I wanted to see the little girl before they took her to the hospital. She was warm in her daddy's arms. He was thanking God over and over in between singing to her. I knelt in front of them and said, 'Hi, precious one. You must be one of God's favorite kids!' She smiled at me as her daddy rocked her.

'The mother said, 'This is the nice lady who helped you. Can you tell her thank you?'

'Thank you,' she said, reaching out her arms.

'I took the sweet little girl in my arms and whispered in her ear. 'You are quite welcome. What is your name, little surfer girl?'

"I couldn't believe what I was hearing as Vanise told the story. Before she could tell me what the little girl said in response, I said, 'I remember! It was *me*! But it wasn't you, Vanise. It was a lady, like my mommy. You don't look like the ladies in Haleiwa. It couldn't have been you.' I was confused and wanted my mom more than ever."

Gracie squeezed her daughter's hand.

"Vanise calmly said, 'Let me show you something.'

"She stepped back from me and closed her eyes. Seconds later, her appearance changed to the human woman I remembered from the beach three years before. It confused and scared me.

"Vanise said, 'Don't be afraid. This is how I look when I'm on your planet, Earth. That's how God made it possible for people here to visit people where you live. If I went to Hawaii looking like I do here, I wouldn't be very welcome, would I?'

"I shook my head no, then asked her, 'The lady on the beach, was really you? Does my mommy and daddy know? Do they know where I am?'"

Gracie's eyes filled with fresh tears.

Axl and I are right there with her.

"With a concerned look on her face, Vanise answered, 'Your parents don't know yet that you are here. But you can be sure God will take good care of your mom, dad, and brothers. And He will take good care of you. You will be with your family again, Lexi, I promise. I know it is all very confusing. You will understand one day. Please trust me, little one.'

"With crying eyes, I nodded my head in reluctant agreement. I didn't really have a choice, so it made no sense to argue. I told Vanise, 'Thank you for saving me that day at the beach. I didn't forget you.'

"Her eyes filled with tears, and she said, 'I never forgot you either, little surfer girl.'"

Gracie was *done*, brah!

Axl says he doesn't know how much more he can take.

Hang tight, dude. It gets better.

35

Becoming The Vinga

Lexi continued, "After the heart-wrenching storytelling, Vanise took me to her home. She already had a bed set up for me in Pime's room. It was different from my *Finding Nemo* room at home, but it was quite welcoming. Pime had been on pins and needles waiting for me to arrive at the house. She grabbed me and hugged me as soon as we walked in. As different as she and I were on the outside, we were a matched pair otherwise.

"Vanise bought a closet full of clothes and shoes for me. Of course, I preferred bare feet, but I would adjust. Vanise and Pime took me on a tour of their house, yards, and gardens. Afterwards, Vanise cooked a delicious meal for us. I was so emotionally exhausted from the events of the day that I crashed shortly after we ate.

"The next few days were a lot of fun. Pime showed me her favorite places, including a huge castle. It was the most amazing thing I had ever seen. Tumah isn't like Earth, where parents have to monitor their kids' whereabouts all the time. It's a very relaxed planet where everyone looks out for everyone else. That permitted bookoos of all-day adventures for me and Pime. We left footprints all over the place from sunup to sundown.

"I quickly grew very close to Vanise and Pime. Pime was my best friend and sister from another world. Vanise was my teacher, my mentor, and my comforter when I was missing my mama. But there was always something else about Vanise. She treated me like royalty from day one. Not the special guest kind of treatment. But literally, like royalty.

"I didn't really notice her behavior at first. But after a couple of years, I began to catch on to some things. For instance, only months after my arrival, Vanise started calling me Vinga. Pime told me it meant 'Queen.' I thought it was just a nickname or a term of endearment, but she was actually calling me Vinga. She would remind Pime to speak to me with respect. She also told Pime to act quickly when I asked anything of her.

"I knew Vanise was on a deadline to teach me tons of important stuff, but it was more than lessons. Vanise was preparing me for something big.

"On my thirteenth birthday, Vanise and Pime took me to the castle I had admired since I arrived on Tumah five years before. The giant doors opened as we approached them. We walked through the enormous entrance, where I was welcomed by a whole staff of castle keepers. They were all lined up to greet me. Much to my surprise, they each gracefully and respectfully bowed and said, 'Welcome, Vinga' as I walked past them. Once I reached the end of the welcoming committee, there was another group. Leaders from other planets had come lightyears to meet me and to bring lavish gifts.

"I thought Vanise had planned it all for my birthday. I was hugely mistaken.

"On my thirteenth birthday, I was inducted as the Vinga of Tumah, appointed by God. No pressure, right?"

Gracie and Mandy laughed.

"'This is your new home,' Vanise said as she and Pime each bowed in reverence. 'By the instruction of our Lord, you are now called Isun, 'Chosen Daughter.'"

"I've got to tell you, it was the craziest but most humbling experience. I suddenly realized this was God's purpose for my life. I determined in my heart to make God proud of me. I also knew it would make you and Daddy proud, too, when I ever got to see you again.

"I've always missed you and Daddy more than I could ever express. I can't tell you how many times I begged God to let me go back to Earth to see you. But He always said, 'It's not time, precious one, be patient. You will be reunited with your family at the right time.'

"God removed my ability to transport shortly after I arrived on Tumah. I decided I was going back to Earth after He said no. Vanise tried to explain, as I cried in her arms, that God had a reason for me to be here and only here until His appointed time for me to travel. This time of learning and growing in His Word and His ways would make me an honorable leader for this planet. He chose *me*, which is more of an honor than I could ever explain."

Gracie said, "I'm so proud of you, Lexi."

Mandy said, "So, what about Pime? How has becoming Vinga affected your friendship with her? Are you still besties? Or is it Vinga versus subject?"

Lexi laughed and responded, "Oh, no, it's not like that here. I'm not some domineering leader who feeds the dragon when someone gets out of line. Everyone on Tumah respects me as their leader, but I am also their friend. Pime will always be my bestie, no matter what. We hang out all the time and do pretty much everything together. In fact, she stays at the castle from time to time."

Gracie said, "I can't believe I'm finally sitting in front of you, listening to you talk, and watching you smile. I have believed for this moment for so many years."

Lexi looked at her mother and replied, "This is the most wonderful day of my life. God has answered my prayers! The only difference is that you came here instead of me going back to Earth! I wish you didn't have to go back.

"I have so many questions! I want to know all about you and your life. How's Daddy? And Austin and Tripp? I bet Austin went on to play for the NBA! He was never without his basketball. I remember he slept with it, took it everywhere, and even took his baths with it!"

Lexi laughed at the memories she had of her brother.

"And Tripp? she added. "What's he doing these days? Remember the time I colored his butt with a black marker after he got out of the bathtub? I got in so much trouble!"

She couldn't help but smile at the memory. Mandy giggled at the thought.

Gracie attempted to smile with her but couldn't.

Lexi asked, "What is it, Mom? Did something happen to one of them?"

Gracie answered, "Honey, your brothers' bodies, along with yours, were never recovered after the plane crash."

"What?" Lexi exclaimed. "What do you mean?"

"We searched for months and months until no one would help us anymore. Too much time had gone by. The ocean was too big for us to look by ourselves. The search teams told us there was no way you kids were still out there. They said we needed to accept that you were gone. God helped us to continue living but it was very difficult.

Your little sister, Chelsey, was born only a couple of months after the crash. The doctors were very concerned she wouldn't make it full term because of my stress level. She fought, thank God. She's amazing. Chelsey has kept us strong all these years. She refused to let us lose faith concerning you and the boys.

"I can't wait to tell her where you are! You girls will have so much fun getting to know each other. Chelsey is no stranger to people of other worlds, either. We just found out recently she has been Universe traveling since she was five years old. Arëk is her BFF from Schmec. They're quite a pair! Like you and Pime!"

Then, an imaginary lightbulb lit up over Gracie's head!

She said, "Oh, my gosh, I'm an *idiot*!"

"Why?" Mandy asked.

"Chelsey has traveled the Universe since she was a little girl. Lexi was saved by someone from another planet! She's lived on another planet since she was a little girl. It makes perfect sense! Austin's and Tripp's bodies weren't recovered either because there weren't any bodies to find! My sons could be out here in space somewhere! They must be! This explains everything!"

Mandy and Lexi looked at each other. They shrugged their shoulders as if to say, "Why not?"

"They'll turn up, Mom, don't worry. God always has a plan that works out perfectly. Now tell me about Chelsey! I want to know all about her. Does she look like you or Daddy? Where is she? What did you say her BFF's name is?"

Gracie spoke my name, setting a whole tornado of thoughts into motion.

"Arëk," she answered. "Hmmm..."

She tapped her fingertips on her lips like she was on the brink of genius.

36

Lightbulb!

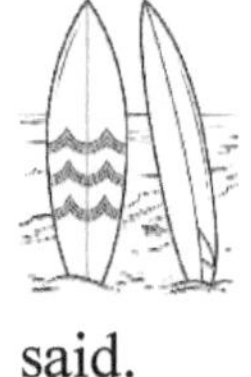

"Lexi, do you remember a kid named Kix that Austin was friends with? He was at our house all the time," Gracie said.

"Yes, of course, I remember him. He practically lived with us! He liked to eat the dog treats, remember?" Lexi said.

The three girls laughed.

Axl laughs, too. He says he tried a Pup-Peroni once because it smelled like a Slim Jim.

Dude, Pup-Peroni's are legit!

Axl and I laugh at ourselves.

Gracie said, "Your dad and I used to discuss Kix after he would go home. He was such an odd little guy. He and Austin were best buds for two years before you kids disappeared in the plane crash. We never saw Kix again after that. Strange, don't you think?"

"What are you getting at, Mom? Why are you thinking about that kid?"

"I think Kix was Austin's 'Arëk.' It makes so much sense now. I wonder if Kix rescued Austin from the crash like Pime rescued you? Maybe that's why he was in Austin's life. Are you sure you'd never seen or met Pime before the crash, Lex?" Gracie asked.

"I'm positive! But you've kind of got me curious about Kix. Since so many people visit Earth from other planets and galaxies, it wouldn't be the strangest idea. Did Kix ever say where he was from?"

"I want to say he told us he was from Kahala. But that would make him Hawaiian, not otherworldly," Gracie said, kind of disappointed.

"Unless he said Nahala," Lexi said, "which could mean he is from a large planet about five galaxies and an oversized wormhole away from Tumah."

Gracie's eyes lit up.

"What do you know about the people of Nahala?"

"You mean besides that, they like dog treats?" Mandy interjected.

They all laughed.

"The two people I've met from there are super friendly, but I really don't know anything else. Since wormholes are so iffy, not many people I know have attempted to travel through them. I wouldn't even consider it if it's what you're thinking, Mom."

Gracie felt deflated. She wanted so desperately to have her family back together she was grasping at straws.

"Don't worry, Mom, God brought you to me, right? He will take you to Austin and Tripp, too. The most important lesson I've learned in my whole life is to have faith in God's plan. It's impossible for Him to fail," Lexi said, taking her mother's hand in hers.

"You're right. Thank you for encouraging me, my wise and beautiful daughter," Gracie said, smiling.

Lexi wrapped her arms around her mother from behind and pulled her close.

"Do you remember the song you used to sing to me if ever I was sad or having a bad day?" Lexi asked.

Gracie smiled and started to softly sing, "Don't worry about a thing 'cause every little thing is gonna be alright."

"Great song!" Mandy said. "Never gets old."

"Good old Bob," Gracie said with a warm heart.

"Rumor has it, Bob used to spend a lot of time on Cozy," Lexi said. "He was quite a pleasure to hear the Coziens tell it."

"I bet he was," Gracie added.

The girls laid back on the grass and stared at the moonlit sky.

"I wonder what Chelsey's doing right now," Gracie said. "I bet she and Arëk are surfing their butts off. Those two can't go a whole twenty-four hours without 'feeling the waves' as they say."

Mandy laughed, "Yeah, they seem like quite a pair."

"Lexi, you and Chelsey will have so much fun together. You are tons alike! Do you want to see some pictures of her? I only have like a thousand of them on my phone," Gracie said, quickly sitting up.

Mandy added, "It's true! And she can't show them enough! Chelsey is one beautiful and special girl! And Arëk is a character!"

Mandy shook her head, laughing at the thought of something cute I did, I'm sure.

Axl rolls his eyes and shakes his head.

"I can't wait to meet her! And him!" Lexi said enthusiastically.

Gracie swiped passed picture after picture of Chelsey and me. Lexi enjoyed looking at her little sister and envisioning their first introduction and how wonderful it would be.

37

Change Of Plans

After only four hours of searching planets, asking hundreds of people a thousand questions, and begging God for ideas as to how to find Austin and Lexi, my best friend had a change of heart.

"Arëk?" Chelsey started.

"Chelsey?" I answered.

"Let's go home. I want to go to the North Shore and sit by the water," she said.

"You feeling ok, buddy?"

"Yeah, I'm good. Let's go home," she said with discouragement in her voice.

"Alright," I conceded.

When we arrived on Oahu, we found our favorite spot on the beach, close to the water. I sat quietly, waiting for Chelsey to explain what was going on.

"You know what would be totally awesome, bestie?" Chelsey asked.

"What?"

"If the Universe had Google," she answered.

"What?"

"If the Universe had Google, we could do tons more educated research. It would make it so much easier to narrow down which planets my brother and sister might live on. I wish I knew something about them."

"What happened to you today, dude? You started off pumped and determined. Now, you sound like your drive is gone. What's up?"

"I don't know, Arëk. This all just seems kind of pointless, doesn't it? We search and keep coming up empty-handed. I want to find them so badly, but it feels like we're just setting ourselves up to fail repeatedly."

"How can you say that? We already found Tripp! One down, two to go, remember?" I encouraged.

Chelsey looked sadly down at the sand.

"You're right. Maybe I'm trying too hard. I just want my family back together so bad, Arëk," she said as her chin quivered.

"I know you do. I do, too. I say we relax and pray about it. God took us to Tripp, didn't He? The Universe is way too big for us to *accidentally* meet someone who had seen your brother. *God* did that. We need to let go of the controls and allow God to lead us again," I said from my heart.

Axl nods in agreement.

"You're right, Arëk. I let my determination get ahead of God's plan. We'll never find them that way. Thanks, buddy, you're so good at talking me off the ledge."

"It's what besties do. You know what else besties do?" I asked, smiling.

"If you tickle me right now, I'll knock your block off!" she responded with a look warning she would literally *kill* me.

"No, crusty butt, I was going to suggest getting a *smoothie*! Besties get *smoothies*! You better ditch your sucky attitude before I feed you to the volcano or something else big and scary! EWW!" I said with a scrunched-up face.

Axl laughs.

She gave me an apologetic smile and took my hands to be helped up.

"A smoothie sounds good, actually. I'll buy," she said in place of an apology.

"Dang right, you will, you grouchy old shark!" I accepted.

She giggled.

Axl laughs.

We walked down the beach to our little smoothie shack.

"So, buddy, since we're going to chill on the sibling search for now, what would you say to hanging out around the beach the rest of the day?" Chelsey asked.

"I like it!" I said, giving my bestie a fist bump.

38

Time To Return To Zooch

One of the most remarkable sights to see on Ack is when the sun transforms into the moon. Light of day to dark of night with a side of oohs and aahs from tourists. It's the only planet I've ever seen with that phenomenon. It's like God hits the dim switch on the wall, and day becomes night.

Axl gives me a "no way" look. Yes, way, brah!

Dracula made sure he and the guys were outdoors for the event. He knew it would be entertaining to see Micah's reaction. The three men strolled near a park where tons of people were enjoying the day. Dracula looked at his watch and then at Booka, who quickly figured out what Dracula was up to.

Dracula said, "Hey, Micah, you want to see something cool?"

"I always want to see something cool," Micah answered.

"Watch this! In three, two, one!" Dracula counted down.

Right on time, the sun began to dim into the moon. The day became night right before their eyes. And speaking of eyes, Micah's grew as huge as vinyl records!

Axl chuckles.

"What in the world?" Micah asked.

He looked in every direction, trying to decide if he was really seeing what he thought he was seeing or if he was losing his marbles.

Dracula and Booka laughed.

"Pretty cool, huh?" Booka asked the bewildered Micah.

Micah looked at each of them, neither of which seemed shocked at the weird happening. They stood there with their hands in their pockets, smiling.

"So, y'all just going to leave me hanging?" Micah asked.

"It's nighttime!" Dracula answered matter of factly.

"But it was *daytime,* like seventeen seconds ago!" Micah said emphatically.

"Welcome to the Universe, buddy! Lots to see out here," Dracula said.

Once Micah decided he wasn't crazy and this was just one more weird thing about his day, he relaxed and enjoyed it.

"I can't wait for Gracie to see this! Has Mandy seen it?" Micah asked.

Dracula laughed.

"Dude, she thought the planet was under attack!"

All three laughed.

Axl laughs, too.

"I thought the same thing!" Micah said laughing at himself.

"Well, bro, have you had all the fun you can stand on this awesome planet?" Dracula asked Micah.

"This day was epic, dude!"

"Booka, my friend, we've got to get back to Zooch to meet the ladies. You're welcome to join us," Dracula said, patting Booka on the back.

"I appreciate it, but I'm meeting a few of my littermates tonight for our monthly tahves game. Ack has the best field to play on. And if we clean up before we leave, they're cool with us playing here," Booka answered.

"What's tahves?" Micah asked.

"Dude, you don't want to know, trust me! It's like Earth's rugby combined with UFC. But it's substantially rougher and with fewer rules. It's played by giants whose goal is to see how much blood they can draw from their opponent. It's super gruesome," Dracula said with a scrunched-up face.

Booka laughed, "It's not that bad, Micah."

"It's worse!" Dracula shouted.

Micah and Booka laughed.

"Dude, seriously! The one time I accepted Booka's invitation to watch him and his brothers play tahves, I got sprayed with blood when they ran past the stands! Thinking back on it, *splashed* might describe it more accurately. That's when I decided tahves was a little too much for this Flunian."

Axl says, "OMG! That's crazy!"

"Yeah, I think I'm ready to *never* see that!" Micah said, giving Booka a hard time.

Booka laughed and patted Micah on the shoulder.

"Alright, man, we're going to head back to Zooch," Dracula said to Booka.

"Great meeting you, Micah," Booka said with a fist bump.

"We'll hang out again sometime," Micah answered.

"You guys take care!" Booka said and turned in the other direction.

"Let's get back to our girls, buddy," Micah said to Dracula.

The wives had not yet arrived at the Mima Café in Rew.

"Would you care to try a famous Zooch yubl while we wait?" Dracula asked.

"Say again, chief?"

"A yubl! Do you remember Orange Julius? The old school frothy drink from the 80s?" Dracula asked.

"Yeah, in every mall!"

"Well, it's kind of like an Orange Julius, only better. It'll surprise you," Dracula said.

"Yeah, I'll try one. Where does one go to get a famous Zooch yubl?"

"You can actually get them right here at the Mima Café," Dracula answered.

"Awesome! Let's yubl!"

Moments after the server took their order, a familiar face walked up to the table.

"Hey, Chelsey's dad! What's happenin'?" Fot asked.

"Howdy, Fot! What are you doing in Rew? I thought you lived in Brint," Micah said shaking Fot's hand.

"I live in Brint, but I hang in Rew most of the time. My brother lives here. It's a sweet setup. So, I've got to ask," he continued in his extra dramatic surfer voice, "did the Fot-ster hear you ordering the totally mouth-watering famous Zooch yubl?"

"Yes, you did," Micah replied, "My friend, Dracula, says it's a must-try!"

"Oh, for sure, dude! I mean, Mr. Wick," Fot corrected himself. "I was the lucky one to introduce the yubl to your daughter, Chelsey. She loved it so much she drank like three of them, one after another!"

Once Chelsey's name was spoken, Fot became a blabbering idiot.

Axl laughs.

"Sweet Chelsey," Fot said with a heavy sigh. "I love her so much! If I could get one chance, I would totally steal her away from Arëk! I would marry her, and we would have like ten little wave riders! It would be a dream come true!"

Axl mouths a big wooow!

Dude, you don't even know half of his stupid crush.

"Alrighty then!" Micah responded as Fot realized what he'd just said, out loud, and to whom.

"Where is that beautiful goddess today? Is she hanging out in Rew with you guys?" Fot asked hopefully.

Micah and Dracula could almost see the bubble hearts bursting over both of Fot's bald heads.

"Umm, no, not this time. But it was great seeing you again, Fot. We'll tell Chelsey you asked about her, ok?" Micah said, hinting to Fot to move along.

"Oh, ok and will you tell her I wrote a poem for her?" he asked as he began to slowly walk backwards.

"Oh, you *bet* I will! I can't wait to tell her!" Micah said facetiously as Fot waved goodbye.

"Wooow!" Dracula said after Fot was out of sight.

"I'm telling you, bro! He's not the only one, either. He's the oddest one, by far, but Chelsey has quite a fan club across the Universe! There will be a lot of crying boys, both human and alien, the day she decides to get married."

Dracula laughed.

Axl says he's even more excited to meet her now. Don't step on my toes, brah!

"Here you go," the server said as she delivered two tall glasses full of frothy, slushy blue liquid. "And here are your straws, enjoy!"

She laid two colorful crazy straws in the center of the table and walked away.

"These goofy crazy straws remind me of Chelsey and Arëk," Micah said. "I hadn't seen one since I was a kid until she and Arëk brought me a Frappuccino with one sticking out of it. Now, you can find one in almost every drawer in our kitchen."

Dracula chuckled as he watched the yubl rush through the twists and turns of his straw.

"Now you've got me wondering if it was Chelsey who introduced these crazy straws to the Mima Café. They didn't always have them but now every yubl is served with one. I must admit, yubls are much more enjoyable with a crazy straw," Dracula said.

Micah chuckled and agreed.

"This is delicious!" Micah said.

Dracula agreed with a nod as he stirred the froth with his straw.

"We'll have to get the girls one when they get back from wherever they're at," Micah said looking at his watch. "Where do you think they are, anyway?"

"There's no telling! But I'll bet they're having fun burning up their credit cards!" Dracula replied and they both laughed. "No, I'm joking, Mandy is not a big spender. I mean, don't get me wrong, the woman likes expensive things, but she's frugal."

"You know, I've got to brag on Gracie, too, as far as frivolous shopping goes. She's not a heavy spender," Micah said smiling. "She loves simple things. A lot of women are all about expensive jewelry and clothes and stuff but not Gracie. Do you know what her favorite, most prized pieces of jewelry are? You probably saw them on her. She never takes them off."

"What are they?" Dracula asked.

"First, a little history. So, one morning Gracie and I got up early, made our lattes, and decided to go down to the beach to watch the sun come up. It was a perfect July morning. We walked next to the water picking up tiny seashells. We had a wonderful conversation about how much we love our life and how blessed we are.

"When we got back to the house, Gracie got in the shower while I put our shells in a small bowl to wash them off. Gracie is always doing thoughtful little things for me, so I decided to do something for her.

"I went to her craft cupboard and found some fishing line and a jewelry clasp. I guessed, by measuring my own ankle, how big around hers might be. Then I started stringing tiny shells on the fishing line until there were enough to go around her dainty little ankle then clumsily attached the clasp. I worked frantically on it the whole hour it took her to get her face and hair done. When she came into the kitchen, I presented it to her. She cried as if it were made of diamonds. I put it on her, and it fit perfectly. She's never taken it off in two years."

Dracula raised his eyebrows in amazement.

Micah added, "She's also never taken off the puka shell necklace Chelsey made her years ago. Those are the things Gracie loves. Things that don't cost a penny. Things from the heart."

The thought of his Gracie made him smile, all cheesy.

"Wow, that's cool! I bet Mandy would like things like that."

"Dude, *every* woman likes things like that. Things that show her you're thinking about her. Thoughtful things. Creative things," Micah said.

"I'm glad you told me about that, Micah. I'm always looking for things to *buy* for Mandy, instead of taking the time to create something special and original for her. I'm going to spice things up, moving forward. Thank you, bro. You're a good inspiration."

Fist bumps.

39

Exciting Story To Tell

With proud tears in her eyes, Gracie said, "My beautiful daughter, I have missed you so much for so long. I am incredibly grateful God has put us back in each other's lives. I love you so much, Lexi. My heart always knew you were alive."

"I never gave up on you either, Mom," Lexi replied, embracing her mother.

Gracie asked, "You know how you said, when you met Pime she had been waiting for you all her life? And Jesus had spoken to her about you from birth?"

Lexi nodded yes.

"Well, as soon as Chelsey was born, Jesus started talking to her about Arëk, her future best friend from Schmec. She waited patiently until he finally showed up when she was five years old. Your dad and I didn't know anything about Arëk or their friendship until just a few years ago. The two of them have been inseparable since the first time they met, just like you and Pime.

"Your little sister has been traveling the Universe since she was an itty-bitty thing. She's been looking for you, Austin, and Tripp for a long time. So have your dad and me. We didn't know about Universe travel until Chelsey and Arëk came forward and informed us about it. And it still took us a little while to get up the nerve to try it. Now we take trips all the time. But *this* trip, I have to say," taking Lexi's hands in hers, "is the best one yet! I can't wait to tell Chelsey I found you! It will make her the happiest girl ever!"

"Where is she?" Lexi asked.

"I don't know. She's off running around with Arëk somewhere. They pushed your dad and me into taking a vacation on Zooch. So, I'm sure they're up to something they didn't want us in the way for," Gracie said with a chuckle. "We've learned we must trust Chelsey and Arëk when they go on their adventures. After all, she's been a Universe traveler since she was in kindergarten!"

"I can't believe our stories are so much alike; Chelsey knowing about Arëk, and Pime knowing about me. I can't wait until the four of us get together and tell our stories!" Lexi said with excitement.

Mandy spoke up and said, "Gracie, I don't mean to be a party pooper, but don't you think we should head back to Zooch to check in with the guys? We've been gone all day. I know Drac will worry if I'm not back soon. The sun has already set in Rew."

"Yes, you're right, we do need to go. Lexi, I promise to come back very soon. And I'll bring Chelsey and your dad! We'll have a big family reunion!"

Lexi grabbed her mother and held her close.

"I love you, Mama. Please come back as soon as you can. I finally have you back. I don't want to be without you for long."

Gracie held her daughter's beautiful face in her hands.

"I love you, Lexi, so, so much. You will never be without me again. *Never.*"

Tears fell from everyone's eyes.

"A new beginning for us, no more goodbyes," Lexi said and pulled her mother close to her.

"No more goodbyes, I promise," Gracie agreed.

"I'll see you, girls, soon," Lexi said to Gracie and Mandy.

"Very soon," her mother said happily.

Gracie blew her daughter a kiss as they disappeared.

Axl gets all teary again. He's as sappy as I am.

Within a blink, they were back on Zooch.

"We have to find the guys!" Gracie exclaimed.

"The Mima Café is right around the corner," Mandy said.

The girls quickly walked down the street and turned the corner.

As soon as the Mima Café was in sight, they heard, "Hey, beautiful!"

Gracie knew that smooth voice by heart. They entered the café where Micah and Dracula stood up to greet their wives.

"We were wondering about you," Micah said just before he kissed Gracie. "We were afraid you might have been kidnapped by some crazy scary movie aliens who were sucking out your brains!"

"And eating your eyeballs!" Dracula added.

Mandy laughed and kissed her husband.

Axl laughs.

Gracie kissed Micah again and said, "Yeah, you look super worried, slurping up your blue smoothies. Is that a…? Did you bring crazy straws from home, silly?"

She laughed out loud.

Axl laughs again.

"No! They serve them here! Honey, you have got to try this! It's called a yubl. It's so good!" Micah said.

Gracie sat down in the chair next to him.

"Just wait until you hear about our awesome dude's day!" Micah added.

"Wait! Can I go first? Please, please?" Gracie interrupted, "It's important. You'll never believe what happened today!"

She looked at Mandy, who was so excited about her friend's news. Gracie's eyes started filling with tears and her chin started to quiver.

"What's wrong, baby, why are you crying? What happened?" Micah asked as he pulled his wife close to him.

"I don't even know where to start or how to say this," Gracie said.

"Just tell us, sweetheart, what is it?"

Gracie looked at Mandy for support. Mandy smiled and nodded her head encouraging Gracie to go on. She took as deep a breath as she could muster and wiped the tears off her cheeks. She had every intention of staying calm and slowly describing the events of their day. But her words didn't come out calm or slow. Instead, she spoke through hard sobs. Micah tried several times to slow her down so he could understand her, but she couldn't be stopped. He was uncertain if she was sad or happy as the tears streamed down her face. All he knew was Gracie was crying about Lexi, but he didn't understand why.

With tears dripping from his eyes, Micah grabbed his wife and pulled her close to him. He held her tight, as she cried on his chest.

Once she caught her breath, he asked her to start again from the beginning, only slower. As Micah listened to the details of Gracie's reunion with their daughter, her voice seemed to turn into slow motion.

"Could it be true," Micah thought. "Could it really have been Lexi? And in all places, out here, in space?"

Then he looked over at Dracula and Mandy, his friends from another planet. He realized, why *couldn't* Lexi be out here? When he returned from the distant place he had drifted off to, he felt elated!

Micah's face lit up as tears dropped from his chin.

He grabbed Gracie's arms with a hopeful smile and asked, "You really saw Lexi? How is she? Did she mention the boys? How are they? Where are they? We have to go! We have to go see them! Let's go!"

Gracie smiled and took Micah's hands in hers.

She said with fresh tears, "Lexi hasn't seen the boys since the plane crash. But don't worry, we will find them, too. We won't give up until we do, I promise. God led us to Lexi and He will lead us to Austin and Tripp! I just know it!"

Micah hugged his wife and sobbed like a baby.

Axl's eyes fill with tears again and he says, "I never cry like this!" Yeah, whatever, dude.

Dracula pulled Mandy close to him as she cried with her friends.

Micah wiped the tears off his face and sternly nodded.

"You're right, we *will* find them! I just can't believe we didn't think to look on other planets after Chelsey and Arëk told us about all their travels! How could we have been so stupid?"

Gracie replied, "Don't be so hard on us, honey, we're still new to this whole *other planet* stuff. Maybe Lexi can give us some ideas about where to look. Or Chelsey and Arëk. Knowing those two, they're probably already on the hunt! We know Chelsey's been looking for them for years. The boys will turn up!"

Micah took a deep breath and said, "You're right! We will find our sons. So, tell me more about Lexi. I bet she's beautiful, like you."

Micah began to weep, along with Gracie and Mandy. Dracula shed a few tears, too.

Axl wipes another tear away and says, "Man, this story!" I nod in agreement.

"She's stunning!" Gracie said with pride.

"Why can't we go there *now*?" Micah asked with frustration.

"It would be unfair to go back without Chelsey. She has been looking for the kids for almost as long as we have. It would break her heart if we went without her."

"You're right. So, let's go to Oahu. We can drop by the Raan's house and tell them what happened. We'll get our stuff and go home to get Chelsey. We can come back here to finish our vacation afterward, right?" Micah looked at Dracula and Mandy.

"I think it's a great plan, buddy," Dracula said, and Mandy agreed.

"Drac and I will be here for another couple of weeks. You guys go have your family time. We'll look in on Friday for you. Just be sure to look us up when you get back to Rew. We'll be waiting anxiously to hear all about your family reunion!" Mandy said.

"You got it! We'll see you soon," Gracie replied as she hugged her friend goodbye.

Dracula and Micah bro hugged and agreed to pick up where they left off.

40

Big News For Chelsey

The parents hoped against all odds that Chelsey and I would be at the house in Haleiwa when they arrived. As per usual, we weren't. They immediately checked the garage for obvious clues. Chelsey's Jeep, our boards, the dogs, and the monkey were gone. Answer: surfing.

Gracie asked Micah if he would drive down to the beach to find us while she did some laundry and repacked. The plan was for the four of us to stay a few days with Lexi on Tumah. Gracie smiled big every time she thought of her family being together again.

Chelsey's dad took off toward the beach on his souped-up shiny black Harley Davidson. It was Gracie's gift to him on his forty-fifth birthday. She knew it would surprise him since he thought he was getting a new set of golf clubs.

His bike made him feel like a king, riding around with the wind blowing against his face and the warm sun tanning his skin. It always felt like a special occasion when he mounted "Jet" but today it would take him to surprise his younger daughter. And that surprise would mean telling her something she'd longed to hear all her life.

Her sister had been found and was excited to finally meet her. He'd never felt as much like a king as he did that day.

As the motor rumbled in his ears, Micah recapped the crazy events of the day. He thought how miraculous it was that "just like that," after all those years they'd found one of their missing kids.

He asked Jet, "I wonder what Tumah is like? The girls didn't really have a chance to tell us. Guess we'll find out here shortly."

A few minutes later Micah parked the motorcycle. As soon as he approached the beach he was greeted with a big loud bark.

"Hey, Booger!" Micah shouted to the giant dog loping toward him. Micah knelt on his knees to lessen the impact of the slobbery monster. As always, he was tackled then slimed by Booger's huge drooling tongue.

"I love you, big guy, but you are so gross!" Micah said laughing in between slobbery licks.

Axl scrunches up his face.

"Ok, buddy, get off! Where's Chelsey? Take me to Chelsey," he said to Booger. The Mastiff/Great Dane clumsily ran toward the beach where Chelsey and I were coming out of the water.

"Dad? What are you doing here? Why aren't you on Zooch? Is everything ok?" Chelsey asked as she squeezed water out of her hair.

"Yes, everything's fine. Great, in fact," her dad replied as he hugged his daughter and offered me a fist bump. "Grab your stuff and come to the house. I'll help you load up your boards."

Chelsey and I gathered up our towels and the pets and we followed Micah to the Jeep.

"So, what's going on? Is Mom at the house?" Chelsey asked.

"Yes, she is. Mom and I will tell you what's going on when we get there."

"This is weird," Chelsey mouthed to me as we walked with her dad.

"I know, right," I mouthed in response.

After a short drive, we walked into the house. Gracie grabbed Chelsey right away.

"Hey, Angelfish! How's my girl?"

"Suspicious," Chelsey replied.

"Hi, Arëk!" Gracie said as she hugged me next and kissed me on the forehead.

I love that, brah. So, so much.

We put our wet towels in the basket by the washer in the laundry room. Then we went back to the living room where her parents were waiting for us.

"So, what's up, guys? Why are y'all here?" Chelsey asked.

"Have a seat," Gracie said.

She motioned toward a blanket on the floor since our swimsuits were still wet. We sat down and looked at each other with apprehension.

"Your dad and I have something to tell you. Something happened today, something wonderful."

"Mom, just spit it out, whatever it is, please. The suspense is torture," Chelsey said.

"Ok," she said and then looked at Micah. "We found Lexi."

Chelsey couldn't speak. Or think. Or anything else, but cry. She sat perfectly still as her green eyes filled full of big heavy tears. Finally, she blinked, and tears turned into streams down her cheeks. She covered her face with her hands and began to sob. I wrapped my arms around my bestie and held her tight. She started shaking her head and mumbled in her hands what sounded like, "Thank you, God, thank you." Her mother knelt in front of her on the blanket and held her close to her chest. Seconds later, Micah came over and hugged the three of us.

"God led us right to her. She has been waiting for us all this time," Gracie said.

Axl wipes away a tear before it falls from his eye. He says, "Geez, this family!"

"Where is she?" Chelsey asked in between sobs.

"She lives on Tumah. Have you been there?" Gracie asked.

"I don't think so," she replied looking at me for confirmation.

I shook my head no.

"We came home from Rew to get you so we could all go see Lexi together. Mandy and I are the only ones who have seen her so far. Your sister is so excited to meet you, baby."

"When are we going?" Chelsey asked as she wiped her face.

"As soon as we get a good night's sleep and repack our stuff. Why don't you two take showers and wash off the ocean while Dad and I make something to eat."

Gracie helped us up off the floor and we hugged her parents and cried some more.

After we were showered and dressed, I asked Chelsey if we should tell them about Tripp since they told us about Lexi. She thought it would be best to handle one big surprise at a time. Besides, she wanted Tripp to be available when they found out about him. I agreed it was the best idea.

After a quick supper with the parents, we all turned in for the night. I don't think any of us slept a wink, dude. We were all up before the sun the next morning, excited about the big day.

"Ok, we're ready!" Chelsey announced as we entered the kitchen where the folks were finishing their lattes.

"Eat some breakfast first and then we'll be on our way. We've already eaten. I made your favorite, buttermilk pancakes and there's warm syrup by the stove. Do you want me to make you lattes?" Gracie asked us.

"Yes, please, with an extra shot of espresso. We didn't sleep all night. This adrenaline will wear off eventually and we'll wish we'd had an extra caffeine boost," Chelsey said.

"Lattes coming up!" Gracie said.

It didn't take long for me and my bestie to inhale a stack of pancakes and a latte.

"Ok, we're done!" we said at almost the same time.

"Alright, rinse your dishes and put them in the dishwasher. The animals have lots of food and water. Micah, honey, please make sure all the lights are turned off, and we'll be out the door," Gracie said.

"So, Captain Blackbeard, what's up with the fishhook?" Chelsey asked Micah, giggling.

"I was wondering when someone was going to bring it up. Cool story! I'll tell you about it later!" he answered.

41

Reacquaintance With Lexi

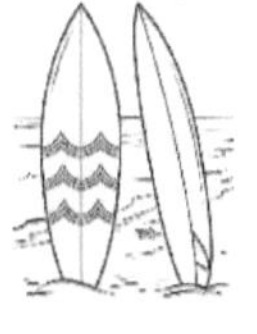

"This place is beautiful!" Chelsey said, looking all around. "I can't believe we've never been here, Arëk."

"I know, and we've been in this galaxy lots of times," I responded.

"Maybe it just wasn't the right time yet," Gracie interjected.

"Maybe," Chelsey said as she took in all the beauty of this welcoming planet.

"Hello!" from a woman Mandy and Gracie met the previous day.

She gently hugged Chelsey's mom and kissed her cheeks.

"I spoke to Isun after you left and was so honored to find out you are the Vinga's mother! The resemblance is unbelievable!"

"Oh, thank you! This is Isun's father, Micah, and her sister, Chelsey," Gracie said with pride.

"Ahem!" I cleared my throat, hoping to be acknowledged.

"And this is Arëk, Chelsey's best friend," Gracie smoothly added and smiled at me.

"It is such a pleasure to meet you all. Welcome to Ci!" the woman said with arms stretched out toward the village.

As our little group began to walk down the street, Chelsey asked, "So, what's this Vinga business, and who is Isun? What was she talking about, Mom?"

Gracie stopped everyone and said with a mischievous smile, "Did I forget to mention that Lexi is the queen of this planet?"

"Wait, what?" Chelsey asked. "What do you mean, *queen*?"

We all looked at Gracie and each other curiously.

"Lexi is the Queen of Tumah! Here they call it Vinga," Gracie said proudly. "She can tell you the whole story when we see her."

Micah stuck his chest out, put his hands on his hips, and said, "My daughter is the *queen*!"

Chelsey and I giggled at how silly he looked.

After walking about a block, we stopped where a group of people were gathered. Gracie saw a man she recognized from the boutique the day before. She asked if he knew how they could find the Vinga. He said he saw her going to the castle a couple of hours ago.

"The castle? Really?" Chelsey asked.

"Yep, the castle!" Gracie replied.

"So, my brain's not wrapping around this whole queen thing. Are you sure you found *our* Lexi, Mom? Because, for starters, how can a human be a queen on another planet?" Chelsey asked.

"Trust me, honey," Gracie said, putting her arm around Chelsey's shoulder. "This is *our* Lexi. As soon as you see her, you'll know. She looks just like us girls. A mirror image almost."

"And President Trump, remember?" Micah interjected.

"Good point!" Chelsey and I said together.

"Alright! So, are we going to the castle or what?" Micah asked, trying to move the show along.

"Yes! Let's get moving! Most of the people of Ci walk everywhere they go instead of using vehicles, so we're going to get some exercise," Gracie said.

"Why?" Chelsey asked.

"Why, what?" her mother responded.

"Why don't they drive?" Chelsey asked.

"Because it's so beautiful here and they take time to enjoy the scenery," her mom answered.

"Okey, dokey," Chelsey responded with a sarcastic thumbs up.

"And here we go!" Micah said, rubbing his hands together.

The castle was visible from anywhere in the village. It was much more modern and welcoming than you'd expect. The enormous stones forming the outer castle walls were not gray or solid in color like you see in movies. These stones looked more like frosted glass. You could even see movement on the other side of the wall through them, although not clearly.

Axl asks about the bridge and slimy mote. He also wants to know about the dragon in the dungeon and the fair lady imprisoned in the tower. Slow down, Prince Charming, we're getting there!

There was, in fact, a bridge to cross, and it was over water. But the bridge was clear like glass. And the water beneath it was pure enough to drink. Colored stones, like the ones in the Wuvet River, showed off in the water surrounding the castle. Real proud of themselves for being more beautiful than the other planets' stones.

The inside of the castle was even more spectacular. The same frosty glass-like stones made the steps on every staircase and composed many of the walls. The sky replaced the ceiling in most of the rooms of the ginormous structure. It was one of Lexi's personal remodeling ideas. She loved the sun, the moon, the stars, and the music of nature, so she had the ceilings removed. I'll tell you more about the place as we go along. I just wanted to give you an idea of what we were all about to experience for the first time. It was awwwesome! You'll have to see it sometime!

Axl says, "Definitely!"

After walking a couple of miles toward the castle, an old man riding in what looked like a floating golf cart passed us on the road.

"So much for the natives walking everywhere, huh?" Micah said sarcastically in Gracie's direction.

"I'm as surprised as you are, smarty pants," she replied.

"We need one of those!" Micah said to his wife. "The castle is so big, it looks closer than it really is. It could be several more miles of walking."

"Ok, fine. Let me see if we can get the man's attention," Gracie said, looking back down the road.

"Sir? Sir! SIR!" she shouted to the man in the floating golf cart.

He finally looked behind him to see what all the shouting was about. Gracie motioned for him to turn around and come back to them. He smiled and gladly went back.

"Hello there! Headed to the castle today?" he politely asked.

"Yes, sir, we sure are. We're going to see our daughter, the Vinga," Gracie answered proudly.

"Oh, my! Yes, I see the resemblance! Uncanny, it is!" he said, smiling.

"Sir, we were wondering where we might find a vehicle, so we don't have to walk the whole way up there," Gracie said.

"Oh, sure! But what you folks need is a carriage! Old Grint is going to take care of you. I'd like to invite you to take in the beauty of what surrounds my wonderful village while you wait for my return. Be sure to notice the flowers to your left. They're my favorite of all the flowers on Tumah. They're called Starlights, and they smell good enough to eat!" He chuckled at his own comment, then said, "I'd better be on my way to find you some transportation. I shouldn't be gone long."

"Ok, we'll be right here waiting. Thank you for your help, sir," Gracie said and patted him on the arm.

"My pleasure! It's not every day an old guy like me gets to assist royalty!"

"Royalty," Chelsey repeated, "I could get used to that."

"Lady Chelsey, I presume?" I said jokingly while bowing to her.

"Yep, I like it!" Chelsey answered and curtsied.

After about twenty minutes, we heard who we assumed was Old Grint coming down the road. We couldn't believe our eyes when we finally saw it. It was a procession of three fancy floating carriages. They were like something you'd see in Cinderella, minus the mice and pumpkins. When the carriages stopped in front of us, we were greeted by six well-dressed young chauffeurs.

"Good day to you all! Please allow us to escort you to the castle," one of the men said, motioning toward the middle and last carriage.

Two passengers fit comfortably in each. Chelsey's parents paired up as did Chelsey and me. There were two chauffeurs at the front and back of each carriage. As they assisted each of us into the carriages, they bowed and called us "Majesty." Chelsey's head swelled up to the size of the Sphere in Las Vegas. She did the dumb princess wave all the way to the castle. Ugh, obnoxious.

Axl does the wave.

Yep, that's the one, brah.

When the procession turned onto the road leading to the castle, we were stunned at its size. Talk about feeling microscopic, dude! It was the most magnificent architecture any of us had ever seen. The way it glistened in the sunlight made us feel like we were in a dream. It was crazy! The carriages stopped under an arch of trees in front of the glass bridge. The chauffeurs stepped down to help us out.

"Would you like us to escort you into the castle, your Majesty?" one of them asked Gracie.

"Oh, no, thank you. I think we can handle it from here. Quick question, though. When we get to the gate, how do we get in?"

"You will find a gate watch standing at the entrance. He will escort you inside," the chauffeur answered.

"Thank you! And please thank Mr. Grint, as well," Gracie said.

"Certainly," he said and bowed.

The chauffeurs mounted the carriages and began to float away.

Gracie led the way across the shiny, clear bridge with Micah at her side. Chelsey and I followed a few feet behind them. We all wowed at the dreaminess of it all as we slowly strolled and enjoyed every little detail. Gracie immediately noticed the colored stones in the water.

"Oh, yeah," Gracie turned to Micah and said, "I forgot to show you the necklace Lexi made me! It's the same kind of stones as those!" she said, pointing to the water.

"I saw it last night, but we were so quickly distracted with the story about Lexi that I forgot to ask you about it. Then, we were in such a hurry to get ready to leave this morning I didn't think about it. I'm sorry. Let me see it, love. Wow! Those stones look expensive! What are they?" Micah asked as he examined them closely.

"Sapphires, I think, only better and purer," Gracie answered. "I'm so proud of it."

She touched the necklace and thought back to the precious time she and Mandy spent at the Wuvet River with Lexi. Or Isun, at the time.

Gracie turned to Chelsey and said, "I gave her the puka shell necklace you made me when you were a little girl as a trade gift. I told her how it was a reminder of hope from you."

"Did she wear it?" Chelsey asked hopefully.

"I put it on her myself. She loved it! It made her cry," Gracie answered.

Chelsey smiled, imagining the shells on her long-lost sister whom she was about to meet for the first time.

Then she put her hands on her hips and said, "Alright, so how do I get a shiny river necklace?"

"You have to be friends with the Queen," Gracie winked and brushed off her shoulder as if she were privileged.

We all laughed.

Axl says he likes Gracie.

We continued our journey toward the castle. About a block past the bridge, we came upon ginormous double gates appearing as swirled frost. We wondered if they would be cold to the touch. There was a man standing just inside a partition next to the gate, unseen until we were right in front of it.

"Who may I tell the Vinga is visiting?" he asked, startling us.

We all grabbed our chests and gasped.

"You scared me!" Gracie shouted impulsively.

"My apologies," he responded with sincerity.

"We would like to surprise the Vinga. I'm her mother, and this is her father, her sister, and a dear friend," she said, winking at me.

I love her.

"Oh, yes, I see the resemblance," he said.

"I get that a lot," Gracie responded.

"Please go on ahead. I am sure the Vinga will be happy to see you."

He smiled and motioned us onward.

"Thank you," we all said.

"I wonder if Lexi looks anything like Mom," Chelsey said sarcastically.

We all chuckled.

The castle was ridiculous, brah! None of us had ever seen anything so marvelous before. The courtyard, just inside the gates, was what the Garden of Eden must have looked like in its prime. There were fountains, trees, flowers, and gardens. We all turned circle after circle looking around and above us, trying to take it all in. Plush grass and designed stone pathways curled around like ribbons through the courtyard and into the castle. The flowers were planted strategically by color, shape, and size. And there must have been fifty different species of trees shading most of the courtyard. It was breathtaking, dude! Oh, and there was music all around us in the courtyard, too. It sounded like perfectly tuned chimes.

We finally made it into the castle, which had no doors to push open. It was a huge, open, and welcoming entrance for all who visited. We saw people of different species tending the gardens and others moving around inside the structure. Gracie decided it would be best to ask where Lexi was instead of spending all day wandering about.

"Excuse me," she said to a woman who was polishing a beautiful sculpture, "We're here to see the Vinga. Do you know where we can find her? We'd like it to be a surprise."

"Oh, my!" the woman said, smiling, and then covered her mouth with her hands. "You must be her mother! The two of you look so much alike! The Vinga has been dancing and singing around the castle since she saw you yesterday. She even asked the orchestra to play music to dance to today! We are all so excited for her! She has talked nonstop about seeing you again for the first time after so many years. I have never seen her so happy!"

Gracie's eyes lit up, and her heart was filled to hear her daughter was so excited to have her back in her life.

"Let me take you to her! She's probably still on the dance floor," the woman said.

We all looked at each other with excitement and took nervous breaths. We were finally going to see one of the siblings we had searched so long for. I couldn't have been happier for my bestie. Chelsey took my hand as we followed the lady into another vast area of the castle.

Axl says he's so excited! He's sitting on the edge of his seat.

Just as the nice lady said, Lexi was singing and dancing to the music of cellos, violins, and piano. Initially, we stood and watched her, admiring her gracefulness and joy. Plus, she was unbelievably *hot*, dude!

Axl smiles and raises an eyebrow.

I'm telling you, brah. The Wick women are on a whole other level of gorgeous. They make guys act stupid.

Axl laughs.

Gracie had an idea. She whispered in Micah's ear, and he smiled. The next thing we knew, he was walking toward the dancing beauty. When he got close enough, he cleared his throat to get her attention. She turned around and saw a man standing to the side with his head bowed. She walked over to him and smiled her beautiful smile.

He held out his hand and asked, "May I have the pleasure of this dance, my lady?"

Without even a second's thought, she took his hand and accepted the invitation. I suppose she assumed he was someone from the village who had come to see her about something. After about a minute, Micah pulled away from her just enough for her to see an older but very familiar face.

She gasped and said, "Daddy?"

Axl's eyes fill with tears. Mine, too. Every time.

He immediately started to cry and pulled his long-lost daughter close to him. She hugged him tightly and cried against his chest.

When they released each other, Lexi said, "I can't believe it's you!"

Micah replied, "And I can't believe it's you! You are so beautiful!"

They hugged again.

"There's someone else who has been waiting a long time to see you, too," he said as he looked toward Chelsey.

Lexi looked in the direction in which he was looking.

"Chelsey?" she asked, hoping it was her little sister she was looking at.

Chelsey didn't say a word. She just ran to Lexi, grabbed her, and held her tight. The sisters cried and hugged. Their dad joined in, wrapping his arms around them both.

"I can't believe it," Chelsey finally said, still holding Lexi. "Thank you, God. Thank you so much."

Axl wipes tears out of his eyes before they have a chance to fall.

When everyone let go of each other, Lexi saw her mom standing outside the group, witnessing a miracle.

She grabbed Gracie, hugged her tightly, and said, "Thank you, Mom. You can't imagine what this means to me."

"Oh, yes, I can, baby! Believe me, we've all been waiting for this moment as long as you have! This is an answer to all our prayers!" Gracie said.

I wiped away tears and cleared my throat, wanting to be a part of this long-awaited occasion.

"Oh, my goodness! Lexi, I want to introduce you to Arëk, my very best friend," Chelsey said, holding her hand out to me.

Lexi hugged me and said, "It is wonderful to meet you, Arëk. I heard all about you yesterday."

"I've heard all about you for years!" I replied with a smile.

She hugged me again. Duuude! She's crazy hot! I could've hugged her all day long.

Axl laughs.

"I didn't expect to see you again so soon, Mom! I'm so happy you're all here! This is the best day of my life! And I can't wait to get to know you, little sister!" she said, turning toward Chelsey. "I have wondered about you all your life!"

"Likewise!" Chelsey responded. "Arëk and I have been looking for you, Austin, and Tripp for years. I guess it just wasn't God's timing until now."

"Today was the perfect time!" Lexi said.

"It's an awesome day!" Gracie said.

"Well, let's get you settled in. You *are* staying, aren't you?" Lexi asked hopefully.

"Yes!" Gracie answered. "At least for a few days, right, everyone?"

"Absolutely! We have a lot of catching up to do!" Micah quickly answered, and the rest of us agreed.

"Good! Then I'll take you to the rooms you'll be staying in. Chelsey, I want you to stay in my room with me," Lexi said.

"I'd love to!" Chelsey readily accepted.

"Arëk, do you think you'll survive without Chelsey?" Micah asked sarcastically.

"Well, I'll try," I said with pouty lips and sad eyes. Then I smiled and said, "Are you kidding me? My bestie has been waiting for this forever! I couldn't be more excited for her!"

"Arëk, you'll have your own room with all the best amenities, I assure you," Lexi told me.

"Bring it on, girlfriend!" I said, literally wishing she was my girlfriend.

"Our bags are back in the other room. Should we go grab them?" Micah asked.

"No, no, I'll have them delivered to your rooms," Lexi said, smiling at her dad and then giving a staff member her request.

Chelsey walked between Lexi and me, with the parents following.

"Your sister's smoking hot!" I whispered to Chelsey as we walked up the wide curving staircase.

She punched my arm and jokingly whispered, "Shut up, creep!"

We both laughed.

Axl laughs.

"What are you two doing up there?" Gracie asked, assuming we were goofing off.

"Arëk thinks Lexi's hot," my bestie announced to the whole group.

My mouth fell open, and suddenly, I couldn't look at Lexi, who was grinning. The parents rolled their eyes, shook their heads, and laughed.

Axl says, "Duuude!" And laughs.

"Wow, thanks, bestie. Remind me to get you back later," I said.

Chelsey smiled a cheesy smile, which told me she was up for the challenge.

Once we finally reached the top of the stairs, Lexi led us to the left, where the castle seemed to go on for even more miles. Luckily, Gracie's and Micah's room was only four rooms down the long hallway from the staircase. When we entered, we were all blown away, dude. It was basically a penthouse apartment! It had two huge bathrooms, one with a huge tub and a huge window facing a huge garden. Then there was the ginormous bedroom with a ridiculously comfortable bed, a retractable ceiling, a glass-walled sitting room with a view of a different huge garden, a ginormous walk-in closet, and a balcony.

Axl's mouth falls open.

Dude! I know!

"Do you think you'll be comfortable?" Lexi asked her parents with sarcasm.

"Oh, we'll try to manage, I suppose," Micah replied, smiling.

When we had gotten an eyeful of Gracie's and Micah's room, Lexi said, "Now, let's venture on to Arëk's room."

"That's what I'm talking about!" I said with excitement about my mammoth guest quarters.

"Onward, ho!" I shouted with a fist in the air.

"I prefer Vinga, thank you," Lexi responded with quick wit.

It took a second then everyone busted with laughter.

"Good one. She's quick!" I said to the group.

Axl laughs, too, and says, "I like her!" Grrrrr.

We walked for what seemed like a mile down the same hallway. Then we walked down a set of stairs, then all the way down another long hallway to the last room. Lexi opened the door, and I walked into what I presumed was the smallest room in the entire castle.

"Here you go, Arëk!" Lexi said, trying not to laugh at my appalled expression.

Let me tell you about this room, brah. Number one, it was the size of an elevator car. I don't even know what purpose such a small room could possibly serve in a castle. It couldn't even pose as a mop closet.

Axl is laughing.

"You got jokes, girlfriend?" I asked Lexi.

Everyone tried to hold in their laughter, and finally, Lexi said, "You don't like it? Well, I guess you can bunk with the dragon down in the dungeon. Henry hasn't had company for quite some time. I'm sure he'd be ecstatic to eat you! I mean to see you."

Everyone laughed.

Axl laughs, too.

Then she added, "On second thought, you look a little too chewy for Henry's taste. He fancies meaty snacks."

"Hey! I'm not chewy! See, solid muscle!" I said, flexing my sad little biceps.

Micah and Chelsey looked at my muscles, then at each other and laughed together.

"Really?" I said with disgust.

Axl laughs at me again.

"I don't know, Arëk, I'd say you're pretty gristly," Micah jousted.

"Kind of gangly," Chelsey added with a scrunched-up face.

"Anyone else want to chime in? Gracie?" I asked sarcastically.

"Oh, honey, I'm sure you wouldn't be *that* tough for Henry to eat. You got any tenderizer, Lexi?" Gracie joked.

"Nice!" I said to the woman who was supposed to love me like a mother.

Axl laughs while clapping.

"Oh, Arëk, you know you're adorable. Lanky but adorable," Gracie said, hugging me from the side.

Everyone laughed except me.

"Y'all are just mean to an alien," I told them.

Axl laughs again and falls backwards.

They all laughed. But then Chelsey and Lexi tag teamed me with a hug. My best buddy and her hot sister. My life was golden.

"Ok, ok, follow me," Lexi said as she tussled my hair and commented about how cool it felt.

I told her she could touch my hair anytime.

We followed her back down the hallway, up the stairs, and back toward the grand staircase.

"I have a special room just for you, Arëk," Lexi said.

"Yeah, I think we've already seen the *special* room," I replied sarcastically.

She smiled back at me, and I fell in love a little.

Axl is still laughing and says, "The special room!" and laughs some more.

After you reach the top of the huge staircase, you can walk a complete circle around the grand room, which is open all the way up to the sky. There are wings and hallways in every direction. Lexi led us about halfway around the circle before making a left turn into a short hallway with only two rooms. One on each side. We stopped at the room on the left.

"I think this will be more to your liking," she said to me as she swung the large door open.

Brah, I thought I was hallucinating when I saw the inside of the room! This guest room had no ceiling and it had trees growing in it! It was an enormous, wonderful room with all the benefits the parents had in theirs. I was a happy little Schmecum. Chelsey ran past me and dove onto the super huge bed.

"Have you ever seen a bed this big in all your life, bestie?" she asked.

"Never!" I responded. "Thank you, Lexi, this is awesome!"

"You're welcome, Arëk. Only the best for my little sister's BFF," she said, then winked.

I was in love for sure, brah. No question about it.

Axl says Lexi sounds amazing!

"So, where's your room, Lexi?" Chelsey asked, excited to see where she'd be staying.

"Not far from here, actually," she said with a playful smile.

"Awesome!" Chelsey and I said to each other in unison.

We walked out of the room and waited for Lexi to lead the way. She walked directly across the hallway and opened the second door.

"This is my room. Well, the one I stay in most of the time, anyway," she said.

We entered the room and were all blown away, like each time before. Just as in my room, there were trees growing up through the floor and up to the sky. I loved the whole no-ceiling idea. What better way to fall asleep than to be staring at the stars? Chelsey's parents oohed and awed at the size of the room and all its comforts and conveniences. It was quite a sight to behold!

"This is beautiful!" Chelsey commented as she turned in circles, taking it all in. She mouthed, "WOW!" when she and I made eye contact.

I readily agreed.

"We'll do lots of catching up in here tonight," Lexi told Chelsey.

"I can't wait!" Chelsey responded.

Lexi asked, "Is anyone hungry? I thought we could eat and then sit in one of the gardens to catch up."

"Food sounds good!" Micah said enthusiastically, and everyone agreed.

Then he turned to Gracie and said, "That reminds me, don't let me forget to tell you about the dajan steaks Dracula and I ate for lunch yesterday! OMG!"

"Ok," she said with a look of curiosity. "Then you can enlighten me on your cool new earring."

Gracie touched the hook in his ear.

"Ow!" he said, grabbing his sore ear.

"I'll check in with the chef to get something delicious started," Lexi said. "Please make yourselves at home. You are welcome to wander around if you'd like. I'm going to run to the kitchen and be back in a blink. Daddy, I have a physician on call who can remove your fishhook. I'll send him this way," she said, winking at him.

I'll fast-forward a little bit. We all gathered in the grand dining hall and sat at the longest table I had ever seen. Of course, we all sat at one end so we could visit without yelling across the room. The chef prepared courses none of us recognized, but altogether, it was one of the most delicious meals any of us had ever tasted. I could totally get used to the royalty kind of living.

After our bellies were stuffed, Lexi led us to one of her favorite places in the castle. It was a garden that seemed almost dreamlike. An oversized tree that resembles Earth's Weeping Willow grew right in the center of the garden. Its branches and leaves hung all the way to the grass, creating a curtain. Inside the curtain hung a simple hammock. It was Lexi's favorite reading spot. Other species of trees grew randomly around the area, along with flowers of every color and kind. There were rocking couches under several shade trees, which made it perfect for visiting with company. Lexi had six of her staff members move several couches together under a huge tree so all of us could gather comfortably around.

Chelsey seemed preoccupied almost immediately after we began our trek across the beautiful lawn.

I asked, "What's on your mind, buddy?"

She pulled me away from the group and whispered, "Tell me if I'm crazy, but I think this is the time to tell my parents and Lexi about Tripp. They won't be as shocked since Mom found Lexi. I think we should sneak off and transport to Smithers to see if he's there. If so, we'll see if he can get away and return with us. It would be the best surprise for my parents and for Lexi, too!"

"I think it's an awesome plan!"

"Let's tell them we're going to explore and check out the weeping tree. Once we're inside its curtain, we'll go to Smithers and hopefully come right back with Tripp," she whispered loudly.

"Good plan!"

"Hey guys, we'll be back in a few. We're going to check out the huge willow," Chelsey announced to the group.

"Ok, honey," Gracie said.

"Enjoy!" Lexi added with a smile.

"Ok, Arëk, let's go!" Chelsey said quietly.

We walked about five blocks to the tree. I'd have given anything for a floating golf cart. My belly was too full for a lot of walking. Once we got inside the curtain, we transported to Tripp's house on Smithers.

"Please be here, please be here, please be here," Chelsey said as she knocked on the door.

The door opened after about a minute, and Tripp's eyes lit up with joy.

"Hey! What are you guys doing here?" he asked as he hugged his sister. "Come on in! Wow, you look great! You're always so tanned!"

Chelsey giggled at the same words she heard everywhere she went.

"Lots of surfing in the sun," I answered.

Chelsey interjected and said, "Ok, Tripp, so here's the dealio, bro."

She gave her brother a super-fast rundown of the day's events, about finding Lexi, about her being Vinga, the whole castle thing, and about our plan to surprise the parents and Lexi by emerging from the willow with him. All in one breath.

"Awesome plan! I love it! And it's perfect timing, too. I won't be leaving Smithers again for five days," he said with excitement.

"Pack clothes and stuff for as many days as you can stay so we can all catch up," Chelsey said.

"You're going to love the accommodations! The castle is *swanky*!" I added, wiggling my eyebrows.

"You're going to love the accommodations! The castle is *swanky*!" I added, wiggling my eyebrows.

42

Sibling Surprise #2

After Tripp packed a bag, we transported to Tumah. When we opened our eyes, we were inside the curtain of the big willow tree.

"So, how are we going to do this?" Tripp asked Chelsey. "Are you going to go out first and then present me, or are we all just going to dive in with both feet and go out there together? Wow, I'm nervous!"

"I think Arëk and I should go first, don't you think, bestie?" she asked me.

"Yes. So, Tripp, you just wait for us here, ok? Don't disappear on us," I said as I elbowed his arm.

It made him smile.

"Ok, here goes," Chelsey said and grabbed my hand.

We walked the long distance between the big tree and the rocking couches where Chelsey's parents and Lexi sat visiting. They all acknowledged us when we arrived.

"Hi, Angelfish!" Gracie said and pulled her daughter by the hand to sit next to her.

"So, listen, Arëk and I have a little surprise for you all. It's something we've wanted to give you for quite a while, but it just hasn't been the right time. We'd like to present it to you now. And to you, too, Lexi."

"What is it?" her dad asked.

Chelsey looked at me and smiled a big cheesy smile.

"Ready, Arëk?"

"Ready!" I replied.

"Ok, everyone, come with us!" she said, grabbing her mother's hands to pull her up, then her dad's.

"What are you two up to?" Micah asked.

Chelsey smiled at him. He looked over at Gracie, and she shrugged her shoulders.

Once the group was about a hundred feet from the tree, Chelsey said, "Ok, wait here."

We entered the leafy curtain, and Chelsey asked, "Are you ready, Tripp?"

He took a deep breath and answered, "I'm ready."

Chelsey took her brother by the hand, and the three of us emerged from behind the veil.

After only a few seconds, we heard Lexi say, "Who's with them?"

The three of them tried to focus on the third person with us.

"Oh, my gosh, Micah, is that…?" Gracie started.

Micah answered, "Tripp? Son!"

"What?" Lexi gasped.

Gracie, Micah, and Lexi ran toward us then Tripp ran to meet them.

"Mom! Dad!" Tripp shouted as they finally reached each other and embraced with tears of joy.

"Is it really you?" Micah asked, crying and gasping for breath.

Axl's all teary-eyed again.

Gracie pulled back and took Tripp's face in her hands.

"Let me look at you!"

She began to cry even harder when she looked into the big brown eyes, she had missed all those years.

"It's really you!" Gracie whispered.

"Tripp?" Lexi said, barely able to speak through her sobs.

Her brother hugged her and lifted her off the ground.

"Lexi! Look at you! You're all grown!"

"I can't believe this! Two of them in one day! Thank you, Jesus!" Gracie cried as she looked toward Heaven.

Tripp hugged his parents again and then turned to Chelsey, hugged her, and said, "Thank you so much for this."

"It was time," she replied.

Then she looked at her parents and Lexi and said, "Two down, one to go!"

They all laughed as they wiped tears off their faces.

"Let's go sit and catch up! Tripp, are you hungry? We just ate, and there is plenty left," Lexi said to her brother.

"Maybe in a bit. Right now, I just want to sit here in this beautiful place and talk to you all. There is so much catching up to do. I don't even know where to start!" he said, and we all agreed.

We all got comfortable on the outdoor couches where Lexi's staff brought us drinks. Gracie, Tripp, and Lexi sat on one couch facing Micah, Chelsey, and me. It was a glorious reunion with everyone talking and laughing all at the same time.

At one point, Chelsey said, "You know what we should make today? Yubls!"

"I had a yubl yesterday!" Micah enthusiastically responded. "It was delicious! Dracula introduced me to it!"

"A what?" Lexi asked.

"Did you say *Dracula*?" Tripp added.

"A yubl. It's like an Orange Julius on Earth, only way better, and blue! And, yes, I did say *Dracula*," Micah answered.

Lexi and Tripp looked at each other and giggled.

"Is that what you guys were drinking at the Mima Café when we got back to Rew last night?" Gracie asked.

"Yeah!" he answered.

"If we knew what was in it, I bet we could ask the chef to make us some," Lexi said.

"Oooh, that's not a bad idea!" Micah said, and Chelsey and I agreed.

"I love those things!" Tripp piped in. "I go to Zooch just for that, sometimes."

"You go to Zooch?" Chelsey asked.

"Yeah, occasionally. It has a great culture," he responded.

"I started a crazy straw madness there!" Chelsey said, laughing at herself.

"Dracula was right!" Micah said. "We talked about the crazy straws they brought us for our yubls and how they reminded me of Chelsey."

"Chelsey always puts two crazy straws in her backpack for us when we go anywhere. When we took them out to drink our yubls on Zooch, everyone asked about them. The next thing we knew, there was a crazy straw served with every yubl at the Mima Café. My bestie's famous!" I bragged, bumping her shoulder.

"And speaking of the Mima Cafe," Micah said, looking at Chelsey, "Dracula and I ran into your spacey little friend, Fot, yesterday. He's got it *bad* for you, Chels," her dad said, wiggling his eyebrows.

"Yeah, I know, poor guy. He drives Arëk crazy with it," she responded, shaking her head.

"He said he wrote you a poem about your soft, tanned skin and your silky golden hair," Micah said, laughing. "He said he's going to steal you away from Arëk and have ten alien babies with you!"

Micah fell over, laughing at the look on Chelsey's face. His laughter made the rest of us laugh, too.

Axl chokes, he's laughing so hard.

Chelsey jumped up and tackled her dad for giving her a hard time.

"It wouldn't be the first one of those stupid poems he wrote," I contributed and rolled my eyes.

"Sounds like someone's a little jealous," Micah said, still laughing.

"She's *mine*!" I said, pounding my chest.

Everyone laughed and pounded their chests, too.

43

Meanwhile, On Oahu

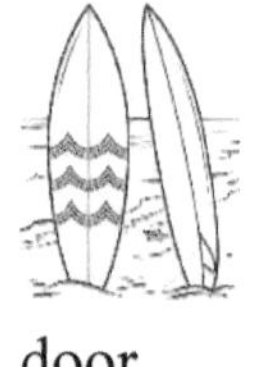

Knock, knock, knock…

"Coming," a woman's voice said, approaching the glass door.

She opened the door to the stranger and said, "Aloha!"

The man said, "Hi, sorry to bother you, but I'm kind of lost. Yours was the first house I came upon. I was hoping you could help me. I'm looking for a lady named Gracie Wick. She's a writer from this island."

"Oh, yes, Gracie, of course! Everyone on the islands knows her. Are you here for an interview or an autograph or something?"

He chuckled, "An autograph would be a bonus, but I really just need to talk to her. Do you know where she lives or where I can find her?"

"She spends a lot of time on the beaches with her husband and daughter. You might check there first," she said, trying to be helpful.

"Any beach in particular, to narrow it down?" he asked, hoping for a little more information.

"She ventures all over the island, but Waimanalo Beach seems to be one of her favorites. I'm sorry I can't be more help."

"No, no, you've been very helpful. Thank you so much," the stranger said as he walked down the steps of her porch.

"Good luck! Aloha!"

He waved goodbye.

The man walked through the small town, stopping at a fresh produce market. After checking out the fruit, he decided on a mango. He was surprised as the juice squirted and ran down his chin with the first bite.

"Oh, my Lord, this is amazing!" he said out loud to himself.

He had always been a lover of fruit, but after eating the mango, his new love was Hawaiian fruit. He was determined to taste every flavor the islands had to offer.

During his search for the Oahu writer, the stranger took in every detail of the beautiful island. He was delighted by the lush green vegetation and the variety of colorful flowers. As he walked through the small country town, he thanked God for this amazing experience. Once he reached the outskirts of the town, he found himself standing in front of the mammoth Pacific. The smell of it was so familiar and nostalgic. He had an impulsive urgency to feel the water on his skin. It was as if the ocean was calling to him. He pulled his leather backpack off his shoulder and laid it on the sand. He took off his shoes, socks, and t-shirt, leaving only his cargo shorts.

He closed his eyes and listened to the roar of the distant waves and the quiet splashing of the water on his bare feet. When he opened his eyes, he realized he was smiling. He walked into the warm water until he was waist deep. He seemed to know the ocean, and the ocean seemed to know him. He immersed himself in the water and felt it embrace him.

The stranger swam out a little farther, where several kids and their parents were floating on boards.

He asked from a short distance away, "Excuse me! Do you live here?"

The man of the family replied, "No, but we vacation here twice a year. It's our favorite spot!"

The stranger asked, "Have you, by chance, heard of a local author named Gracie Wick?"

"Oh, yeah, of course! We've met her several times over the last two or three years. We have her sign a book for us every time one comes out. She's super friendly, and all the locals love her. Have you had the pleasure?" the man asked.

"No, I haven't, not yet. That's why I'm here on the island. I'm trying to find her."

"It's not unusual to see her or her daughter out here on a surfboard," the man said. "That daughter of hers could probably go pro if she wanted to."

"Yeah, she's awesome!" one of the kids interjected. "She's even surfed on tv!"

"She's pretty, too, and nice," a younger girl added.

"And she has a monkey and two dogs that surf, too! You should see them!" the first kid added with excitement. "They were out here yesterday. It's so cool!"

"Really? So, they're on the island then. That's good news," the stranger said.

"Keep your eyes open, buddy. Maybe you'll see them out on the waves today," said the father of the kids, "I can't imagine anyone missing out on this perfect day."

"I'll look for them, thank you! It's been a pleasure chatting with you all!"

"Bye!" they all said and waved.

"Ok," he said to himself, "at least they're somewhere on the island. It's a start."

After swimming for quite a while, he exited the water, looking like a shriveled-up prune. The stranger found his belongings and dried off with his t-shirt. He looked around as the sun began to set, trying to decide what to do next.

He spotted a smoothie shack up the beach. His growling stomach gave a thumbs up. He grabbed his stuff, walked to the shack, and reviewed the menu. And just as you discovered, brah, there were so many combinations to choose from he couldn't decide. He asked the guy behind the counter which flavors tasted the best together.

Makaio, the tattooed smoothie maker, replied, "It depends on what you like, brah."

"Well, I like every fruit and most vegetables."

"I tell you what. I'll make you a smoothie I'm certain you'll like. If I'm wrong, which I hardly ever am, it's on the house," Makaio said, leaning on the counter.

"Deal!" he replied.

After about five minutes, the man delivered the stranger's orange-colored smoothie topped with a slice of mango, pineapple, and kiwi.

"Tell me what you think, brah," the smoothie maker said.

The stranger took the first drink of the cold, thick smoothie. His eyes immediately closed with pleasure. It was the most delicious creation he had ever tasted.

"You like?" Makaio asked.

All he could do was slowly nod his head yes. He didn't want to take his lips off the straw for a second. Makaio laughed and started wiping down the counter.

Finally, he spoke, "Oh, man, this is incredible! I've never tasted anything this good before! What do I owe you?"

"Don't worry about it this time, it's on me. Come back later, and I'll make you something different," Makaio said, confident he could wow the stranger again.

"Hey, before I go, where's a good place to stay the night around here? I'm visiting, and I'm not familiar with the area. I really don't want to pay for a pricey hotel room, if you know what I mean."

"I get you, brah. My tutu rents out a condo she owns close to the beach just up the way," he said, pointing in the direction of the house. "You can go ask her if it's available. Her name is Meleah. Here's her address."

He handed the man a napkin with the information scribbled on it.

Axl asks if she's the same Meleah as Vanise's Maleah. Yep, same lady.

"Awesome! Thanks, man! I'll see you tomorrow for another smoothie! And maybe a surfing lesson?" the stranger asked and smiled as he started walking away.

"I'll look for you, brah!" Makaio said.

The stranger followed the directions to the lady with the condo. He made it there just as porch lights began to light up around the neighborhood. He knocked on the screen door. After about half a minute, an elderly lady answered the door.

"Aloha!" she said through the screen.

"Hello, ma'am. I was wondering if your condo was available to rent for the night, maybe two. Your grandson sent me over here from the smoothie shack. I need a place to stay," he said, hoping for a vacancy.

"Are you on vacation, young man?"

"No, ma'am, not really. I'm looking for someone who lives on the island. I'm kind of flying by the seat of my pants, to be honest."

"Well, I do have a vacancy and you are welcome to stay in it. Let me get the key for you," she said and disappeared into the next room.

Moments later, she appeared back at the door.

She stepped outside onto the porch with the stranger and asked, "Are you going to watch the sunset tonight?"

"Oh, yes, ma'am, I'm told it's gorgeous here! I've seen sunsets from many different places, but I'm told there's nothing like it from Hawaii."

"The Lord is quite a painter, isn't He?" she asked.

"Yes, He sure is! It's always a pleasure to meet someone who knows the Lord," the stranger said, smiling.

"I wish everyone knew Him. Those who don't are missing out!"

"Agreed!" he responded.

"Well, son, you better get on down the road so you can find the house before it starts to get dark. Get yourself settled in for the night and enjoy! My name is Meleah. If you need anything at all, you just let me know," she said as she shewed him off the porch.

"Thank you, I will," he said, smiling back at her.

"By the way, who's the person you're looking for? I might know them," the woman asked.

"She's a local author. Her name is Gracie Wick."

The elderly lady smiled and slowly nodded her head up and down.

"Everyone knows Gracie. She's one of the most generous and loving people I have ever known," Meleah said.

"She sounds wonderful."

"Oh, she is! And her daughter and husband, too! They're a gift to this island," she said with warm sentiment.

"I talked to someone earlier who said they saw her daughter out on the water yesterday. I was relieved to know they were on the island. I've traveled a long distance to meet Mrs. Wick."

"I see Gracie and her husband take their morning walk almost every day as soon as the sun comes up. You might look for her then. Other than that, the water is your best bet. Gracie and her daughter are always on a wave somewhere," she said, laughing to herself.

"Since you see them walking in the mornings, do they live near here?" he asked with hope.

"Well, not exactly in the same neighborhood," she chuckled. They live a couple of miles up the road. You can't miss their house. It's the biggest house on the island. Gracie and Micah have done well for themselves."

"You've been very helpful. Thank you, Meleah. Oh, what do I owe you for renting the condo? I'm not sure if I'll be here just tonight or if it will be an extended stay. It'll depend on whether I have luck finding Mrs. Wick."

"Don't worry about it, sweetie. Any friend of the Lord's is a friend of mine. Just leave it like you found it, is all I ask."

"Yes, ma'am! Thank you again! You're a real blessing, Ms. Meleah!"

"My pleasure! Go get some rest!" she said.

He smiled at her and then turned to step down from the porch.

When he arrived at the condo, he felt right at home. It had everything he would need for his stay except food. The smoothie would hold him over until the morning. He decided to sit on the porch to watch the sun sink into the ocean. Once the moon lit up the sky, he turned in for the night. He lay in the comfortable bed and prayed for a successful day ahead.

44

Catching Up At The Castle

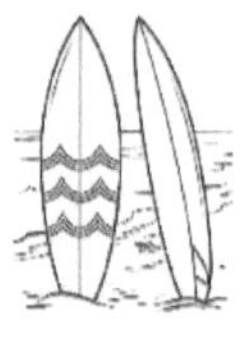 "So, you guys want to hear something really awesome?" Chelsey asked.

"Always!" Gracie answered with interest.

"Tripp's a medical scientist!" Chelsey announced with pride over her brother.

"You're a scientist, really?" Gracie asked her son.

"Yes, ma'am," he replied.

"A good one, too!" I added. "He's on the hunt for a root which will cure terminal diseases on Earth!"

"I'm believing it will. The root I've been researching contains all the ingredients for the perfect recipe to cure several human diseases. Unfortunately, I only ran across a small root of its kind to perform testing on and research. I haven't found another like it since. When I do find it again and perfect the solution, I'll deliver it to Earth. I pray it will be approved so it can be administered. It seems difficult to get an effective drug approved on Earth. Sickness is such a lucrative business there. It's sad and criminal how the big pharmacy companies prefer to make and sell drugs that don't fix the illness!"

"Or that cause additional health problems that require more drugs and cause even more sickness," Gracie added.

"Exactly! I want to be a part of the solution!"

"I'm so proud of you, son!" Micah said.

"Me, too!" Lexi interjected.

"So am I! We'll pray you find that root *and* get it approved on Earth!" Gracie said.

"Prayer works every time! You kids are proof," Micah said, looking at Lexi and Tripp.

"Now tell me again what planet you live on, son," his mother asked.

"I grew up on Ustak then started university on Smithers. I've lived there ever since."

"What's a Smithers person like?" Lexi asked.

"SNOOTY!" Chelsey and I said in unison, then laughed.

Tripp nodded and said, "I can't deny it."

"You don't fit in there at all, as far as attitude is concerned," Chelsey said.

"Thank you, sis."

"What about you guys?" Tripp asked. "What do all of you do for a living?"

We all looked around at each other then Micah said, "Babe, why don't you start?"

"Ok, well, I write fiction novels, mostly humorous. I also write children's books. I worked several jobs before I had my first best seller, and then God blessed me with the opportunity to write full-time. I love it," Gracie said with a warm smile.

"How many books have you written so far, Mom?" Lexi asked.

"I write at least one book a year and sometimes two. So, I guess around twenty-three or twenty-four?"

"Wow, Mom, impressive!" Tripp exclaimed.

"Thank you, son."

"And since she won't brag on herself, I will. She's also won several prestigious awards for her novels," Micah said, winking at his wife, making her smile.

"Mom even has a huge fan base across the Universe, come to find out!" Chelsey announced proudly. "Ask her about her encounter with Mark Wahlberg on Zooch!"

"Mark Wahlberg! What?" Lexi shouted. "He's been to Tumah several times. He's…wow!"

Micah rolled his eyes.

"He's not *that* wow," Micah answered.

Axl says, "Jealous much?" I laugh and agree.

Gracie mouthed to Lexi, "He's *super* wow!"

Lexi nodded her head in agreement.

I interrupted, "Marky Mark's not the only celebrity on the wall of fame in Gracie's fancy office. She's got Keanu, The Rock, Donald Trump…"

"Keanu Reeves, too? Are you kidding? Oh, my gosh, Mom!" Lexi interrupted excitedly.

"It's pretty cool!" Chelsey added.

"Micah, honey, you go next," Gracie said.

"I also worked several 'going nowhere' jobs before I found my niche. I invented a robot designed to assist me with my garage projects. It was very basic and unsophisticated. But your mother thought it was worthy of a patent. So, I hired an engineer to help me refine 'Mack,' and he became my first patented product. After Mack, God started giving me one idea after another to patent and sell. So now, my job is basically to create what the Lord puts in my head! You can't have a better boss than God!"

"Dad has made some super cool stuff!" Chelsey bragged.

"And you, Chelsey? What do you do all day? Besides surf!" Tripp asked his sister.

"I finished high school a year and a half early and started college right away. I had already taken all my basics in high school, so I went straight into studying marine veterinary. I love the ocean and everything in it. Well, except sharks. I don't like sharks. But I've learned to respect that the ocean is their domain, and to them, I'm the intruder."

Chelsey raised the side of her shirt and the leg of her shorts to reveal her worst scars.

Lexi gasped, and Tripp turned his head away.

Axl shakes his head and says, "That's awful."

"I'll tell you about it sometime," she said, smiling.

"I almost had a shark encounter once, too, remember?" Tripp asked his parents.

"Oh, yeah, we remember," Micah answered. "A very close call! You have your brother to thank for knowing what to do when the shark got close enough."

"What did he do?" Chelsey asked.

"He waited until just the right moment, then jabbed his paddle into the shark's gills. It swam away after that. Austin was one fearless little boy! He was always looking out for you two."

Gracie's eyes welled up with heavy, warm tears at the memory of Austin's sweet little face.

Chelsey crawled over to her mother and hugged her.

"We'll find him. Promise," Chelsey said.

Gracie wiped tears from her face and asked, "Who's next?"

Tripp said, "Lexi, I think your job speaks for itself!"

Everyone laughed.

"Overachiever, much?" he added.

"Ha-ha," she said. "It's not like I stood in a long line with my resume and applied, wise guy."

She pushed Tripp playfully.

Axl chuckles.

"I was appointed as Vinga by God, apparently at birth. I found out about it on my thirteenth birthday. SURPRISE!" she said, throwing her arms in the air.

Everyone laughed at her expression.

"It's still so hard for me to wrap my head around!" Micah said, shaking his head. "My baby girl is a *queen*! And of a whole other *planet*! How many dads get *those* bragging rights?"

"Yeah, most dads just get to say, "My daughter's a nurse! Or my daughter is the best lawyer in town!" Chelsey said, attempting a dad's voice.

"Or my daughter's a pro surfer!" Tripp jumped in and winked at his sister.

Micah smiled big and cheesy with pride for both of his girls.

"Oh, stop it! It's not a big deal," Lexi said jokingly.

We all laughed.

"Yeah, she's only a *queen*! Piece of cake! Anyone can do *that* job!" I said, rolling my eyes.

Lexi winked at me. I like that. *A LOT!*

Axl says he's jelly.

Micah piped in, "I also get to say my younger daughter is a marine veterinarian who saves the lives of precious ocean inhabitants! And my son is a medical scientist who is going to cure humans of deadly diseases! And my older son does something very important, too! I'm so proud of all you kids!" he said, reaching out to touch each of them.

"Arëk, what about you, dude?" Tripp asked me last.

"Mafia boss," I answered matter of factly.

Chelsey, Micah, and Gracie whipped their heads around to look at me.

"Ever heard of the Godfather? Yeah, I'm kind of like that. I'm also Chelsey's bodyguard. I shoot bad guys and stuff," I finished.

Chelsey and her parents stared at me blankly.

Axl sits, waiting for the punch line.

"What?" I asked seriously.

Tripp and Lexi sat quietly, waiting for someone to say something.

"You're an idiot!" Chelsey said, laughing, and everyone joined in. "But you're *my* idiot! I love you, Arëk!"

Chelsey hugged me from the side, and Gracie threw her flip-flop at me.

"He makes me laugh for a living. That's what he does!" Chelsey said.

"The pay is terrible, though!" I said, dodging another shoe.

Everyone laughed.

Axl laughs.

By then the sun was beginning to set on Tumah. Lexi invited her family to go inside.

"I think I might grab the snack you mentioned earlier, sis, if the kitchen's still open for business," Tripp said.

"I'm kind of snacky, too," Chelsey agreed.

"There are three main kitchens, four grand dining rooms, five outdoor cafés of different cultures, and four breakfast nooks," Lexi responded. "I'll bet we can find something to eat around here."

Everyone looked at each other with wowed expressions.

"Who's up for French? Francois is an excellent chef!" Lexi said.

"You have a French café in your house?" Gracie asked her daughter with raised eyebrows.

"Ooo, la-la!" Chelsey said.

"I'm all about trying something new," Tripp commented.

"Then let's try French!" Micah said.

Lexi led her family through the enormous castle. We walked up a spiral staircase, just as large as the one we'd climbed earlier. It took us up to a middle level, enormous enough to be its own castle.

There were gardens, trees, and a gorgeous grand room without a ceiling where an orchestra played. Two beautiful Grand pianos, one black and one white, posed elegantly in the center of the room. They were surrounded by strings of every kind.

Finally, we walked into a section of the middle level which seemed set apart from the rest. The rooms were still huge but smaller and quainter than most of the other rooms we had seen so far.

"This is one of my favorite cafes in the castle," Lexi said as two men opened the tall doors.

It looked and sounded just like a cozy small café you'd see in France. It housed twenty small round tables, accompanied by four chairs each. A single flower in a simple vase graced the center of each table along with pristine glassware and silverware.

The band in the corner played softly as the host greeted us in perfect French. He escorted us to our tables and then announced the chef's special menu for the evening. Moments later a waiter came to welcome us and ask for our drink orders.

Chelsey and I both knew Gracie was going to love this café. She had been taking a French course off and on for about six months. She loved the language but didn't have anyone to carry on conversations with until now! She was bursting to use her new skills.

"Je voudrais un thé non sucré avec du citron vert, s'il vous plaît," Gracie uttered with a perfect French dialect.

Micah looked at his wife with surprise, as did Chelsey and me.

Lexi said, "Very impressive! Où avez-vous appris Français?"

"En ligne dans mon temps libre," Gracie responded.

"Interpretation, please?" Micah asked.

"I ordered an unsweet tea with lime. Then Lexi asked me where I learned French, and I told her I learned it online in my spare time," Gracie answered.

"Wow, Mom, impressive!" Chelsey bragged.

"It sure was!" Tripp added.

"Yeah, I think I could get used to hearing you speak French!" Micah said wiggling his eyebrows.

"Thanks, guys. I think Italian will be next," Gracie said.

Micah kissed his wife's hand.

While we ate amazing food, we talked, told stories, laughed, and caught up on each other's lives. It was a wonderful family reunion! I had never seen my bestie so happy before.

"Well, I hate to be a party pooper, but this has been an exciting and exhausting day! I think I'm ready to turn in and get some sleep," Gracie said.

"Me, too," Micah agreed then the rest of us followed suit.

"I think I'll have Tripp stay in the room next to you guys, so you'll be close enough to visit," Lexi said.

"Sounds good to us," the parents said, and Tripp agreed.

"I think you should offer Tripp the *special* room you had planned for me," I said sarcastically.

"Oh, no, Arëk, that room is only for our chewy guests," Lexi said with a big smile.

"You're a mean woman, Lexi Wick," I said jovially.

Everyone but Tripp laughed.

He looked curiously at Chelsey, who was walking arm in arm with him.

She said, "Lexi was going to put Arëk in the janitor's closet."

Tripp laughed along with everyone this time.

"She also offered him the dungeon, but Henry the dragon doesn't like gristle. So, Arëk didn't qualify," Micah said laughing.

"You people are *horrible*!" I shouted.

Everyone laughed at my expense. Then Lexi apologized and kissed my cheek. I decided she can be mean to me every second of the day if that's the apology I'll get. Hot, dude, she's so smoking hot.

Axl laughs and shakes his head.

Lexi led us on a different route to the section of the castle where the parents were staying. Being the owner of the joint, she knew every secret passageway and shortcut. When Lexi showed Tripp his quarters next to Gracie and Micah, he was just as blown away as we'd been.

"What in the world?" Tripp said as his eyes wandered all over the outrageous room.

"I know, right?" I replied.

"This is incredible!" he added.

"I'll send someone to wake everyone up in the morning so we can meet together for breakfast," Lexi said. "Sound good?"

"It sounds great!" we all agreed.

"There is so much I want to show you all!" Lexi said with excitement.

"We're excited, too!" Micah said.

"Ok, hugs, everybody. We'll see you in the morning," Lexi said.

Love and hugs were exchanged all around.

Lexi, Chelsey, and I headed to our rooms. Gracie and Micah stayed behind in Tripp's room to visit for a few more minutes.

"Can you believe this place, son?" Micah asked Tripp.

"No, I absolutely *cannot*!" he responded, looking at the open ceiling.

"I'm so happy you're here, sugar!" Gracie said and hugged her son for the hundredth time since he arrived.

"Me, too, Mom. This is the best day of my life! God is so good!" he said.

"I'll say a big amen to that!" Micah interjected and joined in for a group hug.

The parents left Tripp to get settled in. Once the girls and I arrived at our section of the castle, I hugged them goodnight. We went to our separate rooms for a restful night under the stars.

45

The Stranger Wakes Up On Oahu

After a big yawn and a hard stretch, the stranger woke to the smell of rain. He hadn't smelled rain since he was a little kid. It was warm and welcoming, just like the ocean had been the previous day. He sat up on the bed and thanked God for blessing him with another day.

"This is going to be a great day!" he said out loud.

He took a shower and brushed his teeth. He wondered if Gracie and her husband would take their morning walk in the rain or if they'd wait until the sun came out. He hoped the rain would stop, ensuring the couple would be out and about as usual.

He sat on the porch for about half an hour, then the rain stopped. He walked to a nearby coffee shop to kick-start his morning. With coffee in hand, he began his walk down the street where Meleah said Gracie and her husband might be taking their morning stroll.

He took his time looking for the couple, but he didn't see them. He wondered again if maybe the rain had kept them inside. He continued to walk up and down the street for about an hour and a half, with no results. The stranger was becoming a little discouraged, but he was determined to meet this famous author.

He walked further down the street into the neighborhood Meleah indicated the Wick's house was located. Sure enough, he found the enormous structure. She wasn't kidding when she said it would be impossible to miss!

"Wow," the stranger thought, "Nice house!"

He stayed in the area long enough for a couple of the neighbors to become suspicious.

A man who lived down the hill from Gracie and her family drove his golf cart up to the stranger and asked, "Can I help you, mister? I've seen you hanging out over here for quite a while."

"I'm hoping to run into the author who lives in that house. I've traveled a long way to meet her. I was told she and her husband take a morning walk every day, so I was hoping to see them out."

"Well, you're making the neighbors a little edgy, hanging out like this. The Wicks have had some crazies up here stalking them before," the man said.

"Oh, wow, I'm so sorry! It's nothing like that, I promise. I just need to talk to Gracie Wick. I don't mean to upset anyone."

"I'm sure it's true but hanging around their house and making the neighbors nervous isn't going to help your cause. Why don't you go get some breakfast and give them some time to come out of their house? The beach is usually a good place to find them. They're friendly folks. I'm sure Gracie will talk to you," the neighborhood man said.

"Thank you, and I'm sorry again for freaking anyone out."

He began to walk back in the direction he came from and reminded himself he needed to be patient. God was helping him. This was going to be successful.

He took the man up on his breakfast suggestion. He stopped at a diner he'd seen the day before. While he enjoyed scrambled eggs, crispy bacon, and toast, he sat at the table and made a mental plan for the day. First, he would rent a bicycle or a car so he could get around more efficiently. Then he would visit the fresh market he had found the day before to buy some fruit and veggies. Afterward, he would find a grocery store and get some staples like peanut butter, bottled water, and milk. He noticed a grill outside the condo, so he decided to buy some chicken to cook, Hawaiian style.

After breakfast and grocery shopping, the stranger glanced at his watch. It had been a little over four hours since he started his search for Gracie Wick. He wondered if she had ventured over to the ocean yet. He found it a little frustrating having to search for her blindly, but he was willing to do whatever it took to find her.

46

Wakey, Wakey!

Knock, knock!

The sound was heard on each of the four doors at the same time of the morning.

"It's time to wake up, everyone! Breakfast will be served in one hour," the voice of a staff member announced.

We all stretched and yawned as we opened our eyes to another wonderful day.

"Good morning, babe," Micah said to his wife as they both climbed out of bed.

"Good morning, love," she responded, "how'd you sleep?"

"Better than I have in my whole life, I think. I'm digging this whole no ceiling thing! If the inside of the house back home wouldn't be instantly covered in geckos and rain, I'd suggest we install a retractable ceiling."

Gracie laughed and said, "Cool idea, but you're right, the critters would take over the house!"

Tripp slowly crawled out of his oversized comfortable bed and ventured to the bathroom.

"Good morning, Lord! What do you have in store for us today?" he asked God through a big yawn.

"Oof! Morning breath! Got to brush my teeth before I talk to the Lord in the morning! Where'd you put the toothpaste? Oh, there it is!" Tripp said to himself.

Axl comments on how he's glad he's not the only one who carries on full conversations with himself in the mornings.

"Ahhh! Much better!" Tripp told his reflection in the mirror after brushing his gnarly grill.

He turned on the rain shower to wash off his good night's sleep. He was pleasantly surprised to find it smelled and sounded like rain!

"Are you kidding me? It's so good to be the brother of the queen!" he said out loud.

I woke up to my bestie pouncing on me after busting in like a wild animal through the big doors of my room.

"Wake up, Arëk! It's a beautiful day! Look!" she said pointing up to the sky.

The stars were still out, and the sun had just started to rise. What a view, brah!

"Wow! The stars are even bigger and brighter than on Oahu. How is it possible?" I asked.

"I don't know but I love it! Lexi and I fell asleep talking last night. I still can't believe Mom found her! I thought for sure it would be us, didn't you?"

"I think we thought so because we found Tripp. Also, your parents weren't Universe travelers until recently, so we thought it had to be us," I answered.

"Yeah, you're right. I'm glad Mom found her, though. It was really special. We found Tripp, Mom found Lexi, I wonder who will find Austin," Chelsey said as she plopped next to me on the bed.

"I don't know but it'll happen. It all seems to be falling into place!"

"You're right! I can't wait to see how it happens!" she said then jumped off the bed. "Come on, get ready! I'm going back to Lexi's room. I'll see you in an hour!"

After an hour, everyone filed out of their rooms. The parents and Tripp joined together at the top of the grand staircase. It took a little wandering for them to recall the location of Lexi's room, but they finally started recognizing a few landmarks. Luckily, we found them before they got lost.

Hugs and good mornings were exchanged. Then Lexi escorted us to a breakfast nook, a.k.a. beautiful balcony facing amazing scenery, on the upper level of the castle. She thought it might be nice to eat breakfast in the light of the sunrise.

Just like the French café the night before, this outdoor balcony had its own waiters and kitchen staff to treat us like royalty. Our menu was basically anything we wanted. Plus, there was fruit of every kind on the table and freshly squeezed juices. The food we ate set such a high standard it made me never want to eat at a chain restaurant again. So good, dude.

Axl says, "Yum!"

We talked and caught up some more over breakfast. Chelsey's family is comedy central, dude! There was a lifetime of stories to hear and tell. Some were funny, and some brought tears. All were good, except for the story of their separation.

"So, what's on the agenda today, sweetheart?" Micah asked.

"Well, I'd like you to see some other parts of the castle at some point. But for sure I want you all to meet Pime and Vanise."

"Who are Pime and Vanise?" Chelsey asked.

"My bestie and her mother, the woman who raised me."

Gracie interrupted Lexi to tell Micah, "Mandy and I didn't have time to tell you guys the whole story when we got back to Zooch yesterday. There's a whole lot to hear."

"I'd also like to show you around Ci, the capital city of our beautiful planet," Lexi added.

"Awesome! Does everyone bow when they see you?" Tripp asked.

She shook her head and laughed.

"Not by decree. Many of my citizens do bow their heads out of respect when they see me, but I've never required it of them. We're all one people."

"Very cool," he responded.

"So, are you guys ready to go?" she asked with excitement.

"Yeah! Let's do it!" Gracie said.

Lexi led us all the way back down to the castle entrance, where four carriages were waiting for us.

"Whoa, what's all this, sis?" Tripp asked.

"This is our ride!"

"I could get used to this!" he replied.

"That's what we said!" coming from Chelsey and me.

We boarded the carriages and Lexi took us into the village. Our first stop was at Pime's and Vanise's house. As soon as Pime heard the carriages, she came running out of the house.

"Bestie!" she said with arms stretched out wide.

"Bestie!" Lexi answered with the same gesture, clearly their signature greeting.

They hugged and Lexi said, "I want you to meet some of my family, the ones I've told you about all these years. This is my mom, Gracie. My dad, Micah. My brother, Tripp. My little sister, Chelsey. And her bestie, Arëk."

"What a pleasure it is to finally meet you all! I've heard about you for so long! Wait, isn't there another brother?" she asked.

"Yes, Austin. We haven't found him yet. Soon, though, right, Mom?" Lexi encouraged.

"Right! And Pime, it is a pleasure to meet you, as well! You are so cute!" Gracie said.

Everyone either hugged Pime or shook her hand as we were introduced.

"Where's Vanise?" Lexi asked her friend.

"She's at the market."

"Well, get in, Pime! We'll go find her!" Lexi said.

The carriages took us further into the village to where the fresh market was located.

"There she is!" Pime said pointing.

"Vanise!" Lexi shouted.

Vanise waved, paid the man for her fruit and veggies, and then walked over to her Vinga.

"Hello, Isun!" she said, bowing her head.

Lexi got down from the carriage and met Vanise with a hug.

"I want you to meet some of my family. They're finally here!"

"Yes, I heard! They're the talk of the whole capital!" she said.

"Vanise, as a favor, would you mind appearing human for my family?" Lexi asked her quietly.

"As you wish, Vinga," Vanise answered, bowing her head.

Suddenly, the beautiful Tumahn woman became a beautiful human woman.

As soon as Gracie and Micah saw her, they recognized her from the day at the beach so long ago.

Micah said to his wife, "Isn't she the lady who…"

Gracie finished, "helped save Lexi's life? Yes, it's her."

"How is it possible?" Micah asked with confusion.

"It was all just part of God's plan. It was her daughter, Pime, who rescued Lexi from the plane crash and brought her here. Lexi's been with them ever since," Gracie answered as she watched Lexi interact with Vanise.

"I am so confused," he said.

"She'll explain everything to you like she did to me yesterday. Then you'll understand better."

"Vanise, this is my mother, Gracie. And my dad, Micah," Lexi said proudly.

"It is an honor to meet you, *again*," she said with a curtsy and a bow of her head.

"Yes, we remember you from the beach. Lexi told me the story yesterday. It's a pleasure to meet you again, Vanise," Gracie said, taking the woman's hand.

Micah added, "That was quite a day. And so is this one! My head is spinning, seeing you here. I'm hoping for an explanation to make sense of it somehow."

"I understand, and I'm sure Isun will explain everything in a way which will bring you comfort," she replied in her soothing voice.

"Vanise, this is my sister, Chelsey, and my brother, Tripp," Lexi said.

"You have a beautiful family, Isun. I am overjoyed for you all. See, I told you God would reunite you with them. Patience, my love, always patience," Vanise said.

She placed her hands on her Vinga's arms then kissed both of her cheeks.

"Am I invisible? I mean, really?" I said jokingly, throwing my hands up in the air.

Axl laughs and tells me I'm ridiculous.

"I was saving the best for last, Arëk!" Lexi said, reaching over to grab my hand.

I decided she could save me for last every time if it meant getting to hold her hand. Seriously, dude, my crush on her is insane! She makes me stupid.

Axl laughs again.

"Vanise, this incredibly amazing, legendary, handsome Schmecum is Chelsey's BFF, Arëk. He's her Pime!" Lexi said bumping her bestie's shoulder.

My love for her inflated with every word, brah.

"It is certainly a pleasure, Arëk," Vanise said as she curtsied in front of me, clearly overdoing it since I was last.

I didn't mind.

"Likewise," I responded with a dramatic bow and a kiss on her hand.

"Oh, give me a break!" Chelsey said rolling her eyes.

Everyone laughed.

"Well, I must get these beautiful veggies and fruit home," Vanise said to the group. "Enjoy your stay in our beautiful capital! Pime, will you please assist your mother?"

"With pleasure," she answered her mother with a smile.

"Later, bestie!" Pime said as she hugged Lexi.

"See ya, bestie!" and she returned the hug.

We all waved goodbye.

47

Discouraged Stranger

Another hour passed and it was now around two in the afternoon. The stranger rode his rented bicycle back up Gracie's street, hoping to see some movement. To his disappointment, it was the same as before, still and quiet.

He took a deep breath and prayed, "God, I feel like I'm supposed to be here. I feel like You led me to this island and to this writer. I know You have a purpose in it and I am doing my best not to get discouraged. Please help me."

The stranger turned around and rode toward the ocean. Once he arrived, he kicked off his flip-flops and walked into the water. The sun shone brightly, warming his wet skin. He swam and turned flips in the water. He caught himself smiling at the pure pleasure of it. He felt totally carefree in the clear water.

Then from a distance, he heard, "Hey, smoothie! You still up for a surfing lesson?"

He shaded his eyes with his hand and saw the tattooed guy from the smoothie shack standing on the shore with a surfboard. He swam back to the beach to greet the man.

"Hey, dude, how's it going?" the stranger asked, happy the man remembered him.

"It's all good, brah! All good! So, were you serious about surfing lessons? The waves are perfect today!" Makaio said.

"Yeah! I'm in!" He replied with enthusiasm.

"Cool, man, let's get you a board. I've got another one behind the smoothie shack," Makaio said.

They retrieved the board and headed out into the water. Makaio coached the stranger on how to paddle out into the rolling waves, and then how to stand up and balance. After the stranger watched his new friend a couple of times, he was ready to try it.

When the perfect wave came rolling in, Makaio said, "That's the one, brah! Take it!"

The stranger paddled out, and then let the wave carry him. He stood up with perfect balance and rode the wave all the way in. Makaio clapped his hands, cheering him on from his board a little way off.

"You were awesome, brah! Are you sure you haven't surfed before?"

"It was crazy! I totally surfed! It's like my brain and my body already knew what to do! It was awesome, dude!" the stranger said excitedly.

"Ok, so you're a natural. Let's get back out there. Let me know when you want to tackle some *real* waves!" he said jousting.

"I'm ready! Let's do it!" the stranger said with excitement.

"Ok, if you're sure."

The two new friends paddled out into deeper water where the bigger waves were rolling and crashing. The stranger wasn't the least bit intimidated.

Makaio and the stranger stood up on their boards at the same time, riding the daunting wave toward the shore.

"Woo-hoo!" the stranger shouted with his fists high in the air.

"You're no pro but you're not a beginner, either! Where do you surf, brah?"

"I swear, I don't! We don't even have oceans where I live," he replied.

"Well, you can borrow my board anytime! You up for another smoothie, brah?"

"Oh, yeah!" he answered.

The two friends hung out, surfed, and drank smoothies all afternoon. The stranger was having the time of his life. And Makaio was happy to have a new friend.

Later, the stranger asked his new Hawaiian friend, "Hey, do you know the famous writer who lives in the big house on the hill?"

"Gracie?" he answered. "Yeah, of course, everyone does, why?"

"Have you seen her today?" the man asked.

"You know, come to think of it, I haven't. It's pretty unusual, too. She and her daughter are normally out on the water long before now," he said looking around. "You'd know if they were out here. That girl of hers has everyone's attention when she's on her board. We've all tried to talk her into competing for pro, but she won't do it."

"Why, is she afraid of sharks or something?" the stranger asked, knowing it was a stupid question.

"Naw, brah, the sharks are afraid of *her*!" he said laughing. "She was attacked by a shark when she was a little girl. It took a bite out of her board and ripped up her thigh and her side. She has some killer scars to show for it. But the shark attack didn't scare her off. She got right back in the water as soon as she was healed. She *belongs* in the water, brah," Makaio said with admiration.

"Whoa! That's crazy!" the stranger said picturing the scenario in his mind. "So, I wonder where they are today?"

"Why, dude, you want a book signed or something?"

"Maybe, but it's not why I'm looking for her. I just need to talk to her. I have some questions I think she can answer."

"Well, if they're on the island, you'll see them," Makaio said.

Then he noticed the location of the sun and said, "Oh, no, man, I think I'm late for my shift at the smoothie shack! I still need to buy fresh fruit and veggies for the smoothies. Catch you later, brah?"

"Yeah, for sure! Maybe I'll drop by for another smoothie."

"Cool, man, I'll catch you later," Makaio said and gave shaka.

The stranger rode his bike back toward Gracie Wick's house.

48

God's Blessing On Lexi

One of the stops on our "kingdom tour" was the Wuvet River, where all the beautiful stones exist. As she did with her mother the previous day, Lexi made two beautiful keepsakes for Chelsey. The first was a ring, which she duplicated so they could wear matching ones. The other was a bracelet for Chelsey's right ankle. They'd be worth millions on Earth, no doubt.

"What an exciting day this has been! I'm so proud of you, Lexi. You are the epitome of a godly leader," Gracie said, bragging on her daughter after she'd introduced us to her kingdom.

"Thank you, Mom. It's easy when everything you do is for the Lord. I love being the Vinga here. I love these people.

"So, there's something important I want to tell you guys. I was going to wait until we got back to the castle this afternoon, but I don't think I can hold it in one more second. I'm about to burst!" Lexi said, clasping her hands together.

"What is it, baby," her dad asked.

"Last night, after Chelsey and I went to bed, I had a very sincere conversation with God. I asked Him to honor my obedience and give me the one thing I've asked of Him the whole time I've been on Tumah."

Every one of us listened intently.

"I asked God to allow me to go back with you to Hawaii. Until this morning, the answer has always been, 'Be patient, my child.' When I woke up, I went onto my balcony to watch the sunrise. I stood in the fresh morning air and closed my eyes. Before I even had the chance to tell God good morning, I heard Him speak to my spirit.

"He said, 'My precious and honorable daughter, I grant you this day what you have asked for so long. You have honored and served Me with your whole heart. You may go and be with your family for short periods of time. But you must always return to serve the people I have placed in your care.'"

"I almost fell off the balcony when I heard it!" Lexi said, with tears in her eyes.

Axl says, "Whoa, that's awesome!"

"Sooo?" Gracie encouraged.

"So, I want to go to Hawaii. Today. ASAP!" she said begging.

"Oh, my gosh! Let's go!" Gracie said with excitement.

Brah, I was *stoked* that Lexi was coming home with us to Hawaii.

Axl shakes his head at me.

Lexi bounced up and down and said, "Let's get back to the castle to pack!"

We decided to skip the scenic route this time and just transport. The carriages wouldn't be able to float to the castle fast enough! When we arrived, we laughed and ran up the stairs to our respective rooms.

Everyone packed as quickly as we could. We all met in one of the grand rooms.

Lexi said, "We'll transport from here! All together on one, two…"

352

49

Determination

The stranger arrived on the street below the humongous house. He took a deep breath and started up the long, palm tree-lined driveway.

"No more waiting," he thought.

It seemed like the longest walk of his life. He trekked until he reached the large steps in front of the tall wooden double doors.

"Ok, God, here goes," he said out loud.

Ding dong.

He waited.

Ding dong, ding dong.

He waited. No answer at the door.

Knock, knock, knock, knock.

He waited. He took a deep breath and knocked again. No answer. The stranger sat on the top step in front of the doors.

His mind was set to wait as long as it took for someone to open the door. He would be a fixture on the porch until he got the answers he came for.

50

Home

"…three!"

Seconds later, our whole group was standing in Chelsey's living room. Home sweet home. Lexi looked around at her family's beautiful home and smiled.

Her eyes filled with tears as she said, "I can't believe I'm finally here. It's been so long."

Her mother embraced her, then kissed her on the forehead.

"Arëk, will you please take Tripp to the guest room next to yours? Show him around a little bit. Then will you please make sure Booger, Poot, and Charlie have plenty of food and water? Lexi, Chelsey can show you to your room right next to hers," Gracie said.

"Booger, Poot, and Charlie?" Lexi quizzed her mother.

Axl laughs, as usual, at Poot's name. Dude.

"Chelsey's dogs and monkey," Gracie answered.

"Monkey?" she asked.

Gracie nodded yes.

"I should go grab Friday from the Raan's house! She should be a part of our family reunion, too!" Micah told Gracie.

"I love the idea! Come back quickly," she said.

Gracie kissed her husband.

"Who's Friday?" Chelsey asked.

"Just a little gift we picked up for you on Zooch."

Chelsey's eyes lit up with excitement.

About twenty minutes after we got Lexi and Tripp settled in, we all met back in the living room.

Micah arrived with Friday only minutes before.

"Chelsey, meet Friday!" her dad said.

Friday ran and jumped into Chelsey's arms, licking her face as if it had been ages since she'd seen her.

"I *love* her!" Chelsey shouted.

Micah brought cold iced tea from the kitchen while everyone played with the new dog.

"Oh, thank you, babe!" Gracie said as Micah passed out glasses.

"The service here isn't *nearly* as good as at the castle!" I said, expecting a shoe.

"Oh, yeah?" Micah said with attitude.

He pretended like he was going to pour tea on me.

I jumped, and he said, "Mouthy kid!"

We all laughed.

Axl laughs.

"And thank you, sir," from Chelsey, Lexi, and Tripp, as they were handed their tea.

"I was thinking that we might put on our swimsuits and head out to the water in a little while," Gracie said, looking around at each one of us.

"You know *I'll* never say no to the water!" Chelsey said immediately.

She stripped off her tank top and shorts to reveal the bikini swimsuit underneath. My bestie is always prepared for surfing.

"Great idea, honey!" Micah replied.

"Kids? Water sound good?" Gracie asked Lexi and Tripp.

"Are you kidding? I've only been begging God for it most of my life! You better believe it sounds good! You in, brother?" Lexi asked.

"Heck yeah! I'm ready!"

"Awesome! Whenever you guys are ready to get changed, we'll go! Chelsey has drawers full of bikinis, Lexi. You can borrow one unless you brought your own," Gracie said.

Then a sound interrupted the excitement.

Ding dong, ding dong.

Everyone looked at each other, and then Micah said, "I'll get it! Y'all go get changed."

He walked through the house to the front door. When he opened it, a stranger was standing in front of him.

"Aloha!" he said, "What can I do for you?"

"Hi, is Gracie Wick here?" he asked.

"Uh, yeah! Hang on a sec," he replied and yelled, "Gracie, it's for you!"

Gracie excused herself from her children and walked toward the door.

She mouthed, "Who is it?" to Micah as she got closer.

Her husband shrugged his shoulders and mouthed, "I don't know, it's some guy with sunglasses and a backpack. Probably wants a book signed or something."

"Ok, thank you, babe."

Gracie approached the doorway to find the tall stranger standing there.

"Aloha!" she said.

The moment the stranger heard the voice of the author he had so desperately searched for, everything became crystal clear. He suddenly knew why he was in Haleiwa. He knew why he knew the ocean and why it knew him. He knew why the face on the back of the book he was given as a gift a month prior was so familiar. And he knew why God had pushed his faith not to give up until he found her. His eyes filled with tears and his chin quivered as he looked down at Gracie.

Her immediate instinct was to step out onto the porch and hug the stranger. She didn't know why but she knew he needed it. As soon as he wrapped his arms around her, he began to weep.

Then something happened inside her.

God spoke to her spirit, saying, "My third gift to you, my daughter."

Her eyes opened wide and began filling with tears. She quietly spoke the first word between them since she greeted him.

"Austin?" she whispered.

Axl says he knew it!

He sank to his knees, sobbing harder. He embraced her tighter at the sound of her voice saying his name.

"You've come home to me," she said in between gasping sobs.

As she knelt in front of him, she whispered, "Thank you, Jesus! Thank you so much for bringing my children home to me!"

She couldn't express enough gratitude.

Axl is wiping tears away. I'm right there with him.

Gracie pulled back from his embrace. She removed his sunglasses and cupped her crying son's face in her hands. He looked at his mother, who he hadn't seen since he was ten years old.

"Mom," he finally spoke as streams of tears flowed down his cheeks.

She had waited so many years to hear that word come from the lips of her lost son. She smiled at him with fresh tears falling from her eyes.

"I missed you, Austin. You can't imagine how much," she said to the handsome face looking at her.

Tears flowed from both.

And Axl. And me.

"I didn't know. I lost my memory when the plane crashed. I didn't get it back until I heard your voice. I didn't know, Mom, I promise I didn't know," his pleas were stopped by raw emotion.

"It's ok, son. You're here now," Gracie said hugging her son tightly against her.

They had been on the porch for about fifteen minutes before Chelsey realized her mother hadn't come back inside.

She asked Micah, "Is Mom still out there talking to that guy?"

He replied, "I don't know. Maybe I should go check."

"Did he say who he was or what he wanted?" Chelsey asked.

"No, he didn't."

Micah, Chelsey, and I headed toward the front of the house. Lexi and Tripp followed right behind us. We wanted to know who the stranger was. When Micah opened the door, he saw Gracie and the man on their knees holding each other.

"Uh, honey, what's going on?" he asked.

"My boy came home," she quietly answered without looking at us.

"What did she say?" I asked.

"Mom? What's going on? Are you ok?" Chelsey asked.

She and Lexi walked around the two hugging bodies so they could see their mother's face.

"Austin," Gracie answered.

"Say again?" Chelsey asked, thinking she heard her mother say "Austin."

Gracie nodded her head and smiled.

Chelsey covered her mouth as her eyes immediately filled with tears. She fell to her knees and hugged her long-lost brother from behind.

Lexi couldn't even speak when she realized who it was. She just began to sob as she joined in the embrace.

"Will someone please tell me what's going on?" Micah asked.

Gracie looked up at her husband and son, who were wondering what was happening.

"Come here, Tripp," Gracie said holding out her hand.

He walked over to the hugging foursome.

His mom said, "Look who's here."

Tripp knelt to look at the face of the person who was on his knees, wrapped around Gracie. With Austin's face buried in Gracie's shoulder, all Tripp could see were tear-filled hazel eyes. It only took him a few seconds to recognize who they belonged to.

Tripp gasped and said, "It's *you!*"

He immediately joined in the hug while heavy tears filled his eyes.

"Dad! Look!" Tripp urged.

Micah walked closer to the stranger who was now covered in bodies and arms. He knelt to try to get a glimpse at the man's face. When he saw his eyes, he immediately knew.

Micah lifted his arms to the heavens and shouted, "Thank you, God, thank you!"

Gracie said, "Ok, let's give him some air. Let's get you up, honey."

They all stood up and offered helping hands.

Immediately, Micah grabbed his eldest son and hugged him. Father and son clung to each other like they were afraid to let go.

"Sweetie," Gracie said, making sure I was immediately included this time, "you finally get to meet Chelsey's brother, Austin."

"What? Oh, my gosh, I can't believe it! *All* of them? They're all here!" I said, finally understanding what the fuss was about.

I walked around the hugging duo to see Austin's face for the first time. Little did anyone know something strange was about to happen.

"Hoops?" I questioned with surprise when I saw the face of the man attached to Micah.

Axl says, "WHAT?!"

My eyes were clearly deceiving me. I closed them and shook my head to clear out the muck. I reopened them expecting to see a totally different face than the one I *thought* I had just seen. But again, it was the familiar face of someone I knew. I felt like I was in the Twilight Zone, dude! I looked around at everyone else to see if I was the only one experiencing a hallucination or if it was a group thing. Lexi, Tripp, and Chelsey were hugging their mother with joy over their long-lost family member coming home. Micah was hugging his son. And then there was psycho me, looking and feeling like I had officially lost my mind. I took another look at the closed-eyed man embracing Chelsey's dad.

"No way!" I thought.

It was still him. Was it possible this guy was freakishly identical to my Rondoan friend? After all, everyone has a twin somewhere, right? That could explain it. That *had to* explain it. Austin and Hoops were universal twins, that's it. I felt satisfied with my conclusion until I saw proof which removed coincidence from the equation. How is it possible that Austin and Hoops, two totally different dudes from two totally different planets in the Universe, could have the same tattoo of a Rondoan symbol meaning "breathe easily" on their right shoulder? It's him! AUSTIN IS *HOOPS*! HOOPS IS *AUSTIN*!

Axl says, "No way!"

"Hoops?" I finally said out loud to see if he would open his eyes to the sound of the name.

He opened his eyes, clearly not expecting to hear his nickname.

"Arëk?" he responded with confusion at the sight of me.

"You're Chelsey's brother?" I asked.

"Uhh, no," he answered with a look which said, "that's a stupid question."

"Yes, you are," I corrected him.

"No, I'm not," he argued.

Axl laughs.

I turned and pointed toward the group huddled together next to us.

He let go of Micah when he recognized Chelsey from the side.

"What's happening?" he asked with confusion.

He touched Chelsey's arm to get her attention.

She was surprised to see him standing there.

"Hoops? What are you doing here, buddy?"

She hugged him around his waist from the side.

"I'm Austin," he answered.

At first, her light bulb didn't turn on. She was just happy to see her friend. Then about five seconds later, her smile turned into an open mouth and her eyes widened. She looked up at the face she knew as her friend from Rondo.

She squeaked, "What did you just say?"

He turned her around by her shoulders to squarely face him.

He answered, "I'm Austin."

Chelsey looked at her parents and then at her siblings, none of whom knew what was happening. Then she looked at me. I held my arms out and slowly nodded my head up and down to confirm the question in her mind.

"Austin is Hoops," I finally said.

She looked at him again, this time deep into his eyes.

"You're my brother?" she asked as her green eyes dropped big heavy tears.

"I don't think so," he said, then looked back at me for another argument.

Axl laughs again.

"Maybe?" he said wondering if it could be true. Then conceded, "Apparently so," and pulled her close to him.

She began to sob loudly as his tears dripped off his face onto her hair.

"Can anyone tell me what's happening?" Tripp asked, looking at Lexi and his parents.

"I want to know the same thing," Micah said.

"Austin is our friend, Hoops, from Rondo. You've heard Chelsey and I talk about him a hundred times!" I said, addressing Gracie and Micah.

"Hoops?" Tripp questioned, only knowing of "Hoops" the famous sportscaster.

"Yes, Hoops. I'm sure you've heard of him, Tripp. He's the Universe's favorite sportscaster from Rondo!"

"No way!" Tripp responded.

He walked around Chelsey to get a better look at Austin's face. His shocked expression needed no explanation.

He looked back at the rest of his family and shouted, "Austin is Hoops!"

"Why do I feel stupid right now," Lexi asked her parents.

"Don't feel like the lone ranger, kiddo, we're just as lost as you are!" Micah said.

"Ok, you kids need to fill the rest of us in. What's going on?" Gracie asked.

Austin, Tripp, Chelsey, and I all started talking at the same time with individual versions of who Hoops is. Chelsey and I mentioned how we met him. Tripp went on about him being a famous sportscaster. Chelsey and I talked over each other about how we've been friends with him for a couple of years...

"Whoa, whoa, whoa! One at a time! We can't understand any of you!" Gracie shouted.

Chelsey started, "Arëk and I met Hoops, or, I guess, Austin, a couple years ago on Schmec. He was doing a live promotion for a kids' basketball camp. We went there to get his autograph."

"Autograph?" Gracie and Micah asked at the same time.

"Yes, autograph. But the promotion was canceled at the last minute, so he was on his way off the planet for his next show. We caught him before he got too far."

"His next show?" Gracie and Micah asked at the same time again.

This time they got a chuckle out of Austin.

"Yes, Hoops, or Austin, is an awesome sportscaster on ESPNU. He lives on Rondo, the basketball planet," Chelsey continued.

"Sportscaster?" Micah asked with enthusiasm.

"The Universe favorite! He's like the darling of the sports world out there!" Tripp bragged.

"That might be a little generous," Austin responded.

"Anyway, the day we caught up with him on Schmec, we ended up scrimmaging him and his crew at a park. That's when we became friends. Since then, we've hung out a hundred times!" Chelsey said.

"Only we didn't know who he *really* was!" I added.

"The amnesia," Gracie said, remembering what Austin told her.

"Amnesia?" Lexi asked.

Austin started, "I lost my memories and any knowledge of who I was or where I was from when the plane hit the water all those years ago. I've had so many unanswered questions throughout my life. All I knew was I woke up one day all bruised up in a strange place with non-human people who took care of me.

"I became the adopted child of a couple on Roiva. I lived with Tay and Yim until they disappeared forever into a wormhole on a vacation to another planet. I was about fifteen when I lost them. They wanted me to go with them on the trip, but I begged them to let me stay behind to play in a basketball tournament on Rondo.

"The couple who lived next door went with them and only one of the four made it through the wormhole. The surviving wife told me when I got back from the tournament. I didn't say a single word. I packed my things and went back to Rondo. I lived on my own, finished school, went to university, and landed an epic career in sportscasting after busting my knees just after my NBA draft."

"NBA draft?" Micah asked with pride.

Austin smiled at his dad.

"Then one day, about a month ago, a friend of mine gave me a book as a gift for watching her house while she was out of town. I didn't recognize the name of the author nor her face on the back of the book. But immediately I felt the weirdest sensation. This will probably sound stupid, but the author's name lit up like it had a light behind it. Then I heard the loudest whisper telling me to find this author, Gracie Wick.

"I couldn't sleep. I couldn't focus on work. I couldn't concentrate on even the most mundane routines of the day. I burned all the food I cooked. I haven't cleaned my house for a month. I've been a mess!

"Finally, I asked God to help me find this Gracie Wick lady. I didn't know why I was supposed to find her or what I was supposed to say to her if I did. I just knew I was going to lose my mind if I didn't follow the Lord's leading. When I arrived on Oahu, I developed brand new weird feelings inside. Things and places were oddly familiar, although it seemed completely impossible. The ocean, surfing, the sunset, all these things knew me already. They were a part of who I am somehow," Austin said.

He inhaled deeply and exhaled. All the truths of his life were unfolding as he spoke. We listened intently as he continued.

"I found out where Gracie Wick lived and was run out of the neighborhood once for looking like a stalker," Austin said jovially.

Everyone chuckled.

"I was determined not to leave this island without answers. Then, you answered the door," he said, looking at Gracie. "The very moment I heard your voice, I knew exactly who I was, who you were, and what I was doing here. God brought me home!"

His voice quivered as he began to cry again. We all did.

"It's still so crazy to me! I've been looking for you all my life and I found you two years ago! I didn't even know it!" Chelsey said.

Austin pulled his little sister into a hug.

"I can't believe you're my sister! That's awesome! And it kind of makes sense considering our amazing basketball skills!" he said, trying to make her smile.

"I can't believe my big brother is Hoops from Rondo! I should have known you'd end up in sports somehow," Tripp said.

"Right?" Lexi agreed. "You couldn't tear his basketball away from him when we were little. I'm just sorry I haven't had any exposure to the Universal sports world since I've been on Tumah. I've never even heard of Hoops before today. Sorry, brother."

Austin laughed, "Don't worry about it, sis. It's not that big a deal."

Chelsey, Tripp, and I all shouted over each other, "Not that big a deal? Yeah right! You're only a celebrity!"

"So, let's talk more about *that*!" Micah said, patting his famous son on the back.

"How about we talk more about it inside the house," Gracie said.

We all entered the Wick residence as one big complete family. I don't remember ever having a better day than that one.

Axl says he wishes he could've been there to witness the reunion.

"We need to get you settled in, son," Gracie said, wrapping her arm around Austin's waist. "We've got lots of catching up to do! Are you hungry?"

"We should have a celebration BBQ!" Chelsey suggested.

"Your dad can cook some mean BBQ ribs," Gracie said, bragging on her hubby.

"That's right! Texas-style ribs slow-cooked on the fire. Mmmm, the meat just falls off the bone!" Micah responded.

"Oh, my goodness, ribs sound good. You're making me hungry, dude!" I said.

"We're all home together. Can you believe it?" Lexi said excitedly.

"And all in two days' time!" Micah exclaimed.

"Two days' time? What happened in two days?" Austin asked.

"There's a lot of catching up to do!" Chelsey said. "Mom just found Lexi the day before yesterday. Then you showed up today! And it hasn't been long ago since Arëk and I found Tripp!"

"Found? Where were you guys?" Austin addressed Lexi and Tripp.

"Well, I've been living on Tumah since the plane crash," Lexi answered.

"And I lived on Ustak as a kid and have been living on Smithers since I started university," Tripp said.

Austin looked around at the group and said, "Sooo..."

"All three of you kids disappeared when the plane crashed into the water. We've been searching for you guys all this time. Apparently, Chelsey and Arëk found Tripp a while back. But we hadn't seen him until yesterday when he and the kids surprised us at Lexi's place. And just two days ago, God led me and my friend, Mandy, to Tumah where we found Lexi. And now we've discovered Chelsey and Arëk found you a while back but didn't know it!" Gracie said, smiling. "This couldn't be more wonderful and more planned out by God!"

Austin expressed his surprise, "So, you guys have been gone all this time, too?"

Lexi and Tripp nodded their heads in unison.

Then he readdressed his parents, "It had to have been awful for you! Oh, Mom, Dad, I'm so sorry you had to go through such heartache!"

Austin walked over to his parents and held them both close to him.

"It was horrible. I can't tell you how much. But God was there with us the whole time and kept us intact. We had to stay sane. There was a baby on the way who needed us to be loving strong parents. Chelsey is the biggest reason your dad and I made it through after losing you kids. God works everything for good for those who love Him. Your baby sister refused to let us lose faith. She knew we would find you, your brother, and your sister again. And look at us today!" Gracie said, looking around the room at each of her family members.

"We have so much to be thankful for!" Micah told his family.

We all agreed.

Axl shakes his head and says, "Wow!"

"So, Mom, where do you want Austin to sleep? You know what would be fun? If all the bros and sis's camped out in the living room so we can talk and catch up all night!" Chelsey said.

"I'd love that!" Tripp replied.

"Me, too!" Lexi agreed.

"Yeah, I'm totally in!" Austin said.

"Well, then it's settled," Gracie answered Chelsey. "But until bedtime, let's get Austin set up in a guest room next to Tripp and Arëk. Austin, honey, do you have a bag or anything?"

"Yes, ma'am, my stuff is in a condo I'm staying in. I'll have to go get it."

"Are you staying at Meleah's place?" Micah asked.

"Yes, how'd you know?"

"She's helped so many people throughout the years. God sends them to her, we're convinced," his dad said.

"We can get his stuff after we come in from the water, can't we?" Chelsey asked her mother.

"The water?" Austin asked with bright eyes.

"Yeah, we're all about to go down to the beach," I answered.

"I just came from there! I could *live* in the ocean! And I found this awesome smoothie shack on the beach!"

"Oh, yeah! So, you probably met Makaio, the tattooed smoothie master!" Chelsey said.

"Yeah! We never told each other our names, but we hung out today and surfed!"

"Makaio's a cool dude. He's never made a less-than-perfect smoothie, *ever*!" I said.

"Agreed!" Austin said.

Axl agrees, too.

"I want a smoothie on the beach!" Lexi said.

"I want to surf!" Tripp added.

"I think the kids are ready to get in the water, what do you think, babe?" Gracie asked her husband.

"Go get changed, everyone! I'll grab the towels!" Micah shouted.

"Family time at the beach, just like old times!" Tripp shouted, as he ran through the enormous house to his room.

"Woo-hoo!" cheered Austin, who was running just behind Tripp. "Coming, Arëk?"

"Right behind you, Hoops!" I answered.

The girls rushed to the other side of the house to Chelsey's room.

"Think you'll remember how to surf, sister?" Chelsey asked Lexi.

"Well, in case I don't, will you have my back?"

"Always!" she said.

Twenty minutes later, the seven of us grabbed towels and ran out the door. Gracie's and Chelsey's Jeeps were loaded with people, animals, and boards in less than five minutes.

"Did someone grab sunscreen for the pasty kids from other planets?" Chelsey teased her siblings.

"Very funny, Banana Boat!" Tripp retorted.

Axl laughs.

"Hey! Chelsey, tell your thieving little monkey to give my sunglasses back!" Lexi shouted as she fought with Poot.

"But he looks fabulous in them!" Chelsey laughed.

"Very funny!" Lexi responded sarcastically.

"There's a bag of banana chips in the glove box. Make a trade with him. Poot would rather eat his favorite snack than wear your fancy sunglasses!"

"It's pretty crowded back here, sis!" Tripp said, trying to push Booger off his lap.

"Mom! Dad! Booger needs to ride with you! There's not enough room for his big ole butt over here!" Chelsey yelled.

"Come on, Boogie! Jump in! Good boy! Want a snack?" Gracie said to the giant dog.

"Charlie, you can ride with us, too! Come on, girl! Booger, make room for Charlie," Micah said.

"Friday, you can help me drive. Then I'll teach you how to surf," Chelsey said to the little dog, rubbing her head.

"Hey, it worked! He gave my sunglasses back," Lexi said happily.

"See, I told you! You've got to be smarter than the monkey!" Chelsey jousted.

"Hey, bestie! Are we going to sit in the driveway all day, or are we going to SURF?" I shouted.

"Woo-hoo! Yeah! Let's go!" Austin and Tripp cheered from the back seat.

"You guys ready to go?" Chelsey asked her parents over the excited shouting in her back seat.

"Let's do it!" Micah shouted back.

The Wick family pulled away from the house and drove down the long driveway to the road. Chelsey's noisy crew led the way, with parents, Charlie, and Booger close behind.

Gracie grabbed her husband's hand and said, "Can you believe this is happening? Look at this!"

She pointed at the Jeep full of their kids in front of them, happy, shouting, laughing, and singing.

"It's the best day of my life!" Micah answered.

Axl says he wishes he was part of the Wick family.

It didn't take as long as usual to find parking since it wasn't as touristy a season. We all poured out of the Jeeps, grabbed towels, and unstrapped boards.

"Come on, guys!" Chelsey encouraged the dogs and monkey. "Let's go surfing!"

The pets raced Chelsey to the water.

"The last one in the water buys smoothies!" Austin shouted.

The sound of laughter filled the air as brothers and sisters ran toward the mighty Pacific. It was the most epic of days.

Epilogue

Axl says he's never heard such a miraculous story.

Pretty great, huh, dude? Chelsey's family is such an awesome example of determination and love. It's super fun to be a part of that crazy bunch.

Axl tells me he was at the end of his rope when he came to Hawaii. But hearing about the Wick's struggles and victories has given him a new perspective.

I'm glad you came to the islands, brah. I believe in God's timing. He has a plan for everyone. Who knows what kind of knucklehead life I'd be living if Chelsey hadn't been a part of it? Maybe you were supposed to run into me on purpose, too.

Axl says he totally believes it. And he also believes everything I've told him over the past couple of days.

Brah, I have a stellar idea!

Axl is all ears.

Let's go to Zooch and have a yubl. Then we'll talk about your new life on Oahu.

Axl closes his eyes and says, "Let's go, brah!"